# THE
# FAT YEARS

NAN A. TALESE

*Doubleday*
NEW YORK
LONDON
TORONTO
SYDNEY
AUCKLAND

# THE FAT YEARS

## A NOVEL

CHAN
KOONCHUNG

*Translated from
the Chinese by
Michael S. Duke*

*with a Preface by
Julia Lovell*

Translation copyright © 2011 by Michael S. Duke
Preface copyright © 2011 by Julia Lovell

All rights reserved. Published in the United States by Nan A. Talese / Doubleday, a division of Random House, Inc., New York, and in Canada by Random House of Canada, Toronto.

www.nanatalese.com

DOUBLEDAY is a registered trademark of Random House, Inc. Nan A. Talese and the colophon are trademarks of Random House, Inc.

Originally published in Hong Kong as *Shengshi: Zhongguo 2013* by Oxford University Press (China) Ltd., a subsidiary of Oxford University Press, in 2009. Copyright © 2009 by Chan Koonchung. This translation was originally published in Great Britain by Transworld Publishers, an imprint of the Random House Group Limited, London, in 2011.

Book design by Maria Carella
Jacket design by Michael J. Windsor

Library of Congress Cataloging-in-Publication Data
Chen, Guanzhong.
  [Sheng shi. English]
  The fat years : a novel / Chan Koonchung ; translated from the Chinese by Michael S. Duke ; with a preface by Julia Lovell. — 1st U.S. ed.
    p.  cm.
  1. Beijing (China)—Fiction. 2. Political fiction. I. Duke, Michael S. II. Title.
PL2840.G84S5413 2011
895.1'352—dc22        2011014043

ISBN 978-0-385-53434-5
EBOOK ISBN 978-0-385-53435-2

MANUFACTURED IN THE UNITED STATES OF AMERICA

10  9  8  7  6  5  4  3  2  1

First American Edition

# CONTENTS

Zhongguancun, China's Silicon Valley in northwest Beijing, is a fine place to visit these days. In the thirty-odd years since China abandoned Maoism for market reforms, glass- and marble-fronted malls and five-star hotels, brimful of balloons, promotions, and the promise of the good life, have sprung up all over the capital; and Zhongguancun has its fair share of such high-rent establishments. The district's grand shopping plaza sprawls across two hundred thousand square meters packed with boutiques, supermarkets, cinemas, eateries, and eager consumers. The area happens also to be the center of China's elite institutions of higher education, home to China's most privileged scholars and students. With its glittering temples to self-gratification and to state-approved academic endeavor, Zhongguancun is one of the flagships of the contemporary Chinese dream.

On December 23, 2010, at one of Zhongguancun's police stations, a less harmonious episode was taking place. That evening, a Beijing law professor called Teng Biao decided to pay a visit to the mother of a friend. The friend, it so happened, was a human rights lawyer called Fan Yafeng, currently being held under house arrest by the authorities. Since Fan's mother was at home on her own, Teng thought it would be courteous to look in on her. As soon as he entered the apartment, however, a plainclothes police officer stormed in and loudly demanded his ID, pushing him for good measure. Not long after, a gang of Public Security reinforcements arrived and dragged Teng back down the stairs (confiscating his glasses in the process, leaving him extremely shortsighted) and into a police van, and drove him to a nearby police station. There, more violence ensued—in which Teng's hand was injured, his tie was violently yanked off, his legs were kicked, and he was sworn at—while he vainly quoted his citizen's constitutional rights. "Why waste words on this sort of person?" one police officer asked in front of him. "Let's beat him to death, dig a hole to bury him in, and be done with it." Eventually they let him go but only, Teng suspected, because they were a little intimidated by his academic status and, more importantly perhaps, because a timely tweet—before the police tried to remove his mobile phone—had gathered some of his supporters outside the police station. Teng was lucky: one of his peers, the lawyer Gao Zhisheng, has been imprisoned for years, multiply beaten, burnt with cigarettes, and tortured with electric shocks on account of his advocacy on behalf of groups persecuted by the regime; another human rights advocate, Ni Yulan, has been crippled by her police interrogators and is currently under house arrest in a Beijing hotel lacking electricity and running water.

A short walk from Zhongguancun's glass and neon palaces, another face of the contemporary Chinese miracle was showing itself. Welcome to the world of *The Fat Years*.

Chan Koonchung's *The Fat Years* describes a near-future world that, to a significant degree, already exists. This is a China in which a dictatorial Communist Party has guided the country safely through

a global economic meltdown that has weakened the liberal democratic West but strengthened the appeal and prestige of an authoritarian Chinese model, enabling China to reassert its premodern
status as the economic, political, and cultural center of the world.
This is a China in which the majority of the urban population—
despite the Party's repressiveness and corruption, and ruthless cen-
soring of history and the media—seem happy enough with a status
quo that has delivered economic choice without political liberties;
in which many once-critical voices have been marginalized or co-
opted.

In early 2011, two years before the novel begins, the world is
rocked by a second financial crisis that makes the shock of 2008
resemble a mere wobble, and during which the dollar loses a third
of its value in a single day. Somehow sidestepping the economic
Armageddon that hits the West, the People's Republic of China
instead immediately enters what its communist government officially names a "Golden Age" of prosperity and contentment. No
one in a placid Beijing of 2013 seems to have anything negative to
say about the country; all unhappy memories have been erased, as
urbanites busy themselves with self-gratification. Our guide to this
paradise on earth is Chen, a Taiwanese–Hong Kong writer who has
over the past few years made China his new home. He spends his
time socializing, going to literary events and parties, browsing in
bookshops, or sipping Lychee Black Dragon Latte in Beijing's Starbucks (which, following the collapse of the dollar, has had to sell out
to a Taiwanese snacks consortium). "I felt so spiritually and materially satisfied," he summarizes, "and my life was so incomparably
blessed, that I began to experience an overwhelming feeling of good
fortune such as I never had before." China's awkward squad—the
minority of critics who have poked and jibed at the regime since
public opposition became possible again after Mao's death—has

been intimidated, isolated, or mainstreamed into silence, leaving an intellectual establishment dominated by complacent national treasures, trendy young things, or fascistic Party ideologues. The novel's atmosphere of overwhelming self-congratulation is resisted only by a handful of individuals determined to remember less happy times and to ask why everyone else has forgotten them. We meet an old flame of Chen's, Little Xi, a drop-out lawyer-turned-democratic-protestor of the 1980s; Fang Caodi, a hippie globetrotter who is looking for China's "lost month"—the four hellish weeks of martial law imposed after the economic collapse of 2011 in which countless civilians died, and which is now mysteriously wiped from public memory; and Zhang Dou, a former victim of government-condoned slave labor.

It was, Chan Koonchung has observed, China's current situation that inspired the novel. "I got the idea for the book from responses to the financial crisis of 2008—I'd been plotting a novel about China for some time, but that gave me a moment, a focus. That year, as the West reeled from the financial mess while China escaped unscathed, it seemed that everyone—from officials down to ordinary urbanites—began to feel that China was doing well for itself, that there was nothing more to learn from the West, that China can argue back . . . The public have now bought enthusiastically into China's authoritarian model." The construction of an authoritarian harmony has always been implicit in communist theory and practice, but this became official policy after 2007, when President Hu Jintao exhorted "all people [to] coexist harmoniously, love and help each other, encourage each other, and make an effort to contribute to the building of a harmonious society."

In recent years, China's communist government has indeed succeeded—perhaps beyond its wildest dreams—in muffling critical voices. The 1980s were choppy times for the regime, as

China's chattering classes debated the disasters of Maoism, and whether there was any place for Marxism in economic and political liberalization. As China stumbled toward a market economy and as inflation rocketed throughout the decade, the conviction grew that the government's reforms weren't working and the leadership had not persuaded the populace that they could lead. The most avant-garde rebels—such as the 2010 Nobel Peace laureate Liu Xiaobo—speculated that China could experience "great historical change" only if it had been colonized like Hong Kong was after the Opium War of 1839–42. ("China is so big," he added as a provocative after-thought, "that naturally it would need three hundred years of colonization to become like Hong Kong.") From the middecade onward, urban China was given pause, every year, by student protests—over the lack of government transparency; over the rising cost of food; over the rats in their dorms—culminating in the two-month occupation of Tiananmen Square from April to June 1989. The demonstrations' bloody denouement was an international and domestic PR disaster for China's communist government: while Western politicians and overseas Chinese called for economic and political sanctions, hundreds of thousands of sobbing Chinese people came out in protest in Hong Kong, Macao, Taiwan, and Western cities, comparing the People's Republic to Nazi Germany and spray-painting the national flag with swastikas.

Fast-forward to the present day, and China's communist rulers have effectively neutralized many of their former opponents. "For years," as one analyst has observed, "the Beijing regime has stayed in power using a basic bargain with its citizens—tolerate our authoritarian rule and we'll make you rich." Confounding Western prophets of communist apocalypse, China's post-1989 leaders accelerated economic reforms, while backpedaling on political liberalization. In China 2011, as in *The Fat Years*, much of the urban

population seems to have tacitly agreed to forget past political violence, and to concentrate on enjoying the fat times of the here-and-
now. Not only sharp businessmen, but also many of China's writers
and thinkers have benefited, enjoying generous research grants,
conference budgets, and travel opportunities, as long as they do not
break taboos on open discussion of issues such as official abuse of
power, the need for political reforms, human rights abuses against
critics of the regime, ethnic tensions (especially in Xinjiang or
Tibet), and widespread censorship. This unspoken consensus also
demands public amnesia about communist-manufactured cata-
clysms: in particular, the man-made disasters of the Maoist era (the
brutal excesses of Land Reform, the Great Leap Forward, the Cultural Revolution) and, of course, the bloodletting of 1989. "Many
of those who were once critical of the regime are now part of the
system," Chan Koonchung has observed. "The Party has absorbed
the elites by handing out funding, positions, and employment. Those
in universities are getting government projects so they don't want
to be vocal. Many people depend on money from the state to build
their careers. So the intellectual center is mainly employed by the
state, which is now rich enough to attract it with apparently limit-
less funding. More and more people are buying into this now. It's
very difficult to find people to make a challenge" while critics of the
government are becoming "increasingly marginalized."

   Although communist control might be far less visible in contemporary China than it was during, say, the Maoist era, it is quietly ubiquitous: through public and private businesses, local politics,
media, and culture. The Party, Chan Koonchung points out, is "the
elephant in the room of contemporary China—no one discusses it
but it's always there. The country's like a Rubix cube—enormously
complex, but with one organizing principle: the Communist Party."
When I met him in Beijing in the summer of 2010, he invited me to

lunch at a fashionable East–West fusion restaurant in Sanlitun, one of the city's best-heeled commercial quarters, littered with high-end bars, cafés, and designer stores, through which *The Fat Years'* own hero, Chen, regularly strolls feeling "incomparably blessed." After a smiling, smart-casual young Chinese waiter introduced himself to us in English ("Hi, I'm Darren, I'll be looking after you today") then disappeared again, Chan Koonchung conspiratorially reminded me: "There'll be Party members in this joint venture too, keeping an eye on things."

Much of the force of *The Fat Years*, then, springs from its unusual honesty about certain aspects of contemporary Chinese reality. For Chen is almost unique, among his mainland-Chinese novelist contemporaries, in confronting the political no-go zones of life in China today. By 2000, according to many critics, Chinese writers could write about anything they wanted without fear of severe reprisal, and even with the prospect of financial gain—*if* they did not write directly about politics. What has resulted is a culture often rich in commercial shock value—in its explicit descriptions of sex and violence—but frustratingly weak in its grasp of the political roots of China's problems. China's leadership remains a taboo subject—on the Chinese Internet, even writing the names of China's rulers is prohibited. Acclaimed mainland novelists such as Yu Hua write bestselling books about communist China that evoke the chaos of war and revolution, but that pull their punches when it comes to seeking the deep, institutional causes of post-1949 China's ills, and that avoid—for censorship reasons—even the most veiled reference to the suppression of the 1989 protests. The violence of the Cultural Revolution, for example, is portrayed as an irrational explosion of thuggery, without any attempt to search for longer-term origins (in, say, communism's normalization of violence and in mass resentment of its castelike system of class designations). *The Fat Years*, by contrast, directly faces up to the marriage of mass acquiescence and violent political intimidation that keeps China's authoritarian show on the road. One contemporary writer did not wholly identify with Chan Koonchung's vision of China's near future, but admitted that "at least he's willing to point out some of the holes in our fancy tapestry. He's the only Sinophone author to make the attempt, unfortunately. And it's we mainland-Chinese writers who are to blame for that."

The mainland-Chinese response to Chan's novel was revealing. With its explicit references to the 1989 crackdown and to Party censorship, the book—published in Hong Kong—was of course not officially distributed on the mainland. But the Communist Party's control on information—although extensive—is nowhere near as absolute as portrayed in *The Fat Years*, and the book was sold under-the-counter in some Beijing bookstores, or by mail order from Hong Kong; each copy that reached the mainland, one estimate ran, was passed between at least six or seven readers. Its mainland audience was seriously shaken by the novel's "authenticity" (*kaopu*); by its discussion of how the government has silenced or absorbed its opponents; by its descriptions of collective amnesia and compromise with the regime, and of the fascism implicit in China's brave new world. "It's a long time since I read anything that made me think so much," wrote a reader. "I almost forgot that it was science fiction," admitted another. "It's more like a documentary." "Now we know what China's near future will be like," observed one blogger, while chic party hostesses slipped copies of the book into guests' take-home bags. "Starting from today," decided one journalist after finishing the novel, "I have no friends and I have no enemies. I now divide people into two categories—those who have read *The Fat Years* and those who haven't." "The book is hot," a publisher anonymously declared, noting the resonances between Chen's fictional diagnosis of China's political landscape and recent headline controversies such as the eleven-year sentence handed down to Liu Xiaobo in 2009 after his calls for constitutional human rights, or Google's 2010 confrontation with government censorship. "It's very clear that things are getting harsher and harsher." Others again read it as utopia, rather than dystopia. "If only China could be *just* like this!" sighed another blogger. "It would be wonderful." Chan reported that officials at the very pinnacle of China's political hierarchy had told him that "the political situation in the novel summarized their basic difficulties and plan . . . And ordinary readers seemed quite happy that a former radical from the 1980s like Little Xi was marginalized as she was—they thought that was fine. Many mainland readers felt that cracking down with martial law was fine, too—that it was an appropriate response to civil chaos."

But *The Fat Years'* power to unsettle goes beyond its uncomfortable proximity to reality. It sketches a credible likeness of China, then pushes it a touch beyond credibility. Chan's China is self-satisfied to an uncanny degree. "Now everybody's saying there's no country in the world as good as China," Chan's hero remarks early in the book, noting "so many celebrated members of the intellectual elite . . . harmoniously gathered together in one place looking genuinely happy, even euphoric . . . This really must be a true age of peace and prosperity . . . Every day I read the papers, surfed the net, and watched the TV news, and every day I congratulated myself on living in China; sometimes I was moved to tears I felt so blessed." The puzzle of Chan's blissed-out China is unraveled only at the end of the book. This fictional China is also intellectually repressive and conformist way beyond contemporary standards. Although for well over a decade, for example, the Chinese government has been one of the world's most assiduous censors of the web, in reality the Chinese Internet still seethes with potential dissent and capacity to organize

against the regime, with a lawyer like Teng Biao only one representative of China's awkward squad. At one point in the novel, Chen
tries to find a restrained satire of intellectual life under Maoism,
Yang Jiang's *Baptism*, which is at present easily found in Beijing; the
assistant in the bookshop tells him that not only is it not available in
that bookshop, but that officially it does not exist—all digital record
of the book has disappeared. Chan's fictional regime has, more-
over, apparently erased from mass memory a whole, brutal month
of government violence and civil war from just two years earlier.
(Although public discussion of the bloodletting of 1989 is impossible
in contemporary China, it assuredly lives on in private memory.)
Chan Koonchung's dystopian China of 2013 represents a degraded
version of a recognizable state: the iron fist of a harsh, Leninist dictatorship lying inside the utopian velvet glove of communism. To
one mainland blogger, the novel seemed both "extremely realistic"
and an allegory of "everyone's common fate. [It] painfully describes
the fears that lie deep in our hearts, [convincing us] that the world
described in the book is quickly bearing down on us."

Although the autocracy of *The Fat Years* is less shockingly brutal
than Orwell's Ingsoc in *Nineteen Eighty-Four*, the restrained plausi-
bility of Chan's dystopia brings with it a clear warning about China's possible near future. Nearing the end of his torture by O'Brien,
Orwell's hero Winston Smith asks his captor why the Party seeks
power, expecting some self-loving sentiment about dictatorship
being for "the good of the people." His persecutor has no such illu-
sions: "The Party seeks power entirely for its own sake. We are not
interested in the good of others; we are interested solely in power. Not
wealth or luxury or long life or happiness: only power, pure power . . .
The object of torture is torture. The object of power is power." He
Dongsheng, the representative of the communist leadership in *The
Fat Years* who finally reveals the government's grand scheme "for

Ruling the Nation and Pacifying the World," is an altogether softer dictator, whose policies—like those of China's government today— rely more heavily on the active agreement of his Chinese subjects. The China that he has created, he believes, is "the best option in the real world": "there is no possible way for China to be any better than it is today . . . Can China be controlled without a one-party dictatorship? Can any other system feed and clothe one billion, three hundred and fifty million people? Or successfully administer an 'Action Plan for Achieving Prosperity amid Crisis'? . . . there *must not be* [democratic] reform because any reform would lead to chaos." In *The Fat Years*, rulers and the ruled are locked in collusive harmony. Did the Office of Stability Maintenance, Fang Caodi asks, inject everyone with a drug created "to make us all forget" the terrifying month of martial law imposed in 2011 during which many more will have died at the hands of the People's Liberation Army than perished in the notorious suppression of 1989? "It would be wonderful if we did have one," He Dongsheng wistfully responds. "Then our Communist Party could rewrite its history any way it wanted to . . . If you ask me for the real reason [why everyone forgot], I can only tell you that I don't know! You shouldn't think that we can control everything." The Chinese of *The Fat Years* have, according to the logic of the novel, the rulers that they deserve: they have deliberately chosen to forget. "The people fear chaos more than they fear dictatorship," He Dongsheng summarizes. "The vast majority of the Chinese people crave stability."

Chan Koonchung has himself felt the ambivalent pull of the contemporary "Chinese model." The son of refugees from Maoist China, product of Hong Kong's Anglicized education system, he is an unlikely sympathizer with authoritarian methods. "I grew up listening to the Beatles, watching French films, reading Camus, J. D. Salinger, Jane Austen, Agatha Christie, Raymond Chandler,

Dashiell Hammett," he recalled. "My friends and I would have worn black polo-necks, but we couldn't get hold of any in subtropical Hong Kong, so we had to make do with white T-shirts instead." But the open-ended questions he scatters through the book express his own uncertain position vis-à-vis contemporary Chinese politics. "Between a good hell and a fake paradise—which one would *you* choose?" Little Xi demands of Chen at one point. He has just said to her that "no matter what you might say, many people will believe that a counterfeit paradise is better than a good hell . . . But there's always a small number of people, even if they are only an extremely small minority, who will choose the good hell no matter how painful it is, because in the good hell at least everyone is fully aware that they are living in hell." Outside the book Chan is selectively critical about China's capacity for mass amnesia: "This is a place where memories get terribly distorted: people in their fifties now say that the government was right to crack down in 1989. And many people forget that 1989–92 was an ice age, before China began marching toward the market. I don't think ordinary people should have to concentrate on remembering—it's not good for them, and it's not their job. It's intellectuals who shouldn't forget. These days, they can't say anything, though. They know the risks of speaking out: that there's a huge difference between having government approval and losing it, in terms of the housing you'll get, access to international funding, and so on." Chan is even able to see the pluses of He Dongsheng's "Action Plan for Ruling the Nation and Pacifying the World." "I saw the economic crisis of the novel as the government's great opportunity to take control. That was the best way that things could have worked out; mine was the most optimistic scenario."

Both Chan Koonchung and his fictional namesake in *The Fat Years* voted with their feet by moving to Beijing from Hong Kong a few years ago; both are, to an extent, seduced by the lure of a rising

China: "This place is too fascinating to ignore," Chan confesses. "The Beijing I described in *The Fat Years* is basically the Beijing in which I live. There's nowhere quite like it." Is it also as frightening as his fictional Beijing? I asked as we left the restaurant after lunch. He gazed about the airy, glazed mall, as we glided down the escalator back to street level on a perfect, blue-skied August day. "Not today. I don't know about tomorrow, though."

JULIA LOVELL, FEBRUARY 2011

This book uses the *pinyin* Romanization system. Only a few letters
sound very different from normal English. They are:

c = ts (*Fang Caodi* sounds like Fang Tsao-dee)
q = ch before i (*qigong* sounds like chee-gong)
x = sh (*Xiao* sounds like Shee-ao)
He in *He Dongsheng* is pronounced something like Huh

THE
FAT YEARS

## LIST OF MAIN CHARACTERS

Lao Chen, the protagonist, a journalist and novelist with writer's block

Fang Caodi, an erstwhile friend of his, who has led a globe-trotting, jack-of-all-trades life

Little Xi, another old friend of Lao Chen. Had a short-lived career as a lawyer, now has a marginal existence as an Internet political activist

Big Sister Song, her mother, the owner of the Five Flavors restaurant

Wei Guo, Little Xi's son, a law student and ambitious Party member

Jian Lin, an acquaintance of Lao Chen, a wealthy real estate entrepreneur, and holder of cinema evenings

He Dongsheng, his cousin, a high-ranking government official

Zhang Dou, a former child slave-laborer, now an aspiring guitarist

Miaomiao, his girlfriend, formerly a journalist

Ban Cuntou, another cousin of Jian Lin, and once a classmate of Little Xi; now a highly influential figure in government circles

Wen Lan, a former girlfriend of Lao Chen; an international jetsetting political adviser

Dong Niang, a high-class prostitute

Zhuang Zizhong, an elderly editor of a literary journal

Hu Yan, an academic, member of the Chinese Academy of Social Sciences, expert on rural China

Gao Shengchan and Li Tiejun, organizers of an underground Protestant church, the Church of the Grain Fallen on the Ground, in Henan Province

Liu Xing, a former classmate of Gao Shengchan, and a local government official

County Head Yang, a young and ambitious local government official

# PART ONE

1.

TWO YEARS
FROM NOW

*Someone not seen in a long time*

One whole month is missing. I mean one whole month of 2011 has disappeared, it's gone, it can't be found. Normally February follows January, March follows February, April follows March, and so on. But now after January it's March, or after February it's April . . . Do you understand what I'm saying—we've skipped a month!"

"Fang Caodi, just forget it," I said. "Don't go looking for it. It's not worth it. Life's too short; just look after yourself."

No matter how clever I was, I could never change Fang Caodi. Then again, if you really wanted to search for a missing month, Fang Caodi would be the one to do it. In his life, he'd probably spent quite a few missing months just existing. He was always turning up unexpectedly in odd places like he had vanished for a million years and was being reborn just when you were least expecting him. Maybe someone like him really could accomplish such a politically unfashionable task as restoring a missing month.

The thing is, at first I didn't really notice that a whole month was missing. Even if other people told me about it, I wasn't ready to believe them. Every day I read the papers and checked the Internet

news sites; every night I watched CCTV and the Phoenix Channel, and I hung around with intelligent people. I didn't think that
any major event had escaped my notice. I believed in myself—my
knowledge, my wisdom, and my independent judgment.

On the afternoon of the eighth day of the first lunar month of
this year, as I left my home in Happiness Village Number Two and
set out on my usual walk to the Starbucks in the PCCW Tower Mall
of Plenty, a jogger suddenly pulled up in front of me.

"Master Chen! Master Chen!" the jogger gasped while trying
to regain his breath. "A whole month is missing! It's been missing
for two years today."

The jogger was wearing a baseball cap, and I didn't recognize
him at first.

"Fang Caodi, Fang Caodi . . ." he said as he took off his cap to
reveal a bald head sporting a short ponytail held at the back with a
rubber band.

Suddenly, I knew who it was. "Fang Caodi. Why are you calling
me master?"

He ignored me. "A whole month is missing! Master Chen, what
can we do about it, what can we do?" he repeated rather desperately.

"It's been more than a month since we last met, hasn't it?" I
said.

"Longer than that. Master Chen, you know, a whole month has
disappeared! It's terrifying. What should we do about it?" Fang said.

I tried to change the subject. "When did you get back to
Beijing?"

He didn't answer and then suddenly he sneezed. I handed him

my card. "Don't catch cold. You shouldn't be running around. We can meet later. My phone number and e-mail are on the card."

He put his cap back on and took my card. "We can look for it together," he said.

As I watched him jog off toward the Dongzhi Menwai Embassy Row area, I realized he wasn't just out for a jog, he was on a mission.

### Another person not seen in a long time

A couple of days later, I found myself attending the *Reading Journal* New Year's reception on the second floor of the Sanlian Bookstore on Art Museum East Road. The reception was an annual affair. In the 1990s I used to drop in off and on, but since I moved to Beijing permanently in 2004, I've come up every other year to shoot the breeze a while with the older writers and editors, just to let the cultural world know that I'm still alive. I never bother with the younger ones—I don't know them and they don't seem to feel any need to know me.

The atmosphere at the reception was somehow different from previous years; the guests seemed quite elated. For the past year, I've noticed that I, too, have often felt some sort of unaccountable cheerfulness, but the high spirits that day still took me aback. That day everybody was so euphoric it was as if they'd just knocked back a few shots of Jack Daniel's.

The venerable founder of *Reading*, Zhuang Zizhong, hadn't made an appearance at a reception for a while, but this time he turned up in his wheelchair. There was quite a crowd jostling around him, so I didn't go over to say hello. Besides Old Zhuang, all the staff at the journal—those who were still alive, that is—had all showed up. That was no minor miracle. In all the years I've been associated with the Sanlian and its journal, *Reading*, I've never seen such a grand occasion. It left me pleasantly surprised. I'm quite cynical about human nature. I've never believed that the inner workings of any organization were completely harmonious, especially not any mainland-Chinese organization, and particularly not state-operated enterprises, including state-operated cultural units.

That day all the writers and editors whom I knew greeted me with excessive enthusiasm; but when I started to strike up a proper conversation, their attention had already shifted and they hurried off to someone else. This sort of treatment is pretty common at receptions and cocktail parties, especially when you're not a star. After being greeted and then snubbed two or three times, I readjusted my attitude and returned to my usual one—that of an observer. I have to admit I was pretty moved by what I saw: so many celebrated and diverse members of the intellectual elite gathered together in one place looking genuinely happy, even euphoric . . . This really must be a true age of peace and prosperity, I thought to myself.

I was feeling pretty good, but very quickly I got the feeling that it was time to leave. I walked out of the reception intending to browse around in the bookstore. I took a look at the art books on the second floor, and then glanced at the new bestsellers and the business and travel books on the first floor. The bookstore was teeming with browsers. So people are still reading books. Terrific! "The sweet smell of books in a literary society," I thought. As I made my way downstairs toward the basement, students were crowding both sides of the stairs, sitting and reading, almost as though they didn't want anyone else to go down there. Feeling cheerful, I picked my way down the stairs. The basement level is where the Sanlian keeps its extensive collection of books on literature, history, philosophy, politics, and the humanities, and that's why it's my number-one destination every time I visit. I've always believed that the generous display of these humanities books is one of the things that make Beijing a city worth living in. A city that reads books on literature, history, philosophy, and politics is definitely a special place.

The basement level was very quiet that day. No one was around, and strangely enough, when I got down there I didn't really feel like browsing anymore. I just wanted to lay my hands on one particular book, but I couldn't remember what it was. I walked into the room thinking that when I saw it I would know. As I walked past the philosophy section and moved on to the politics and history sections, I suddenly felt I couldn't breathe. Was the basement air that bad?

So I decided to make a quick exit. I was walking up the stairs trying not to bump into any of the youngsters, when suddenly somebody grabbed the cuff of my trousers. I looked down in surprise, and that person looked up at me. It was not one of the young people.

"Lao Chen!" She seemed surprised to see me.

"Little Xi" is all I said, but I was thinking, Little Xi, where have you been all these years?

"I saw you go downstairs and I thought, that must be Lao Chen!" From the way she said it she seemed to imply that running into me was quite important.

"Didn't you go up to the reception?" I asked.

"No . . . I didn't know about it till I got here. Are you free now?" She leaned toward me conspiratorially.

"Sure," I said, "I'll buy you a cup of coffee."

She paused a minute before she said, "Let's just walk and talk." Then she let go of my trouser leg.

We started strolling toward the National Art Museum. I walked beside her, waiting for her to start a conversation, but she didn't, so I asked her about her mother. "How's Big Sister Song?"

"She's fine."

"She must be over eighty now?"

"Yup."

"And how's your son?"

No answer.

"How old is he?"

"Over twenty."

"That old?"

"Yup."

"Is he at university or working?"

"He's at university. Look," she said, "can we change the subject?"

I remembered how much she doted on her son and was startled at her reaction. "Let's go to the Prime Hotel and have a cup of coffee," I offered.

She didn't want to, so we walked instead into the small park next to the National Art Museum.

Little Xi stopped suddenly. "Lao Chen, have you noticed anything?" she said.

I didn't know how I should respond, but I knew I couldn't say, "Noticed what?" She seemed to be testing me. If I gave her the wrong answer, it was unlikely she'd open up to me. As a writer, I like people to tell me their innermost thoughts. As a man, I wanted this woman to tell me her innermost thoughts.

I paused, feeling a little awkward, and she asked, "Is it kind of hard for you to express your feelings?"

I gave a small nod. I've often felt nothing at all when people have asked how I feel about a work of art or a piece of music. I hate this feeling of feeling nothing, but I'm pretty good at faking an acceptable response.

"That's great, I knew it," she went on. "When I saw you going down the stairs, I thought to myself, Lao Chen will understand. Then I sat there waiting for you to come back up the stairs."

In Little Xi's mind I'm probably a reasonable, mature, and fairly knowledgeable person.

At least, that's what I'd like people to think.

"Let's sit down on this bench," I suggested gently.

It seemed to work, because after we sat down she relaxed, closed her eyes, sighed deeply, and said, "At last."

Little Xi was definitely my type. After so many years, her looks and figure hadn't changed much, but wrinkles had begun to appear on her face from neglect. She also looked pretty depressed.

She kept her eyes closed, trying to regain her composure. I looked at her intently and I suddenly realized how much I still liked this woman. I like melancholy women.

"I don't have anyone to talk to. I feel like there are fewer and fewer people like us . . . There are so few of us left that life hardly seems worth living anymore."

"Don't be silly," I said. "Everybody's lonely, but no matter how lonely you are, life still goes on."

She ignored my banal response. "No one remembers, except me. No one talks about it, except me. Does that mean I'm completely mad? There's no trace of it, no evidence, so nobody can be bothered."

I was enjoying the sound of her Beijing accent.

She briefly opened her eyes before closing them again. "Well, how about it? We were such good friends. Why haven't I seen you for so many years? What happened?"

"I thought you'd gone abroad."

She shook her head. "No."

"Well, it's good that you didn't. Now everybody's saying there's no country in the world as good as China."

She opened her eyes once more and gave me a look. I didn't really understand what she was getting at, so I didn't react. She broke into a smile and said, "It's unbelievable that you can still make jokes."

I hadn't been joking, but I immediately went along with her and smiled, too.

"You sound just like my son," she added.

"Your son? You seem not to want to talk about him. What's up between the two of you?"

"He's doing really well," she said in an ironic tone. "He's studying law at Peking University and he's joined the Communist Party."

"That's good," I said vaguely. "It will be useful when he tries to find a job."

"He wants to go into the Chinese Communist Party Central Propaganda Department!"

At first I thought I hadn't heard her clearly.

"The Central Propaganda Department?" I ventured.

Little Xi nodded. "He says it's his life's ambition. He's got big ideas! If you ever meet him, you'll know what I mean."

I was enjoying a feeling of happiness sitting there next to Little Xi. It was such a beautiful spring afternoon; the sun was so bright and warm that many elderly couples were strolling around the park. There were also a few smokers . . . smokers? Two of them were standing close by chain-smoking. I like to read detective stories and I've even written a few myself, and so this situation left plenty of room for the imagination. It could have been a surveillance scene, but as I was nothing more than a self-indulgent writer of very ordinary bestsellers, why would anyone want to spy on me? Wherever there are people in China there are smokers.

I listened as Little Xi continued to pour her heart out to me. "Am I causing trouble, making a fuss? I know it's none of my business, but I can't act just like nothing's happened. How can things change just like that? I don't get it and I can't stand it."

I was still wondering what had made her so upset. Her son, or the after-effects of her own nightmarish experiences?

"One day in a small restaurant in Lanqiying," she said, looking directly at me, "I went on a blind date with one of you Taiwanese men—he was a businessman. He was a terrific talker, there was nothing he didn't know: astronomy, geography, medicine, divination and horoscopes, finance, investments, and world politics, you name it, he just wouldn't stop and I was bored to death. When I managed to get a word in edgeways about our government's failings, he called me ungrateful and said I didn't know just how good I had it. He made me furious. I really felt like giving him a good slap."

"Taiwanese men are not necessarily all like him," I said. I felt I had to stick up for us Taiwanese men. But I was also curious. "So what happened?"

She smiled broadly. "He was so busy leaning over to tell me off that his butt was barely on the edge of his chair. When a tall, muscular young guy from the table next to us walked by, he deliberately bumped into his chair and knocked him off onto the floor."

"What about this young guy?" I asked, still curious.

"He was just a strong young man."

"But did he say anything?"

"He just walked out. And I felt delighted."

"Did you know him?"

"No, but I'd like to."

I felt a twinge of jealousy. "You can't go around being violent like that."

"Well, I thought it was great. I seem to feel like slapping people in the face all the time these days."

Little Xi had seen a great deal of violence in her life, and some of it must have rubbed off on her. I remembered then why I hadn't dared get too close to her. "What did that Taiwanese guy do after that?"

"He got up, absolutely livid, and looked around for someone to swear at, but he couldn't see anyone, so he just muttered 'philistine' under his breath. You see, you Taiwanese still look down on us."

"Not anymore, we don't." I know there used to be a certain amount of mutual contempt between people from the mainland, Hong Kong, and Taiwan, but I think all that has changed now.

I said, "So how are things for you now, Xi?"

She knit her brows and pursed her lips. "Things are okay, but the people around me have changed and I feel pretty low. I feel a lot better now talking with you. I haven't had anyone to talk to for a long time . . ."

She suddenly turned her gaze into the distance, her expression quite blank. Her behavior puzzled me. What on earth was she looking at? The scattered shadows of the leaves on the ground as the slanting sun filtered through the branches? Or had she suddenly thought of something that threw her into a daydream? After a minute or so she abruptly said, "Oh, I've got to go, the rush-hour buses will be packed."

I quickly got to my feet and gave her my card. "Let's have dinner sometime, with your mother and your son."

"We'll see," she said rather noncommitally. Then, "I'm off," and away she went.

Little Xi still walked quite fast. I took a good look at her from behind—she could definitely turn heads. Her figure and swinging stride were still youthful. Xi left by the south side of the park while I happily ambled along toward the east-side exit. I suddenly remembered those two smokers, and looking back, I saw that they were already at the south-side exit. Little Xi turned right toward the National Art Museum and walked out of my line of sight. The two smokers waited a couple of seconds and then followed her in the direction of the museum.

### Fat years in Sanlitun

I don't feel like going home right away, so I catch a taxi to the Swire Village in Sanlitun and go to Starbucks. Ever since the Want-want China Group acquired Starbucks, many Chinese drinks have gone global. Take this great-tasting Lychee Black Dragon Latte I'm drinking now. I've heard that Wantwant Starbucks together with a Chinese investment consortium called EAL Friendship Investments (EAL for Europe, Africa, and Latin America) have opened outlets in several Islamic cities in the Middle East and Africa, including Baghdad, Beirut, Kabul, Khartoum, and Dar es Salaam. This is one big new global market guaranteeing that anywhere the Chinese live in the world there will be a Starbucks. In business never forget culture—a wonderful expression of China's soft power.

Coming here was the right thing. I feel better and that familiar feeling of happiness comes flooding back. Look how busy the mall is. The young people look great, and there are so many tourists and visitors from abroad—what an international city. And everybody's shopping—stimulating domestic demand and contributing to society.

I remember that a couple of months ago, a friend of mine studying rural culture at the Chinese Academy of Social Sciences asked me a favor. Her niece from Lanzhou was in Beijing for her winter vacation and staying with her. When she asked her niece where she fancied going, she said she wanted to go to Y-3 to buy some clothes. My friend hadn't a clue what Y-3 was, so she asked me. She's such a bookworm. It didn't even occur to her to look it up online. Y-3 is a new clothing brand started as a cooperative venture between Adidas and Japan's celebrated Yohji Yamamoto. "Y" stands for Yohji and "3" is probably for the three leaves of the Adidas trefoil logo. The Y-3 brand is really hot here. In fact, they say the biggest Y-3 market in the world is in China, and its flagship department store is right in front of me now, opposite the Swire Village Wantwant Starbucks.

When they opened just before the 2008 Olympics, they occupied only about one-third of the fourth floor of the five-story Adidas outlet. Now one whole floor belongs to Y-3. Of course Adidas also expanded its Swire Village area by taking over the floors once occupied by Nike. This was all due to the merger and reorganization of the local brand Li Ning with Adidas, but the thanks should go to the Chinese government's new policies. Every brand that wants to enter the Chinese market has to have at least 25 percent Chinese-owned capital; with 50 percent or more, they can receive even more favorable terms. If they want to be listed in Shanghai, they have to meet extra requirements, I can't remember exactly what. Any foreign brand that does not meet these conditions has to wait for the Ministry of Commerce to grant it special permission; if it doesn't receive special permission, then it has to remove itself from China's 1.35-billion-person market.

I've lived over half my life in Taiwan and Hong Kong, and I always used to believe that for any place to develop it had to rely on exports. The population had to depend on living frugally and getting rich through thrift in order to fill the first bucket of gold. But now I finally realize how important domestic demand and consumption are. If the Chinese are willing to spend money, they may not be able to save the world, but at least they can improve their own situation.

I'm not blindly praising China. I know China has many problems. But just think about this. There was the 2008 financial tsunami, when the developed capitalist countries, led by the United States, began to self-destruct. They enjoyed only a couple of years of slight recovery before they fell into stagflation again in 2011. This new crisis spread right across the globe, leaving no nation untouched. And now there's no end in sight to this depression. Only China has been able to recover, surging forward while the others are on the decline. With domestic demand filling in for the dried-up export market, and state capital replacing evaporated foreign investments, the current forecast is that this year will be the third successive year of more than 15 percent growth. Not only has China changed the rules of the international economic game, we've also changed the nature of Western economics. Even more importantly, there has been no social upheaval; in fact, our society is even more harmonious now. You can't help accepting that it's all really incredible. Now I'm beginning to get emotional. It's been happening to me a lot recently, being so easily moved that I actually start to weep.

Then I remember how depressed Little Xi looked and it makes me sad. Everybody around us is living the good life, while she's becoming more and more despondent. I take a couple of deep breaths and fight back my tears. I used to be a very cool guy. Why am I so sentimental these days? I quickly fly out of Starbucks.

### A future master

Ever since the All Sages Bookstore, the best one in Beijing for humanities and academic books, had been forced to close down, I hardly ever went to the Haidian area near Peking University's east gate. But about a week after the Sanlian *Reading Journal* spring reception I found myself over there. Things had been fine all week, nothing unpleasant had happened. Every day I read the papers, surfed the net, and watched the TV news, and every day I congratulated myself on living in China. At first I didn't think about Little Xi. I figured her attitude was out of tune with my life and my present state of mind. But then for a few nights in a row the last dream I had before waking up was about her, and it got me all aroused. I guess it had been too long since I'd been with anyone. I also dreamed about Fang Caodi, a repetitive dream of walking up and down in the same spot. I was sorry I hadn't taken their cell phone numbers. But they hadn't contacted me, either—I guessed I wasn't that important to them. I didn't know how to track down Fang Caodi and actually I didn't really want to. But I still had an idea of how to find Little Xi and that's what brought me to the east gate of Peking University.

In the 1980s, Little Xi and her mother were *getihu*, self-employed entrepreneurs. They ran a small restaurant called the Five Flavors in a one-story temporary shack outside some apartments near the university's east gate. I called Little Xi's mother Big Sister Song; her Guizhou-style goose was very popular, but the main attraction of the Five Flavors was that Little Xi and her mates hung around there all day. They chatted all day and all night, so that the restaurant became a sort of Haidian salon for foreigners and intellectuals. They went out of business for a few years, but after Deng Xiaoping's 1992 southern tour called for continued economic reforms, they found a place nearby and started up again. Whenever I came to Beijing, I would go over there to eat, but I hadn't been there for years and didn't even know if the restaurant was still there.

As soon as I reached the east gate, I knew I was out of luck. The surrounding apartments had all been torn down to build office towers. The Five Flavors was gone, the All Sages Bookstore was gone, too, so I left without a backward glance. I decided to walk over to the Photosynthesis Bookstore in the Wudaokou district and browse around. It was better than nothing, and I could kill some time having a cup of coffee. This used to be the rock-music center of Beijing's

Westside, with quite a few performance venues, but I hadn't followed those guys in recent years and didn't know if there were any venues left. On Chengfu Road just before Wudaokou, I passed by a restaurant and then felt like I'd missed something, so I stopped. Turning back, I saw that the front was extensively decorated. The place was simply called Five Flavors, with no indication whether it was a Chinese restaurant, a Western restaurant, or some kind of club. I decided to go in and investigate.

The inside was also elaborately decorated, though the tables and chairs were quite ordinary. There was a stage that could just about accommodate a four-man rock band. The front hall was empty, but I heard the sound of a loud, resonant, and very familiar voice ringing out from the back room. I drew the curtain and marched in. "Big Sister Song!" I called.

"Lao Chen!" Little Xi's mother recognized me instantly.

"I came to see you, Big Sister Song." It felt a little hypocritical saying that.

"It's good to see you after all this time!"

She picked up a room-temperature bottle of Yanjing beer and led me into the front hall. "It's so great to see you, Lao Chen, I've really missed you."

I felt a little ashamed that I'd lived in Beijing for so many years and had never come to see the old lady. "I ran into Little Xi last week," I said.

Big Sister Song suddenly lowered her voice. "You should talk to her, try to get her to stop all her antics."

"I only ran into her briefly at a bookstore. Will she be coming over?"

"Definitely not."

"But do you have her cell phone number so I can give her a call?"

"She doesn't use a cell phone." Big Sister Song kept her eye on

the door as she spoke. "She's on e-mail. She spends all her time arguing with people on the Internet, and she keeps changing her address.
I wish you'd talk to her."

I figured dropping her an e-mail would be better than not being
able to reach her at all.

Big Sister Song stood up purposefully. "I'll get you her new
e-mail address."

"There's no rush, you can get it later," I said rather insincerely.

"I'm afraid I might forget." And she hurried off to the back.

Big Sister Song is still so gracious, I thought, an old-style
Beijinger.

At this point, a young guy walked in. He was the kind of
young guy who would have all the girls chasing him—tall and
muscular like an athlete. He was wearing white high-top sneakers.
There is so much dust in Beijing that most men don't wear white
sneakers. He looked me over very confidently like he wanted to
know who I thought I was, but then he said politely, "Hello. Are
you . . . ?"

"I'm . . . a friend of Big Sister's." The penny dropped. "You're . . ."
I was going to say "Little Xi's son," but for some reason I didn't.

"Grandma!" The young man greeted Big Sister Song.

"Hey, you're back. This is my grandson. This is Master Chen."

I acted surprised. "Your grandson!"

"Master Chen, I'm Wei Guo."

"Pleased to meet you. What a handsome young man you are."
We shook hands. I remembered that when I'd last seen this boy over
ten years ago, Little Xi had told me he used her maternal surname,
Wei.

"Master Chen is Taiwanese and an old customer," Big Sister
Song said about me.

"I don't think we've ever met."

"He used to come to the old place," Big Sister Song explained. "Master Chen hasn't been in Beijing for years."

"Big Sister, I *live* in Beijing now."

Wei Guo didn't ask me what district I lived in. Instead, he asked, "What do you do, Master Chen?"

"I'm a writer."

This seemed to pique his interest. "What do you write?"

"Everything, fiction, reviews, criticism . . ."

"Criticism about what?"

"Food, drink, entertainment, cultural media, business management . . ."

"And what do you think about China's current situation?"

This was turning into a cross-examination, so Big Sister Song broke in. "Stay here for dinner!"

"I've got something on tonight—maybe next time, Big Sister!"

"You two keep talking," she said and went into the back room.

Wei Guo looked at me with a very steady gaze that bordered on intimidation.

I wanted to know why Little Xi said she could not talk to her son, so I said quite deliberately, "Today everybody says that no country is as good as China." Little Xi had said this would sound like something her son might say.

"That's right, quite correct. Ji Xianlin said the twenty-first century is the Chinese century."

I decided to tease him a little. "Well then, what do you intend to do in this Chinese century?"

Most young people would act a little bashful before answering such a question, but Wei Guo did not hesitate. "Right now I'm in the Faculty of Law at Peking University. After I graduate, I'm going to take an exam to become a government official."

"Do you want to be an official?"

"Yes, I do. The country needs talent."

"Wei Guo, if you could choose, which ministry would you like to join?" I remembered Little Xi mentioning the Central Propaganda Department, and so I wanted to sound him out.

"The Central Propaganda Department."

I hadn't expected him to be so frank.

"Of course, one can't just join the Propaganda Department, but it's my ideal choice."

"Why the Propaganda Department?" I persisted in this line of questioning.

"The people cannot rely just on material power; they have to have spiritual power, too, for the people to be united. Hard power is important, but soft power is equally important. I think the Propaganda Department is vital, but it's not doing as well as it could; it could do even better."

"How could it do better?" I asked. He seemed to have it all down pat.

"For example, they don't understand the Internet and netizens well enough; they don't really know about the trends in national youth culture. I could make a real contribution in these areas. I'm studying law and I could provide solid legal backing for the Propaganda Department's policy decisions. That would contribute to the state's 'rule of law' policy. Of course I'm still young and I have my immature and romantic idealist side—but I think the Department is very romantic and idealistic." He began to look a little embarrassed.

"Romantic? Idealistic? What do you mean?"

"You're a writer, you should know. The Propaganda Department guides the spiritual life of the entire nation."

I begin to tire of this topic. "Do you ever have live gigs here?" I asked, gesturing toward the stage.

"New bands and some community groups play here every night. I gave Grandma the idea. All sorts of young people come here, and that gives me a chance to understand what they're thinking and doing. If you don't do any survey work, you don't have any right to talk about anything."

"In a place like this you're going to have some bad elements mixed in with the innocent kids. Won't that influence your future?"

"You underestimate our Party and our government. Everything is under the Party's and the government's control; they know everything."

"Well, it's been great talking to you, Wei Guo, but I need to get going." He must have thought I was pretty backward.

"Have a good time in Beijing. Write more articles on the true face of China so our Taiwanese compatriots won't so easily believe the Western media."

I was about to ask him to tell his Grandma I was leaving, when she appeared.

"Leaving already?"

"I have some business on the Eastside, so I'd better leave early to beat the traffic."

"Come back when you can and have some Guizhou goose."

"Of course . . . You take care of yourself, Big Sister."

As we shook hands, Big Sister slipped me a piece of paper. We both felt a little reluctant to part.

Just as I was reaching the door, Wei Guo turned to me with a cold look. "Master Chen, have you seen my mom lately?"

"No," I lied.

He said good-bye politely, and I nodded back. I couldn't help taking another look at his snow-white sneakers.

*The year of Lao Chen's zodiac sign*

This year is the year of my zodiac sign, and a lot of strange things are bound to happen. Things like getting so worked up that I burst into tears, or like meeting Little Xi and Fang Caodi one after the other after such a long time—I think all these things are vaguely connected.

It's been a long time since I've run into anyone so completely out of tune with the prevailing mood as Little Xi and Fang Caodi. Of course, China is a huge country and you can meet all sorts of different people. From the mid-1980s, when I first came to the mainland, up until a few years ago, I knew quite a few dissatisfied people like them, but there are fewer and fewer of them now. I have not associated with such out-of-sync types since the global economy went into crisis and China's Golden Age of Ascendancy officially began.

Let me describe for you the three types of people I most frequently come into contact with now:

The first type is made up of people like my cleaning lady. I hire only laid-off female workers who live in Beijing with their families. That's because I'm away from home a lot and it makes me feel safer. My current cleaning lady's daughter is a graduate and works for a foreign company, so her finances aren't a problem, but she likes to keep busy, likes to work. While she's cleaning, she tells me all about her daughter and her boyfriend. Such details as how much her daughter spends at the hairdresser, or that her daughter's boyfriend might be transferred to Shanghai. She also tells me all the Taiwanese news that she sees on Fujian's Southeast Satellite Television. I just sit there working at my computer and listening. Sometimes it gets a little irritating, but sometimes I'm grateful to her for keeping me in touch with ordinary folk.

The second type is made up of media reporters. Most of them

are young and dynamic, and they know everything worth knowing in China: who's hot and who's not, which nightclub is in and which one's out, which year-end blockbuster film is great and which one is a dog, and where to go on holiday if you want to be cool. When they write a special report that needs an outsider's opinion, they may well call on a famous Taiwanese cultural personality who lives in Beijing like me. Hey, it's convenient. I'm also happy to talk with them so that I can get to know what the young people are wearing, what's on their radar. You know, so I won't get passé.

The third type is made up of publishing-house editors. Some of my books have been published in simplified-character editions and have sold pretty well, so editors often approach me wanting my next book. The problem is, I've not been able to write a single sentence for the last couple of years now; the best I can do is market a few of the older works I wrote in Taiwan that haven't yet been published on the mainland. I've repackaged a couple more of them and they're due out soon in simplified characters. Sometimes they take me to meet their editors-in-chief—who used to be nobodies, but who have become managing directors. Most of the time they're not interested in my books; they're concerned just about market share and the next big thing. Once in a while, as a major figure in the Taiwanese cultural world, I get to meet some officials of the Chinese News Service, the Ministry of Culture, the Taiwan Affairs Office, or the United Front Work Department. It's terrific to be an official in China today. They all cut quite a figure and, no matter what rank they occupy, when they talk they're all very impressive. They treat the Taiwanese like their little brothers, and all they ask is that we treat them like our big brothers.

I'm not being immodest when I say I'm a major figure in the Taiwanese cultural world. I was born in Hong Kong, and it was only after I finished elementary school in Tiu Keng Leng refugee camp that I followed my parents to Taiwan. Still, I have always genuinely thought of myself as Taiwanese. I've always loved to read, and I decided I wanted to be a writer while still at secondary school. While studying journalism, I came second in a short-story competition. I know it was because I went to Cultural University instead of National Taiwan University that I didn't win the first prize.

It made me so angry that I wrote a satirical story called "I Want to Go Abroad" in the style of Chen Yingzhen, but I didn't dare get it published. I circulated it among my classmates, who really liked it. Some dissident students tried to enroll me in their group, which made me both excited and anxious. I was just a student, my parents had worked their fingers to the bone so that I could go to university, and I had to watch out for my future. I didn't publish that story until after the media controls were lifted many years later. It came out in the *New Life* evening paper, but by then it was no longer topical and young people didn't understand what I was satirizing.

After graduation, I got lucky with a scholarship to a Catholic university in Jamaica. I practiced my English every day and devoured novels in the library. I was obsessed with the hard-boiled detective novels of Raymond Chandler and Dashiell Hammett. My MA thesis compared the logic of Charlie Chan with Western detective novels. I slogged for a year and a half, right through the summer vacation without taking a break, and got my masters degree.

In the library one day I read in the Hong Kong *Mingbao Monthly* that an overseas Chinese in New York was starting a Chinese-language daily called *Huabao*, and his managing editor was one of the judges who had given my student story its second prize. I got in touch straight away and was given a job. That's how I finally made it to Manhattan.

The *Huabao* was really small fry—it wasn't even on sale outside Chinatown. After working there a couple of years, I got pretty depressed. I was so bored that I wrote a novel called *The Last Grey-hound to Manhattan*. I never imagined that this overseas-student novel would allow me to squeeze into the ranks of Chinese-language writers for the rest of my life. I wrote it in the modernist stream-of-consciousness style, and I still don't know how I did it. Most people don't know that over the years this book has sold a hundred thousand copies in Taiwan. While I was in New York, the famous martial arts novelist Jin Yong visited America. I interviewed him for the paper. The ban on Jin Yong's works had just been lifted in Taiwan, and his name could be mentioned in the media. My interview was circulated, attracting a huge number of readers. It made me into a famous reporter.

Jin Yong also liked my interview. He knew I'd been born in Hong Kong and spoke Cantonese, so he invited me to come and work for *Mingbao*. I became an editor there and wrote articles about the mainland for the China section of the *Mingbao Daily*. From the mid-1980s to the early 1990s, I interviewed quite a few famous members of the older generation of mainland writers and artists. I established a network of contacts, witnessed a number of major events, and deepened my understanding of the mainland. In 1992, Jin Yong retired and I was given a post on the mainland. At the same time, my mainland girlfriend, Wen Lan, decided to go abroad, basically breaking up with me, so instead I decided to go back to Taiwan.

Now I was at the Taiwanese *United Daily*. I collected the articles I'd already written and planned to publish a volume of interviews with famous mainland cultural figures. I thought at the time that it would be my greatest contribution to posterity. These venerable personages ranked as national treasures—and where they had already died and my interview represented their parting words, its worth would be beyond question. I probably worked too slowly, revising the book over and over, and so I missed my opportunity. When *Endowment and Remembrance: In Search of One Hundred Forgotten Mainland Masters of Art and Literature* was finally published, the atmosphere in Taiwan had changed. The book didn't even make the Kingstone Bookstore's bestseller list; it was featured in the weekly book-review section of the *United Daily,* but nobody discussed it again after that. Lee Teng-hui was the president of Taiwan and ethnic conflict was growing increasingly acrimonious. The people of Taiwan were concerned about the dangers of a cross-Strait war and not about mainland-Chinese culture.

After the publication of my book, everybody in the trade labeled me as a "China expert" or "an expert on mainland issues"—in other words, they were not interested in me.

So I decided to change my image. If I couldn't write a literary masterpiece, I could at least write popular bestsellers. Books about war in the Taiwan Strait were big sellers at the time, so I read up on the nationalist and communist militaries to see what sort of angle I could take. I decided there were too many books following this trend and so I gave up, but I did learn something: if you want to ride a wave, you better get on early.

I wrote a detective novel called *Thirteen Months,* but it bombed.

People were becoming instantly famous by writing about their philosophy of life, so I wrote a book on life philosophies, but it bombed, too.

Management studies were all the rage, so I wrote several books on secret workplace-survival strategies, but they bombed, too.

My books on life philosophies and office management were really opportunistic works; they wouldn't sell, and I had to admit it. But *Thirteen Months* should not have been confined so easily to oblivion. It was certainly an excellent piece of innovative Taiwanese detective fiction. Unfortunately, contemporary Taiwanese readers were used only to Japanese detective works or Agatha Christie who-dunnits. They didn't know how to appreciate the black humor and ironic worldly sophistication of American-style hard-boiled detective novels. Perhaps I wasn't a first-rate writer, but I consoled myself with the self-mocking words of Somerset Maugham: among second-rate writers, I was definitely first-rate.

Finally, an opportunity came my way when some foreign author published a book on emotional IQ, or "EQ," and it sold like hot cakes in Taiwan. I immediately pulled together all the information I'd amassed over the years about Chinese culture, from philosophies of life to business management, and quickly came out with a book entitled *The Chinese EQ*.

Just as I expected, *The Chinese EQ* was on the Kingstone best-seller list for six weeks in a row, peaking at number two. To see my work displayed in the place of honor every day in bookstores made me feel great.

By that time I was a celebrated journalist, a novelist, an expert on mainland China, and a self-improvement specialist. I was also a bestselling author, and this status gave real meaning to everything else I wrote. Most people had never read my books and had no idea what I'd written; they just knew that I was a bestselling author. In the 1990s Taiwanese society still had a certain amount of respect for bestselling authors.

My luck held. After the millennium year of 2000, my books were published on the mainland one after another.

Then in 2004, Chen Shuibian was reelected as president. I received a retirement package from the *United Daily* and moved to Beijing.

When I first arrived, I had a feeling of urgency and started to write very industriously. I wrote about Taiwan and Hong Kong culture for the mainland, and about Beijing and Shanghai for Taiwan and Hong Kong. The most important thing I did was to bring out my *Comprehensive Cultural Guide to Beijing* well before the Beijing Olympics. I was interviewed on a China Central TV books program, and thus you could say that I had received Chinese government approval.

At that point there was only one thing that I wanted to do, write my *Ulysses* or *In Search of Lost Time*—my literary masterpiece. In an age when there are no first-rate writers, I still wanted to prove that I was the best of all the second-rate writers. I refused all further requests to write journalism and started to concentrate solely on my novel.

Since then, I have not written a single word.

I have to confess that I don't have to worry about meeting my living expenses. Western philosophers say that happiness consists in being moderately famous and moderately well-off, but not too famous and not too well-off. I don't depend on royalties to get by; they don't amount to much, anyway. The thing is, back in the early 1990s, when I was still working in Hong Kong and planning to get married, I bought a ninety-square-meter apartment on Hong Kong island, in Taikoo Shin. After my girlfriend went to Germany and married a German, I handed the apartment over to an estate agent to rent out for me and returned to Taiwan. Every year after that when we negotiated a new rental agreement, both the rent and the value of the property had soared. When I sold it just before Hong Kong's 1997 retrocession to China, it was worth almost ten times what I had paid for it. In all my working life I could never have made enough money to buy such an apartment at a later date. When the Asian financial meltdown hit, the Taiwanese dollar depreciated, but fortunately all my money was safely in Hong Kong dollars with the HSBC. In 2004, when I moved to Beijing, I bought three apartments in Happiness Village Number Two, just ahead of the government prohibition on foreigners, including people from Taiwan and Hong Kong, purchasing more than one residence. I lived in one apartment and rented out the other two. I converted all my money to Chinese renminbi and it appreciated in value. As the world economy continued to be hit by wave after wave of crises, only China continued to flourish, and my small earnings were enough to live on quite well.

I've worked very hard on my writing, but I have lost all inspiration. It disappeared exactly two years ago, just as official Chinese discourse announced that the global economy had entered a period of crisis while China's Golden Age of Ascendancy had begun. From that time on, I began to see that everyone in Beijing, and everywhere in China, was living well. I felt so spiritually and materially satisfied that I began to experience an overwhelming feeling of good fortune such as I never had before.

### An insomniac national leader

For more than a year, except for the New Year and other holidays, I'd been going to Jian Lin's firm's restaurant on the first Sunday of every month to have dinner, drink red wine, and watch old movies. Jian Lin is the owner of the Capital BOBO Properties Corporation. He is a member of the "old three classes"—the three secondary school classes of 1967, 1968, and 1969 that never graduated due to the Cultural Revolution. In 1978, when the college entrance examinations were reinstated, he went to university. He later became an official and often associated with artists and writers. Then he plunged into business in Hainan and somehow made it big in real estate, but he still has an air of culture about him and regards himself as "a scholar and a merchant." He likes to discuss national affairs, and every year at Chinese New Year he writes a few traditional-style poems and sends them off to his friends and customers.

Jian Lin is a workaholic, but two years ago he started a new custom. He began to have dinner with his friends and family and afterward show an old movie—on the first Sunday of every month. At first his movie evenings were very popular, but gradually his relatives cried off, and then his friends wanted to choose the films they liked before they would show up. By the start of winter, Jian Lin and I were often the only ones there.

After the first time a friend took me along, I became a regular. I had a lot of spare time, I lived fairly nearby and I loved to watch those post-1949 Chinese films. I hadn't got to see them in Hong Kong and Taiwan, so it was a new experience for me.

I was the only one who never missed a screening. Jian and I didn't have any connections on any other level—I didn't want anything from him and, because I wasn't especially important, he didn't have to be on his guard with me; I was the best sort of person for him to have a friendly social relationship with. In the winter, when there was just the two of us, Jian would bring out a bottle of red wine—always the finest-vintage '82, '85, or '89 Bordeaux. Sometimes we'd go through two bottles in one evening. The Taiwanese had started drinking high-quality red wines fifteen years before the mainlanders got in on the act, so I could join him in appreciating his wines, and I would willingly listen to him showing off the enological knowledge he had picked up in books. He had found an ideal wine-drinking partner. But whenever a crowd turned up, I noticed he was pretty parsimonious—for them, he brought out a few bottles of only ordinary vintage. This, to me, indicated our greater friendship.

The only thing that concerned me was that I couldn't pay him back. That made me feel like a freeloading literary type. Jian Lin always served Bordeaux, never Burgundy. After looking up Burgundy on the net, I told him about it; he seemed curious and wanted to know more. I hit on a plan. When I want back to Taiwan for the Lunar New Year, I looked up my secondary school classmate Ah Yuan.

Ah Yuan is the largest collector of Burgundy in Taiwan. When the global economy hit the skids, Ah Yuan's wealth shrunk, but his Burgundy collection was still intact. I had never asked Ah Yuan for anything before, but this time I asked him to give me two bottles of good Burgundy. He gladly told me to take a few more bottles, but I declined because of customs duties. I took just two bottles, one white wine and one red.

I sent Jian Lin a short message asking him what was showing the following Sunday. I told him I was bringing a Bâtard-Montrachet 1989 and a Romanée-Conti 1999.

When I took the two bottles over to the restaurant, there weren't any other guests, just me and Jian Lin. He carefully examined them, exclaiming, "Great wine, great wine . . . Let's open it and let it breathe."

"What's on tonight?" I asked while he gently poured the red wine into a crystal decanter.

It was the 1964 film *Never Forget Class Struggle*, directed by Xie Tieli. "Have you ever seen it?" he asked.

"Are you kidding? If I'd seen it, Chiang Kai-shek would have had me shot."

"Those were good times, 1964," Jian Lin said. "The Three Years Natural Disaster was over, people's living conditions were beginning to recover, and the Cultural Revolution had not yet started. But in 1959 Old Mao was unhappy. He had nothing to do after resigning his post as National Chairman, so he put out the slogan 'Never forget the class struggle.' And this film responded to his call to remind the masses never to forget that there were still class enemies concealed among the people. It was advance notice of the coming Four Cleanups Movement to cleanse politics, the economy, Party organization, and ideology. It was also a prelude to the Cultural Revolution."

"I've invited my cousin to watch the film and taste your wine," Jian later said as we were eating.

I didn't remember ever meeting his cousin and I wasn't particularly happy about sharing my expensive wine with someone I didn't know.

Just then a rather stern and pale-faced man with sparse hair came in and greeted Jian Lin as "Elder Brother."

"This is my cousin, Dongsheng. This is my good friend from Taiwan, Lao Chen."

"He Dongsheng, we've met before," I said as we shook hands. "It was at the Macao session of the Prosperous China Conference in 1992; you were the representative from Fudan University."

"Yes, yes," He Dongsheng said softly.

Jian Lin looked puzzled. "Do you two know each other?"

"Yes, yes," He Dongsheng repeated.

We all felt a little awkward. "We met twenty years ago," I said.

A wealthy Taiwanese named Shui Xinghua—meaning "prosperous China"—had set up a foundation that held four Xinghua, or Prosperous China, conferences in the early 1990s. The idea was to invite a dozen or so promising young people from China, Taiwan, and Hong Kong to get together and exchange ideas and experiences. In Macao in 1992, He Dongsheng was a mainland delegate and I was a Taiwanese delegate. He Dongsheng was just a young scholar at that time and didn't give us the impression that he was particularly outstanding, but then later he became a high-ranking official in the Communist Party.

We all raised our glasses to each other, and after that we watched the film. Nobody said a word throughout the entire thing except once when Jian Lin commented, "The woman playing the mother-in-law of the counterrevolutionary was really very young at the time. You can still see her quite often these days on TV."

During the screening, I took a look at He Dongsheng. He seemed to have fallen asleep. Jian Lin was very conscientiously watching the film—he really did love those old Red Classics.

*Never Forget Class Struggle* was about an electrical-machinery factory in the Northeast. The workers were all striving to improve production, but then one young worker married a woman with a petit bourgeois family background. She urged her husband to buy himself a suit made of extremely expensive material, costing about 148 renminbi. The young worker's mother-in-law also urged him to hunt wild ducks during his free time and sell them at a profit on the black market. He took so much time off that his absence from work almost caused a major accident and harmed the national interest. All this was because of a loss of revolutionary vigilance—they had forgotten about the class struggle. At the end of the film, five big, blood-red words filled the screen: NEVER FORGET THE CLASS STRUGGLE!

"Pretty good," I said, "interesting, but when young people see it now they probably won't understand it. They'll need someone to interpret it for them."

Suddenly He Dongsheng spoke up. "It's easy to make them work for eight hours, but it's hard to control them after those eight hours. Old Mao never solved that problem."

I was rather surprised that He Dongsheng would come right out and call Mao Zedong "Old Mao."

"Did you know, after Deng Xiaoping's 'Reform and Openness' started," he continued, "there was a magazine in Tianjin called

*After Work?* Eight hours was work time and after eight hours—*after work*—was leisure time, but nobody knew then what to do with leisure time. Socialism had totally transformed work time, but was unable to handle after-work time, the time *after* those eight hours of work . . .”

"After they work eight hours, let capitalism take care of them," Jian Lin quipped.

"Yes, definitely," He Dongsheng continued—the alcohol had loosened him up. "Your Old Mao cannot ask people to grasp revolution and increase production twenty-four hours a day. You have to let people go home and have something tasty to eat, buy some nice clothes, and indulge in some petit bourgeois fun. The people want all this and you can't deny them it. If you don't let them enjoy themselves, who's going to work for you? Just having a good life is not too much to ask."

Most officials, when they open their mouths, seem to come out only with conventional bureaucratic patter, but what He Dongsheng was saying sounded quite normal.

He began to grow on me.

After expressing his opinions, he gloomily sipped his wine.

"This is very good wine, very good wine," Jian Lin said again after a while. "It's better now than it was before. The flavor has completely opened out. We've been mixing white and red, and it still tastes great."

We all fell silent again. I thought He Dongsheng would leave after the film ended, but he just sat there with us. He didn't speak anymore and he didn't touch the huge assortment of snacks that Jian served with the wine. He just kept on slowly sipping his wine. Jian brought out some big cigars, but we didn't want any, so he was too embarrassed to smoke alone.

After the bottles and our glasses were all empty, Jian served up some famous Wuyi Dahongpao tea. He Dongsheng didn't touch it. He didn't seem to need even any water. It was just about midnight when He Dongsheng stood up and went to the toilet.

"He suffers from insomnia," Jian Lin whispered. "He doesn't need any sleep, and I was afraid he'd stay here forever. I can't stay up all night; these days I go to bed early and get up early."

"I go to bed early, too—I hate staying up all night." I recalled that He Dongsheng had dozed off during the film.

"How about I give you a ride home?" said He Dongsheng when he got back.

"There's no need," I replied, "I live nearby. I'll walk home." Then, without thinking, I asked, "Is your driver still here?" Of course, as a high official, his driver would always be there.

I never imagined he would respond the way he did. "At night, I drive myself, I like to drive. Sometimes I drive around until morning; if I'm tired, I take a nap in the car." He seemed to think that he had said too much, muttered, "I'm going," and then left.

I sort of regretted not letting He Dongsheng drive me home. I really didn't live that close. In the daytime, I would have walked it, but so late at night, I had to take a cab. It was Jian Lin who really lived close, on the top floor of a building in the same neighborhood.

"We hadn't seen each other for a long time," Jian Lin explained, "when I saw him recently at a memorial service for my aunt, and so I thought I'd invite him over."

"You're cousins on your father's side," I said, "but your last name is Jian and his is He. Why is that?"

"My father had two younger brothers who both joined the Revolution and changed their last names. Dongsheng's last name was originally Jian."

Apparently, it was quite common for second cousins in old revolutionary families to have different surnames.

"What about your other uncle?" I asked.

"I don't have much contact with that side of the family," Jian Lin answered.

I was uncomfortable delving any further into Jian's family, so I said, "I never imagined that you and He Dongsheng were related. How high up is he now?"

"How high?" exclaimed Jian Lin. "Right now he is a member of the Politburo—a veteran of three Party Congresses. That's no mean achievement."

"Does that make him a national leader?" I asked.

"Strictly speaking, they should be called 'Party and national leaders,'" Jian Lin said. "On the Party side, everyone from the secretaries in the Party Secretariat on up should be regarded as Party and national leaders. That would, of course, include members of the Politburo."

Most national leaders I had seen had well-groomed black pompadours and ruddy complexions, and they were always in high spirits. I'd never imagined I would run into a pale, balding, insomniac national leader.

### A titillating spring night

Standing on the pavement waiting for a cab on that early-spring morning after watching an old film and drinking so much wine, I had lost all desire for sleep. I phoned a friend of mine and went over to her place. I'd first met her over ten years ago when she was still working at the Paradise Club—a popular Beijing nightclub and disco famous for its beautiful and cultured escorts. I am a man of modest appetites, but sometimes I have my desires, and so I looked her up. I figured it was over two years since I'd last seen her, and I hadn't even thought of her, not until that morning . . .

When I returned home from my visit, I still couldn't get to sleep. I had only one question on my mind: should I send an e-mail to Little Xi?

Big Sister Song had said Little Xi often changed her e-mail address. So there was no point writing one—her address had probably already changed. And if I did write, I might be inviting trouble. She'd always been the type of woman I like. When she was running the restaurant, I was strongly attracted to her, but there were always too many customers after her. Although we'd known each other for twenty years and could be considered old friends, there'd never been anything sexual between us, not even flirting. She was always surrounded by a circle of men—some of them were her friends and some were suitors; there were also some unsuccessful suitors who then joined her gang of friends. She was one of those women who had only male friends and, at the same time, seemed quite unaware of the fascination she held for men. She actually believed that all her male friends were just mates. I never pursued her romantically, and she never showed any interest in me, either. Later on I thought she had married a foreigner and moved to England, but now it looked like that had fallen through. Anyway, it had been seven or eight years since I'd had any real contact with her.

I'd been worried about her being a troublemaker. She wasn't one of those intellectual-style dissidents, but political trouble had been dogging her for decades, all because she was too outspoken and too stubborn. She hated injustice and thus easily offended people. In the past, many people had been willing to help her, including some foreigners. But today foreigners like that have disappeared—none of them want to upset the Chinese Communist Party. Foreigners willing to risk offending the CCP don't get a visa. Everybody around her was living the good life and couldn't be bothered with her. They were all avoiding her, and that's why she'd told me last time that everyone around her had changed.

After talking to Big Sister Song and Little Xi, I'd felt that Little Xi must be in trouble again. Now I was convinced that she'd been under surveillance there in the park next to the National Art Museum.

If I hooked up with her, wouldn't she bring me trouble? My life was so good now; everything was going along smoothly and I felt extremely happy. Why should I risk it? If I saw her and she expressed the least bit of interest in me, I wouldn't be able to control myself. I found her sexually very attractive, which scared me. I hadn't felt like this about someone for a long time. If I took an emotional leap and we really got together, I could guarantee that we would not be able to get along. She still imagined me the way I'd been ten years ago, when I'd agreed with her on everything. But I'd become one of those people she said had changed. Our present frames of mind were as different as our understandings of China's current situation. I was certain that we would never be able to agree on anything. I remembered when Chen Shuibian had run for reelection in Taiwan—many of my male friends supported the Nationalist Party while their wives supported the Democratic Progressive Party, and they split up over this.

I sat there in front of my computer staring blankly at the piece of paper Big Sister Song had given me. Suddenly it dawned on me that I had not been able to write a really good novel. Perhaps my life was too peaceful, I just felt too happy. I felt no pressure. Who was it that could tear me away from this excessive feeling of happiness and good fortune? Little Xi, obviously.

Written on the scrap of paper was the yahoo.com e-mail address *feichengwuraook*. Next to it were the words "If you're not sincere, don't bother, okay?"

*Little Xi's autobiography*

I am Wei Xihong. Everyone calls me Little Xi.

I don't know where to start; I don't know how the world has become what it is. I'm just afraid that many things may be forgotten later, so I want to write them all down and store them in this Google file.

Somebody is following me. But I haven't done anything wrong. So why are they on my tail?

Maybe I'm just too nervous. Maybe there is nobody following me at all, and I'm just overly suspicious.

If somebody is following me, it's bound to have something to do with Wei Guo. How did I ever give birth to such a monster?

Ever since he was born, he has frightened me. He had a face like a little angel, but he lied, ingratiated himself with his teachers, ingratiated himself with anyone who could do him any good, and bullied anyone weaker than he was. His character was just naturally cruel. Okay, so he was like that from childhood. Now he writes letters informing on his classmates, getting them into trouble with the authorities, and persecuting them. He is always spouting empty slogans, pretending to embrace a wonderful idealistic morality.

Does he have his father's genes, or my genes, or has he inherited his character from my father? Or is he just the result of the worst possible combination of bloodlines?

He blames me for not telling him who his father is, and I can understand that. He actually curses my friends using the Cultural Revolution term "monsters and demons"! He says they are dubious characters who could have a bad influence on his future. He laughs at me for resigning my position as a judge and says that I'm too stupid to be his mother.

If that 1983 crackdown on "spiritual pollution" and crime had not made me understand clearly that I was not suited to be a judge, I would still be part of the Public Security system today. I think I'm constitutionally unable to adapt to this political system. I studied law only to please my father.

My father can probably be considered one of the first judges in the New China. In the 1950s, he participated in the drafting of the new Constitution. I remember when I was a child and my father came home, Mother would tell us not to make any noise. We were all afraid of my father. He never once gave me a hug. My mother was probably more afraid of him than anyone else. I remember my mother never smiled if he was around. After he died, she became another person. She was reborn, and even her voice seemed louder. My mother didn't say much about the things my father did, but no doubt he must have persecuted and ruined quite a few people.

My father himself was persecuted and put in prison during the Cultural Revolution. He was released only when he became ill. In 1979, after the college entrance examinations had been reinstated, I graduated from Number 101 Secondary School. Fully aware of my father's wishes, I listed the Peking College of Political Science and Law as my first university choice. I wanted nothing more than to become a judge after graduation. I thought that, like my father, I was a prime candidate for being a judge in our republic.

My mother had told me in private that my personality was not suited to studying law. She told me to study science and engineering, and keep out of trouble. At the time I didn't agree and felt furious with her. I wanted only to make my father happy and figured that my mother was a housewife with no practical experience or understanding. People are so strange. When people treat us badly, we do what they want us to do; when people treat us well, we pay no attention to them at all.

During the trial of the Gang of Four, I watched the televised proceedings with my father. Father's temper had grown even worse after the Cultural Revolution; he was very hard to get on with and he often swore at us. He didn't achieve the success he longed for in his later years and he took his hatred to the grave.

While I was in college, people had their Rightist status removed and many who had suffered miscarriages of justice during the Cultural Revolution received political rehabilitation. Even the Gang of Four were given a trial, and state-appointed lawyers to defend them. I was full of hope for the future and utterly confident that the Communist Party intended to create a society governed by the rule of law.

I graduated in 1983 and was assigned to a county-level court under the Beijing jurisdiction to serve as a legal clerk-secretary. That was when my nightmare began.

I was twenty-two years old when I arrived at my work unit in August. Everyone else there had just finished studying Party Central's August 25 document "Decision on Severely Cracking Down on Criminal Activity." They briefly explained the "spirit" of the document to me and then they let me get to work. I'd always hated to see the guilty prosper and the innocent suffer, and so I was naturally very much in favor of the Party and government's policy of severely and rapidly punishing criminal activity according to the law. I was certain I would not be soft on criminals. What I didn't know, however, was that the "severely and rapidly" that I had in mind was not the "severely" or "rapidly" that they practiced. Maybe I hadn't had enough psychological preparation, and perhaps my idea of the rule of law was too far removed from reality. In any case, the problems began as soon as I started work.

The correct procedure in criminal cases was for the Public Security Bureau to arrest people, the prosecutor's office to bring charges, and the judges to decide the verdict and the sentence. In order to process cases rapidly the Public Security Bureau, the prosecutor's office, and the legal division each assigned two people. All of us worked in an office of the Public Security Bureau. The arrest, investigation, decision, and the sentencing all took place practically at the same time. In those days, nobody much understood the function of a prosecutor. Our judicial unit assigned two people of the lowest secretarial rank—a retired army officer who was politically reliable but who had had no legal training and me, someone who had just graduated from law school and who was also a young woman. In this way, the chief and deputy chief of the local Public Security Bureau basically controlled everything.

I was ready to fall apart by the end of the very first day. In every case, big or small, the accused was given the death sentence, and not one of the crimes involved murder. Robbery received a death sentence, petty theft received a death sentence, swindling received a death sentence, and no one paid any attention at all when the accused produced solid exculpatory evidence.

There was one case in which a young man had sexual relations with a young woman, her family came after him, the two sides had a fight, and they all received minor injuries. The girl's family went to the Public Security Bureau and had the boy arrested. The boy's family knew that this was potentially a very serious situation for him during this crackdown period. The whole family went over and knelt down in front of the girl's house to beg them to withdraw the charge, but the girl's family refused. When the case came to our six-person group, the Public Security chief asked us, "What is the sentence for the crime of hooliganism?" "This crime does not merit the death penalty!" I exclaimed as soon as I could. The other five group members stared at me in silent rebuke. In the end the boy was given an indefinite sentence of labor reform in far-off Xinjiang Province.

After court that day, the deputy chief of Public Security came over to us clutching a report and said, "Other places are all executing ten or more people by firing squad . . . Just look at Henan Province. Zhengzhou, Kaifeng, and Luoyang all executed forty or fifty people at the same time. Even a place like Jiaozuo executed thirty at the same time. But we haven't even reached double figures. What do you say we should do about it?" Everybody felt under great pressure.

At that point the retired army officer who had been assigned with me said, "The hooligan intentionally injured others. His sentence was too light and out of step with the spirit of Party Central."

"Then we'll just change the sentence to execution and say he made it onto the list." Turning to me the deputy chief added, "Female comrade, you should not be so kindhearted." His reprimand really knocked me back—that's how weak I was.

That weekend we shot ten people in the back of the head. I was ashamed of my cowardice and felt so angry about my compromise. What good is the law? Is this a society that practices the rule of law? I debated with myself. When I returned from the execution grounds that day, I set out on a path from which there could be no return.

In the next round, the court secretaries went together with the district police officers to various locations to investigate cases and arrest people. Then we took the accused to the Public Security Bureau in the county seat for trial. I had already made up my mind: for any crime that didn't deserve capital punishment, I would say so outright. Since there would be a record that one of the two judicial representatives was opposed to the death sentence, the others in the group would be unable to insist on it and would have to change the sentence. But in this way there would be fewer death sentences, and everybody would be afraid of criticism from higher up. Members of my work unit phoned me and tried to dissuade me from acting the way I was, but I just ignored them.

Later on, I came to know that even if I had not had an "accident," my work unit was already planning to transfer me. One night in the county seat, an army vehicle ran into me. This was a common occurrence. In rural areas, army vehicles sped around like crazy and often ran into people. If civilians were killed or injured, they just had to accept their fate. But even though it was a common occurrence, usually if an army vehicle ran into a member of the Public Security authorities, there would be endless wranglings back and forth between these and the military. In my case, however, the army took me straight to Number 301 Hospital, and afterward my work unit didn't inquire further into the incident.

After leaving the hospital, I handed in my resignation and became a person without a work unit. And my mother didn't have a bad thing to say about it.

I became a privately self-employed person by opening a small restaurant with my mother. We mostly served her Guizhou-style goose. In the 1980s, Beijing was a fascinating place, the heart of an era full of promise. Our first regular customers were natives of Guizhou, especially scholars and writers who had moved to Beijing. They brought other Beijing writers, artists, and scientists and foreigners to eat and to talk. My mother loved to entertain guests and I loved the excitement. Everybody called me Little Xi. We expanded our restaurant and renamed it The Five Flavors. In the autumn of 1988, I met Shi Ping and fell in love.

He was a poet. There is nothing at all poetic about me, but we both cherished genuine sentiment. Shi Ping said that someday he would certainly receive the Nobel Prize for literature, and I said I would certainly accompany him to Sweden to attend the award ceremony. That was the happiest time in my entire life.

We didn't really have too much time alone together, though, because Shi Ping liked to spend time with his poet and artist mates. There were quite a few women around him, but, surprisingly, I didn't mind.

Every night The Five Flavors was full of our intellectual and artistic friends debating issues, drafting and signing manifestos, competing jealously for each other's affections, getting drunk and throwing up. The police visited us frequently, but my mother was very adept at getting rid of them.

In the spring of 1989 Shi Ping and a group of his friends went to Lake Baiyangdian and stayed a few days—they had been "sent down" there during the Cultural Revolution. I came back to Beijing early. I had the feeling Shi Ping was seeing one of the other women, so I found an excuse to leave. I guess I didn't want a direct confrontation. That night the authorities closed our restaurant down. They said a group of academics had issued some sort of political statement there a few days earlier, with foreigners present.

I don't know what I was thinking at the time, but I actually went to see Ban Cuntou. He was in my class at university. He grew up in this big courtyard and could be considered a member of China's Red aristocracy. His whole demeanor implied that this world had been created through his force of arms and therefore it all belonged to him. There were many people like him living in Beijing's big, old-fashioned courtyards. I'd heard that he was the highest-ranking official among my former classmates, so I went over to ask his advice. When we were in school, he often hinted that I ought to become his girlfriend. He thought that every woman should like him, but I couldn't stomach his attitude. This time I was really stupid to think that I could take advantage of my "old flame" status to see if he could save my restaurant.

I was in a rotten mood in the first place, and I was overconfident about the drinking capacity I thought I'd built up at the restaurant. That night we didn't drink Chinese rice wine, but we had something called Rémy Martin. I drank too fast, wasn't used to foreign liquor, and before I knew it I was plastered . . . I remember Ban Cuntou pointing at the TV reporting on Mikhail Gorbachev's visit and asking me, "What do you think about Gorbachev?"

When I woke up, I was in bed and he was sitting on the sofa in his underwear reading the paper. I realized I had slept with him. To get even with Shi Ping? I don't think I'd have done it for that. Ban Cuntou had deliberately got me drunk. "Well, this time you finally got to me," he said when he saw I was awake.

"Ban Cuntou, you've gone too far this time!" I said angrily.

"Well, you're no St. Joan the virgin martyr either," he retorted.

Ever since college, I'd always known that guys like him were smooth-talking and insincere, so I shut up. With a terrible headache, I went to the bathroom, had a quick shower, got dressed, and left without saying another word.

In the days after that, everybody was busy going to Tiananmen Square. Shi Ping wrote a new poem in support of the students. I was still furious with Shi Ping, and we were both busy with our own activities on the Square.

Then they started shooting at us, and Shi Ping and I were separated.

A couple of weeks later, I was arrested, but they let me go when they found out I was pregnant.

Actually, I was already three months pregnant. I was so caught up in the June 4 events that I didn't even notice. At the time I believed it was Shi Ping's child, but later on I didn't dare say for certain.

I lived with my mother and waited for the baby. The big courtyard was full of people from political and legal circles, who all knew of my situation; we had to put up with a lot of tongues wagging and fingers pointing behind our backs. Fortunately, after June 4 everyone felt they had just survived a calamity and they didn't want to be too nosy and attract attention.

I didn't hear anything from Shi Ping for a long time. He escaped to Hong Kong in secret. Later on, he went to France and married a Frenchwoman. He never even sent me a single letter to let me know he was safe.

When my son was born, I named him Wei Min, giving him my last name. When Wei Min was twenty years old, he changed his name to Wei Guo, exchanging the word "people"—Min—for "nation"—Guo.

Our restaurant was closed for a year and a half, but the following autumn, we received a notice that we could open again. Did Ban Cuntou help me? I don't think so.

Mother and I became extremely busy reopening the restaurant and trying to make a living. To begin with, business was very slow. The national economy was in decline, and many people were out of work in Beijing. President Jiang Zemin had let it be known that he intended to crack down on private businesses like ours. The people who had made up our most solid customer base couldn't satisfy the thought-police investigators, so their work units fired them, and they didn't have either the money or the spirit to eat in restaurants. A lot of our regulars had been foreigners, but they had not yet returned to China. Needless to say, the winter of 1991 was a cold one.

In 1992, Deng Xiaoping made his "southern tour" in support of continued economic Reform and Openness, and then Beijing's financial conditions started to improve. At that time we worked particularly hard on our business and didn't go in for any more "salon" activities. My mother and I read up on some new recipes, remodeled the restaurant inside and out, trained a new cook from Guizhou, and business gradually picked up, but it was exhausting work. My mother handled the lunch crowd while I took care of my son in the daytime, then I handled the dinner crowd. Gradually some of our old customers started drifting back. They would talk for hours, taking from five thirty to midnight to eat dinner. Sometimes I would sit beside them and listen, but I would close up shop at midnight—no more talking until dawn. Freedom of speech at the dinner table slowly returned in the late 1990s. By listening to them talk and by reading some of the banned books from Hong Kong they gave me, I slowly began to understand what modern Chinese history had really been like, especially the things that my mother and father had been through.

Our Taiwanese and Hong Kong compatriots also started coming back, along with some foreigners. Peter, or Pi-te as we used to call him, arrived around the middle of 1997, when Hong Kong was returned to China. I called him Little Pi. He was slightly younger than me and very shy. He was a reporter stationed in Beijing, working for a foreign news agency, and he especially liked me to tell him about the Tiananmen democracy movement of 1989. After we'd known each other for a year, he very formally asked me to be his girlfriend. I thought he was decent, and nobody else seemed to be after me at the time, so I agreed. I knew that I wouldn't be with him for a lifetime—I didn't love him that much—so I refused to move in with him. Later, when he was transferred home, he asked me to marry him, but I turned him down.

At that time all my friends loved to discuss contemporary politics and criticize the government. That's why I cannot adapt to today's situation. Suddenly in the last two years, since China's so-called Golden Age of Ascendancy officially began, not only has everybody stopped criticizing the government, but they have all become extremely satisfied with the current state of affairs. I don't know how this transformation came about. My mind is a complete blank because I recently spent some time in a mental hospital and the medicine they gave me has left me muddleheaded. My mother tells me that one day I came home and started shouting, "They're going to crack down again! They're cracking down again!" She says I didn't sleep all night and kept mumbling to myself. Early the next morning, I went out into the courtyard and started cursing the Communist Party, cursing the government, and cursing our neighbors, shouting that the law courts are all bullshit. And the courtyard was full of representatives of the Chinese legal system! Not long after that, I fainted, and when I woke up I was in a mental hospital. My son, Wei Guo, said he had arranged it all. He said he had saved my life by preventing me from shouting all that crazy nonsense. Otherwise, if a crackdown really did start, they would probably shoot me in the head.

When I was discharged, everybody around me had already changed. When I asked them what had happened while I was in the hospital, they wouldn't tell me. I don't know if they were feigning ignorance or if they really didn't remember. What astonished me most was their reaction when I started to talk about the past, especially the events around June 4, 1989. They didn't want to talk about it; their faces went blank. When we talked about the Cultural Revolution, all they could remember was the fun they had when they were sent down to the countryside—it had all turned into some sort of romantic nostalgia for their adolescence. They didn't even know how to "remember the bitter past and think of the sweet future" like the Party had taught them. Certain collective memories seemed to have been completely swallowed up by a cosmic black hole, never to be heard of again. I just couldn't understand it. Had they changed or was there something wrong with me?

I also started to suspect that the antidepressants the hospital had given me were having serious side effects.

Now I go on the Internet all day and argue with people under several different names.

I discovered that the nationalistic "angry youth" on the Internet are actually not all youths. Some of them are in their fifties and sixties. They grew up during the Cultural Revolution and heeded Old Mao's call for young people to engage with important national affairs. None of them went to college. They work at the most menial jobs in society and haven't had the benefits of the Reform and Opening policies. Now they are laid-off or retired and they have learned how to go on the Internet, where they can find like-minded people and a place to vent their anger and dissatisfaction. Their language is the language of the Cultural Revolution, they especially revere Mao Zedong, are especially nationalistic, anti-American, and bellicose. The cultural enlightenment movement of the 1980s and the ideological polemics of the 1990s have had no influence on them. Their mode of thinking remains an unreconstructed Maoist Chinese Communist Party mode of thinking. I love to contact them, to join their patriotic forums, old-classmates' Web sites, and argue with them. I present the strict facts and employ reasoned arguments, and I argue exclusively from the point of view of the Constitution of the People's Republic of China. This infuriates them, and they all attack me.

I know only that in doing this I am reminding everyone that they should never forget that the Chinese Communist Party is not the great, glorious, always correct party of their propaganda.

Of course I am also telling myself never to forget this lesson.

Naturally my postings are very quickly deleted by the Internet police; sometimes they block me completely and I cannot even post them. But *their* posts are never ever deleted.

Wei Guo must have found out about my Internet activities and turned me in to the authorities. That's why I'm being watched.

I feel very lonely. I don't trust anyone except my mother. A while ago, I ran into the writer Lao Chen, at the Sanlian Bookstore. He used to come to the old restaurant quite often to talk, and the impression he gave me was that he was one of us. He's also Taiwanese, so I latched on to him and jabbered on for quite a while before I realized that I hadn't seen him in ten years, and he might not be the person he was back then. The Taiwanese and Hong Kong people of today are not like the Taiwanese and Hong Kong people back then. How could he be the same? Eventually I found some excuse and left. I didn't think that he would look up my mother's new restaurant, and then get my e-mail address from her. My mother must still be hoping that I'll find a man and stop doing what she believes are crazy things. She still has another mistaken idea: she thinks I cannot get along with mainland-Chinese men, so she is always introducing me to Taiwanese and Hong Kong men. What can I tell her? I'm such a bad daughter, still relying on her to support me at my age.

My poor mother, she has to deal with Wei Guo every day and take care of him for me. Even when she wants to send me an e-mail, she doesn't dare use our home computer. She has to walk a long way over to an Internet café for fear that Wei Guo will find out where I am. She never gives up on anyone—if I have inherited any good traits, they all come from her.

Should I take a gamble and answer Lao Chen's e-mail? I'm really longing for someone whom I can talk to face-to-face, but everyone I've met in these last two years has disappointed me. We have nothing in common anymore. Could Lao Chen be an exception?

### Zhang Dou's autobiography

I'm Zhang Dou, twenty-two years old.

I'm taping this video now in Miaomiao's house in the rural Huairou district just outside Beijing.

I'm from Henan Province, where my parents were peasants. I've had asthma since I was a child, but I'm quite tall—at thirteen, I looked like I was sixteen. It was then that I was abducted at the railway station and taken to do slave labor in an illegal brick kiln in Shanxi Province. I made bricks for building houses for about three years, and I almost died from several asthma attacks. Once I tried to run away and was rescued by some strangers who took me to the local Labor Bureau, but the Labor Bureau sold me again to another illegal brick kiln. Six or seven years ago the illegal brick kilns in that area were exposed by the national media. Many of them were closed down and many child laborers were saved. Most of them were of the same age and background as me—all of them were missing persons. I met a number of reporters then, and one of them was Miaomiao from a Guangzhou paper. We hit it off especially well, and she told me I should write an article describing what had happened to me. I didn't write anything very good, but Miaomiao really liked it and wanted to help me get it published. Then I was sent back to school. My mother died quite young and my father went south to work. I went back to school to do the first year of middle school over again.

A year or so later, I got a letter from Miaomiao. She said the media had all been told that they were not to publish any more news about the illegal brick kilns because it would damage the nation's image. My piece couldn't be published; it could only be posted on the popular liberal Internet Web site Tianya. I received quite a few comments until it was "harmonized" off the net by the web police.

Miaomiao gave me her e-mail address, and when I went into town I sent her an e-mail to tell her I didn't want to go to school anymore. There was nobody with me at home, and I wanted to go and find a job. Miaomiao wrote back and told me to come to Beijing and stay with her. She'd quit her job on the paper in Guangzhou and moved back to Beijing. She said the office world was too horrible and the pressure was too great. She would rather be a freelance writer and work from home.

Just after my seventeenth birthday, I went to Huairou district outside Beijing to find Miaomiao. She now lived in the countryside.

She taught me how to make love and how to play the guitar. I discovered that she was an excellent cook and baked cakes and cookies, too. She had three cats and three dogs, all strays that she'd brought home with her. She said that before the Beijing Olympics there were so many demolitions and relocations that many people left their dogs and cats behind, and so Beijing was full of stray dogs and cats. Even valuable golden retrievers became dog meat and were sold for only seven yuan a pound in the farmers' market. I was also a stray that she had taken in, and now I didn't have to worry when my asthma flared up.

She wrote articles and television scripts to provide for us. Sometimes I would work at a nearby pet clinic, and I became very chummy with the clinic staff because I was always bringing cats and dogs in for treatment. Miaomiao had bought a small house from some peasants. It had three north-facing rooms, a separate kitchen, and a bathroom with a shower. We lived there very happily with all the cats and dogs for a year and three months, until Miaomiao turned thirty-two.

Then we heard that the whole country was in chaos, and people in Beijing were very frightened. The first thing we worried about was running out of food, both for ourselves and for our dogs and cats. When another crackdown was announced, things settled down, but Miaomiao would not let me go outside for fear I might be arrested. I stayed indoors for a whole month. Food supplies were very short then, and many more people abandoned their pets on the streets again. Every time Miaomiao came home, she brought more dogs and cats with her. Some of them were sick or injured. So we had over a dozen dogs and cats living with us, and I learned how to take care of them.

Winter passed, and people suddenly became more prosperous and everyone started smiling. But then something hard to understand happened to Miaomiao. She suddenly didn't recognize me, didn't recognize anyone. Whenever she met anyone, she just nodded and smiled but didn't say a word. She only took care of her dogs and cats, baking some sugar-free cookies for them every couple of days. She no longer wrote articles or played the guitar. When she felt the need, we would make love, but she no longer discussed anything with me.

I always knew that all the time I was in Beijing she was taking some sort of drug when she thought I wasn't looking. Then she would be completely spaced out for a while and would not recognize anyone. This usually lasted for only about half an hour, but this time she didn't recover.

I knew it was now time for me to take care of her, but I couldn't support us on part-time work alone. So I did something that I hoped Miaomiao would forgive me for—I secretly began to sell off our cats and dogs, beginning with the new kittens and puppies. Of course, I didn't sell them to the dog-meat dealers. Because the economy was good, many people had started to keep household cats and dogs again. I was already very good at breeding and raising them. I would raise a few and sell off a few. We always had cats and dogs in the house, and Miaomiao would feed whichever ones she saw because she loved them all equally.

I still practiced my guitar for three hours a day. Some nights, I would tell Miaomiao I was going out to listen to music, but she wouldn't respond. I took a long bus trip to Wudaokou and went to some places Miaomiao used to take me where I could see live performances. I felt pretty bad if I didn't get to listen to live music. I would always meet some vaguely remembered people there and played a few numbers with them. They often told me how much they liked my Spanish guitar and if they needed a guitarist for one of their gigs they would ask me to join them. Then I went home and practiced even harder—mastering all the chords and techniques you taught me, Miaomiao—and waiting to go to Wudaokou to perform.

I never imagined that something would happen to me the first night I went on stage.

When I got a call asking me to perform, I prepared dinner for you and our cats and dogs at five o'clock, then said good-bye and took off for Wudaokou. As usual the performance would end too late for me to get home, so afterward I was going to find a place to take a nap and wait for the first bus back in the morning. This time when I went into town, I went first to a small restaurant in Lanqiying to have something to eat. The place was small and crowded, with little room between the tables. There was a man and a woman at the next table and the man was talking nonstop in an accent just like that Taiwanese variety-show host. I couldn't understand what he was talking about, but suddenly the woman started talking in a Beijing accent. Then I realized that she was actually cursing the government.

Ever since China's Golden Age of Ascendancy officially began two years ago, I've noticed that everyone was getting pretty strange— everyone I met was extremely happy and you would hardly ever hear anyone say anything unpleasant. I couldn't figure out why everyone was so weird, so I just pretended to be happy, too. So I had a very unusual feeling when I heard this auntie cursing the government. But I never imagined that the Taiwanese guy would actually start having a go at her. "Your government is wonderful," he said, "they take such good care of you. You mainlanders don't know how to be grateful. You think it's an easy thing to feed 1.3 billion people? What right do you have to criticize the government? What do you women know anyway? . . ." Maybe it was because he kept saying "you" and "we" that it made me feel uncomfortable. When I'd paid my bill and was about to leave, I noticed that his ass was only half on his chair, and so I deliberately bumped into his chair on the way out. He fell on the floor, and I just walked on out the door without even looking back. I didn't see anyone rushing out after me either.

I went on to the little restaurant called Five Flavors where I was due to play, and the band performed pretty well. The atmosphere was fantastic, and I made two hundred yuan. Then the guys in the band invited me to drink some beers with them, to celebrate my first live performance, they said. It was two in the morning when we finally broke up.

I thought I'd just tough it out until dawn, but I was a little sleepy because of all the beer, so I sat down against the wall of a building near the bus stop to get a little shut-eye.

I had just closed my eyes, when five or six people started beating me all over with wooden clubs. I didn't even have time to fight back. Was it that Taiwanese guy come back for revenge? I'm pretty strong, but I really couldn't take it. Then the gang suddenly cleared off. I couldn't breathe, and my left arm felt like it was broken. I was lying on my right arm and I couldn't get my asthma inhaler out of my trouser pocket. Just then someone walked by, and I moaned and gestured for him to help me get the inhaler out of my pocket, but he just didn't understand. I knew I was going to die.

Miaomiao, at that time all I could think was, If I die who's going to take care of you? And what will happen to our cats and dogs? Miaomiao, I'm sorry, I shouldn't have been so reckless, I shouldn't have knocked that guy's chair. If I die now, I kept thinking, who'll take care of you? What will happen to our cats and dogs?

Suddenly, somehow, I had my inhaler against my mouth and knew that I wasn't going to die. I'm strong—they can beat me, but they can't kill me.

When I woke up, I was lying in a hospital bed. I heard the nurse calling, "Hey, the boy you brought in is waking up!" Then an older man came up to my bed. I didn't know him. "Please get my trousers," I mustered enough strength to say. He brought them over. I asked him to take five hundred renminbi out of the pocket. Then I asked him for paper and pen and wrote down Miaomiao's address in Huairou, the brand name of the pet food we use, and how much to buy. Also some flour and eggs, and so on, and asked him to buy them for me and take them to Miaomiao. I didn't know whether that man would take off with my money or be willing to go to Huairou. I couldn't even really understand why he'd stayed around at the hospital waiting for me to wake up. I couldn't be bothered with all that. My only worry was what might happen to you if you ran out of food.

The next morning, he came back and told me he had delivered the groceries. He said a woman took them in, and when he told her I was in the hospital, she just smiled slightly and nodded. She offered him some cookies. "You have quite a collection of cats and dogs at home," he said. I was very relieved when I heard that.

He came to see me again that afternoon. "Why are you looking after me?" I asked. He said that when he saw me lying on the ground panting for breath and fumbling for my pocket, he realized I was asthmatic. He was, too, and had been taking corticosteroids for a long time, so he took my inhaler out of my pocket.

"Since I take corticosteroids, too," he went on, "I wanted to know what it was like for other people with asthma."

"What do you want to know?"

"To see if you think other people are different from you."

"Of course they're different. They don't have asthma!"

"Are they happy?"

When he said that, I felt like I'd received an electric shock. It's not that I'm not happy. I haven't been unhappy since I started living with Miaomiao a few years ago. She doesn't talk to me now, but we're still not unhappy. But for the last two years, I've felt that there is something different about the people I meet. I can't say exactly what it is, but they seem to be unusually happy. Whatever it is, I feel like I'm different from them. Even when we're happy, we have a different sort of happiness.

He watched me intently, waiting for my answer, so I nodded.

He looked as excited as if he'd just hit the jackpot, then he glanced around like he was afraid someone was spying on us.

"I've finally found the answer," he said. "It's only those of us who are on asthma medication who are not high. This is our secret."

I hadn't a clue what he was talking about.

"Have the people around you all forgotten that month?" he asked.

"What month?"

"The month when the world economy went into crisis and China's Golden Age of Ascendancy officially began."

I didn't understand.

"Doesn't everybody say that the two events—the world economy going into crisis and China's Golden Age of Ascendancy officially starting—happened simultaneously with no time at all in between?" he asked. "But there was actually a one-month gap between those two events, or, more precisely, there were twenty-eight days, counting from the first working day after the spring holidays."

He continued: "Do you find that when you talk about the whole country being in turmoil, the panic buying of food, the army entering the city, the Public Security forces cracking down, and the entire population receiving the bird flu vaccine, nobody remembers these things?" I guess he said all this because I was slow to respond.

I started thinking how true it was that nobody talked about these things anymore. It certainly was like they thought such things had never taken place, but I didn't know if they really had forgotten.

"Then I guess you've forgotten, too," he said as he sat down and hung his head. "I was wrong. It was so much wishful thinking."

"Uncle," I said, "I remember."

"You remember?" His face lit up.

"Yes. I remember everything that happened that year."

He still looked at me skeptically.

"I remember running around all over buying up pet food, and I remember being afraid to go outside during the security crackdown."

"That's wonderful, wonderful. Thank God I've finally found somebody who remembers!" he exclaimed. "What's your name, little brother?"

"Zhang Dou."

"Little brother Zhang Dou, I'm Fang Caodi, but you can call me Old Fang. From now on, you're my good brother, a brother closer than a flesh-and-blood brother—because you're the only brother of mine who remembers what happened that month. You absolutely must not forget the things you remember now. We've got to find that lost month."

I would do whatever he said because he'd saved me and Miaomiao and our cats and dogs. I also said to myself, "You must never forget that you are a stray that Miaomiao took in, and Miaomiao treats you better than anybody else."


### Wei Guo's autobiography

I'm Wei Guo, twenty-four years old.

I have not kept a diary for a long time, but today this diary has to be written down as a historical record.

Today, I made a great stride toward my life goal because today I became an official member of the SS Study Group. I feel so proud, because I am its youngest member. The SS Study Group brings together political and business circles. Its formal members include government officials of vice-ministerial rank, army officers of major-general rank, directors of major state-owned enterprises, chairmen of sovereign funds, and leaders of China's top-100 private businesses, as well as a few professors and institutional heads from the Chinese Academy of Social Sciences and key universities. In fact, our network of connections extends all the way up to the Heavenly Court.

We are not ivory-tower bookworms. We study political and legal thought and scholarship concerning statecraft, and how to assist the state in governing the nation. Our motto is "perfect wisdom and courage"—we promote a martial spirit, heroism, and the robust qualities of manliness. We constitute a new generation of superior men with a sense of mission. In this age of mediocrity without any sense of honor, we courageously affirm that we are the genuine spiritual aristocracy of China's Golden Age of Ascendancy.

Of course, not all our members come from revolutionary families—some of our academic members are from commoner or intellectual families—but most do. My grandfather on my mother's side was a judge of the Republic and I grew up in a big courtyard full of people from political and legal circles. Still, I could be regarded as the one with the least illustrious background in the Group.

Perhaps I should be thankful to Professors X, Y, & Z—especially to Professor X—because they were the ones who nominated me to be a member-in-waiting a year or so ago. Thus, I was finally able to become an official member today. Professor X brags that he's the one who spotted me first. I let him think so, but in actual fact when I was studying first-year law, I investigated all my professors to see which one had the best future prospects, and which one would go the furthest in the shortest period of time. And *I* chose Professor X.

I made the right choice, too. Professors X, Y, & Z are the founders of the SS Study Group. Their position is that ideas and power should be united in order to make China stronger. Because they had already mastered the Western and Chinese classics, they were able to attract to the Group those government officials, army officers, and business executives interested in political thinking. X, Y, & Z want to become state tutors, and they believe that within ten years their ideas will control the fate of the nation. All this is in perfect accord with my own ten-year plan.

Of the three, X controls an important scholarly journal, has the widest circle of connections, and is the most popular with the media. He has the biggest mouth, too, and is rumored in the academic world to have a national security background. Y has the highest academic standing, is the leader in his field, serves as dean of a newly established faculty in a key university in the south, and is quite well-known in overseas academic circles. Z lectures to a research class on national security strategy at the People's Liberation Army's National Defense University in Beijing. This research class is made up of civil and military leaders and includes provincial officials as well as high-ranking officers.

Z is the more profound individual, farsighted in his views, and he is the one who understands me best. There were two particular initiatives of mine that I reported only to him, and when he didn't respond at first, I was afraid that I had been mistaken about him and regretted being too impetuous. It was Z, however, who argued in the Selection Committee that they should ignore their rules and allow me to become an official member of the Group even though I hadn't finished my studies. X also claimed credit for this, telling me that he and Z argued together on my behalf, otherwise I would have had to remain a member-in-waiting for another three to five years.

Youth is too valuable a commodity, so how could I allow myself to be so easily held back by them? I intend to actively accelerate the achievement of my goals. I discovered that Z was the key to my success, because he has a secret relationship with the one person whom every member of the Group calls big brother, Ban Cuntou. Ban Cuntou is a genuine Red aristocrat. On the surface, he is supposed to be an investor in overseas projects, but in point of fact he is intimately connected with all the legitimate and illegitimate activities of the Party, the government, and the military establishment. He is, as we say, able to "communicate with Heaven itself," and I believe that he will eventually become one of our nation's heads of state. Everyone in the Group is well connected, but they all exhibit reverence and fear when talking to big brother Ban Cuntou. Big brother Ban Cuntou and Z are the real souls of the Group—although I don't believe in the soul. Unfortunately, it is not easy to get close to Ban Cuntou, and so far I have not figured out any way to attract his attention. So I'll just keep working on Z for the time being.

When I was an undergraduate, I already did a lot of running around for X, Y, & Z. They all have different organizations and they control a great many resources. For example, they can allocate funds for research projects to scholars who are willing to be allied with them; they can obtain the support of wealthy foundations to fund high-level academic conferences, support like-minded people, and set up united fronts; they can organize twice-yearly conferences for outstanding graduate students in the humanities, to train the next generation of the academic elite. All expenses paid for. The food and entertainment are superb, but the mentally intensive brainwashing is also terrific; that's why the conferences have been dubbed the Devil's Training Camp, or the New Whampoa Academy.

With so many activities, X, Y, & Z naturally have to divide up the work. For example, only Y and Z lecture at the Devil's Training Camp, while leaving the organizational work to X. X does not appear up front as the organizer. The nominal organizer is Q, because Q is best at shaking things up and at influencing young people, especially passionately enthusiastic new MA students. Q has a very high opinion of himself, and he also aspires to become a state tutor, but X, Y, & Z look down on him. They say his academic qualifications are insufficient, he's had no scholarly publications, and his position keeps changing. In private they call Q the Pied Piper—like the Pied Piper of Hamelin in the German fairy tale who played the flute so bewitchingly that he enticed all the children away from home. X, Y, & Z are clearly aware that in an intellectual revolution— and what the SS Study Group is promoting is nothing less than an intellectual revolution in which the contemporary Chinese world-view will triumph—there are many roles to be played, and a Pied Piper to lead away the children is indispensable.

The first time I confided in Z about my activities was about the first time I implemented the Group's concept that politics is the art of distinguishing between the enemy and ourselves. I told him that from my sophomore year on, I'd organized my classmates to system-atically refute reactionary discourse on the Internet, and to denounce reactionary Web sites to the authorities. After that, we moved on to simultaneously observing the virtual world and the real world. We would report to the university president and the Communist Party Secretary any professor in our university who was promoting the Western system of values or liberalism in class. Our working model spread like a virus and was soon being copied in many other colleges and universities. This clearly made known my operational abilities and demonstrated that many university students listened to me and even worshipped me—I am the charismatic leader of today's youth generation.

After Z listened to all this, he didn't say much, but I knew that he had taken it all in. That's because not long after that meeting he nonchalantly asked, "Have you attended any of Professor Gong's lectures at your faculty?" I immediately understood what he wanted, and, after making some inquiries, I learned that Gong had openly criticized the politics of the ancient Confucian Gongyang School in his class. I brought together all the students who had taken Gong's classes and incited them to denounce him to the university president for slandering traditional Chinese culture. They also launched an online petition demanding that a thorough investigation be carried out and that Gong be fired. This process is not yet complete, but we've given Gong so much trouble he can hardly take it anymore. I'm quite certain that Z is very satisfied with my performance.

What I didn't tell Z was that my yearlong denunciation activities have finally been appreciated by the government. First the Internet Monitoring Department of the State Council Information Office and then the Ministry of State Security formally contacted me— this amounts to saying that I am now an official informer for both Public and State Security units. I didn't tell Z or the other members of the SS Study Group about this either, so that they would not be on their guard with me. When I report to the authorities that I am now an official insider in the SS Study Group, they will certainly have an even higher regard for me.

My second initiative makes an interesting story. Six months ago, some time after I had become a Group member-in-waiting, I went to listen to Z give a public lecture. The topic was "The Role of Love in China's Present Age of Prosperity." In it he said, "Today our society is suffused with 'love' and the media are repeatedly promoting great love, universal love, and love of all mankind. For a while everybody feels good, their hearts are full of 'love,' they experience a feeling of satisfaction and happiness. The entire nation is harmonious, crimes of violence decrease, even domestic violence decreases. Thus, we can see the power of 'love.' "

Every time he used the word "love," Z made hand gestures indicating quotation marks around it.

When I was just about bored to death and thinking that Z didn't have anything new to say, near the end of his lecture he softly came out with the following sentence: "Everybody is busy 'loving,' so the martial spirit is not on display, there are no enemies, and hatred cannot emerge." His words hit me like a bolt of lightning. Z is so profound and he has pondered this topic very deeply, I thought.

I remembered that Y once had said, "The vast majority of the people in the world have not received any rigorous philosophical training and they do not possess the intelligence to understand things clearly. We philosophers cannot tell them the truth, otherwise they would attack us just like they executed Socrates. In a public forum, a philosopher can say only what the masses love to hear and cater to them. Nevertheless, a philosopher may utter a few code words, heeding the difference between insiders and outsiders and permitting the insiders, members of his own party, to grasp his true meaning, as in the traditional phrase 'subtle words carry profound meanings.'"

Z and Y are kindred spirits, and so Z was also employing "subtle words to carry his profound meanings."

He talked about "love" for the sake of the masses, and they thought he was promoting "love," or that he believed China's present Golden Age of Ascendancy needed such "love." But in his entire lecture, Z only *described* "love," he didn't *advocate* "love." He discussed only how "love" was influencing the Chinese people during this age of prosperity, but he never said that the Chinese people should "love" more. That one phrase, "the martial spirit is not on display," was the key; it was a repudiation of all the so-called love that came before it. This phrase was the code meant for people like me to hear, because I know from the SS Study Group that the martial spirit is the virtue that we admire and advocate above all. Z promotes the martial spirit, and if this martial spirit is positive then anything that prevents the martial spirit from being displayed cannot be positive. And just what, according to Z's lecture, prevented the martial spirit from being displayed? It was "love."

Someone like me who has received philosophical training and knows how to read between the lines to find the "profound meaning" understood that Z's "love," in quotation marks, referred to the previously mentioned great love, universal love, and love for all mankind. In theory, the martial spirit does not necessarily require hatred or enemies, but enemies and hatred can strengthen people's martial spirit—enemies and hatred are an aphrodisiac for the martial spirit. The real goal of Z's lecture, his "subtle words carrying profound meanings," was to negate the idea that people should "love" even their enemies—to refute the kind of so-called universal values of great love and love for all mankind that fail to distinguish between the enemy and ourselves. His lecture even implied that we must identify our enemies and let our hatred rise against them so that our martial spirit can be fully displayed. This I understood.

I knew this was also the ingenious method I could use later to earn Z's trust. With his strong idea of the difference between inside and outside forces, he will surely make me a close member of his inner circle. I immediately organized six Peking and Tsing-hua University students who already worshipped me into a group of iron-willed loyal braves and began to practice martial arts with them. I feel that university students today are all lacking in courage and the killing spirit. They've all been overinfluenced by society's general mood of love. They've all been feminized and sissified and have lost the lofty male spirit of machismo. Sometimes I'm afraid that even I am too loving, too indecisive, and won't be able to accomplish anything great. I tried my best to stimulate their killing spirit and told them that they must never forget how to hate, must never forget the distinction between the enemy and ourselves. We watched documentary films on the Nanjing Massacre and the Nazi extermination of the Jews, and I encouraged them to imagine how they would systematically massacre the little Japanese devils. Then on one occasion, when we were camped out on maneuvers, I wanted them to kill a couple of stray dogs in order to build up their courage, but they let the bastards get away. I think university students are all good-for-nothing losers.

Finally, one night, I had the chance to put them through their rite of passage.

Every night in my grandmother's crummy little Wudaokou restaurant, Five Flavors, there is a folk-music performance. It's a good place for me to keep watch on our young people's attitudes and thinking. That night all the iron-willed loyal braves were there, but their morale was pretty low and they were frowning into their drinks. Maybe he had had too much to drink, but one of them, from Tsing-hua University, suddenly pointed at a tall young man onstage playing the guitar and said, "Look at that big shit playing the guitar. One look and you know he comes from the countryside." That Tsing-hua iron-blooded loyal brave also comes from a peasant family, but he hates peasants more than anyone else. He was always saying that peasants are a vulgar social class lower than anybody and nobody should sympathize with them.

I've always known that poor people hate other poor people, peasants despise other peasants, and children love to bully other children. "Look at him and his dark skin! He's disgusting, isn't he?" said the Tsing-hua student. "The tall guy plays pretty well, though," said another brave, but another one disagreed with him. "His body language is so crude and his fingers are as thick as rolling pins. And he still wants to play Spanish guitar? Fuck!" "He's just a fucking peasant!" said the Tsing-hua guy, with anger rising in his voice. All the iron-blooded braves stared at that tall peasant guitar-player in utter disgust. "Maybe tonight we should . . ." I suddenly thought out loud. They all understood immediately, and one of them said, "Let's go pick up our weapons."

We waited outside the restaurant, growing angrier by the minute while that big jerk was still in there drinking and laughing. When he finally came out, we followed him, not knowing exactly how to have a go at him. After a while we came to a bus stop and that dumb prick actually sat down against a wall in a narrow street across from the bus stop and went to sleep. All my crew went after him at once, beating the crap out of him with their clubs until the big bum couldn't move even a muscle. I was standing across the street thinking to myself, This is the real thing. Tonight we're going to beat that fucker to death. But just then a Jeep Cherokee drove up, and everybody scattered.

I hesitated for a long time trying to decide whether or not to tell Z about this action because the result could have been either extremely good or extremely bad. If X knew about it, he might get scared, and Y might even reprimand me, but Z probably would think more highly of me if he knew. I decided to take a gamble and tell Z. I told him that I had been inspired by his "love" lecture. I had understood the true meaning of his subtle words and put them into practice. Hate is absolutely indispensable if we want to accomplish great things. What I made clear, but didn't actually say, was that I could carry out important missions for him. Z listened in his usual way without any obvious reaction and then just walked away. I didn't hear anything from him for quite a few days, but fortunately events proved that I had understood Z correctly. Today I was made an official member of the SS Study Group. I had bet on the right horse.

Now I'm twenty-four. When I was twenty-two, I formulated my ten-year plan, and have been fulfilling it step-by-step, but I must not get too self-satisfied. What was Chairman Mao doing when he was thirty years old? He was one of the five members of the Standing Committee of the Chinese Communist Party Politburo. With this in mind, I know that I have to work much harder.

PS: The "SS" in the SS Study Group refers to two Germans (even though one of them was a Jew) whose last names begin with S. The Group started up by studying their ideas on politics, theology, and philosophy, but later on it was no longer of any importance who they were.

PPS: I suffer from one minor annoyance—unfortunately Little Xi is my "mother." She's the one uncertain element in the progress of my project. I have to eliminate this uncertainty. If we were still living under Chairman Mao, she would certainly long since have been condemned as a counterrevolutionary element. But our government has grown much too lenient. I asked my superior in the Ministry of State Security to lock her up in a mental hospital for a long time, but he told me not to worry about her. He said everything was under control; and they wanted to let her move around freely to monitor those she came into contact with. I had no choice.

### Searching for a lost month

I'm Fang Caodi and I'm making this recording.

I finally found a true brother. His name is Zhang Dou. He is twenty-two years old, from Henan Province, and he lives in the village of Huairou outside Beijing. I'm sixty-five years old, so I have the right to call him younger brother and to occupy the rank of elder brother, ha, ha.

Just like me, he remembers everything about that lost month, those twenty-eight days between the time when the world economy went into crisis and China's "Golden Age of Ascendancy" officially began. Two years of searching has told me that this is very rare and extremely important.

He also has asthma just like me and has been taking corticosteroids for many years. This has led me to the bold hypothesis that our not suffering from memory loss has something to do with our asthma. Ha! This is wonderful news. It proves that within the boundaries of our nation, there are as many people who still remember what happened that year as there are suffers from chronic asthma. It's just that they don't know of each other's existence. If

I can bring together a hundred or a thousand of these asthmatics, then I can prove to all our nation's people that that month did in fact exist. Ha!

Last Friday evening, I went to Wudaokou to see a friend, and the outdoor equipment store on the ground floor of his apartment building was being cleared out and cleaned. I went in to look around and under a pile of junk I noticed an old copy of the popular liberal paper *Southern Weekly* from that lost month. It must have been the last issue they came out with before being forced to stop publishing. I felt like I'd stumbled upon a great treasure, so I just bought a few things and then took the paper along with them. When I compared the printed version of the *Southern Weekly* with the online version, as I expected there were many discrepancies. For example, the printed version carried an article critical of that year's crackdown, but in the online version it had been deleted and replaced by an article explaining why Western universal values are inappropriate for China. I don't know why, but when I saw how the *Southern Weekly* had been defiled and distorted so that it was now opposed to universal values, I burst out laughing. I forgot that the coffee shop was full of other customers.

That lone issue of the *Southern Weekly* was my document No. 71—evidence for the true historical existence of that missing month.

Even more fortunately, in the small hours after I'd left my friend's place and hadn't driven very far, I spotted five or six young men beating up another man who was lying on the ground. When they saw my car, they all took off running. When I stopped the car, experience told me not to get involved, but while I was hesitating, I realized that the young man was gasping for breath, and that was something I am very familiar with. I got out of the car and walked up to him. I saw his arm shaking and then I understood. I reached into his trouser pocket and found, as expected, his asthma inhaler. I shoved it into his mouth, sprayed like crazy a couple of times, and he revived.

Should I continue to help him? I wondered. Suddenly I became extremely curious. What was he like, this kid who took the same medication I did? I've had many bouts of this sort of curiosity in my life. You could say that I've traveled my whole life's road on the basis of this sort of curiosity. So I decided to take care of the kid.

He was so big and heavy! I had a hell of a time dragging and lifting him into my car. Finally I got him in and took him to Peking University Third Hospital. I was afraid he would check out and leave the hospital, so I went to see him the next morning. He was still sound asleep. When he woke up in the afternoon, he asked me in a wheezy voice to buy some groceries and take them to his family in Huairou; he wasn't even afraid that I'd disappear with his money. I decided to do what he asked. I'd wait to see the next card, just like in a poker game. By the third day I knew I'd been right. He remembers that month. We *are* the same, and I've finally proved that I'm not alone. Ha! He is Zhang Dou, and I made him my brother, closer than a flesh-and-blood brother.

In two years, he's the only person I've found who is like me. Everybody else is different.

At first I thought all those other people just didn't want to talk about the events of that month. Then later I realized that they recalled things wrongly, completely differently from the way I remembered them. Finally I came to the conclusion that in all their memories there were twenty-eight days missing. In order to verify this memory loss, I went to the library to look up the daily and weekly newspapers from that year, but the library had only online versions and it was no longer possible to read the printed versions. The online reports of those twenty-eight days were completely different from my memory of them: they held that the world economy had gone into crisis at the same time as the official start of China's Golden Age of Ascendancy. The horrifying month that came between these two historical events had completely disappeared.

For a while I thought that even though the government had distorted the truth, at least the common people would remember what had happened, but later on I had to admit that it was a case of total collective amnesia.

Complete collective amnesia. I suspected that this amnesia was related to the nationwide bird flu inoculation that spring, but I could not confirm my suspicion.

I started to frequent Beijing's secondhand bookstores looking for related reports, but all I could find were official government newspapers and mindless entertainment magazines. There were no publications that carried the truth.

I bought a Jeep Cherokee in Beijing and took off south on the G4 Beijing–Hong Kong–Macao highway to collect more evidence of that month. It was only in rather strange places, though, that I found a few snippets of corroborating evidence. For example, in a guesthouse at the foothills of Mount Huang, I found a complete issue of the financial magazine *Caijing* that reported on how the new round of great economic decline in early February of that year was affecting China; at Hengdian World Film Studios in Zhejiang, I saw part of an *Asia Weekly* magazine from Hong Kong that reported on how the people were hoarding food that year; in a squalid urban village near Wuhan University in Hubei, I picked up half of an old *China Youth Daily*, published by the Communist Youth League, in which the main article, "The Leviathan Has Arrived," introduced the seventeenth-century Western political philosopher Thomas Hobbes; the general theme of the article was that given a choice between anarchy and dictatorship, people will always choose the latter. Another article was a retrospective report describing how the government had failed miserably during the 2008 riot of over ten thousand people in Wan-an in Guizhou Province, when the police were accused of covering up the death of a young girl; in the Tujia ethnic region of Xiangxi in Hunan, I found an incomplete clipping from the *Southern Weekly;* it was an advertisement on how to use a made-in-China radio—because at that time many people were afraid that the power supply would fail and they would not be able to watch TV or surf the net, so they bought radios. On the reverse side of that advertisement was an article discussing the 1983 crackdown on criminality.

As time went by, media evidence was harder and harder to come by. That's why I was so ecstatic when I found that late-February *Southern Weekly* with its clear evidence of that missing month.

I became much more anxious to find people like myself. I made a list of all the people I knew. The ones I believed always to have a clear understanding of things I called clearheaded people. I went to talk to these clearheaded people one by one, but came back disappointed every time. Am I like the lone survivor on earth whom we see in those apocalypse movies? But the heroes in those films are always destined to find other survivors later on. I relied on that idea to persist resolutely in my search.

Finally I met Zhang Dou. We both believe that this is only a beginning. Out of more than a billion Chinese people there must be many more like us.

I told Zhang Dou I'd been going to his home every day to see if Miaomiao and the dogs and cats needed anything. I like his kind and smiling Miaomiao and her pets more and more. Zhang Dou said that when he got out of the hospital I could come and live with them. Ha! I was quite excited. I need a safe place to store my accumulated evidence. I hope Zhang Dou gets out of the hospital soon.

*A supplementary tape recording:* I spent a few days visiting several big hospitals pretending to be sick but actually taking a look at their asthmatic patients. I tried to raise the issue of the missing month, but I was disappointed because none of them remembered it. I thought everyone taking corticosteroids would be just like Zhang Dou and me, but I was mistaken. I told Zhang Dou about my discovery, but I also told him that we must not give up. "We absolutely must not forget how lonely we used to be. As long as there might be Chinese people who have not forgotten that month, we definitely have to look for them."

*To prevent us forgetting, here is another supplementary tape:* Last week on New East Road I ran into Lao Chen, a former journalist for *Mingbao* and the *United Daily*. I remembered that he used to be one of my clearheaded people who once helped me out with something important. Is he still a member of the clearheaded group? From the look in his eyes, I think the chances of him still being one of us are not great, but I should not let any opportunity go by. Look him up when you have time.

## Lao Chen's notebook on Fang Caodi

Little Xi, or *feichengwuraook*, didn't return my e-mail, but Fang Caodi sent me one asking me to come and see him. I didn't answer him immediately.

Recently all I'd been thinking of was Little Xi and I couldn't seem to stop. But what was really weird was that when I thought about Little Xi, I also started thinking about Fang Caodi. I kept thinking about that time I saw him jogging near Happiness Village Number Two and all the *mouleitao* nonsense he kept spouting. For all the many years I've known him, I noted to myself, he's always called me Lao Chen, but this time he actually called me *Master* Chen. I even started to think that Fang Caodi's state of mind seemed to be in some inexplicable manner similar to Little Xi's.

The other day I opened up a box that I have not opened since moving to Happiness Village Number Two and took out my notebooks—one of them was titled "Fang Caodi." I started to read what I'd written:

Fang Caodi, original name Fang Lijun. Later on, when an artist with the same name suddenly became famous abroad, the Fang Lijun I knew changed his name to Fang Caodi.

I first came to know Fang Caodi when I was an editor at Hong Kong's *Mingbao* and frequently received letters from an American reader signed "Old Fang." Sometimes he corrected facts or evidence given in an article, but more often he would be offering us a great deal of related material, most of which was too detailed to print. I came to know that Old Fang understood a great many unofficial and secret aspects of contemporary China. Once I put a notice in the readers' section asking him to give his real name and address, and he did. I even wrote back to thank him.

He paid particular attention to my articles, and he could even spot the ones I'd written under a nom de plume for the China page of *Mingbao*. To use a modern expression, he was my "fan."

We first met in the summer of 1989 in Hong Kong, when he was on his way back to the mainland. I was surprised that he wanted to enter China at a time when so many others were trying to get out. He asked me if I was familiar with the organization that was rescuing leaders of the Tiananmen democracy movement. I told him there was a Hong Kong Alliance in Support of Democratic Movements in China, but at that time

I didn't know there was also a secret organization spiriting people out of China.

I realized that his life experiences were quite unusual, so I invited him to meet me again the next day, and then I made these notes.

Fang Lijun's or (Fang Caodi's) ancestors came from Shandong. He was born in what was then known as Beiping in 1947. His father had joined the Communist Party of the Soviet Union in Xinjiang, the restive northwestern province, together with the Xinjiang warlord Sheng Shicai. Later he went over to the Nationalist Party. In 1949, just before the People's Liberation Army entered Beiping, he boarded a plane to Qingdao, and then took a ship to Taiwan, leaving behind his young third wife and his youngest child—Fang Lijun.

Sheng Shicai's branch of the Communist Party was a quite different affair from the Communist Party of Zhu De and Mao Zedong. The former had once actually advocated that Xinjiang, with almost half its population being Muslim, become independent from China. Fang Lijun's father not only betrayed the Communist Party, however, he was also closely involved with criminal gangs in the Northwest and was responsible for training people with "special skills" for them. Fang Lijun was born in a historic old Daoist temple on the east side of Beijing. After liberation, this temple was taken over by the Ministry of National Security—that shows how vigilant the Chinese communists were about Daoist supernatural techniques.

After they took power across the entire country, the Chinese communists started a Campaign to Suppress Counterrevolutionaries. From 1950 to 1953, they cracked down severely on clandestine nationalist agents, organized crime, and members of religious organizations and secret societies. Anyone possessing

Daoist-style "special skills" was liable to be considered part of a counterrevolutionary secret society. Mao Zedong suggested that one out of every thousand Chinese fitted these counter-revolutionary categories, and that the Party should first execute half that number. Large numbers of people who had worked for the nationalist government but then had surrendered, and even people who had worked underground for the Communist Party in the White areas, were also executed at this time. They included the writer Jin Yong's father, Zha Shuqing, and the essayist Zhu Ziqing's son, Zhu Maixian.

After the Campaign to Suppress Counterrevolutionaries, the criminal gangs and religious secret societies went into hiding and their voices were silenced throughout the land for quite some time. The leaders who had escaped most promptly went to Taiwan or Hong Kong. Fang Lijun's father was implicated in all forms of counterrevolutionary secret activities, and so he went to Taiwan. Fang Lijun's mother, who was a Daoist secret society "Big Sister," was not so fortunate—she died in a Beijing prison.

As for Fang Lijun, the offspring of a counterrevolutionary nationalist spy and criminal-gang member father and a religious secret society mother, he grew up in an impenetrable Daoist temple where there were no longer any religious activities. He was raised by an old gatekeeper, and later helped the old man with many temple repairs. He finished upper middle school in the process.

Fang Lijun was not allowed to go to college due to his shady family background. Because he was a few months too old, he was also not eligible to be sent to the countryside with the "old three classes" of 1967, '68, and '69. He was even less eligible to become a Red Guard. At the start of the Cultural Revolution, then, he'd been assigned to teach in an elementary school in the Mentougou district of Beijing. But before he could even start, the Cultural Revolution reached a more intense level, and he was sent off to work as a coal miner in the Muchengjian mine, and there he stayed for several years.

According to his account, one day in September 1971 he suddenly got the urge to see the Summer Palace. He had heard so much about it, but he had never visited it, and he thought it might be a long time before he would have another chance to go. When he got halfway there, however, the road was closed. He guessed that there was something going on, maybe some troop transfers, at the restricted military area on Jade Spring Hill near the Summer Palace. When he got back to the workers' dormitory, he told everybody something big was going to happen in China. And it certainly did. In a short time the shocking news was broadcast that Chairman Mao's designated successor, General Lin Biao, had betrayed the nation and attempted to flee, but his plane had crashed in Outer Mongolia.

Fang Lijun refused to go to work again after that. He told me that he believed "history had come to an end." He wrote a small note and went to the bridge between Zhongnanhai Party Headquarters and North Lake, where he stuffed the note into a slit in the white-marble railing. The note said, "History has already come to a halt and will no longer move forward. From now on, all new revolutions will be counterrevolutions. Don't try to fool me anymore. What right do you have to make me dig for coal?"

His asthma flared up again and he stayed in the dormitory. No matter how much his work unit threatened him, he would not go into the coal pit again.

He could not be sure whether it was in 1971, when United

States Secretary of State Kissinger visited China twice, or in 1972, when President Nixon came, but anyway the Americans brought with them a list of relatives of Chinese American citizens who were being detained in China. At this time, when American–Chinese relations were thawing out, and in order to show their goodwill, the Chinese allowed a group of people to leave the country. One of them was Fang Lijun—because his father had long since left Nationalist Party political circles, and had been granted asylum by the American government as a pro-American political refugee.

When Fang Lijun received the notice, he went to the Public Security Bureau and was given a folded-up transit pass. He still strolled around the Summer Palace and the North Lake, enjoying the sites for a few days. Then he went back to the Daoist temple on the east side of Beijing to say good-bye to the old man who had raised him.

When the old man heard his story, he was very worried. "Why don't you hurry up and leave?" he asked. "What if the policy changes and you can't get out? Go and buy a train ticket to Hong Kong right away today." The old man dug up a few pieces of gold leaf buried in one corner of the temple grounds. They were left over from some temple repairs, and he'd kept them there all these years. "Take these and trade them for money for your journey," he said. "Your mother was the temple's great benefactor. When she was in prison, she took our secrets to her death and firmly maintained that this Daoist temple was involved only in religious activities and had nothing to do with any reactionary secret societies. It's because of her that this seven-hundred-year-old temple still exists." Today he could finally pay back the temple's godmother by helping Fang Lijun.

The old man had raised Fang Lijun, but he had not revealed the truth about himself and the temple until this last moment. That's how wary people were of each other in those days.

It was a good thing he took some money, because when the train south reached Guangzhou, Fang Lijun had to stay there a week, waiting to join in the quota for Hong Kong passengers. In Shenzhen, he had to wait two more days before entering Hong Kong. Without a passport or an identity card, carrying only a transit pass, Fang Lijun finally went through customs at Luo Wu station, where they took his pass and allowed him to enter Hong Kong.

When Fang Lijun went to the American consulate in Hong Kong to apply for a visa, he ran into a technical problem: he had not entered Hong Kong illegally, but he had left China only on a transit pass, therefore he was not eligible to be a political refugee, and the Americans could not immediately issue him with a visa. He would have to apply formally for a visa on the grounds of family reunification, with his father.

Fang Lijun found temporary lodgings in a cheap guesthouse in the Chunking Mansions in Tsim Sha Tsui. He stayed there the better part of a year while the American visa process dragged on. While living in that guesthouse he certainly broadened his horizons. He met backpackers and small-business operators from as many as fifty different countries. There was an American hippie who was tired after spending several years in Goa and was now going back to America to join a hippie commune and continue to live his carefree, self-reliant life. Fang Lijun was extremely envious of him.

Eventually Fang Lijun went to Los Angeles and met his now quite elderly father whom he hadn't seen since he was a small child. When Fang Lijun's father had run with Sheng Shicai and the Nationalist Party, he had harmed quite a few people. He was very afraid that someone would take revenge on him, and so he hid at home in Monterrey Park most of the time. He built a high wall around his house and even installed an iron door to his bedroom. The father had remarried, and Fang Lijun lived with them less than a month. Then he took his father's advice and moved to Texas, to the Houston Chinatown, to seek help from one of his father's former subordinates. He worked as an accountant on the second floor of this man's furniture and antiques store. There was a teenage daughter, and the two families fondly hoped that Fang Lijun would marry her. She, however, was completely Americanized, and when she got wind of what her parents were up to, she refused even to eat with Fang Lijun at the same table. He took his meals alone in the shop's storage room. This certainly was not the kind of American Chinatown life he had imagined.

A few months later, Fang Lijun made contact with his hippie friend and left Houston for New Mexico to join the commune. It was located on a large piece of agricultural land where the members cultivated fresh organic vegetables. They also made their own clothes, raised bees, and made jam and candles. They felt like they were self-sufficient, but their seeds, raw materials, tools, and other everyday high-tech items, and their medicines, like Fang Lijun's corticosteroids for his asthma, were all purchased in the city.

Living on a farm, they could not escape hard physical labor. Those hippies were all from middle-class urban families and they found it pretty tough going. But Fang Lijun was used to hard work in China and he was good at it, and could fix just about anything without a lot of talk. Because of all that, he was very well liked on the commune and he spent many happy years living there.

Unfortunately, in time the commune began to split up due to squabbles between the hippies, and then the whole movement started to wane and most of the members drifted away. The great majority of communes were unable to keep going after the Vietnam War ended, and Fang Lijun's commune was no exception. There were no new members coming in and although some of the old-timers came back, they soon left again. In the end only Fang Lijun and an older woman everybody called "Mom" remained. "Mom" was resolved to stay on with Fang Lijun. There were only the two of them, and as the years went by they were pretty much the same as a traditional husband and wife.

One day in the early 1980s, "Mom" told Fang Lijun that she was getting too old to be a hippie anymore and she wanted to go back east and live with her daughter. So the two of them shut off the water and electricity, boarded up the windows, and took a train across the United States to Maryland, where they split up. Fang Lijun headed north to New York, Philadelphia, and Boston. There he ended up as a cook in a self-service chop suey joint in Boston's Chinatown. The boss liked him a lot, too, and he worked there for several years.

One day Fang Lijun suddenly decided to go to the Harvard-Yenching Library, and from then on he was hooked. He worked only in the evening at the restaurant, and in the daytime he jogged from Boston Chinatown to Cambridge to read the Chinese periodicals in the Harvard Library. That was when he started writing letters to the editor at *Mingbao*—that was me, Lao Chen.

In 1989, he really did return to the mainland, and in 1992,

when Deng Xiaoping made his celebrated "southern tour" to promote economic development, Fang Lijun left China again—he always moved against the mainstream.

Back in America, Fang Lijun sent me a letter telling me that he was doing odd jobs in New York's Chinatown. At the time I was back in Taiwan working for the *United Daily* and I heard that the *China Times Weekly News* had set up an editorial office in New York. I casually recommended Fang Lijun to them, and they actually brought him in to act as an editorial assistant there. In no time at all, they promoted him to assistant editor. Fang Lijun wrote and thanked me profusely, and I really did feel a special sense of accomplishment. I knew that Fang Lijun, as an experienced and knowledgeable jack-of-all-trades, was perfectly suited to being an editor for a news magazine.

The next time I received a letter from him, Fang Lijun was in Nigeria in West Africa. He later told me that he had always kept in touch with a Nigerian he'd met in the international guesthouse in Chunking Mansions, and he'd invited him to Africa. When Fang Lijun was young, he had always dreamed about going to friendly states like Ghana, Zambia, and Tanzania and making a contribution to their development. So he went without the slightest hesitation. It turned out that his Nigerian friend wanted to trade with China. He asked him to be his partner. Fang Lijun thought of all those red, white, and blue fabric bags the Chinese use to carry goods and other things when traveling. They could buy them in China, ship them to Nigeria, and sell them all over West and Central Africa.

Those red, white, and blue cloth bags were a big hit with the Africans, and so Fang Lijun's partner wanted them to set up their own factory and make the bags themselves in Lagos.

After making money in the Nigeria–China trade, Fang Lijun
visited Ghana, Zambia, and Tanzania, but he didn't want to
end his days in Africa. He went back to live in China with a
plan to set up a small Cantonese restaurant just outside Li Jiang
City in Yunnan.

Luckily for him he was too slow. The restaurant plan came
to nothing long before Li Jiang was devastated by the great
earthquake of February 3, 1996. Fang Lijun then traveled all
over western China. I remember he predicted that when China
started to develop its tourist trade, too many people would
come and ruin China's scenic and historic spots.

He traveled for seven or eight years, visiting Xinjiang, Tibet,
Inner Mongolia, Qinghai, Yunnan, Guizhou, Hunan, and
Sichuan. He went on foot, by train, by long-distance bus, hitch-
ing rides on passing trucks—he even had a ride on a military
transport plane. If you show him any piece of cloth embroi-
dered by any of the minority peoples, Fang Lijun can tell you
right off if it was produced by the Tong of Guangxi, the Yao, or
the Miao or Hmong from the Southwest, and probably exactly
where they made it. Whenever his money ran low, he would
sign on as a cook in tourist areas. Because the tourists never
came back, he told me, it was just like fooling the foreigners in
American Chinatowns with half-Chinese, half-foreign "Chinese cuisine."

In 2006 he moved to Beijing, said he wanted to see what it
would be like to be an Olympic volunteer. When we met again I
learned that he had changed his name many years before from
Fang Lijun to Fang Caodi. According to him, one day he was
walking past the Temple of the Sun in Beijing, when he saw
many parents picking up their children from the Fangcaodi,

or "fragrant grass," Elementary School, and so he decided
to change his name to Fang Caodi. That's just Old Fang's
logic—no logic at all. With his advanced age and his compli-
cated history, I wonder if the Olympic Committee accepted his
application.

I closed the notebook. After I published my *Comprehensive Cultural
Guide to Beijing* well ahead of the Olympics, I wanted to write sto-
ries only about contemporary China's Golden Age of Ascendancy.
I didn't want to discuss past events anymore. I didn't even want to
*look* at the historical materials on the KMT–CCP Civil War, Land
Reform, the Campaign to Suppress Counterrevolutionaries, the
Three-anti and Five-anti Campaigns, the Anti-Rightist Movement,
the Great Leap Forward that caused thirty million people to starve
to death, the Four Clean-ups or Socialist Education Campaign, the
Cultural Revolution, the 1983 Anti-Spiritual Pollution Campaign,
the Tiananmen Massacre, the Campaign to Suppress the Falun
Gong, and so on and so on . . . I just wanted to forget all those things.

If I could rid my mind of it, a new subject would come to me.
My own interests had completely changed, and I didn't believe that
the new generation of Chinese readers wanted to read about all the
wounds and scars of the past sixty years. I really wanted to write
only about new people and new things, to write about the Chinese
people's Golden Age of Ascendancy.

3.
FROM SPRING
TO SUMMER

*A French crystal chandelier*
ittle Xi didn't return my e-mail, so my happy life could continue. I went to the 798 Art District to participate in the
opening ceremony for an exhibition of paper-cutting instal-
lation art by women from the Northwest. My friend from the
Chinese Academy of Social Sciences was the academic cocurator,
and she'd invited me to be one of the ten speakers at the ribbon-
cutting ceremony. In my three-minute talk, I summarized the Taiwan New Communities Movement of the 1990s and discussed how
Taipei artists and local craftspeople had worked hand in hand to
bring cultural production in villages back to life. I spoke so well I got
a little emotional myself. The curator also said this exhibition was a
fine example of the vitality of Chinese folk culture.

A lunch was held at the nearby Golden Chiangnan restaurant,
and I was placed at the same table as the representative of the China
National Cultural Renaissance Foundation. The Foundation had
sent only an assistant secretary-general. He told me how one of their
most important projects was assisting Chinese around the world to
locate and retrieve national treasures that had been stolen from the
Summer Palace and other sites. Besides that, the Foundation was

working to revive China's ancient rites throughout the entire nation by, for example, providing financial subsidies to many elementary and middle schools to carry out initiation ceremonies at the beginning of every school year, usually requiring students to bow and pay their respects to their teachers. The Foundation was also working hard to have various traditional-style rituals declared "national statutory ceremonies."

After eating a few main dishes, I went to the toilet and by the time I returned a big group of people had crowded around my table to listen to the Foundation's representative, so I decided to move to another table.

My Chinese Academy of Social Sciences friend, Hu Yan, was sitting at a table with a French woman from UNESCO and a Thai who was with the One Village One Craft Association. I thought that if I joined them, I'd have to speak English and that would be too much like hard work, so I decided against it. I went over to the Northwest-delegation table, where there were many empty seats because the reporters were all over at the Renaissance Foundation representative's table interviewing him. Only three elderly ladies who were paper-cutting artists, two female elected village heads, and a Bureau of Culture deputy chief from a prefecture-level city were still at the table. The Northwestern women all looked very honest and kindhearted. My Academy friend always let me see the good side of China. Even though, rationally, I realized that this was not the whole story, emotionally I still liked to meet such good people.

The person I really wanted to chat with was the village head, who was only just twenty years old. She was sitting rather far away from me, and I realized I could not understand her rural Mandarin anyway. All I could do was talk to the deputy chief. She came from a place called Dingxi in Gansu Province. It was originally one of the poorest places in China, but with a few years' hard work after Reform and Opening, it finally lifted itself out of poverty. She told me how a few years earlier the government had convinced the peasants to organize specialist cooperatives and implement dedicated planting schemes, pushing Dingxi to develop into a major potato-producing area. All the Kentucky Fried Chicken and McDonald's outlets in the country used Dingxi potatoes exclusively. She also told me how the local leadership, at a time of rail-transport difficulties, used their connections to provide a special train to get the local products to market on time. And also how they organized surplus labor to go to Xinjiang to pick cotton during the cotton-harvest season.

I learned a lot from her, and so I asked her very seriously if she could summarize for me why Dingxi was able to be so well governed while so many places with better local conditions were still unable to rise above the poverty level. "Dingxi is very fortunate, we have leaders who know how to work hard and get things done." I could sense that what she said was very practical and very simple: it's all about people, she implied. If the government officials are willing to work hard to make things happen, the common people can make the rural economy hum. That is to say, if the present Communist Party cadres had a slightly higher standard of morality and were willing to work harder on practical projects, the Chinese people would be able to live well. As lunch broke up, I thanked her and she said she hoped that members of the Beijing cultural and academic worlds would come to little Dingxi and give them some guidance. I hypocritically told her that I would certainly find time to visit Dingxi.

Feeling very happy after lunch, I went back to the 798 Art District to browse around. Today's 798 Art District is not like the 798 Art District of ten years ago. Now it apes fashionable foreign trends and tries to combine the bohemian and the bourgeois. That's why it has been criticized for becoming increasingly gentrified, commercialized, and kitschy. No matter how you look at it, though, having a 798 Art District is still better than not having one. You can't find another art district on this scale anywhere else in the world. When the foreigners see it they are all amazed and their impression of China suddenly changes, from China as a backward country to China as the most creative country in the world.

In the last two years art and design had become so hot that all the important international art galleries had come to China to set up shop. Famous schools, such as New York's Parsons New School of Design, London's St. Martin's College of Art and Design, and Antwerp's Royal Academy of Fine Arts had also established campuses close to the 798 Art District.

Every time I came to 798, I always took a look at what was on at the Dragon Gate Gallery. This gallery had an extensive collection of French Impressionist and Postimpressionist oil paintings, including some small works by famous masters and, more importantly, many works by lesser known figures of that period.

Their collection is really worth looking at, and it suits my increasingly conservative tastes, I pondered. China now matches Japan as a major collecting country for these French Impressionist and Postimpressionist oil paintings because there is a group of rich collectors who are fascinated by French painting of that age.

The Dragon Gate Gallery had real elegance. The chandelier hanging in the major salon was not made from Chinese materials— it was a genuine Baccarat-crystal chandelier.

As I was looking at that chandelier and ruminating on how the style and temperament of Impressionist and Postimpressionist oil paintings were not quite in sync with Baccarat crystal, a man and a woman came toward me, not exactly holding hands but shoulder to shoulder and talking and laughing. I tried unsuccessfully to avoid them. The man was Jian Lin, my movie-night friend. When he noticed me, he quickly said, "Lao Chen, let me introduce you to Professor Wen."

"It's been a long time, Wen Lan," I said as we shook hands.

"Yes, a very long time, Master Chen," said Wen Lan.

"You two know each other?" said Jian Lin, surprised.

"Master Chen is famous in Hong Kong cultural circles," said Wen Lan.

Wen Lan had probably forgotten that I'm Taiwanese. She was dressed expensively but not vulgarly, rather elegantly glittering.

"Can I swap cards with you?" asked Wen Lan.

"I forgot to bring any," I lied.

"I have his phone number," offered Jian Lin.

Wen Lan didn't give me her card.

"Lao Chen, this is a very nice gallery," said Jian Lin, "but Professor Wen thinks the prices are even higher than in Paris."

"The prices are unreasonably high," Wen Lan said with an air of authority.

"Let me see," I said, and abruptly walked away.

I no longer felt like looking at paintings, but I suddenly thought of three words to describe Wen Lan's elegant manner—Baccarat-crystal chandelier.

Let me explain. There was a time when I was ready to marry Wen Lan. I had already bought an apartment in Hong Kong for us. Then I learned that she was going to marry someone else.

In the autumn of 1991, I went to the mainland to interview an old academic couple who were living under house arrest after the events of 1989. A number of their students from Beijing Normal

University had come to visit them. These young people were not so selfishly concerned with their own futures as to avoid visiting their professors in their time of trouble.

The most striking one among them was Wen Lan, a senior-year student, pretty, easygoing, and cultured. She made me feel romantic.

She asked all the students to note down their phone numbers for me, and I knew she did it just so that I would be able to contact her.

I invited her out and we took a walk around Houhai Lake. Her mother was Shanghainese and her father a Beijinger. He edited a journal on theory and worked in the Central Propaganda Department in Shatan. Wen Lan loved Western literature, was concerned with national affairs, and was extremely beautiful—to me she was perfect.

"What is the meaning of existence?" she once asked me. I flailed around trying to think of something profound. Then, I remember, she quoted Jean-Paul Sartre: "We must take responsibility for our own lives." I was in love.

I went back to Hong Kong for a few days and then contrived a reason to return to Beijing. She said she wanted to go abroad, and I screwed up my courage to ask her to marry me. She laughed and cried, and I thought she had agreed. I told her that we would have no problem living on my salary. I had permanent-resident status in Hong Kong, and she could apply to get it as well.

She asked me how long after we were married would she become a permanent resident and I told her if I got help from friends, probably about two years. During that time she could have a multiple-entry pass to live in Hong Kong for short periods, and I could go to Beijing frequently on assignment. We would be together quite often, and besides, I said, "Meeting after a short separation is like a second honeymoon." She seemed excited and full of expectation. We said we'd get married the following summer so she could finish her studies first. I asked her if I should meet her parents and she said she'd arrange it for my next visit.

I thought I was the luckiest guy getting married to such a gorgeous Beijing woman, and she was eighteen years younger than me. After I returned to Hong Kong, I happened to see an advertisement for properties in Taikoo Shin, so I quickly placed a down payment on the apartment I've mentioned before, and started to build a nest for two.

After completing the paperwork on the flat, I made a long-distance call to Beijing. Wen Lan's father answered and told me she had gone to Germany. "When will she be back?" I asked, and he abruptly replied, "After she gets married! Don't call her anymore!"

I hurried to Beijing and phoned her classmates who'd been at the professors' when I'd first met Wen Lan. They said they were really not close friends and hadn't kept in touch since that night.

I remembered that Wen Lan had said her major was French, but she was also studying German at the Goethe Institute. I rushed over there to look up her records. I found out she had withdrawn from her studies. A secretary who knew her told me she was going to marry a part-time German teacher who worked at the institute. She wouldn't tell me his name. I pushed my way into the dean's office. The dean was a well-known China expert with a Chinese wife, so he probably had some understanding of the wiles of Chinese women. He listened very patiently to my story and said he could not give me Wen Lan's German contact information, but he promised that if I wrote her a letter he would forward it to her.

I went into an empty classroom and sat there, staring blankly, for a long time. I picked up my pen several times wanting to write her a few words, but I just couldn't think how to start.

Three months later I received a letter from Wen Lan. She told me she was married to a German who had been her German teacher, an executive in a German firm in Beijing, and it had been love at first sight. The two of them were living in Germany and they were very happy together. She didn't say which city they lived in and she didn't apologize—it was as if nothing had ever happened between us. She explained herself in only one sentence, the theme of which was that she was like a sparrow that wanted to fly away on the wind and was impatiently longing to spread its wings today, because tomorrow would be too late.

Before 1992, a mainland bride married to a man in Hong Kong had to wait two years before she was granted permanent residence in Hong Kong. (After 1992, she would have had to wait *five* years.) This inhuman discrimination policy was a violation of basic human rights and a disgrace to Hong Kong. If Wen Lan had married me, she would definitely have had to wait two years to live in Hong Kong, so I didn't blame her for choosing to marry a German. I even understood why she had chosen to "ride a donkey while searching for a horse." What I was genuinely indignant about was that she had so thoroughly misled me and hadn't even bothered to tell me anything about her change of heart. I realized that she was a woman who cared only about her own personal advancement, and had no concern for other people.

That night I ate alone at the nearby Singapore Restaurant and read an e-book on my cell phone. I use a K-Touch cell phone. K-Touch used to be the king of counterfeit, but now it's a famous international brand. The phone has every function you could want. The interface uses something similar to Sony technology and the functions combine all the best elements of Apple's iPhone and Amazon's Kindle. Although I still browse in the Sanlian Bookstore on a regular basis, ever since I bought my K-Touch e-book digital phone, almost all my books are downloaded from the net. I've already stored the complete works of Jin Yong, Zhang Ailing, and Lu Xun on my phone.

I was trying to understand Lu Xun's essay "A Lost Good Hell," when I received a call from Wen Lan asking me to come out and meet her. I said I didn't have time, but she insisted, asking me to come out for lunch the next day at the Maison Boulud in Qian Men Street. It's not easy to catch a taxi near there and I don't have a driver, and besides I didn't feel like accommodating that Baccarat-crystal chandelier. I changed it to a small coffeehouse in Qianliang Lane.

"Where is Qianliang Lane?" she asked.

"It's off Dongsi North Avenue, close to your Shatan house, you must know it, right?" I said in exasperation.

She deigned to accept my arrangement—so I knew she must want something from me.

When we met the next day, just as I expected, she said, "Jian Lin and I are just good friends. He's got a wife, you know."

So she wanted to shut me up. She had not seen me for twenty years, and this is all she wanted to see me about. But I wasn't really angry. I just wanted to see what other tricks she had up her sleeve.

"Jian Lin is a big real estate magnate," I said to tease her.

"What's a real estate magnate?" she replied. "Just somebody with a lot of money, nothing so great about that."

What an imperious tone. Was she "riding a donkey while searching for a horse" again? I have to admit that although Wen Lan is over forty, she looks great for her age and has all the charm of a continental European woman. I can imagine that quite a few men have been captivated by her.

"Are you still living in Germany?"

She gave me a puzzled look. "I haven't been in Germany for a long time."

"Didn't they tell me you married a German and went to Germany?" I alluded to what had happened twenty years earlier.

"You mean Hans?" She seemed to be scolding me for not being au courant with her activities. "We haven't been together for ages. Germany was a stifling place, bored me to death. I went to Paris; my ex-husband's Jean-Pierre Louis." Seeing that I didn't react, she added, "A *very* famous sinologist." I was definitely not familiar with any French sinologists. "Sinologists are all insane, I can't stand them," she remarked.

"Jian Lin called you *Professor* Wen," I said.

"Professor Wen or Dr. Wen are both fine. I received my doctorate from Sciences-Po in Paris. I'm a specialist in Euro-African affairs and an adviser to the European Union and the Chinese Ministry of Foreign Affairs."

I remembered that her father was in the Central Propaganda Department—the apple didn't fall far from the tree, either inside or outside the organization, and profiting from both.

"So then, you intend to come back home?" I asked.

"You mean, return to China?" she said with an arrogant air. "We'll see. There are people in Europe who are waiting for me now. There's an old aristocrat who keeps asking me to marry him. But now everybody knows that the twenty-first century belongs to China. If a particularly good opportunity came along, I might consider coming back to do something for China. For the time being, I'll just keep going back and forth. I have a house in Paris and another one in Brussels, and I'm just now looking for a suitable place to buy in Beijing. What about you? What are you doing in Beijing?"

"I just sit around at home, and once in a while I write something."

At that, her interest began to wane.

Then she asked, "Where do you live?"

"Happiness Village Number Two."

"Where?"

"Happiness Village Number Two, in Dongzhi Menwai."

She didn't react—it was probably not posh enough for her. After sizing me up completely, her last remaining interest in me evaporated.

"Well, Lao Chen, I have to go."

"Go ahead."

"About Jian Lin . . ."

I made a gesture of zipping up my lips.

"You're an old Beijinger now," she said in a slightly coquettish manner, "when I return to Beijing, you'll have to take me out!"

I almost said, "What on earth for?" but I held myself in check.

She stood up and added, "I expect you to take care of me."

In socialist realist fiction, this is known as finishing with a bright tail. It could also be called buying travel insurance. On the one hand acting like a big important woman, and on the other hand acting like a helpless little girl, and all the time taking and taking. It's amazing that it didn't embarrass her to say such things.

I felt like I had already become her B-list male escort.

I watched through the window as her driver opened the door for her and she got into a black BMW. It had an armed-police WJ licence plate.

She's no longer Chinese counterfeit goods, I thought, now she's a genuine French Baccarat-crystal chandelier. But it doesn't matter whether she's a made-in-China kerosene lamp or a French crystal chandelier, she's still on the market, always on the make, and she still has her price.

## The Second Spring

Nothing happened for several days after that and no one tried
to contact me. Little Xi was still on my mind, but I resisted trying to
get in touch with her.

Two first-Sunday-of-the-month screenings had come and gone.
He Dongsheng, the government official, was still at the screenings,
but nobody else was invited, and it seemed like Jian Lin had arranged
it that way just for He Dongsheng. This time, when I arrived at the
usual reception room, Jian Lin had already been drinking quite
a bit.

"Wen Lan broke up with me," he said as I came in. "She dumped
me," he added with obvious embarrassment.

I could certainly relate to that—a man with a midlife crisis getting involved with a femme fatale.

I knew that a woman with Wen Lan's good looks and culture
could easily bewitch a man like Jian Lin, in late middle age with a
passion for art and literature.

"Who is she with now?" I asked intuitively.

"My cousin," Jian Lin said with a sad smile, "but this time she's
going to get the worse of it."

"He Dongsheng?" I exclaimed.

"No, no, another cousin. We all met at my aunt's memorial service. Wen Lan attended the Foreign Language School in Baiduizi,
and my aunt taught her French."

"Who's your other cousin?" I asked.

"Do you know of the EAL Friendship Investments group?"

"The one that's involved with Wantwant Starbucks' investments in Africa?"

"That's small potatoes," he said. "Think petroleum, mining,
large-scale capital construction . . ."

"So are they also involved in the arms trade?" I asked nonchalantly.

"Of course they're in the arms trade. Africa, Latin America."

"What about the 'E' for Europe?"

"That's Turkey, the Caucasus, the former Yugoslavia, and the former Soviet Union," he replied.

I remembered that the EAL group's CEO was one Ban Cuntou. "Then Wen Lan is with Ban Cuntou?" I asked.

Jian Lin nodded resentfully.

"You mean he's even wealthier than you are?" I was deliberately provoking him now.

"I can't possibly compete with him."

"You mean he has more power than He Dongsheng?"

"He Dongsheng is very concerned about the nation and the people," Jian Lin explained, "but he is only an adviser, at most like a high-level brain trust. There are many, many people who have more power than he does. He can't even match a secretary to the Politburo Standing Committee in influence. But whether or not you have clout depends upon whether or not your faction commands power at Party Central. You don't understand China's state system. There are so many unwritten rules that you can't possibly fathom. You can't judge the current national situation by superficial appearances, and there's no way of really explaining it to someone outside the party-government system." Jian Lin was growing impatient as he spoke.

I am quite familiar with Jian Lin's idea that outsiders cannot understand the Chinese government system, so I just let him go on thinking that I didn't understand. He was out of sorts and finding me a little irritating, so I figured I'd best not say too much because I still valued his friendship, however remote it might be.

"I hope you won't go around writing or talking about any of this," he said very seriously.

"I don't write gossip," I said with some resentment.

After we finished eating, we had nothing more to say.

I was just thinking that perhaps Wen Lan and Ban Cuntou were quite evenly matched. Wen Lan ought to be pretty satisfied now. After so many years of "riding a donkey while searching for a horse," she was probably tired. Was she really planning on becoming the First Lady of China?

When He Dongsheng came into the room, Jian Lin pointed to his own mouth to remind me not to say anything about Wen Lan.

He Dongsheng gave us a bottle of Maotai each and said, "This Maotai comes from the Party leadership's exclusive Zhongnanhai supply, so it should be good. You can drink it without any worries."

We thanked him enthusiastically. This insomniac national leader was not such a cold fish after all.

Jian Lin took out his crystal decanter and poured in a bottle of 1989 Château Lafite, a fine vintage. Then he put on the film: *The Second Spring*. It had come out in September 1975. This was the first film, after the Eight Model Plays, that was produced under the direction of the Gang of Four during the Cultural Revolution. At the time, Deng Xiaoping had returned to office, and had just traveled to the United Nations. When he came back, he said he was going to emphasize technology. The Gang of Four put out this film aimed at criticizing Deng Xiaoping, but it had still not been screened widely around the country when the Cultural Revolution came to an end.

I was quite interested to note that the director was Sang Hu. He had directed many films, including *Miserable in Middle Age* in 1949, *New Year's Sacrifice* in 1956, and *Undying Love* and *Long Live the Wife*, both in 1947 and with screenplays by Zhang Ailing, also known as Eileen Chang.

I looked over at He Dongsheng and saw that he had his eyes

closed again. I realized then why he had been coming to this gathering for so many months. He usually suffered from insomnia, but when he "watched" the films here he could relax and have a good nap.

Then I looked at Jian Lin. He wasn't watching either. He had his head down with his face in his hands. I never imagined that he could be so upset—he had really been hurt in love this time.

As the film ended and the lights came on, He Dongsheng opened his eyes and presented a long critique.

"That was then and this is now—we've gone around in such a big circle just to bring us back to a new stage of history where order has been restored," he said.

Jian Lin and I listened attentively.

"Completely rejecting foreign technology won't do, but completely depending on foreign technology is no good either. Self-reliance is relative, not absolute. A big country cannot be completely dependent on others, but it cannot be completely self-sufficient either. In Old Mao's day, the people's standard of living was low, and so we could be basically self-sufficient in food and consumer goods, but he wanted to be self-sufficient in science, technology, information, and energy and not ask for foreign help. He abandoned external trade and did business only with small third-world countries like Albania. He was seeking an absolute self-reliance that was ultimately harmful to our development and really unnecessary.

"During Old Deng's age of Reform and Opening, the Americans wanted the whole world to abandon self-sufficiency. This kind of free-market fundamentalism is also unscientific—even the United States itself can't do it. At that time we exported like crazy in order to earn foreign currency, and for a while it worked extremely well for us. But in a world where the U.S. dollar is the standard currency, in order to keep the value of our renminbi low to support

our exports, we had to buy large amounts of dollars. Speaking rationally, this policy could not be sustained for very long because in
the end, when the dollar depreciated and the American economy
bombed, we were almost dragged down with it.

"Fortunately, we adjusted our economic policies. To put it simply, we adopted a form of relative self-sufficiency. We exported our
manufactured goods to Russia, Angola, Brazil, Europe, and Canada
and purchased oil, foodstuffs, minerals, wood, and other raw materials that our nation lacks. We also carried on mutual trade with
Europe and America and bought their Boeing airplanes and their
high-tech manufacturing tools. Aside from those things, whatever
we can do ourselves we do—whatever we can grow ourselves, we
grow it; whatever we can research and develop ourselves, we do;
whatever we can consume ourselves, we do so, from potatoes to
small-producer commodities to cell phones and automobiles. We
are a huge country and so we are our own most important market.
We're no longer overdependent on the United States, but we're no
longer blindly practicing either mercantilism or Old Mao's kind of
isolationism. We still go in for plenty of foreign trade, but it does not
amount to any more than twenty-five percent of our GDP. Isn't this
practicing relative self-sufficiency!"

He Dongsheng was quite animated while he was talking, but
when he finished he went back to his deflated-balloon state. We
knew that the lecture was over, so the three of us just drank our
wine in silence. At midnight, as He Dongsheng went to the toilet,
we were all set to go our separate ways.

"Shall we leave together?" he asked when he came back, and
this time I replied, "Yes, thanks." I didn't want to stay behind and
listen to Jian Lin's maudlin ranting about Wen Lan.

I felt a little awkward as we walked down to the underground parking lot. He Dongsheng didn't say anything and I didn't want to start a conversation for fear of being rebuffed, so I just kept quiet.

He drove a black Land Rover SUV, a kind of foreign import that was so common in Beijing that it was quite unobtrusive. His licence plate was also an ordinary Beijing number—somebody had probably loaned him the car.

After he started the engine, He Dongsheng took a small electric instrument, like a TV remote, out of his shirt pocket. One touch and a small green light came on, and three seconds later two more green lights came on. He put the thing back in his pocket and said, "Nothing's going on."

I was hesitant to ask, but he came out with an explanation. "It's an anti-bugging and anti-tracking device."

"Who would dare to bug or track you?" I could not help asking.

"They all would!" he replied. "The Central Discipline Committee, State Security, Public Security, the People's Liberation Army General Staff Department . . . There are so many organizations and so many people, who can say for sure? Who doesn't have enemies? I monitor people and people monitor me. I know your secrets and you know mine, there's a dossier on everybody, that's the way the game is played."

I was learning again. Even the Party and national leaders are afraid they're being watched. As I fastened my seat belt, I acted so cool, pretending that I had seen it all before and nothing could shock me.

"Where do you live?" he asked.

"Happiness Village Number Two."

He knew it well.

I asked him if he'd seen any of our Prosperous China Conference classmates. "No" was all he said.

I thought he was finished, but then he went on. "Shui Xinghua is a concerned capitalist. You know what I learned from that Prosperous China Conference?"

"What?"

"That was when I first realized," he said, "that the intellectual elites of China, Taiwan, and Hong Kong think about things in completely different ways—their awareness, discourse, concepts of history, and worldviews are fundamentally different. And furthermore, not only do *you* not understand *us*, but *we* don't understand *you* either, and, frankly speaking, we don't have much interest in understanding. I mean real understanding—that's virtually impossible. When I went to the Prosperous China Conference, I finally realized that if the intellectual elites of these three places are so different, the common people will be even more so. This was a great help to my later thinking about Taiwan and Hong Kong."

I'd lived in all three of these places and understood what he was saying. It was rather remarkable that he had only to attend one Prosperous China Conference to pick up on this difference.

"The last couple of years the elites of Taiwan and Hong Kong have all been obediently learning from the mainland," I said.

"It is not easy for outsiders to understand Chinese affairs," he responded.

We must have been speeding, because just then a traffic cop pulled us over. I was thinking that this cop didn't know what was good for him. I watched He Dongsheng bring the car to a stop while talking into his cell phone. "I'm at Gongti East Road, almost at Xindong Road—okay."

Then he just hung up his cell phone while a very fat traffic cop asked him for his driving licence. He didn't respond, and when the cop asked him again he simply said, "Wait a minute," without even giving him a glance. I could see that the traffic cop was about to lose his temper, but fortunately just then he received a phone call. As the cop answered his phone, He Dongsheng started his engine and drove off. "My secretary will handle it," he said.

I thought his secretary must have received many late-night calls like this one—then he has to clean up the mess. Being a big shot's secretary is a hell of a hard job.

After all that, He Dongsheng didn't say another word. I was a little bit sorry because I was enjoying his lectures. To tell the truth, I rather liked this insomniac Party and national leader.


### Wudaokoupengyou

One morning after May 1, when I turned on my computer, I saw I had an e-mail from *wudaokoupengyou*, "Wudaokou friend." I always used to delete any e-mails from unknown addresses straight away so I wouldn't get a computer virus, but recently I'd been opening all of them to see who they were from. As I expected, *wudaokoupengyou* was Little Xi.

She was asking me to wait for her in front of the open-air farmers' market near Gongti South Gate.

I always like to browse around these farmers' markets. The north China seasons are quite distinct and have different fruits and vegetables. You can see this most clearly in the farmers' markets— not to mention that the produce is far fresher than in the supermarkets. Farmers' markets make me feel more like I'm making contact with the common people. You can't avoid making contact with them when people crowd around you, pushing and shoving. If you block their path, those big Aunties and Uncles will push you right out of the way with their bags full of vegetables.

That day, as I waited, I was getting a little worried. Little Xi was already over half an hour late. The Beijing administrative authorities are not especially reasonable and would allow this farmers' market to stay open only until ten a.m. It was almost that already when I heard Little Xi call me. "Lao Chen!"

I turned around to see her smiling and looking quite happy. "You made it!" I said.

"I'm here!" she answered.

She was carrying a canvas bag. "Wait here while I go in and buy some vegetables."

"No, I'll go with you."

At ten minutes to closing time, the market was extremely crowded. I followed behind Little Xi. When she moved I moved, and when she stopped I stopped. I felt like I was always rubbing against her and I was conscious of her scent. But she was absorbed in haggling over prices, making her selections, paying and receiving change, and then shouldering her way through the crush of people on to the next stall. The ten minutes flew by quickly in this way and I felt a kind of unself-consciousness that I had not felt in a very long time.

In the e-mail Little Xi had said that she wanted to come to my place and cook me a meal, and that was something I was very much looking forward to.

"All we can eat today are vegetables and fruit," Little Xi said as we left the market.

"That's fine by me," I said.

"You have rice at home, don't you?" she asked.

I told her that I did.

I actually hadn't had any when I received her e-mail, but then I'd rushed over to Carrefour's and bought rice, cooking oil, spices, chicken, beef, and lamb. I even bought some kitchen utensils. I guessed that Little Xi would want to get some vegetables at the farmers' market.

"Were you worried when I made you wait?" she asked.

"Not really," I lied.

"I had to get rid of those guys who follow me," Little Xi said with a marked change in tone.

On the way, she told me all the many things she had done in order to see me. A few days ago she'd been all around looking at houses as though she were intending to move. Finally she found a small furnished room in one of those old dilapidated 1970s Soviet-style block buildings. This morning she'd met with the landlord, moved a trunk full of things in, and paid the rent. Then she took a canvas bag and said she was going shopping.

She figured that one of the two men following her would remain behind to talk to the landlord about installing a bugging device while she was out. It was because her previous landlord suddenly changed his attitude toward her that she learned she was being followed and listened in on. The second guy might not follow her either, because she had just paid the rent and would be coming back from the supermarket soon. Even if he did follow her, there were two entrances and exits to the Jingkelong supermarket, so she could still give him the slip. But she had always pretended that she didn't know they were watching her, and so they were not especially vigilant.

The more she talked, the more alarmed I became. I thought perhaps she was being oversensitive or overimaginative, but then, she really could be under surveillance. Didn't I see those smokers that day in the National Art Museum garden?

"Are you certain no one is following you?"

She stopped, turned to look behind her, and to the left and right. "You see, nobody there."

We were standing on the wide-open Xindong Road and saw there was no one in sight. I felt quite ashamed. Little Xi had gone to so much effort to see me, but I was worried only about her getting me into trouble.

"What's wrong? Relax, there's no problem," she said.

"Little Xi, what are you going to do?" I asked as we stood there on the pavement.

"I'll certainly do *something*," she quipped. "Let's see, maybe I'll leave Beijing this afternoon."

I stopped for a moment, expressionless and a little stunned.

"You want to eat, or what?" she said with a grin.

We started walking again toward Happiness Village Number Two.

It was a warm spring day and the air was filled with the scent of locust-tree blossoms. They gave off a powerful, sensual aroma that made me feel an intense love. All I wanted to say was "Little Xi, let's be together, let's stop tormenting ourselves, and let's just have a good life together."

But I didn't dare say it. I didn't have the guts.

Little Xi worked quickly and skillfully in the kitchen while I stood beside her, clumsily assisting. She'd taken off her jacket and I could see the uneven scar tissue on her shoulder where she had been hit by the army jeep. She really is a good person, despite her drawbacks, I thought to myself.

"Lao Chen, our old friends have all changed now," she said suddenly while she was chopping the bok choy.

I remembered that she had said something similar that day in the park. So I asked her, "How have they changed? Tell me how."

"They've become . . . they've all become very satisfied," she said after a short pause. "Lao Chen, are you satisfied?"

I felt she was testing me, so I asked her, "Little Xi, why are *you* so dissatisfied?"

This really was our conversation.

Little Xi paused, expressionless for a moment, and then challenged me in turn. "Lao Chen, do you remember how it felt back then? When you were here, in 1989, when I had the old restaurant in Wudaokou with my mother? And later in the 1990s, when we opened up the new restaurant—do you remember what we talked about? Do you remember why we were angry, why we struggled, what our ideals were? Do you remember, Lao Chen?"

And I asked her back tenderly, "Little Xi, why can't you forget? This is a different age."

She looked at me with an expression of vague disappointment, and after a while she said, "I've already forgotten too much. When I was locked up in that mental hospital for so long, I forgot so many things. I don't want to forget anymore."

Just as I wanted to ask more questions, Little Xi seemed to want to drop the subject. "Let's just eat lunch," she said, and lowered her head to continue chopping the bok choy.

When lunch was served, Little Xi was still relaxed, but she had already come to a conclusion about me—I was one of those people around her who had changed.

Just before eating, she took her medicine and told me quite frankly, "It's an antidepressant the shrink gave me, but I don't think it does any good. When I finish this batch, I'm not going to take any more."

I told her how good I thought her shredded potatoes with chili peppers and bok choy with vinegar were. She said it was really great to be able to cook me a meal. But really, I sensed that she was saying good-bye.

At the kitchen table, I decided to make a final attempt to redeem myself in her eyes. I now had an idea of what she was thinking. She was feeling that everyone around her was different and she was the only one who was still angry. I sounded her out. "You know, Little Xi, some people are better at pretending about life, and pretending is a good way to protect their real selves." When I saw her eyes light up, I knew I'd hit on something.

"Obviously, if you pretend for a long time, then you're not going to be able to distinguish between what is true and what is fake," I continued. Little Xi listened quietly.

I followed this line of argument, making it up as I went along. "Lu Xun said that some people are nostalgic for a 'lost good hell' because there'll always be a bad hell that's worse than that lost good hell. That goes without saying. But between a good hell and a counterfeit paradise, which one will people choose? No matter what you might say, many people will believe that a counterfeit paradise is better than a good hell. They know perfectly well it's a counterfeit paradise, but they don't dare expose it. As time goes by, they will even forget that it *is* a fake paradise. They start arguing in defense of this fake paradise, asserting that it is actually the only paradise. But there's always a small number of people, even if they are only an extremely small minority, who will choose the good hell no matter how painful it is, because in the good hell at least everyone is fully aware that they are living in hell."

I wasn't sure what exactly I was trying to say, but the more I spoke, the more I felt I was making good sense. Little Xi listened attentively. On the mainland, if you mention Lu Xun, a writer some liken to Dickens or even Joyce, it will strike a chord with people of a certain age and education. At the very least, what I said had brought Little Xi closer to me.

She looked thoughtful for a while before asking, "Are you saying that I'm too nostalgic for my lost good hell, and therefore I'm refusing to accept our counterfeit paradise?"

"I'm talking about two choices," I answered rather disingenuously.

"Between a good hell and a fake paradise—which one would *you* choose?" she asked.

She had gone straight to the heart of it. She had asked the key question, and I had to be particularly careful. I wanted to bring us closer together, so I equivocated. "Perhaps . . . if necessary . . . I'd be willing to try considering the good hell."

This made Little Xi smile. If she'd been standing nearer, I could have kissed her, but unfortunately, the kitchen table was between us.

"Lao Chen, can I give you a hug?" she asked.

I moved around to the other side of the table and held her as tightly as I could.

"Welcome back to our good hell!" she said.

I so badly wanted to say, "Little Xi, let's be together," but the words stuck in my throat.

Just then the intercom buzzed. Little Xi immediately stiffened and I released her. Little Xi, I thought, they've caught up with you, and there's no way out this time.

Readying myself for trouble, I went to the door. When I looked back at Little Xi, she was still standing totally motionless and holding her breath.

I pushed the intercom button and shouted, "Who is it?"

A man's voice at the other end sounded startled. "Er . . . is this Mr. Chen?"

I saw Little Xi hurriedly put on her coat, pick up her canvas bag, and come up to listen in.

I shouted again into the intercom, "What is it?"

"Mr. Chen . . . wait a minute please . . ." The man seemed to have moved away from the intercom.

"Is there another door out of here?" asked Little Xi. I shook my head.

Then a woman's voice came over the intercom. "Lao Chen, open the door! Please open the door," she shouted.

"Who is it?" I yelled back.

"It's me!"

Then I realized it was Wen Lan's voice.

"It's a friend of mine," I told Little Xi.

Little Xi opened the apartment door and said, "I'll hide in the corner of the hall, and then you can open the front gate."

I didn't think that was necessary, but before I could say anything, she had already bolted out.

I pressed the button and heard the iron gate downstairs open. Little Xi was hiding on the stairwell one floor up. My building doesn't have an elevator, so I could hear Wen Lan's high heels clacking briskly up the stairs.

As soon as she got to my floor, she demanded, "Why the hell did you take so long opening the door?"

"What on earth do you want?" I asked, blocking the entrance to my flat.

"Someone's been picking on me, I've been hurt and need a shoulder to cry on," she said.

You really do think I'm permanently on standby for you, I thought to myself.

She was now clearly agitated and tears were welling up in her eyes. "Why are you looking at me so cruelly? You never used to treat me like this. Didn't you say you were going to take care of me?"

What would Little Xi think when she heard this?

"Come in," I hissed.

Wen Lan strode in and I closed the door quickly after her. I knew that Little Xi would take this opportunity to get away, taking with her any misunderstandings about my relationship with Wen Lan.

"What's wrong with you? Why do you look so shocked?" Wen Lan asked.

"How did you find me here?" I said, really getting angry now.

"Dongzhi Menwai, Happiness Village Number Two. I asked the security guard where that Hong Kong writer lives and he brought me here."

"Do you really think I'm going to be on permanent standby for you?" I said, lowering my voice.

"What are you talking about?" she asked.

"I don't ever want to see you again," I said slowly, and then more deliberately, "never again."

"What do you mean?" Wen Lan shouted at me suddenly as though she could hardly believe her ears.

"Just leave," I said coldly, and feeling calmer now I added, "And don't ever come back."

"Say that again!"

"I said, get the hell out of here!" I pointed to the door.

"Fine, you're heartless anyway," Wen Lan said as though she had finally got the message. "But I'm warning you—you've upset me now, and there will be consequences."

Wen Lan waited till she'd got to the door before she turned around and vigorously gave me the finger. I slowly replied in kind.


### Paradise on earth

I shouldn't have let Little Xi leave. I should have declared my love sooner. I regret it all now.

It's been two weeks and there's been no news. I wrote an e-mail to *wudaokoupengyou*, but there was no response. I searched the net for *wudaokoupengyou*, but received only a great deal of information on *Wudaokou* and *friend*. I could not find any posts by Little Xi. This was quite different from the last time, when she used *feicheng-wuraook* for her e-mail address, and her Web site name had been "If you're not sincere, don't bother, okay." Now that Little Xi knows she's under surveillance, her e-mail and her Web site are probably not connected anymore. It's likely she used *wudaokoupengyou* just to make contact with me. What the hell is her current e-mail and Internet name?

It's dawned on me too slowly, but every day since Little Xi left, I've realized how much I truly love her. I'd be willing to go into hell for her. But the weirdest thing is that my two-year-long feeling of happiness has left me. I'm longing for love, and now I'm no longer happy.

One day, when the Beijing air was fragrant with the scent of willow and crab-apple blossoms, I went over to Dong Niang's house, walked dejectedly into her bedroom, took off my shirt and trousers, and flopped down on her bed.

Dong Niang started taking her clothes off in front of me. "Take everything off, baby, tonight it's on the house."

"Why is it on the house tonight?" I asked.

"Tonight is my last time," she said.

"What do you mean, last time?"

"I'm leaving. I'm getting out of Beijing."

"You're leaving Beijing?" I sat up in dismay.

"No crying, no crying," Dong Niang teased me. "Baby, Dong

Niang has never seen you so unhappy in all these years. You're still my fun-loving baby, aren't you?"

"I'm really very unhappy," I said.

"Let Dong Niang hold you," she said.

She kissed me, but I held back. "Little Dong, let's just talk."

She let go of me and got out of bed. "Let me tell your fortune with the tarot cards."

I didn't like to call her Dong Niang. I preferred to call her Little Dong, just like when she was at the Paradise Club. When Little Dong found out that I was a writer, she asked me to recommend novels for her. It wasn't especially necessary as she loved to read fiction, and even before my suggestions had already read many books by Qiong Yao, Yan Qin, Cen Kailun, Yi Shu, and Zhang Xiaoxian. I told her to read some fiction in translation, starting with Jane Austen. She actually read all six of Austen's novels and she read them better than I had. After that, she read quite a few popular novels in translation. I remember asking what her favorite novels were, and she said Robert James Waller's *The Bridges of Madison County* and Qiong Yao's *How Long Lasts the Sunset?* Our tastes were different, but because we both liked to read, I always felt closer to her. After she left the club and started seeing her customers at home, I carried on visiting her for years, but I felt like she was still Little Dong who likes to read novels. For a while there were a number of Taiwanese customers who would play poker and smoke cigars at her place, and I joined them a few times. They talked of Dong Niang this, and Dong Niang that, until I too began to call her Dong Niang instead of Little Dong.

"Where is my lover?" I asked casually.

Little Dong started to place the tarot cards, but I changed my mind. "No, no, no, no, predict something else." I couldn't put my fate in her hands.

I gave her another scenario, a typically tarot-card conundrum. "I'm standing at a crossroads. The first road will lead me toward a stable and a comfortable life, but I'll never feel truly satisfied. The second road will lead me into a lot of trouble, even insurmountable trouble, but it could also lead me to find true love and the greatest happiness. Which road should I choose?"

She shuffled the cards a few times and laid them out in two rows. Then she said, "The first road is very peaceful and prosperous; on the second road, there are obstacles and many uncertainties, but there is love there." Her answer was a complete repetition of my question.

But then she said, "These cards are about change. You've been on the first road for a long time. If you want to change to the second road, then you should follow it. If you don't, you'll regret it." This was probably just what I wanted to hear.

"Little Dong—I still like to call you Little Dong—thank you," I said.

"Lao Chen, this is the first time I've seen you in the last two years . . . seen your true face."

"My true face? Wasn't I real before?"

"Before—before you were the same as everyone else, always, always . . ."

"Full of happiness?" I asked, my heart racing.

"Exactly. It started about two years ago, you and all my other customers. In fact, everybody around me suddenly became extremely happy!"

"Has everybody around you changed?" I quoted Little Xi's words.

"You could put it that way," said Little Dong.

"But you haven't changed, have you? Why not?" I asked.

Little Dong was quiet for a while. Then she said, "Lao Chen, we've been friends for over ten years. Can I tell you the truth?"

I nodded.

"You know I'm what the Hong Kong people call a 'woman of the Dao'—a junkie?"

I was taken aback. I would never have known.

"I don't use needles. If the customers saw them, they wouldn't like it."

"What kind of drugs do you take?" I asked.

"Whatever I can find that can be taken orally," she said.

"Write them all down for me later. I'd like to know what they are," I said with a certain caution. "Go on. What happens after you take the drugs?"

"When I take drugs, sometimes I feel really high, but sometimes I feel down, right? And sometimes I become extremely aware of my surroundings. At those times, I can see that the world has changed, that everybody around me is not quite right."

"How are they 'not quite right'?" I asked.

"They're just not right," she said, "they're different from before, including you, Lao Chen, they're all too . . . they all feel too happy. I can't explain it, but they're different from before. It's not the sort of crazy high like when people like me take drugs. It's a kind of very mild and very small high."

I was trying hard to understand what she meant. I thought I did, but I was not sure.

"My boyfriend and I can't stand it," she went on. "He's from

Australia. He used to write travel guides for backpackers and he's been in China for twenty years. He says that the Chinese mentality transforms itself every few years. It changed in 1992 with Deng Xiaoping's southern tour; in 1994 with economic macro-control; in 1997 with the return of Hong Kong; in 2000 when China entered the WTO; in 2003 after the SARS epidemic; in 2008 with the Olympic torch and the opening ceremony; and now again in the last five years. He says in the past the leading countries in the National Happiness Index were always countries like Nigeria, Venezuela, and Puerto Rico. Their people all reported feeling especially happy. You wouldn't even know how far down the list China was then, but suddenly for the last couple of years China has ranked as number one. Over a billion people all report being very happy! Don't you think there is something wrong with the Chinese? How can they be so happy?"

Being with this foreign boyfriend, I thought, has definitely given her a different perspective.

"My boyfriend also takes drugs," she continued. "Once we got high and had a big discussion about Jane Austen. It was fantastic. After that we became very close. You remember that year when there was a big crackdown? When I was living in Wangjing district? I knew someone might report me to the police, so I hid in my boyfriend's place in the diplomatic quarter. I didn't dare go out for several weeks—otherwise, who knows if I'd still be alive today. You see, you probably don't remember?"

"My memory of that period is very hazy . . ." I said.

"Today, a normal person doesn't remember," she said, "those of us who remember are the abnormal ones. This is why my boyfriend and I can't stand it. For the past two years in Beijing, it's been harder and harder finding the gear we need. It's like there are fewer and fewer dealers. Early this year, we went to a mountainous region of

Yunnan to see if things might be a little better there. We discovered that the people there were a little more like us. Of course we ran into a lot of junkies and some of them were really evil, but there were some nice ones as well. And then there were the mountain people—none of them had that small-small form of high that the plains people have. My boyfriend calls that small-small high 'high lite-lite.' Sometimes he exaggerates and says that everybody now looks like those happy revolutionary workers or soldiers and peasants in those Cultural Revolution posters. Living among them, you probably don't notice it. It's not like that just in Beijing, but everywhere we went all over the country, everybody is high lite-lite, except in those mountainous areas or far off in the Northwest. My boyfriend and I talked it over for a long time and finally decided to move to Yunnan near National Highway 320, along the border with Myanmar." She went silent and waited for me to react.

"I know someone who feels the same as you two do," I said. "She can't stand high lite-lite either."

"Really?"

"She takes antidepressants."

"Maybe antidepressants have the same effect," Little Dong said thoughtfully.

"Maybe so," I said. "She is that second road I've just asked the tarot cards about."

# PART TWO

1.

WANDERING

BACK

AND FORTH

*The Age of Satisfaction*

"T he Age of Satisfaction!"—Zhuang Zizhong, one of the venerable founding editors of the *Reading Journal*, often pondered this term. He heartily congratulated himself on having lived long enough to see this day, on having survived China's various Ages of Trouble to bear witness to this Age of Happiness—China's Golden Age of Prosperity and Satisfaction. He often told himself the most important thing in life was to live for as long as possible. All the other founding editors of the *Reading Journal* were dead and gone, and he was one of the few remaining greats. All the glory belonged to him now.

During the spring festival, the Politburo member in charge of cultural propaganda visited him at home and even brought along a CCTV reporter. Although this could not compare with earlier times when the celebrated Ji Xianlin received visits from the president, it was still a great event in the cultural and publishing world. Zhuang Zizhong was neither a great classical scholar nor a prize-winning novelist. A few years earlier, if you had heard that a Politburo member was going to visit the home of the aged founder of a scholarly journal, you would have said it was a joke. From this event, we could see how much importance this current Politburo attached to intellectuals and thinkers; this was something we had not seen since the end of the 1980s.

At the beginning of the *Reading Journal* New Year reception, Zhuang Zizhong modestly told everyone that all the honor was due to the *Reading Journal* itself. All the efforts of successive editors over more than thirty years had not been in vain, and the *Reading Journal* had finally received positive recognition from the leaders of Party Central. He recalled how the Party had for some time misunderstood the journal and censured it for its tone and direction, and later when they had patched things up with the Party, the latter still didn't genuinely trust the journal. All that had changed in the last two years. First off, all the previous chief editors and assistant editors had miraculously and harmoniously been cooperating with one another. Then all the journal's writers, who previously had held a variety of positions on how the nation should be ruled, suddenly reached a unified consensus. After the new joint editors organized a wide-ranging discussion seminar on "China's New Prosperity" two years earlier, the *Reading Journal* again regained its briefly lost place as the leading scholarly journal of the nation's cultural and intellectual world. It also came to be seen by the Party leadership as extremely important.

Zhuang Zizhong had made ten national policy suggestions concerning China's New Era of Prosperity:

a one-party democratic dictatorship;
the rule of law with stability as the most important element;
an authoritarian government that governs for the people;
a state-controlled market economy;
fair competition guaranteed by state-owned enterprises;

scientific development with unique Chinese characteristics;

a self-centered harmonious foreign policy;

a multiethnic republic ruled by one sovereign ethnic group of Han Chinese;

post-Westernism and post-universalism as the nation's chief worldviews;

the restoration of Chinese national culture as the world's unrivaled leader.

All these positions, now firmly established principles, seemed like perfectly unexceptional common sense. But why did the *Reading Journal* have to argue them for so many years before reaching a favorable consensus? No matter what, Zhuang Zizhong believed, *Reading* had now received positive recognition from the Party, which meant he had the Party's affirmation of his own devotion to the Party and the Nation. Zhuang Zizhong felt that to be the greatest achievement of his later years.

Now he was sitting in his wheelchair as his new young wife wheeled him toward his new car. Ever since the Politburo member had visited him during the Lunar New Year festival, it had been decided that he should be provided with an official car and driver. One of the official duties of this chauffeur is to drive Zhuang Zizhong every Saturday afternoon to browse around the Sanlian Bookstore.

As Zhuang Zizhong came out of his house, Lao Chen, the Taiwanese writer long resident in Beijing, had just walked out of the Happiness Village Number Two compound and begun his daily afternoon stroll to one of the three nearby Starbucks coffee shops. Since it was Saturday, the Sanlitun Swire Village and the Dongzhi Menwai Ginza Starbucks would definitely be too crowded; his only choice was the Starbucks in the PCCW Tower Mall of Plenty on Gongti North Road. He could only hope that all those white-collar yuppies would be in the gym and not at Starbucks occupying all the comfy chairs and surfing the net, using up all the wireless connection points.

The only unusual thing that day was that, in contrast to the previous two years, Lao Chen was not very happy as he left his house. His feeling of happiness had deserted him. You could even say that as Lao Chen came out the door, he was feeling pretty miserable.

Ever since Little Xi had left his Happiness Village apartment, Lao Chen had not felt good. And Little Dong's departure from Beijing had only made him feel worse.

A few days after Little Xi had left, Lao Chen went to Wudaokou to visit Big Sister Song. He carefully chose ten o'clock in the morning, when the talented young Wei Guo would probably be in school. He wanted to ask her if she'd heard anything from Little Xi. Lao Chen approached the back door of the Five Flavors restaurant and skulked around, trying to avoid being noticed until Big Sister Song came to open up. He was wearing a beige trench coat of the sort worn by the Hong Kong comic actor Ng Man Tat when playing a private detective, or Law Kar-ying in the role of a sexual deviant, a flasher. Obviously, Lao Chen was not at all thinking of himself in this light. In his mind, when he put on his trench coat he looked more like Hollywood tough guy Humphrey Bogart or the author Graham Greene. Because of this misperception, when Lao Chen nervously showed himself to greet Big Sister Song, she screamed in fright.

After calming her down, Lao Chen asked if she knew any way to contact Little Xi. Big Sister Song pulled a note out of her coat pocket. "I just knew you would come by. A while back when I could still send her e-mails, Little Xi asked me if she should see you, and I told her she should. After that, she didn't tell me whether she'd seen you or not. Two days ago, I got this text message. I don't know where it was sent from, but I copied it down because I had this feeling you'd turn up here."

"What do these letters mean?" Lao Chen said, looking at the note with four Romanized Chinese words—*mai zi bu si.*

"I don't know," said Big Sister Song.

"Did Little Xi send this to you?"

"Definitely, she must have."

Lao Chen was only half convinced by Big Sister Song until she took his hands in hers, bent her knees in a half bow, and implored, "Lao Chen, you have to save Little Xi, you have to save her."

"Get up, Big Sister, get up," Lao Chen said, helping her to her feet.

Big Sister Song started to cry, and Lao Chen began to tear up, too, so he took out a white handkerchief and dabbed at his eyes.

"Lao Chen, I know you'll save Little Xi," Big Sister Song said. "You're a good man, Lao Chen, you'll save her."

"I'll do my best," Lao Chen said. "I'll do everything I can."

When he got home, Lao Chen sat down in front of his computer and stared blankly at that note: *mai zi bu si.* With the previous message, he had immediately seen that *feichengwuraook* meant "If you're not sincere, don't bother, okay?" But what did this *mai zi bu*

*si* mean? "Sell appearance cloth thread?" "Bury letter enrich posterity?" He tried out some characters, but the problem with Chinese Romanization is that it does not indicate the tone, so each sound can stand for many different characters.

Lao Chen remembered that when he was a child living in Tiu Keng Leng, his mother worked as a cook in a Protestant church. On Sunday mornings she would take him to the church service because afterward they were given a bag of white flour donated by the people of the United States. His mother would usually doze through the service, but he liked to listen to the pastor's sermon. Once the pastor quoted from what Jesus had said about a single grain of wheat: "Unless a grain of wheat falls into the ground and dies, it will be alone, but if it dies, it will bring forth much fruit." In other words, a grain of wheat that falls into the ground does not really die—*mai zi bu si.* Had Little Xi changed her Internet name to *maizibusi,* "The grain does not die"? And yet he couldn't remember her ever being remotely religious.

Lao Chen looked up the four characters *mai zi bu si* on the net and several literary and religious links came up. For example, a book on Zhang Ailing and her banal "boudoir realism" titled *The Grain Fallen on the Ground Does Not Die* by a Harvard professor, Wang Dewei, and a Chinese translation, *Maizi busi,* of André Gide's 1924 autobiographical novel *Si le grain ne meurt.* Lao Chen looked at a dozen or so Web sites, but didn't find any that appeared to be by Little Xi. He didn't have the patience to look at any more. His promise to Big Sister Song that he would try to save Little Xi was beginning to weigh on his shoulders like Jesus's cross. Then again, no matter how heavyhearted he felt, life must go on—so he went out in search of his customary Starbucks Lychee Black Dragon Latte.

❁

What Lao Chen didn't expect was that Fang Caodi, who once used to be Fang Lijun, had been waiting for him on Xindong Road for almost two hours. Fang Caodi had run into him there before, taken his card, and sent him an e-mail, but Lao Chen had not responded. This time, Fang decided to wait for him at the same spot and feign another chance encounter.

By now, Fang Caodi could almost tell by a person's appearance whether he or she was a "nonforgetter," like he and Zhang Dou were. The last time he'd met Lao Chen, his leisurely, contented expression certainly didn't put him in their camp. But Fang Caodi had always thought that Lao Chen was an intelligent guy, and Fang hardly ever changed his opinion of anyone. He was especially happy today to see Lao Chen coming out of the Happiness Village Number Two compound with a frown and an extremely worried look on his face.

"Master Chen," Fang called as he took off his baseball cap and began walking toward him. "It's me, Fang Caodi." He patted his bald head as if to refresh Lao Chen's memory.

"Master Chen, you look great today," Fang said.

"Old Fang, I'm not really in the mood for talking today," said Lao Chen.

"Not feeling good today, Lao Chen?" said Fang. "That's okay. How could you feel good? A whole month is missing."

"I really have things to do, Old Fang," said Lao Chen. "I'll talk to you some other time."

"Where're you going, Master Chen?"

Lao Chen thought for a minute. He couldn't say he was off for coffee at Starbucks. "I'm going to the Sanlian Bookstore."

"I'll drive you, Master Chen," Fang Caodi immediately offered. He opened the passenger door of his Jeep Cherokee as if to say, "Get in."

"That's okay, there's really no need." Lao Chen was still trying to avoid him. "I'll take a taxi. You must have things to do."

"No, I don't," said Fang. "I came especially to talk to you, Master Chen."

Lao Chen got into the car resignedly.

"Master Chen . . ." Fang Caodi started as he drove off.

"Stop calling me Master Chen!" Lao Chen interrupted, irritated. "The Bible says that when the world is full of masters, then the end of our days is in sight."

"That's not a laughing matter," said Fang seriously. "If I can't call you Master Chen, then I'll just call you Lao Chen, okay?"

"What did you want to talk about, anyway?" Lao Chen said, exasperated. "Come on, out with it!"

"A whole month is missing, Lao Chen," said Fang, "and what are we going to do about it? We have to get it back."

"If it's missing, it's missing." Lao Chen was getting really annoyed with this theme. "What's it to you anyway? Surely nobody gives a damn about one month."

But as Fang Caodi went on talking, a few bells rang in Lao Chen's mind and he began to pay closer attention.

"It's very strange for a month to go missing, Lao Chen. Haven't you noticed that everybody around you has changed in the last couple of years?"

This sounded just like what Little Xi and Little Dong had told him.

"Before and after that month, all China changed and so did the Chinese people," Fang said.

Lao Chen always believed that Fang Caodi greatly exaggerated things.

"China is now divided into two types of people," Fang continued. "One type forms the great majority, and the other type is a very small minority."

"How many people are in this very small minority?" asked Lao Chen.

"I only know about two people up to now," answered Fang. "Myself and Zhang Dou, my sworn brother—but we're confident there are others. We're hoping that you're one of us, too."

"Why do you think I'm one of your minority group?"

"Because you're not happy, you look terrible, wet, and bedraggled like a drowned cat."

"Just because I'm not feeling good—does that make me a member of your minority?"

"That's only an outward indication," Fang said. "The key element is whether or not you remember the events of that missing month."

Lao Chen decided to sound Fang Caodi out. "Old Fang, have you been using some kind of drug for a long time, like maybe—"

"So you are one of us!" exclaimed Fang in surprise.

"Don't get so excited. Answer my question first," said Lao Chen.

"Zhang Dou and I both have chronic asthma, and we've been taking corticosteroids for many years."

"Aha!" exclaimed Lao Chen.

"Don't say 'aha' yet," said Fang. "I did a survey and found that the great majority of people who take corticosteroids for their asthma don't fit in our small minority. To this day, I only know of myself and Zhang Dou."

"Perhaps taking some other kind of drug might yield the same result?" Lao Chen suggested.

"What do you mean, Lao Chen?"

"Corticosteroids, antidepressants, painkillers, other analgesics," Lao Chen went on speculating. "Taking illegal drugs or some other type of medicine . . . maybe they all have this same effect. But not everyone who takes drugs or medicine for a long time will turn out this way. It's just that taking drugs or pills may increase the probability. And then we have to look at other variables—for example, what drug someone takes, or what someone's normal diet is, or personality, or just luck. All these things could influence whether or not a person turns out that way. And so what if you do? If you are that way, firstly, you'll feel everyone around you has changed; secondly, that so-called change will be that everyone around you has become happy and may even experience a constant small-small high; and, thirdly, at least one part of the condition is that you will remember things that everyone else seems to have forgotten." Lao Chen was thinking about how Little Dong remembered so much, while Little Xi did not.

"That's it exactly," agreed Fang Caodi. "We really are just like that. We can actually remember many things that other people have forgotten, especially the events of that lost month."

"That lost month?" Lao Chen finally got it. "So what you've been saying is that *a whole month* has disappeared and been completely forgotten?"

"Exactly. It's a case of collective amnesia."

"*Which* month, exactly?" asked Lao Chen, narrowing his eyes.

"It's precisely the month when the world economy went into crisis and China's Golden Age of Ascendancy officially began," said Fang. "Strictly speaking, it was in fact twenty-eight days."

Lao Chen's mind wandered a bit as he recalled the detective novel *Thirteen Months* that he had written at that time. Then, regaining his composure, he asked, "But didn't those two events occur at the same time, not one after the other, with no gap in between?"

"Lao Chen, you're really funny," said Fang, laughing.

Lao Chen fell silent while he racked his brains trying to remember that period, but his memory was a complete blur. This whole thing might just be the result of Fang Caodi's overactive imagination—there might never have been any such lost twenty-eight days.

It seemed Fang Caodi had finally realized that Lao Chen was not joking. "Lao Chen, you mean you really don't remember? But just now I actually thought you really were one of us."

Fang Caodi, Zhang Dou, Little Xi, and Little Dong—they are probably all members of that club, thought Lao Chen.

"Well then, I'm sorry to have bothered you," said Fang disappointedly.

"No, no, no," Lao Chen countered, "I'm definitely not one of you, but listen . . . It's like this: you're aliens from outer space who have accidentally landed on earth and can't go home, and I'm an earthling who's able to communicate with you. I'm your friend on this earth. Do you understand what I'm getting at?"

"I get it," Fang said. "You're a traitor among earth people."

Lao Chen didn't feel like arguing any further. "I know some people, more than one, who might be members of your club."

"That's terrific," said Fang. "Where are they?"

"I don't know where they are. I'm looking for one of them right now."

"Really? I'll help you. We can search together."

Lao Chen looked at Fang Caodi, trying to decide whether to let him tag along, and whether if he did it would cause him any trouble.

"I'm a specialist," Fang said. "For the past couple of years I've been working on this, looking for that lost month, looking for people like me, for evidence. Let me help you, Lao Chen."

"I'll think about it, Old Fang."

Fang Caodi fell silent for a while, but just as they were reaching the Sanlian Bookstore he said, "Lao Chen, there's nothing worth reading in the bookstores these days. I've been all over the country, and it's the same everywhere; all they have are officially doctored books. Don't imagine you are going to find anything about the true state of things. If you don't believe me, take a look yourself. Not only are there no books that mention that lost month, there are definitely no books about the 1989 Tiananmen Massacre. There aren't even any decent books about the Anti-Rightist Campaign or the Cultural Revolution. They're all a pack of lies."

Lao Chen didn't respond. Fang Caodi was beginning to irritate the hell out of him. Do I need him to give me directions on how to browse in a bookstore? he thought. The Sanlian has thousands of books. Has Fang Caodi read them all? Even the memoirs of famous living people would fill up several rows of shelves. I used to come here every week, and have come here every couple of months for the past two years. Am I not a lot better than him at finding books? I'm the expert here. Old Fang has always been such a pain in the ass.

When Lao Chen leapt out of the car as if to make his escape, Fang Caodi immediately dialed his number. Lao Chen answered his ringing phone.

"Now you've got my cell number. Ring me anytime, twenty-four seven. I'll be expecting your call." And just before driving off, Fang leaned his head out the window. "Lao Chen, I'll bet you they don't even sell books by someone as famous as Yang Jiang in there, and especially not her Cultural Revolution memoir."

With that he drove off. Lao Chen carried on ruminating. Besides those banned books published only in Hong Kong and Taiwan, and books printed illegally on the mainland by underground presses, many controversial books that were once legally published in China are definitely unavailable now, he thought to himself. Books like Little Shu's collection of CCP members' writings from 1941 to 1946, *Harbingers of History,* and Zhang Yihe's celebrated memoir of the

Anti-Rightist Campaign, *The Past Is Not a Fog.* Yang Xianhui's 2003 report on the death by starvation of about three thousand Rightists in Gansu, *What Happened at Jiabiangou,* and Wu Si's *Unwritten Rules,* an exposé of official corruption, might or might not be available . . . But bestsellers like Yang Jiang's *The Shower, Six Chapters from My Life "Downunder,"* and *Reaching the Border of Human Life* surely *must* be available. *The Three of Us* is even published by the Sanlian. How could they possibly not sell it?

❖

As soon as Lao Chen entered the bookstore, he asked the sales assistant to look up Yang Jiang's works on the computer. Searching the screen, the assistant said, "There aren't any."

The young people of today really aren't very familiar with books, thought Lao Chen. "Are they out of stock?"

"There are no references here, it looks like we've never had them in."

"Maybe you had them in a while ago?"

"There's no record of our ever having them."

"But *Baptism* is a Sanlian publication!"

"I don't know about that, but there's certainly no record on the computer."

"Where's the manager?"

"Try the coffee shop on the second floor."

Lao Chen was a fairly analytical person, and so he began to reflect on the fact that in the last two years he hadn't read any eyewitness accounts of the history of the Chinese Communist Party, or of the People's Republic. He hadn't even touched any memoirs of the Anti-Rightist Campaign or the Cultural Revolution. He'd read only the classic Chinese novels, celebrated works in Chinese classical studies. For a while now, he'd been paying no attention to what nonfiction books and memoirs the Sanlian had on its shelves. He decided to go downstairs and take a good look.

The basement had been redesigned. The section right by the stairs that had once held the Sanlian's own publications had been replaced by the fiction section, and next to it were sections on Chinese classical studies, religion, entertainment, and popular media. Today there were still plenty of customers in these areas, but their numbers didn't compare to the customers for bestsellers and business, self-improvement, and travel books on the ground floor. Around the corner of the L-shaped basement, the customers thinned out even further. This was the philosophy, history, and politics section where Lao Chen had felt so suffocated after the New Year reception. Now his head ached like it was going to explode. So he quickly gave up his task and raced back up the stairs, where the pounding gradually let up. He was looking for somewhere to sit down and hurried up to the second-floor coffee shop.

Lao Chen was thinking only of finding a nice secluded seat deep inside the coffee shop, when he was surprised to hear someone call out, "Little Chen!" He turned his head and saw Zhuang Zizhong, the venerable founder of the *Reading Journal*, sitting there with the Sanlian manager, a couple of vaguely familiar members of the cultural set, and a young woman. At the *Reading* reception, Lao Chen hadn't greeted Zhuang Zizhong because of the number of people around him, but this time he couldn't escape. He felt particularly guilty as he shook Zhuang's hand enthusiastically and said, "Master Zhuang! I'm so happy to see you here."

Zhuang Zizhong pointed to the young woman. "This is my wife—my present leadership," he said jokingly. "You've probably not met before."

"Mrs. Zhuang." Lao Chen gently shook her hand. "Call me Little Chen."

"Do you all know each other?" Zhuang Zizhong asked his other companions, to which they all nodded.

"I still have the clipping," Zhuang went on, "of when Little Chen interviewed me for *Mingbao*. That was a quarter of a century ago."

Everyone seemed pretty impressed.

"Sit down, Little Chen," said Zhuang. "I have something I want to ask you. How did *Mingbao* report this time on the Central Party leader's visit to my home?"

The *Mingbao* Web site was blocked on the mainland, and Lao Chen had not seen the report, but he said anyway, "Oh, about the same as the report in the *Beijing News*, quite a big spread."

Master Zhuang beamed.

Lao Chen could not help asking a question that had been playing on his mind. "Master Zhuang, is it true that intellectuals today are genuinely willing to be reconciled with the Communist Party?"

He immediately felt he'd been too frank.

"What do you mean," Zhuang said, showing no adverse reaction to the question, "are intellectuals willing to be reconciled with the Communist Party? The question should be, is the *Party* willing to be reconciled with the intellectuals?"

Just then someone else came over to greet Zhuang Zizhong, and Lao Chen took the opportunity to ask the Sanlian manager, "Why don't you stock any of Yang Jiang's books?"

"Which Yang Jiang?" asked the manager.

"Qian Zhongshu's wife, Yang Jiang."

"Oh," the manager said, as if he'd suddenly remembered, "you mean *that* Yang Jiang. Probably because nobody was buying her books."

Lao Chen's head began to pound again. He hadn't read those kinds of books for a while himself, but did it mean that the tastes of the general public had changed, too?

Lao Chen turned to Zhuang Zizhong. "Master Zhuang, I have to leave now to attend to some business. It was wonderful to see you; do take care of yourself." Then he turned to Mrs. Zhuang and said, "Take good care of Master Zhuang, he's a national treasure."

As Lao Chen left the Sanlian Bookstore, he was wondering if he had been too ingratiating, if calling Zhuang Zizhong a national treasure was a bit over-the-top. But then he remembered what the character Wei Xiaobao in Jin Yong's novel *The Deer and the Cauldron* always said: "Of all the things that can go wrong, flattery will never go wrong. What does it matter if you make other people happy?"

### "Blowing in the Wind"

As soon as Lao Chen got home, he took a couple of aspirins, went to bed, and slept until morning; when he woke up, he still didn't feel like getting up. At midday, he made some instant noodles, one of the hundred flavors offered by the Master Kong brand, but he didn't care which flavor he was eating. When he'd finished, he went on to the Dangdang and Amazon China Internet sites to look up Yang Jiang's works—it was true, there really were no entries under her name.

He went on to look up June 4, 1989, and Falun Gong 1999, and just as he expected, no books on these topics came up. But then he found that there were no books listed either about the Yan-an Rectification Campaign, Land Reform, the 1979 Democracy Wall Movement, the April Fifth Movement, and the 1983 Anti-Spiritual

Pollution and Crackdown on Crime Campaign—no books on any of these previously frequently discussed topics of the 1980s and 1990s. The only books that kept coming up were *The China Reader: Contemporary China* and *The Popular Edition of a Short History of China*—two standard tomes on modern and contemporary Chinese history, both authorized by the government in the last two years.

Old Fang really could be extremely perceptive, and this time he was right on target. In all the bookstores and even on their Web sites, where they claimed to stock every book in the world, of all the thousands of titles listed, Lao Chen could not find one single book that might explain the true facts about contemporary Chinese history. Why hadn't he noticed this a long time ago?

During the Cultural Revolution and at the beginning of Reform and Opening, there were very few books in the bookstores, and everyone knew that the true facts were being suppressed. But today, thought Lao Chen, there is a profusion of books everywhere, so many they knock you over, but the true facts are still being suppressed. It's just that people are under the illusion that they are following their own reading preferences and freely choosing what they read.

Continuing his web search, he discovered he couldn't find anything by using key phrases like "June 4, 1989," "Tiananmen Incident," and so on. Even the items that came up on the Cultural Revolution were terrible—just a load of nostalgic guff for an adolescence spent in the brilliant sunshine of the glorious past. The few items that discussed the history of the Cultural Revolution were only simplistic, officially sanitized versions.

Lao Chen was aghast. No wonder young people today cannot even say who belonged to the Gang of Four, he thought, and people born after 1980 have never even heard of Wei Jingsheng, the early dissident who called for democracy as the Fifth Modernization, or

Liu Binyan, the most celebrated *People's Daily* investigative reporter of the 1980s; and no wonder whenever the June 1989 student leader Wang Dan lectures overseas about the Tiananmen Massacre, there are always Chinese overseas students in the audience who jeer at him. Today's younger generation has no way of knowing.

What a tremendous generation gap in knowledge of contemporary Chinese history there is. For people in their fifties and sixties, these important events are part of their general knowledge. When they get together now, they still talk about them, and they even have several books and periodicals about those times that are no longer available. Because they share this knowledge, they really haven't noticed how they've become increasingly marginalized. They ceased representing the mass of society long ago. There is no longer any channel for them to pass their understanding on to the younger generation. Lao Chen reflected on Lu Xun's "counterfeit paradise" and "good hell." In a good hell, people are aware that they are living in hell and so they want to transform it, but after living for a long time in a fake paradise, people become accustomed to it and they actually believe that they are already in paradise.

All this was quite obvious to him—Lao Chen himself was a living example, he had to concede. In the last couple of years, he'd had no stomach for reading about China's painful contemporary history; all he'd wanted to read were famous Chinese classics and romantic fiction. He hadn't realized that history had been rewritten and the true facts had been airbrushed away. Lao Chen was a writer of fiction, someone who told stories. He also knew that reality could be regarded merely as a construction, and that history was subject to different interpretations. Truth itself could be a field of contested knowledge. Nevertheless, when it came to lying with one's eyes wide open, squinting to deliberately alter reality, distorting the true facts of history without the least scruple, and nakedly falsifying the records—Lao Chen had to feel at least a twinge of uneasiness.

But it was only a twinge.

If Lao Chen had not been a reporter, he probably wouldn't have felt any need to respect historical reality. Most people don't care much about the truth, he pondered. There is, in fact, no way for the average person to care about these things—the price of maintaining a firm commitment to truth is too great. Besides that, the true facts are often painful to recall, and who doesn't prefer pleasure to pain?

At this point Lao Chen wanted to lay down the heavy burden of history. Can we really blame the common people for their historical amnesia? he asked himself. Should we force the younger generation to remember the suffering of their parents' generation? Do our intellectuals have a duty to walk through a minefield in order to oppose the machine of state?

Who has the leisure time to mess around looking up those few historical facts? And furthermore, it's not that all eyewitness accounts and historical memoirs have been banned; there are plenty of books still available. Only those books that contradict the Chinese Communist Party's orthodox historical discourse are totally banned.

Lao Chen then considered a new concept: "90 percent freedom." We are already very free now: 90 percent, or even more, of all subjects can be freely discussed, and 90 percent, or even more, of all activities are no longer subject to government control. Isn't that enough? The vast majority of the population cannot even handle 90 percent freedom, they think it's too much. Aren't they already complaining about information overload and being entertained to death?

The more he thought about it, the more Lao Chen felt he was

right. He had a very long list of unread books that he wanted to read, including Chinese classical studies, such as the twenty-four official histories, and classic European fiction, such as the nineteenth-century Russian novels. He regarded these as the high point of Western fiction, but because the reading priorities of Taiwan and mainland China had been different back then, while mainland intellectuals of his generation read the fiction of imperial Russia, Lao Chen read American fiction. Lao Chen felt somewhat guilty about being a writer of fiction without having read the great Russian novels. He had always told himself that one day he would make up for this literary lacuna. Now old age is approaching, so what am I waiting for? It's enough for me to have these classics, I don't need too much freedom.

And furthermore, when the national situation permits, the state can always relax its restrictions and permit up to 95 percent free-dom. Maybe we already have 95 percent? That would be very little less than in the West. Western nations also have some restrictions on freedom of speech and action. The German government restricts neo-Nazi organizations, and many states in the United States deny homosexuals the freedom to marry. The only disparity is that, theo-retically, the power of Western governments is given to them by the people, while in China the people's freedom is given to them by the government. Is this distinction really that important?

Now even his cleaning lady tells him, "Things are much better today than they were before."

It's all that bloody Fang Caodi's fault, grumbled Lao Chen, with his nonsense about a missing month and Yang Jiang's books being unavailable—he's messed with my mind.

Now Lao Chen had only two worries, both of his own mak-ing: what to write about in his next novel, and how to find his long-delayed love.

He phoned his friend Hu Yan from the Chinese Academy of Social Sciences.

Hu Yan had also come to understand that she should stay at home and rest at the weekend and not go to work. She was reaching late middle age, her children were all in university, and she didn't need to work so hard, or so her husband had been telling her for some time.

She also knew that she could never expect to finish all her projects. Things were very different for her now. In the past, her research projects had not been considered important, she couldn't find funding, and the projects often got her into trouble. But now she could be considered as a leader in her field, and research on rural society and culture had become an important field of study.

She remembered that in the early 1990s, when she'd been investigating in southeast Guizhou how the girls of minority peoples were unable to attend school, she had had to rely on money donated from Taiwan and Hong Kong to fund the project. In the mid-1990s, when she'd studied the lack of access to schools for the children of peasant workers in urban areas, Beijing academic circles had deprecated such projects, and various levels of government had resisted and even tried to suppress her investigations. It was not until 2000 that things took a 180-degree turn, when the central government announced its new rural policies. Local administrators all had to develop corresponding policies, and so they sought out many academic specialists for consultation. Hu Yan received large government grants to investigate construction and the circulation of goods and capital in rural areas, grants large enough to make many of her colleagues jealous.

In more recent years, while conducting field research, Hu
Yan had become aware of an interesting phenomenon: the very
rapid growth of Protestant churches. According to the figures in a
2008 survey, the combined number of adherents to the Protestant
"underground churches," to the government-sanctioned Protestant
Three-Self Patriotic Church, and to the Catholic Patriotic Church
was 50 million, but in Hu Yan's mind the figure should have been
100 million; this 100 percent increase had all taken place in the
last two years. But Hu Yan was concerned that she already had so
many big projects in hand, more than she could handle; she wondered whether it would be worth the trouble to study informal
rural churches. Especially because the sociology of religion was not
her specialty, and if she successfully set up a project and obtained
government funding, even more people would be green-eyed with
jealousy. The gossip and innuendo bruited around would be pretty
nasty—accusations of academic hegemony or intellectual imperialism would be the most polite of the lot.

Hu Yan had always maintained a good reputation and had
never provoked any academic gossip, and so she had to seriously
consider the consequences of pursuing her research on the underground church movement. The temptation was too great, though.
Out of China's 1.3 billion people, 100 million were Christians—one
out of every thirteen—the government could not but consider them
important. Hu Yan knew the underground church movement was
soon to become an extremely hot social topic. How could she stand
not to forge ahead with such research?

Late one Sunday afternoon, while her husband was in the
kitchen cooking dinner and singing revolutionary songs, Hu Yan
was in her study trying to figure out how to launch this research.
Just then she received a call from Lao Chen. He needed her input on

something. They arranged to meet for lunch at the Sichuan restaurant next to the Academy.

The following day, Lao Chen took Fang Caodi with him to see Hu Yan explaining that if he wanted to know the real situation in China, he could do no better than ask Hu Yan. "Nobody knows more about the lower strata of society than she does," he told him. "If Hu Yan says she has not heard of something, then that something does not exist."

"When I remember something," Fang Caodi said peevishly, "no matter what anybody says, I won't forget it."

Lao Chen also had another important reason for seeing Hu Yan. A few days earlier, she had sent him an e-mail with a report about research on Chinese Christian underground churches, and he wanted to ask her what she thought about *maizi busi*, "the grain does not die."

Over lunch, Hu Yan explained what she was working on: helping the government draft policies for the administration of agricultural cooperatives and rural financial institutions, and investigating the social effects of the circulation of goods and capital in rural areas.

"If you sum it up simply," Lao Chen asked, looking for a straight answer, "is the situation in the countryside getting better or worse?"

"Of course there are still problems," answered Hu Yan, "but overall we've entered a period of positive feedback."

Having asked for and received this conclusive answer, Lao Chen was perfectly satisfied and content. He'd visited several cities in China and he knew that first-, second-, and third-level cities were all extremely prosperous, even county-level cities were all developing very nicely. The urban people were living well and the government's goal of a moderately good standard of living had been easily achieved. What Lao Chen was not so sure about was the rural situation. He had visited only villages near major cities and had never lived in the proper countryside for any length of time. Every so often he would phone Hu Yan and ask her if the rural situation was getting better or worse, as if he were making a long-distance call home and gaining peace of mind on hearing that things were indeed improving. Secure in the knowledge that the rural situation was now better, Lao Chen told himself that on the whole China was constantly improving, and so he could go on living his good life with a clear conscience. As far as asking for the details of the positive feedback Hu Yan had mentioned, Lao Chen didn't need information overload; he would leave that to the experts.

"Professor Hu," Fang Caodi asked, interrupting Lao Chen's musings, "what do you think about the time between when the world economy entered a new period of crisis and China's Golden Age of Ascendancy officially began?"

Hu Yan looked like she didn't quite understand what Fang Caodi was saying.

"I mean that month in between," Fang went on, "twenty-eight days, to be precise."

"The front page of the *People's Daily* reported," Hu Yan said very patiently, "that the world economy entered a period of crisis and China's Golden Age of Ascendancy officially began on the same day. That was the day that the American dollar lost one-third of its value in one go, and the Chinese government announced its New Prosperity Policy, or NPP. Everybody knows this. I don't know, Mr. Fang, how you arrive at this twenty-eight-day figure."

Fang Caodi was silent, and Lao Chen thought to himself, Old Fang, this time there is nothing you can say.

Lao Chen asked about the report Hu Yan had written on her research on the Christian underground church movement.

"We recommended," Hu Yan said, "that the central government desensitize the question of religion—that is, abandon their sensitivity to religion. We advised the government not to treat it as a question of 'the enemy versus us,' or not even as a 'contradiction among the people.' They should normalize the question of religion—that is, they should regard religion as a normal part of life. We should learn a lesson from previous policy and not make another mistake like the 1999 suppression of the Falun Gong."

"They absolutely should not," Fang Caodi chimed in, "they absolutely should not make that same mistake, it would be too evil."

Hu Yan nodded her agreement.

"Hu Yan." Lao Chen finally came to his main question. "What do you think about the words *maizi busi*, the 'grain does not die'?"

"I'm not too familiar with the Christian Bible," said Hu Yan, "but I think this statement is from the Gospels, something like 'the grain that falls upon the ground does not die.' All Christians are aware of this passage. There is an underground church in Henan Province that is called the *luodi maizi*, the Church of the Grain Fallen on the Ground."

"Where in Henan?" Lao Chen asked quickly. "Find the exact location for me, will you?"

"No problem."

After they had parted from Hu Yan, Fang Caodi said, "Professor Hu is a good person, but she is not one of us."

"Thank God," said Lao Chen, "that there are still people in the world who are not like you."

"I could tell from her expression," Fang Caodi said, "she was so happy. And as I expected, she didn't know about that lost month."

"Fang Caodi," Lao Chen urged him, "forget all about that so-called lost month. It's not worth it. Life's too short; just look after yourself."

Fang Caodi didn't answer. Lao Chen knew that no matter how clever he was, he could never change Fang Caodi.

Once they were sitting in the car, Fang Caodi said, "Lao Chen, do me the honor of coming to Miaomiao's house to have dinner with Zhang Dou, Miaomiao, and me, okay?"

Lao Chen didn't much want to go there, but since he might need his help to find Little Xi and he didn't have anything else to do, he agreed.

His acceptance pleased Fang Caodi. "This whole area," he said, pointing to Chang-an Boulevard as he started the car, "used to be full of out-of-town petitioners come to state their grievances to the government. I once went over there specially to see if I could find any people like me among that big crowd of people. What do you think happened? There isn't even a single petitioner anymore, and the shacks they used to live in on the Southside have all been demolished. At first I was thinking maybe that friend of yours was hiding there."

It had been years since Lao Chen had given any thought to all those out-of-town petitioners, but he was sure of one thing: even if there still were petitioners there, Little Xi would not be one of them. That area was close to the prosecutor's office and the law courts, and Little Xi would stay far away so as not to be seen by anyone who knew her.

Fang Caodi continued rattling on about everything under the

sun while Lao Chen more or less ignored him. In fact, he would not have agreed to dinner if he had known Fang lived so far out of Beijing.

When they arrived at Miaomiao's house in Huairou, Fang Caodi introduced him to Zhang Dou, Miaomiao, and their pack of dogs and cats. Then he took Lao Chen into the living room. The four walls were lined with metal shelves on which were piled newspaper clippings, magazines, and other miscellaneous junk. In the middle was a desk, a folding chair, and a camp bed.

"Lao Chen"—Fang Caodi pointed to the newspapers and magazines—"these things are all the evidence I've collected for over two years. They prove what really happened during those twenty-eight days. You're an intellectual. You've spent your whole life seeking truth and beauty. You've struggled to uphold what is true . . . you ought to be able to understand all the work I've done on this. Take a good look at it while I fix our candlelit dinner."

Lao Chen was left standing by himself, grudgingly, in the room. Miaomiao came in and put a plate of chocolate cookies on top of the desk for him and then abruptly left.

Lao Chen was feeling bored. He popped a cookie into his mouth, and picked up a few out-of-date periodicals and a couple of small local newspapers, which he flipped through at random. He really couldn't see how Fang Caodi could discern the true facts of history in them. He went on to look at odd half-pages from editors of the *Southern Weekly*, *Southern Metropolis Daily*, and *China Youth Daily*, and incomplete issues of the *Caijing Magazine*, *Southern Window*, and *Asia Weekly*.

Lao Chen recalled that everything had been calm in Beijing during that period, there had been no big disturbances; if there had been even one, it would have left some impression on him. From the so-called evidence that Fang Caodi had collected, it would seem that there had been some sort of unrest in other areas of the country, but that was nothing unusual. China is so big that it's not unusual for there to be some kind of turmoil somewhere every day, he thought. He never looked for that kind of news, and even if it did catch his eye, he would just skip over it. China is such a big country, there are so many things one doesn't know about. These little bits and pieces of evidence collected by Fang Caodi don't explain anything. In fact, to say that one whole month has gone missing isn't strictly accurate, it's just that people's recollections of that month are different, he insisted to himself. Furthermore, if you deliberately looked for bad things happening in China, you could find plenty of examples. If you looked only for good things, you'd find a whole panorama of them. Big countries are all like that. Look at the United States or India. What's so unusual about China? The most important thing today is that the world economy has fallen into a period of crisis everywhere, except for in China.

Little Xi, where are you? I hope you can put the past to rest, and return to the good life of the present. If you want to live with me, then we can live well together.

Perhaps it was due to the chocolate cookies, but Lao Chen began to feel better, and he became even more firmly resolved to locate Little Xi.

As the early-spring evening fell, the atmosphere of their outdoor candlelit dinner was very conducive to happiness. Fang Caodi cooked dish after dish and piled them on the table. He invited Lao Chen to taste them first and asked Zhang Dou to play his Spanish guitar for atmosphere. Nearby in the yard, Miaomiao began dancing with her dogs and cats.

Lao Chen had a few mouthfuls and thought each dish tasted pretty good. "What part of China are these dishes from?" he asked Fang Caodi.

"Chop suey vegetables," said Old Fang. "Look closely, I'm using Sichuan peppers, Hunan black bean sauce, Guangdong shrimp sauce, Thai lemon grass, and our own coriander, sweet basil, lemon leaf, and leeks. They're all organic. We just pick 'em and eat 'em. And we fertilize them with our own and the cats' and dogs' poo."

Conversation over dinner was pleasant, and what was most surprising to Lao Chen was when Fang Caodi told him why he admired him so much. Lao Chen had always thought it was because his literary style impressed Old Fang, but Fang Caodi said it was because of something Lao Chen had once said, though he couldn't remember it. In 1989, when Fang Caodi allowed himself to be interviewed, he insisted that he was genuinely clairvoyant. When he'd seen the military blockade on the road to the Summer Palace in 1971, he'd known the Mao Zedong–Lin Biao incident had happened. When he'd looked out of the window of Hong Kong's Chungking Mansions onto Nathan Road and seen a man jump to his death across the street, he'd known that something was about to go wrong in Hong Kong, and, sure enough, the Hang Seng Index collapsed from seventeen hundred points to only slightly over one hundred. In that American commune in 1975, when his hippie friends were beating on pots and pans to celebrate the end of the Vietnam War, he'd had a vision of refugees swarming out of Vietnam, and, of course, his vision became reality. As he went on talking and talking, Lao Chen had interrupted him and asked, "What's the significance of these premonitions? Did they change anything later?"

"Lao Chen," said Fang Caodi, "with that one question you woke me up from my dreams. When I thought about it, my powers of premonition that I thought made me different from other people never had the slightest influence on the world, and never even changed my own fate. They really didn't have any significance at all." From that time on, Fang Caodi no longer considered his premonitions to be of any importance and no longer put himself under any point-less pressure. This was all due to that one question of Lao Chen's. From that he knew that Lao Chen was an extraordinarily talented person.

"Little brother," Fang Caodi instructed Zhang Dou, "Lao Chen is far wiser than we are; we should listen to him, you understand?"

When Lao Chen, who was eating with great gusto, heard Fang Caodi say this, he felt a little embarrassed. He stood up to give Old Fang a hug.

Lao Chen found he was enjoying the flavors of their long dinner very much, so much so in fact that some of his lost feeling of happiness started to come back. He felt so good that he actually found himself telling his two companions how he'd come to know the insomniac national leader He Dongsheng. He explained how He Dongsheng would sleep through the films Jian Lin showed, but could not sleep at night, and so drove his own car all over town, and when he was pulled over by a traffic cop, he phoned his secretary, who then wiped his ass for him.

After dinner, Zhang Dou carried on playing his guitar, and Fang Caodi sang Bob Dylan's "Blowing in the Wind." Old Fang sang it perfectly in the style of the young Dylan.

As they continued drinking Yanjing beer and eating cookies, Zhang Dou took out his computer and went on the Internet. Fang Caodi asked Lao Chen to show him how to look up his friend.

"I'm not exactly sure," said Lao Chen. "I only have this note." He took it out of his pocket.

"What does it mean?" asked Fang Caodi.

"I think it is *maizi busi*, 'the grain does not die,' in Romanized script," said Lao Chen.

Zhang Dou took a look.

"Let's go to Henan and look for her," said Fang Caodi. "I'll drive. Professor Hu said that church is in Henan—we can find out where exactly when we get there."

"Whoa. Don't get too excited," said Lao Chen. "That church is called the Church of the Grain Fallen on the Ground, but I don't even know for certain that Little Xi *is* called *maizi busi*, not to mention whether or not the two names are related."

"I found *maizibusi*!" exclaimed Zhang Dou suddenly. Lao Chen and Fang Caodi gathered around the computer.

"You just put in *maizibusi*?" asked Lao Chen.

Zhang Dou nodded.

Lao Chen had only guessed at Chinese characters for *maizibusi* and had never thought to just look up the Romanized text.

There was only one link, a post put up two weeks before on the club3.kdnet.net "Cat's Eye" server:

> Idiot Numbskull, you say you are so brokenhearted you'll never post another message. Well, I'm pretty brokenhearted too, but I understand—all your thoughtful articles are willfully deleted by the Internet police and maliciously attacked by a gang of "angry youth" thugs (those people in their fifties and sixties who act like thugs when they go on the Internet). You never use malicious language and you always present the facts and make reasonable arguments, so I greatly admire your firm resolve; it encourages me to keep on going. I'm not afraid of the angry youth, and I'm even less afraid of those aging hoodlums. I will persevere to the end because I believe that human beings are rational and that the truth cannot be suppressed forever. Good-bye for now, friend, we'll meet again in this virtual world. *maizibusi*.

"Is that her?" asked Fang Caodi.

"It certainly sounds like her," said Lao Chen.

"From her tone, she's one of us," Fang said.

"From the tone, the writer is not young either," said Zhang Dou.

"Where was it sent from?" Fang Caodi asked Zhang Dou.

"I don't know. I'll have to ask someone online to help me find out."

When Lao Chen saw that it might be Little Xi, he was so overcome with emotion that he had to sit down and hold back his tears.

"Let me tell you about those twenty-eight days," said Fang Caodi as he handed Lao Chen another bottle of beer and sat down in front of him. He took a few deep breaths, like an athlete warming up before a race.

"That year, just before the Spring Festival, I took a trip to Macau, and on the way back I stayed in Zhongshan in Guangdong for a change of scene. Zhongshan was once a very prosperous area, but people from Hong Kong and Macau were no longer coming to buy houses or holiday there, the factories had shut down, the peasant workers had to stay in the countryside rather than return to work in the city, and university graduates could not get jobs. I had been cooking for a baked-squab restaurant for only a few days when I was let go. I didn't care, I could just enjoy myself. On the eighth day of the first lunar month, I noticed that the *Southern Daily* and all the other papers at a newsstand had the exact same headline: 'World Economy Entering Period of Crisis.'

"Everybody was feeling worried, the atmosphere became extremely tense, and my landlady came looking for me. 'Did you register at the police station before you moved in?' she asked. 'What kind of age are we living in?' I asked. 'Do outsiders have to register to live in Zhongshan?' She retorted that if I didn't register I couldn't stay, and I said she was violating our contract. At this point the neighbors came over—the local authorities had told them to. They actually said that my landlady could pay for me to stay in a small inn, but I could no longer stay in their courtyard, and they made me hand over my room key immediately. I asked for my deposit back and told them I'd move out."

"What point are you trying to make?" asked Lao Chen, growing impatient.

"Paranoia," said Fang Caodi, "it was like that for at least a week. Everybody said China was going to fall into chaos, the machine of the state was nowhere to be seen, the situation was approaching anarchy. It was lucky the peasant workers had not come back to the city, or there would have been serious trouble. But I should never have left Zhongshan. If a city like Zhongshan was that tightly wound up, I should have known that the farther inland I went the worse it would be. As I made my way over the hills, I felt like a mouse crossing a busy street and I acted quite recklessly. I still wanted to go sightseeing, to visit Jinggangshan, Mao Zedong's revolutionary base in Jiangxi, as well as Mount Longhu. When I passed Shaoguan and came to the outskirts of a town called Meishang Fork (where the three provinces of Guangdong, Hunan, and Jiangxi meet) the bus was stopped and everybody had to get off. Outsiders were not allowed to enter the town. We were not stopped by police, but by a temporary detachment of townspeople. I slipped away and stayed in a peasant's house—until two days later when I was picked up by the Public Security police. The peasant had turned me in because the People's Liberation Army had already begun a general crackdown.

"Then they discovered," Fang went on, "that I was carrying an American passport. It wasn't that I didn't want to be Chinese when I came back from the U.S., but it's a hell of a lot harder to regain Chinese citizenship than it is for a Chinese to become an American citizen. So I'd registered myself in Beijing as a corporation and hired myself as a manager; I renewed my contract regularly, and so I had a work permit. Once in a while I went to Hong Kong or Macau, but I could return and live indefinitely in China.

"Back to my being arrested. There was a six-person joint hearing in an office of that Public Security Bureau. There were two Public Security police, two prosecutors, and two judges. One of the prosecutors was a formidable older woman, and one of the judges was a very young woman.

"'Look at you,' said the female prosecutor, 'you don't look like an American. Say something in English for us.' I recited a section of Bob Dylan's 'Blowing in the Wind,' and I did it quite fluently.

"But the prosecutor was not having any of it. 'You're obviously Chinese. You can't fool anybody by pretending to be American. Why would an American hide in a peasant's house? What the hell is an American doing here anyway? There aren't any tourist attractions or investment opportunities here. You look like an American spy to me.'

"'Captured foreign spies are to be executed,' said the male prosecutor.

"'You have no objections?' the female prosecutor asked, looking at the young female judge.

"'He can't be executed,' said the young female judge.

"'Why not?' asked the male prosecutor. 'We're supposed to punish criminals *severely* and rapidly.'

"'If we capture an American spy,' the young judge said, 'we are supposed to report it to the higher authorities.'

"The two prosecutors immediately responded that that would take too much time.

"'Then let's pass sentence,' said the male prosecutor.

"'You can't pass sentence,' said the young female judge.

" 'Why can't we pass sentence?' asked the male prosecutor. 'The Americans sent a spy over here, and we Chinese are not happy. Isn't that so?'

" 'You can be unhappy,' the young female judge countered, 'but you can't be stupid. If he's a spy, we have to report it to the higher authorities; if he isn't, we have to let him go.'

" 'Americans no longer have extraterritorial rights,' said the male prosecutor.

" 'It has nothing to do with extraterritoriality,' said the female judge. 'It is not a crime for a Chinese person to carry an American passport in China—and that's according to our own Chinese law.'

"The two prosecutors looked very unsettled at what the young judge was saying.

" 'Comrade,' the female prosecutor said, 'stop arguing. You know perfectly well you're wasting police time. They worked so hard to arrest this guy and now you want to let him go. This is a waste of our group's time, too. And furthermore, you're interfering with our work schedule. At this rate we won't be able to reach the target set by the higher authorities.'

"The other prosecutor nodded in approval, while the two Public Security officials and the other judge had yet to open their mouths.

" 'I can't worry about that,' said the stubborn young female judge, 'I operate on the basis of our national laws. If he's a spy, report him to the higher authorities. If he's not a spy, set him free.'

"The female prosecutor stared fiercely at the young judge. She was so angry she was about to explode, but the men just bowed their heads in silence. I was stunned. Then the female prosecutor shouted, 'Get him out of here!' and they escorted me off the premises. My life and freedom had been saved. Even in a deserted little town like that, China has outstanding talent like that young woman. Even if it's just for her sake, I cannot allow the world to forget what happened during that lost month."

Lao Chen was moved by Fang's story and longed even more for Little Xi.

"I knew," Fang Caodi continued, "I couldn't keep running around wildly; if I was picked up again, I might really be executed. There was a Daoist temple near the town, and when I recited the names of a few old Daoist monks I'd heard of, the old monk there let me stay. Some other time I'll tell you about my monastic seclusion and the practice of *inedia*. You've heard of *inedia*, haven't you? It basically amounts to fasting. Would you believe that I can practice *inedia* for fourteen days? We could have a competition and see who can practice it for the longest time . . ."

"Forget it," said Lao Chen, looking at a text message, "you win already. I can't stand missing a single meal. Finish your story. I need to talk to you about something."

"I wanted to practice *inedia* in the temple for twenty-one days," Fang went on, "but when I reached the fourteenth day, the old monk came in with a bowl of gruel and told me that I should go outside and see what was happening in the world. What he said made sense, so I went back to the county seat, where the atmosphere was still extremely tense, and the papers announced that there was no end in sight to the crackdown. Fortunately, transport was running again, and so I went to Zhangzhou in Jiangxi. It was eerily quiet. People were avoiding each other's eyes in the street, just like in Beijing after June 4, 1989. At the beginning of March, the evening papers announced that the crackdown had come to an end, and the following day all the papers carried the same headline: 'China's Golden Age of Prosperity Has Officially Begun.' Now everyone was smiling and taking to the streets to set off firecrackers. So you see, there were twenty-eight days between the time the world economy entered a period of crisis and China's Golden Age of Ascendancy was officially announced. The nation went from potential anarchy and terror to the comparatively lesser fear of a police crackdown. China's Age of Ascendancy was not announced until after the crackdown, and not, as everybody today says, on the same day that the world economy went into crisis. That's the end of my story, Lao Chen. Now, what did you want to talk to me about?"

"I've had a text message from Hu Yan. She says the Grain Fallen on the Ground underground church is in Jiaozuo in Henan. Old Fang, let's take a trip to Henan."

*The grain fallen on the ground does not die*

Fang Caodi had been all over, north and south of the Yangzi, and as he drove his Jeep Cherokee at high speed along the G4 highway, overtaking every car he came to, he told Lao Chen about some of the strange and fascinating things he had witnessed.

Fang Caodi said there was a place called Happy Village in the Mount Taihang area of Hebei; everyone in the village was exceptionally happy, but the media had been repeatedly ordered not to report this. Probably because upstream from the village was a huge, secret chemical factory. After he heard about it from a reporter in the provincial capital, Shijiazhuang, Fang Caodi went directly to Happy Village. Everyone in the village really was smiling and extraordinarily friendly. They all looked pretty healthy, too. The men wore flowers in their hair, and there were old women sitting around, bare to the waist and sunning their droopy breasts; they didn't seem to mind at all when strangers walked by. It was a spectacle virtually never seen in China. He followed the river upstream from the village, and after about five kilometers he saw a huge chemical factory with a wide-perimeter barb-wire fence and warning signs all around it. There was no way to get any closer, but he could see small planes flying in and out of what looked like a private landing strip.

Lao Chen listened to Fang Caodi; he didn't dare say a word, even though he felt like it, for fear that Fang Caodi would take his attention off the road. He was driving so fast and talking so much that several times they came very close to an oncoming vehicle. Lao Chen vowed that, if he arrived in Henan alive, he'd give thanks to God *and* Buddha.

Lao Chen didn't want to die before he had found Little Xi. If he were to die in an accident, he hoped it would be while holding her hand, and facing their last seconds of life together. If he were to die a natural death, he hoped that Little Xi would be sitting at his bedside watching over him. He wanted to grow old with her. But now she was almost definitely living in her own personal hell, unable to see any way out. He had to give her hope, had to end her loneliness, had to do everything in his power to bring her out of her shell, so that she wouldn't feel so exhausted.

He took a bite of one of Miaomiao's cookies. Outside the window was the unending North China Plain, and inside his heart was full of unending love; he never imagined he could feel this way at his age.

Driving south from Beijing past Baoding, but before they reached Shijiazhuang, Fang Caodi pulled over to the side of the highway near a slip road.

"Follow the highway from Shijiazhuang and we'll be there," said Lao Chen, looking at the GPS.

Fang Caodi didn't respond.

"What's wrong?" asked Lao Chen.

"I'm sorry," said Fang Caodi, "but I'm having a premonition."

"A premonition about what?" Lao Chen asked.

"A premonition," Fang said, "about that Happy Village I told you about."

"What about it?" Lao Chen was outwardly relieved it was nothing to do with Little Xi.

"I don't know," Fang said, "but I'd like to take a look. It won't take long, it's not very far."

Lao Chen could only agree with him.

They turned off on the side road and headed west on a paved road for about half an hour, and then went into the hills for about twenty minutes on a gravel road. They got out of the car and walked another half an hour on a mountain road until they reached Happy Village.

It was completely deserted. Fang Caodi went into each house one by one. "The villagers didn't even take their farm tools or kitchen utensils," he said. "It looks pretty suspicious."

Lao Chen noticed that all the houses in Happy Village were the typically simple and crude constructions you see in rural North China, especially in Hebei. The peasants of Hebei were not the poorest in China, but Lao Chen believed that of all the rural architecture in China that of Hebei was the most unsightly; they made no stylistic demands, and generation after generation they continued to build crude and simple houses; it was easy to see that the peasants of Hebei didn't care much about aesthetics. Yet there were colored paintings on the outside walls of every house. The paintings had the flavor of those New Year pictures called *nianhua*, but their style was much freer, and some of them even exhibited some charmingly sexual poses. In Lao Chen's present state of mind, he could see feelings of love in the paintings. On one wall was a very colorful life-sized flower. This kind of extra decoration and attempt at adornment was something rarely seen in a primitive Hebei village. These peasants had become graffiti artists, and perhaps Happy Village really lived up to its name.

Lao Chen thought it would be interesting to meet the peasants who had made the paintings, but some other time. "What's wrong?" he asked Fang Caodi, who was staring blankly upstream. "Let's go."

"It's been less than a year," said Fang, "and they're all gone."

"Don't ask me to walk another five kilometers upstream," said Lao Chen. "I can't even walk one more kilometer."

"There must be a road," said Fang Caodi, "that leads to the chemical factory."

"That road probably comes from the Shanxi side," said Lao Chen, trying to dissuade Fang Caodi from the trip to the factory he knew he was about to suggest. "I can think of a hundred reasons why the villagers moved, and none of them have anything to do with that factory. You shouldn't always be trying to find some sort of conspiracy."

Fang Caodi stubbornly refused to move, so Lao Chen played his trump card. "Old Fang," he said, "you know that your premonition can't prevent something from actually happening."

"Yes, you're right," said Fang Caodi, "let's go."

Wei Xihong, female, from Beijing, also known as Little Xi; most recent Internet name *maizibusi;* last-known employment: selling ice-cream bars in the Yellow Emperor's hometown of Xinzheng in Henan Province; previously employed as a ticket seller in three villages claiming to be the original home of the mythical Pangu. Based on this itinerary, her next stop would be either Mount Shennong, named for the legendary founder of agriculture, or one of the various places that claimed to be where the Great Yu parted the waters and created the Chinese continent.

Indeed, she went next to Jiaozuo, known in ancient times as Huaichuan. There are six old cities in this region, and local legend has it that nearby is the place where Emperor Yandi or Shennong planted the five grains and tasted the hundred grasses. It goes without saying that there are many parks with historical themes in the area, and no shortage of jobs in the tourist trade. She didn't, however, immediately look for employment, but wandered around somewhat distractedly because Jiaozuo brought back some deeply personal memories.

She thought of her first posting as a judicial clerk-secretary in that county-level court. And of the pressure on her to agree to all those executions. The examples her colleagues brought up to sway her were of Zhengzhou, Kaifeng, and Luoyang, all of which towns had executed forty or fifty people. Even a backwater like Jiaozuo had executed thirty people. When Little Xi visited Luoyang, Kaifeng, and Zhengzhou, the events of the 1983 crackdown never entered her head. But when she went to Jiaozuo the events of that year appeared right before her eyes.

Those events had changed her life forever and proved she was not cut out to be a judge in the People's Republic of China.

Little Xi stayed in bed for two days in a small inn in Jiaozuo before coming to a decision. She resolved to rid herself of the ghosts of the 1983 crackdown. In the early morning of the third day, she took a small bus toward Wen County, Jiaozuo, and went to the Warm Springs township. She walked around aimlessly until she passed a big house where the front gate was open and a number of friendly-looking, elegant people were milling around in the yard.

There was a spring couplet pasted on the gate. The top line read: "Heaven bestows the Tree of Life / Faith, hope, and love abide eternally." The bottom line read: "The Spring of Life gushes from the earth / Body, mind, and soul dedicated completely."

Is this a home church? wondered Little Xi. Aren't they supposed to be underground? How can they be so open?

At that point, the people in the yard disappeared into the building, leaving only one middle-aged man standing by the gate looking at Little Xi. He took a few steps toward her, and she saw that he was lame. "Please come in," he said to her. Little Xi walked slowly into the yard with her eyes fixed on the banner on the house front: GRAIN FALLEN ON THE GROUND DOES NOT DIE.

She thought to herself, I've only ever heard that the spirit does not die, or that matter cannot be destroyed, but this says that a grain of wheat never dies—it certainly accords with philosophical materialism.

The man responsible for the Church of the Grain Fallen on the Ground was called Gao Shengchan. From his name, meaning "high level of production," one could easily tell that his parents had been minor local officials who had given their children names like "Production" and "Planning" in accordance with government policies at the time of their births.

Two years earlier, Gao Shengchan, Li Tiejun, and three others had organized an underground Protestant church in Jiaozuo City. But they soon came into conflict with the government-run

Three-Self Patriotic Church, were arrested by the Public Security police on orders from the local Bureau of Religion, and were sent to prison. There they dubbed themselves "grain fallen on the ground," from Jesus's parable that if only one grain of wheat fell on the ground and died, it would then give birth to a great deal more wheat. They had already resolved to die for their religion and they grew even stronger in prison; they would never abandon God's work. After their release, they were all the more resolute. Li Tiejun, who had made some money in business, bought a piece of land in the Warm Springs township, built a big meeting house, and established a Christian fellowship. Four leaders set up fellowships in the villages around Jiaozuo and put into practice Mao Zedong's policy of "the countryside surrounding the city." Gao Shengchan traveled between these four fellowships preaching the gospel. Nowadays the Bureau of Religion and the Public Security police no longer bothered them as before. Even more unusual was that almost more people than the fellowships could handle were asking to join their church.

More than thirty people now participated in the Warm Springs fellowship's daily witness meetings and Bible-study sessions, and there were upward of two hundred people at their weekend revival meetings. The parishioners introduced new members every day, and some, like Little Xi, just walked in off the street.

Gao Shengchan had once worried that if the church was too active it might attract the attention of the authorities. But Li Tiejun and the other three leaders had already dedicated their lives to God's work and they wanted to press forward with no regard for the consequences; there was no way Gao Shengchan could restrain them. For example, when Li Tiejun wanted to put spring couplets with Christian themes up on the church gate, Gao Shengchan opposed this as being too conspicuous. In China there are things that you can do, but you cannot be too loud about doing them, he thought.

Gao could not change Li's mind, and Li Tiejun said that they not only had to have a good product, but they also needed some good propaganda, and the spring couplets were an advertisement. What Li Tiejun said also moved Gao Shengchan: "Our mission is just and honorable, and I refuse to hide our light under a bushel." In the end, Li had been right. Many people learned about the church from the spring couplets; they came in to listen to the revival meetings and ultimately joined.

Later on, officials from the Bureau of Religion had come to the church and asked them about their activities. But the officials' attitude was not at all antagonistic; they didn't say much, and after they'd gone, nothing more was heard from them. Over the last two years, the government had been keeping a very low profile.

Gao Shengchan was a graduate of the provincial university. Before going to prison, he'd been a middle-school teacher and an avid reader of the *Reading Journal,* right up to the moment he came to believe in Jesus Christ. He was an intellectual, not from a peasant background like Li Tiejun and the others, and so he worried a lot more than they did. He was particularly concerned that the government's lenient policy might not last long, because the number of believers in the whole country was growing very fast, especially in the terms of the membership of Buddhist organizations and Protestant churches. Gao Shengchan had a number in mind: 150 million. Most of them had joined in the last two years, and the so-called home churches accounted for 80 percent of them. Ever since Liberation, except for the worker and peasant classes, there had never been an interest group that made up such a large proportion of the national population. During past crackdowns on the landlords and rich peasants, on the capitalist class and Rightists, it had always been the great majority against a small minority—but now a divided majority of 1.3 billion was faced by a united minority of 150 million religious believers. Surely the Communist Party could not suppress Christianity the way they had the Falun Gong movement? But how could the Communist Party not be apprehensive about so many Christian believers? Gao Shengchan both hoped that the number of Christians would continue to increase rapidly and feared that the Communist Party might turn on them. He prayed to God to give the Christian churches another ten years of peace in which to develop, and swore that he would work in those ten years to see that the number of Christians reached 350 million. That would equal one-fourth of the population, a critical number that he thought would ensure the security of the church.

In order to protect their long-term development, Gao proposed that each Christian order or sect attend to its own affairs only. The Evangelicals, the Liberals, the Fundamentalists, and the Charismatics should not meet together, and churches within the same sect should not come together too often. He didn't want the government to have the impression that the home churches were developing into province-wide or even nationwide organizations. Many people who attended the churches didn't understand his concern, and they criticized him for being insufficiently open, or caring too much for his own church group, or even for trying to set himself up as a supreme leader. Gao Shengchan told them, however, that the main thing was to communicate directly with God and not to communicate with each other.

Another thing that Gao Shengchan himself could do, however, was to write articles and circulate them to the various believers; this was actually a way of sending information to the government. His most important theme was "God is God and Caesar is Caesar." He wrote that the Christian church did not seek secular political power; it was a force for social stability, and thus the secular government should not interfere with religion. His hope was that he could influence the government to change its usual policy and accept the idea that politics and religion were separate realms. He wanted to erect a firewall between the political regime and his religion, and that would be of great assistance to the development of religion at this point in time. He also wrote blogs under several names to support those Beijing scholars who advocated the desensitization of religion.

However, Gao Shengchan didn't advocate putting extra pressure on the government during the desensitization process, and he was opposed to the demands of urban radical Christian intellectuals for official recognition of the home-church movement and for the legalization, open operation, and free publication of formerly underground churches. He believed that the government could not officially recognize the home churches; desensitization was their bottom line. After desensitization, the best thing would be for the government to act as though it were unaware of the underground churches, and for the Bureau of Religion to act as though it had never heard of any home churches outside of the Three-Self Patriotic denomination. The home churches should not do anything to embarrass the government. If they didn't cause any trouble, everybody could save face and everybody could function well.

Gao Shengchan thought that later generations would probably look back and say that this was the purist age of Chinese Protestant Christianity. Because it operated outside the Three-Self Patriotic Church, Protestant Christianity still retained its underground character, and there were very few secular benefits to becoming a member of the church. So most of the new members joined the church with a pure heart; they were practicing faith for the sake of faith. If some church leaders or volunteer workers became corrupt, they were the exception and not the rule. People in China who were genuinely ambitious for fame, profits, or power joined the Communist Party, the so-called democratic parties, commercial-interest groups,

organized-crime gangs, or the entertainment industry; comparatively few would choose the religious arena. Even if they did, they
would join the government-recognized religious organizations or
found a sect of their own; they would not be very likely to join a
Protestant denomination. On the other hand, in a country like the
United States, where Protestant Christianity was the mainstream
religion, the churches could hardly avoid being associated with
fame, profit, power, and interest groups. Gao Shengchan hoped that
Chinese Christianity could continue to develop underground for a
long time so that ambitious characters would not be interested in
the home-church movement and Chinese Christians would be able
to remain as pure-hearted as they were now.

The Church of the Grain Fallen on the Ground had quite a good
reputation in Chinese Christian circles, and, since all its leaders had
spent time in prison, many foreign Christians came to see them.
Li Tiejun and the others were particularly happy to associate with
foreigners, but Gao Shengchan was quite wary of this; he was afraid
that the Communist Party would charge them with the crime of
collaborating with foreign powers. From his exchanges with visitors from abroad, Gao Shengchan realized even more clearly that,
although the Christian churches didn't aspire to secular power, they
could still be drawn into politics as in America, where the Evan-
gelical Christians frequently worked on issues with the Republican
Party and its right-wing factions that supported the interests of big
capitalists. Some Americans had actually come to Henan to see Gao
Shengchan and urge him to oppose the Chinese government's birth-
control policies, but he had refused to do so. To this day American
Christian church groups have never invited this excellent Chinese
Christian intellectual and charismatic leader of the underground
church movement to visit the United States, not to mention visit the
White House and meet the president.

What Gao Shengchan was able to do was to insist that the Church of the Grain Fallen on the Ground should not accept monetary contributions from abroad, nor receive Bibles illegally smuggled into China, nor invite non-Chinese pastors to preach in their churches. Some people had actually accused Gao Shengchan of promoting a "No No No" Patriotic Church. Fortunately, up to this point, Li Tiejun and the others had agreed with Gao Shengchan on these important policies; the main reasons being that the Chinese economy was very strong, church members donated a considerable amount of money, and the church had no need of foreign donations and even less need of foreign Bibles.

There was one sort of positive development that sometimes, however, gave Gao Shengchan a major headache. After joining the church, the faithful had a natural cohesion based on their common identity, and they wanted to express Christ's spirit of universal love by collaborating on common goals and mutually protecting one another. If some brother or sister in the Lord was in trouble, they felt duty-bound to rush to his or her aid. Gao had heard that there had already been many occasions when collusion between businesspeople and government officials had infringed the rights and well-being of the common people, and when members of the underground churches were among those ordinary victims, their brothers and sisters in the faith organized themselves to resist the business and bureaucratic interest groups. In the mind of the government officials, these incidents could easily be regarded as a confrontation between the believers and the regime. Some local officials already regarded the home churches as a thorn in their flesh and they had put a great deal of pressure on the Bureau of Religion to do something about them. If these incidents kept occurring, they might cause the government to reverse its present relatively lenient policy.

This was precisely why the appearance of Little Xi caused Gao

Shengchan both joy *and* anxiety. His face became flushed. The Lord must have guided her to them, thanks be to the Lord.

Ever since the Warm Springs fellowship had been established, he had stood in the yard and guided many lost sheep back into the Lord's embrace. The difference was that as soon as he saw Little Xi he knew she was not local; she had a certain air of culture about her; she was an intellectual like himself.

After Little Xi had been in Warm Springs a while, Gao Shengchan saw that she read the Bible quite seriously, and that the questions she asked were very sophisticated and not at all trivial. What she most wanted to understand was why they all believed in God and why the church members, after being suppressed and forced underground, didn't harbor any hatred—on the contrary, they were even happier than anyone else.

"Because we have love in our hearts, because we have the Lord Jesus Christ," said Gao Shengchan in his sermons.

Little Xi appreciated the mutual concern the brothers and sisters of the fellowship had for one another; it was much more sincere than the class solidarity she had been taught since childhood. This kind of loving friendship recalled to her the intellectuals she'd met in the Wudaokou restaurant during the 1980s. They had also had a similar sort of kindred spirit. Now it was all gone with the wind.

She could not help wondering to herself, If they didn't have religious faith, could good people in China still keep on being good? In China's current conditions, with this political system and prevailing social mood, it's not at all easy to "guard one's own virtue alone," as the Confucian philosopher Mencius advised. What kind of moral and spiritual power can make one want to be good? Without religious faith, it's just too difficult to be a good person.

Little Xi didn't, however, have the urge to believe in religion. All her life she had been a faithful disciple of materialism and atheism and she could not change her mind. Her reason made her resist the claims of theistic religion.

The only person in the fellowship with whom she could have a high-level discussion was Gao Shengchan, but as the main preacher for all four fellowships, he couldn't stay in Warm Springs all the time. So Little Xi decided that wherever Gao Shengchan went, she would go with him, listen to his preaching, and ask him further questions.

There was something else about the fellowship that Little Xi was only vaguely aware of. Those humble and devout disciples of Christ also exhibited a mild form of dogmatic self-satisfaction—we alone know the truth—that made her feel somewhat uneasy. Although Gao Shengchan was very enthusiastic when he preached the gospel, in everyday life he seemed to carry a great load of care and a certain melancholy; he also had to cope with his lameness, and Little Xi felt it was very easy to communicate with him. She decided to get closer to him.

Little Xi had no romantic notions, but Gao Shengchan certainly did and was even thinking that it was about time for him to take a wife. But Little Xi was not yet a Christian, and all those posts she put on the Internet under the name of *maizibusi* might cause trouble.

It was at this stage in their relationship that the Zhang Family Village incident occurred.

Many peasant families in Zhang Family Village were members of the Christian fellowship. A short while earlier the township

government, in collusion with a business interest group, had vio-
lated their rights and enclosed their land. When the other brothers and sisters in the fellowship discussed this situation, Little Xi
was particularly enthusiastic. She explained many legal concepts to
them and urged them to defend their legal rights. When everybody
learned that she had studied law, they greatly admired her knowledge. They planned out a three-part strategy. First, they would go
to the county court and file a suit against the township government;
second, they would stage a protest demonstration in front of the
township-government headquarters; and third, they would make a
real-time record of the demonstration and put all the evidence of the
township government's corruption on the Internet for wider distri-
bution. This last move was because Little Xi told them, "The Internet is the people's Central Discipline Committee and virtual Public
Security authorities." But some were worried that if they acted this
way, the church would be drawn into the peasants' rights defense
movement, with hard-to-predict consequences.

Gao Shengchan talked to Li Tiejun about these developments
and asked Li to dissuade the fellowship members from broaden-
ing the scope of the Zhang Family Village incident. Who would
have imagined that Li Tiejun would turn around and criticize Gao
Shengchan? "Old Gao," he said, "when I have something to say, I
say it. Everybody now believes that you and Little Xi are a couple.
But she's become Big Sister Gao—she's the outside, and you're the
inside. This *maizibusi* woman is speaking on your behalf!"


### A love that passeth all understanding

As they entered Henan Province, Fang Caodi began to recount
the many coincidences that had occurred in his life. "Lao Chen, do
you believe in coincidence?" he asked.

Lao Chen thought that as a writer of fiction he had to rely on coincidence, but in real life he felt that the value of coincidence was overestimated. He didn't need to answer Fang Caodi very often because Fang would just keep on talking anyway. Fang had not stopped talking since they had left Beijing that morning. So in answer to this particular question, Lao Chen just shrugged.

"I knew I didn't have to ask you," said Fang Caodi. "As a writer, you must believe in coincidence. You know that life is just like fiction, everything is coincidence—if not I would not be driving into Henan with you today."

"Have you read the American writer Paul Auster's novels of coincidence?" Lao Chen asked out of curiosity.

"No," said Fang, "but I've read the mystery stories of Seichō Matsumoto. Without coincidence there'd be no fiction."

"Fiction is one thing," said Lao Chen, "and real life is something else. Most coincidences are probably predestined. On the surface they look like coincidence, but in the background, 'Heaven's net is wide-meshed, but nothing can escape it,' as old Laozi said. Cause and effect are always there, and there are always clues, but most of the time we can't see the clues."

"A really perceptive analysis, Lao Chen," said Fang, "really perceptive."

"Wow!" exclaimed Lao Chen, looking at his cell phone. "Zhang Dou has found new posts by *maizibusi* on three Web sites. One says that she's finally swept away the ghost of 1983. Another says that she's in W County in J City in H Province helping some peasants defend their legal rights. Hu Yan's text said that that church is in Jiaozuo in Henan. That's J and H. All we have to do is find W County."

"Wen County," said Fang, "it must be Wen County. Because I've been there—it's another coincidence."

"Then let's just head for Wen County," said Lao Chen, reluctant to dispute Fang's logic, and setting the GPS.

Gao Shengchan's college classmate Liu Xing was the vice minister of the Jiaozuo Municipal Committee Propaganda Department. He was in charge of media propaganda. When Gao Shengchan called him in the morning, Liu Xing immediately and with no hesitation invited him to the Yiwan Hotel for dinner. "We can have a good talk then," Liu said.

If it had been two or three years earlier, Liu Xing would not have wanted to be seen in public talking to Gao Shengchan, but after the last change in the local administration, when he hadn't been promoted, he knew now that his career had reached its high point. He was already fifty years old. He hadn't made it into this new leadership group, so he didn't have any future prospects for promotion. So now what difference would it make to be seen having dinner with his old college friend?

Fang Caodi and Lao Chen had lost a few hours visiting Happy Village, and so it was already nine o'clock in the evening when they reached Jiaozuo City, too late to go on to the Warm Springs township. They had to stay overnight in the Jiaozuo area. By the time Fang Caodi, at Lao Chen's insistence, had registered at the four-star Yiwan, in a private room in the hotel's restaurant Liu Xing and Gao Shengchan had already had a few rounds of drinks and were about to begin a serious discussion.

Gao Shengchan told Liu about the trouble his church was

facing—that some of the brothers and sisters in the fellowship had become involved in the Zhang Family Village land-rights dispute, and that things were likely to get more heated. Religious affairs came under the Bureau of Religion and not under Liu Xing's department, so Gao Shengchan could discuss the situation with him just as an old friend. Gao Shengchan knew that he could not start off by asking Liu Xing to show him how to solve his problem. If he did, Liu Xing certainly would not want to tell him the truth about anything. Gao Shengchan simply told his friend about his problems and then they went on drinking and chatting, waiting for Liu to say something important.

Although Liu Xing had downed quite a few drinks, he had been a seasoned bureaucrat for so many years that getting him to talk was like getting blood from a stone, and nobody could get the goods on him. He said that all levels of government were now studying a document from Party Central and they were going to be tested on it. He could recite it by heart:

"'Our Party's governing philosophy in the present stage of development is to practice virtuous government for the people and to manage the relationship between the Party cadres and the masses. The Party cadres are the servants of the people and the people are the parents of the cadres. The Party cadres must correctly handle contradictions among the people, establish a dispute-resolution mechanism for contradictions and disputes throughout the entire society, establish an early-warning mechanism to maintain social stability, work actively to prevent and to handle properly all types of collective incidents, maintain a stable and harmonious society, follow the law to crack down severely on all types of illegal criminal activities, and above all, always make the protection of our nation's security and fundamental system China's priority number-one core interest.'

"In other words," explained Liu Xing, "the government now wants to maintain a posture of solving the common people's problems. Thus they must not allow the outbreak of any collective incidents to disrupt their harmonious society. The Party officials not only must not provoke the common people, but they must also remain vigilant and have advance warning to head off any possible mass demonstrations, resolve issues before anything happens, make big problems small, and small problems disappear. If the Party cadres lack this early-warning sense and an incident of collective protest occurs, no matter how it is finally resolved, Party officials will have to take the blame in the end.

"What is one-party dictatorship? Dictatorship simply means that the ruling party has the absolute power to practice strict dictatorship whenever it wants to. At that point, the entire apparatus of state can practice dictatorship against the people or a portion of the people without authorization or any limitation by the people. By the same token, under a one-party dictatorship, when the ruling party wants to avoid trouble, it will try to make the people everywhere feel the paternalistic solicitude of the party-state government. Today China is in a period when the Party wants to avoid trouble. Only the core interest of the Communist Party's fundamental one-party rule must not waver, however flexible its maneuvers or moderate its methods."

Gao Shengchan understood all this only too well. His church had been able to develop without government interference for the past two years because the government's present policy was to avoid trouble. The officials were all afraid that some mass incident might occur in their jurisdiction, afraid of losing their positions, and so nobody dared to poke any hornets' nest. And the underground churches were just such hornets' nests.

What Liu Xing was saying at this time was quite deliberate,

and Gao Shengchan interpreted his words very correctly. His unspoken message was that although the people were afraid of the officials, the officials were also afraid of the people. If news of a possible mass protest became known, it was quite possible that local officials would want to resolve the situation before it escalated. During the preparatory stages of a protest both sides still had room to maneuver, but after the protest broke out, the outcome was unpredictable. If the protesters were charged with "beating, smashing, stealing, and fighting," suppressed, and thrown into jail, both the officials and the people would suffer. Even if, after the protest, a few officials lost their jobs and were replaced, it would be of no real help to anybody.

But who should one inform about the possible outbreak of a mass protest? Gao Shengchan pondered. If you're too open, it'll become a public incident, and the local officials will lose face; if you're not open enough, you'll be ineffective. For example, Liu Xing will just pretend he doesn't know anything about it because it's not under his department. Gao Shengchan gloomily ate his after-dinner fruit and wondered, Which official would be worried about this impending incident?

Of course the township Party leadership was the most directly involved, but if they hadn't been so fixated about making money in the first place, they would not have created the situation. With the prospect of great financial gains, they would not "shed tears until being measured for their coffins"—they would not give in. There would have to be a real mass protest before they would change their tune. But that was just what Gao Shengchan was trying to prevent in order to protect the interests of his church. He thought it over and concluded that if he was going to let the cat out of the bag he would have to go to a higher level of government—to the county government.

So then he changed the subject and casually said, "Our Wen County Head Yang is very capable and has a good reputation, no?"

"Little Yang is young and talented. He's only in his thirties and has a great future," said Liu Xing, who had just been waiting for Gao Shengchan to mention County Head Yang.

Gao Shengchan understood that Liu Xing was telling him who he should go to—to a young official in charge of the county's various townships and anxious about his future career.

"Did you know," Liu Xing said with an upward gesture of his hands, "our mayor of Jiaozuo was transferred here from Fujian? And did you know that County Head Yang was selected for promotion by the mayor? And did you know that at this latest change of government the mayor was promoted again to provincial level?"

He really is my old classmate, Gao Shengchan gratefully thought to himself, and so he's making everything clear for me. A new mayor has been promoted from outside the province and he will certainly promote some cadres to fill up his staff, but he won't use men like Liu Xing who were loyal to the former mayor. County Head Yang is a follower of the present mayor, and as soon as the present mayor is promoted and warms his seat at the provincial government he will move Yang to work alongside him. All that the young County Head Yang has to do is to make certain that nothing big happens in the county in the next couple of months and he can be smoothly promoted to serve as a provincial-level official.

In other words, if a mass protest were to break out in the county, regardless of whether it were handled badly or well, County Head Yang's chances of a provincial-level promotion would be ruined. So County Head Yang was the ideal candidate to be informed about the possibility of such a protest. How could a young and able man like him allow his official career to be put in jeopardy by the actions of a couple of corrupt township officials?

When it was clear Gao Shengchan had completely understood what he was telling him, Liu Xing seemed to experience a pleasing sense of pride; then he stood up and staggered over to the bathroom. Gao Shengchan took immediate advantage of his absence to phone Li Tiejun and tell him to make an appointment as soon as possible with County Head Yang.

Fang Caodi knew that Jiaozuo was an important producer of Chinese medicines such as foxglove (*Rehmannia glutinosa*), *Doscorea opposita* yams, *Achyranthes bidentata* root, and chrysanthemums, so he had already planned to buy some supplies, to cure Zhang Dou's internal injuries and Miaomiao's strange sort of idiocy. He got up at four thirty, completed his *qigong* exercises, and went out before dawn without disturbing Lao Chen's sleep.

After their long drive the day before, Lao Chen was extremely tired, but he didn't sleep well all the same. He got up at six and had breakfast in the hotel restaurant, but he had to wait until nine before Fang Caodi finally arrived, carrying a big backpack full of herbal medicines. At that point, Lao Chen looked quite annoyed. The two of them left hurriedly and set out for the Warm Springs township.

When they reached the center of the provincial city, Fang Caodi asked a taxi driver if he knew if there was a Christian church called the Grain Fallen on the Ground in Wen County. The taxi driver said it was only a short distance away and told Fang Caodi to follow him and he would take them right to the front door free of charge.

"Isn't it an underground church?" asked Lao Chen. "How come everybody knows the address and there are Christian spring couplets openly displayed on the front gate?"

"The Henan people have not offended anybody," said Fang

Caodi, "but everybody criticizes them. Look how generous this driver is."

Gao Shengchan and Li Tiejun were in the yard preparing to leave for their meeting with County Head Yang.

"Our fellowship has a thousand members in the Wen County area alone," said Li Tiejun proudly. "How could the county head dare refuse to see us?"

Gao Shengchan kept reminding Li Tiejun that when they met with the county head to leave the talking to him. He felt confident that he could persuade Yang to solve the Zhang Family Village land-rights encroachment, so he asked Li Tiejun not to interfere.

As they were thinking and talking, the four men met at the front gate.

"Morning, friends!" Fang Caodi spoke up, afraid that Lao Chen's Taiwanese accent might give rise to suspicion. "Sorry to trouble you, but is this the Church of the Grain Fallen on the Ground?"

"That's right," Li Tiejun answered somewhat warily. "Who are you looking for?"

"We're looking for a woman called *the grain does not die*," said Fang Caodi. "Her real name is . . . er, what is it?"

"Wei Xihong, Little Xi," Lao Chen said.

"Do you know her?" asked Fang Caodi.

"Wei Xihong, Wei Xihong." Li Tiejun didn't want to lie, so he just repeated the name. "Little Xi, Little Xi . . ."

"She's from Beijing," offered Fang Caodi.

"From Beijing," Li Tiejun went on repeating as though he was thinking about it, "from Beijing, come to Henan from Beijing . . ."

"Who's in charge here?" asked Fang Caodi impatiently.

"God is in charge here," said Li Tiejun.

"Don't talk nonsense," said Fang Caodi.

"Forget it, let's go," said Lao Chen, pulling Fang Caodi away.

Li Tiejun turned around, closed the front gate very purpose-fully, and walked off with Gao Shengchan toward the township. The shepherd has a responsibility to protect his sheep, he thought. "Those two," he said to Gao Shengchan, "might be Public Security informers, so I didn't want to tell them anything, but I didn't lie either."

Gao Shengchan had not said a word, but he had a different opinion of Chen and Fang. He knew where Little Xi was, and he didn't want to help them find her. He knew that they would come back, and he felt a little uneasy about his refusal to talk to them. He had to handle things in the order of their importance, and the most important of important things he had to concentrate on now was to prevent his fellowship from being drawn into a protest.

If Lao Chen had not received Zhang Dou's text message he would not have known for certain that Little Xi was there and he might have had his confidence shaken by this encounter. Now that they had located the church, he knew for certain that Little Xi was there somewhere. Those two fellows were simply unwilling to tell them the truth. He told Fang Caodi to stay there at the church and watch for Little Xi to come out while he himself returned to the township center, found an Internet café, and tried to communicate with *maizibusi* online.

Lao Chen and Fang Caodi didn't know that Gao Shengchan and Li Tiejun were fully aware that Little Xi was at that very moment inside the church attending a Bible-reading class. She would not leave the church that day, but would eat lunch there and in the afternoon she would go on the Internet and surf the virtual world, or perhaps use her *maizibusi* web name to write a blog on the peas-ants' rights defense movement. She might even receive an answering post accusing her of being a *sonovabitch* who turned the truth upside down. Dinner in the village at five p.m., participation in the fellowship witness meeting at six-thirty, and at eight a discussion with the most enthusiastic brothers and sisters of the plans for the final meeting on the Zhang Family Village land-rights protest. Little Xi felt that her life was richly rewarding.

The population of the Warm Springs township was less than a hundred thousand, but there were quite a few Internet cafés. As Gao Shengchan and Li Tiejun were going into the county head's office in the county government building on Yellow River Road, Lao Chen was entering an Internet café that had just opened for business. He was extremely excited when he found *maizibusi*'s blog and comments. Little Xi was so far away and yet so close, but four hours passed before Lao Chen posted his first comment.

At first he thought he would play it cool, so he wrote a post saying that he was traveling with a friend in Henan and visiting Jiaozuo to buy Chinese medicines. He disingenuously asked her if she was still in Beijing and said he'd like to meet up with her. He probably thought that she would respond to this by saying what a coincidence that she was also in Jiaozuo, and why didn't he meet her for dinner at the Yiwan Hotel? Fortunately he didn't send this message. Who was he going to fool? It was too ridiculous.

So he wrote a different message, apologizing for when Wen Lan had suddenly appeared, and saying he hoped he could see Little Xi. To such a message, however, she would probably just respond that it was no big deal, no need to apologize, never mind, see you sometime when we have the time. He still would not get to see her—given her assumptions about his relationship with Wen Lan, she probably would not want to be alone with Lao Chen again.

He would have to tell her the honest truth—that he had

come to Jiaozuo in Wen County deliberately to see her . . . that he wanted to see her because he wanted to be with her. He decided it was time to declare his love. If he could do so openly, everything else could be talked through in more detail later. Some twenty years earlier, he had fallen in love with Wen Lan and she had hurt him badly. For many years after that, he didn't dare have any feelings for anyone else. To open his heart now to Little Xi would certainly take a great deal of courage. Lao Chen sat there blankly for two hours before he finally wrote a nearly five-thousand-word post titled "A letter to *maizibusi* from someone who is not a stranger," in which he poured out his thoughts and feelings in fast-flowing prose.

The first line of Chen's letter was: "When you open this letter, I will be at the Modern Fuxi Internet Café on Yellow River Road in Warm Springs township, Wen County, Jiaozuo City . . ." Next he told her that after he'd met her at the Five Flavors restaurant in Wudaokou in the 1990s, he had always loved her. He'd never expressed himself at the time because she had so many male friends around her all the time and then later she had an English boyfriend. Still later, because he'd been hurt so badly he was afraid to ever try to have another serious relationship. Lao Chen described how he and Wen Lan had met, become engaged, how she'd dumped him, and how, twenty years later, he ran into her by chance as a French crystal chandelier.

Most importantly, he told her how very recently he had lost his heart to another woman whom he had not seen in a long time, how he had learned to get in touch with her, how he had waited for her reply, how they had met again, how he had lost contact with her again because of Ms. Wen's barging in, how he had looked her up on the Internet, how he had followed a possibly unreliable lead and come to Henan, and how he had put the pieces of the puzzle together and learned that she was in Warm Springs—and that woman was

Little Xi. Now he only hoped that she would give him a chance, would communicate with him, would give him time, in Henan, in Beijing, or anywhere else to prove his love. He had also brought along a friend who could help restore her memory.

Lao Chen even told Little Xi of his thoughts about death on the drive to Henan, that if he were to die in an accident, he hoped it would be while holding her hand and facing their last seconds of life together; or if he were to die a natural death, he hoped that she would be sitting at his bedside watching over him. He wanted to live out his last years with her.

Lao Chen wanted to post the letter as a comment on Little Xi's blog, but it was much too long. He had to divide it into several smaller sections and post each one separately while leaving a notice that he had a blog on the Sina network where the entire letter could be read as a whole.

After Lao Chen had finished pouring his heart out, he sat very calmly in front of the computer and checked every few minutes to see if there was any answer.

Shortly after lunch Little Xi had indeed gone online and very soon noticed Lao Chen's post, after which she went to his Sina blog and read the entire letter. It made her whole body feel totally paralyzed. For the past two years, she had wanted so badly to find someone she could really communicate and share her feelings with, but every time she'd been disappointed. After meeting Lao Chen again, she had fantasized that he was different from other men, but in the end, or so she thought, she had become another woman. As she was despairing more and more, she discovered the church fellowship. She didn't really believe in religion, but what she had found was a large extended family. Then when the Zhang Family Village rights-protection movement had come along, it made her feel useful. She never imagined that at this point Lao Chen would come into her life again, to declare undying love.

Little Xi sat blankly in front of her computer for over an hour. She knew that at another computer someone else was also sitting there blankly.

Finally, she posted an answer: "I'm no longer the Little Xi that you knew."

"I like the present you even more" was Lao Chen's immediate answer.

"I suffer from clinical depression," she wrote.

"I know. I'll take care of you," he fired back.

"My body is decrepit beyond repair."

"I'm proof of your beauty."

"I'm not sure I want a relationship."

"I'll wait patiently until you decide."

"I'm sure I don't have time for a relationship," Little Xi wrote.

"I can wait as long as you want, in Henan or anywhere else," Lao Chen answered.

They went back and forth like this until after five in the afternoon, when Little Xi sent her last post: "I have to go off-line. Give me some time to think things over, then we'll talk again."

Little Xi went to help the fellowship prepare dinner, and Lao Chen closed down the computer; he decided to go to the church and look for her.

What the two of them didn't know was that during the entire afternoon many netizens were following their posts with bated breath. After they left their computers, the netizens' comments on their dialogue took over. Some said it was very moving, some said it was schmaltzy, some said it was cute, and some even said it was disgusting. Taiwanese netizens said they had to admire this romantic auntie and uncle, while mainland netizens said that no matter how you looked at it, it was amazing how they kept going. On the whole, though, these netizens reached a pretty unified verdict: "Stop messing around, Little Xi, make up with Lao Chen and everything will be okay!"

At around six the brothers and sisters of the Warm Springs fellowship finished their evening meal and came to the church with their hearts full of thanksgiving to wait for the witness meeting to begin.

Gao Shengchan and Li Tiejun had also just emerged from the county-government building and decided to say a simple prayer then and there on the street to thank the Lord for His grace. That morning at the meeting with the young and able County Head Yang, Gao Shengchan had said what needed to be said as though with the Lord's help, stating his case thoroughly and in a dignified manner. Although the county head had remained silent throughout, Gao Shengchan was confident that Yang had listened to him attentively. As for how the official would evaluate the pros and cons of this case and what the fate of the church might be, Gao Shengchan left that in God's hands.

When they left the morning meeting, the head's secretary had come to find them, and advised them not to go too far and to be ready to be called back; this was a good sign. The two of them waited in a small restaurant near the government building. "Let's say a prayer," Gao Shengchan said, taking Li Tiejun's hand.

County Head Yang conferred with his advisers, and then called the township leader and the businesses' representative to an immediate meeting. The meeting lasted until after five, then Yang summoned Gao Shengchan and Li Tiejun to his office. Yang thought like a bureaucrat, but he was also pretty smart. He knew that Gao Shengchan was trying to force his hand, but he also knew that for the sake of his future career he had to back down somewhat. He informed Gao Shengchan and Li Tiejun that the Zhang Family Village land-requisition program was definitely going forward as planned, but, with the good offices of the county government, every family would receive increased compensation for their land. Furthermore, due to a revision in the amount of land required, the land occupied by the homes of the church members was no longer within the scope of the plan. In this way, the business-interest group had been made to give up some of their large potential profits, and the township leaders who had failed to stop corruption had been thoroughly reprimanded; the government's credit with the people had been maintained and an organized mass protest had been prevented.

As County Head Yang formally escorted Gao Shengchan and Li Tiejun to his office door he reflected that when promoted to provincial level he would no longer have to deal with the schemes of these church people. Gao Shengchan, aware that he had achieved his goal, offered up a few words of praise: Yang was a genuine mother and father to the people, he said. And Yang replied that it was the people who were *his* mother and father, and it was his duty, as a mere public servant, to serve them. In this fashion, with a mutual acknowledgment of their insincerity, they bid each other a cool good-bye.

Walking back to the church, Gao Shengchan felt he had accomplished something very good. The rights of his parishioners had been restored, and a direct confrontation between the church and the government had been avoided. His only worry was in facing those of his flock who had been so enthusiastically preparing to mount a protest, especially Little Xi. Nevertheless, Gao Shengchan never wavered as to what was important and what was not.

Meanwhile, Lao Chen and Fang Caodi were sitting in the chapel among the worshippers and looking all around for Little Xi. She was in the kitchen, and while helping prepare refreshments, she was just managing to calm herself after the emotional turmoil of the afternoon—when she looked out and spotted Lao Chen among the faithful, her heart immediately started to race again. She hid behind the door, not daring to enter the chapel. Just then she heard the sound of the Canaan hymn "What Am I?" and felt deeply moved.

Gao Shengchan and Li Tiejun entered the chapel and Gao instructed Li to ask the congregation to settle down because they had something to tell them. Then Gao Shengchan announced the new decision taken by the government on the Zhang Family Village land issue. This decision in favor of the brothers and sisters of their fellowship, he said, was an example of God's grace, and demonstrated that God had heard everyone's prayers. Finally, he led them all in giving thanks, shouting, "Thanks be to the Lord!" Some of the faithful were moved to tears of joy. Many of them, however, were there precisely to witness such moving reactions.

When they had settled down again, Lao Chen stood up and proclaimed in a loud voice, "Everybody, I have something I want to say to you."

Li Tiejun tried to stop him, but Gao Shengchan indicated to Li to let him speak. Gao Shengchan knew that such events could not be prevented by force, but had to be handed over to the Lord for His disposition.

"Fellow countrymen," said Lao Chen, "I am on the lookout for someone. Her name is Wei Xihong, also known as Little Xi."

The people stared quietly at the stranger, but did not respond.

"I am a friend of hers," added Lao Chen.

Still no response.

"If you know where she is," Lao Chen continued, "please tell me. Please let me see her, because . . . because I love her very much and I can't live without her. I hope you . . . hope you can tell me if she is here or not."

The entire fellowship of the good people of Henan looked back intently at Lao Chen.

Lao Chen waited with rising emotion, fighting back his tears.

All he received in return was a deep silence.

Finally, he calmed himself down, nodded slightly to them to indicate that he would not persist. He turned and walked slowly toward the door.

"Lao Chen!"

Little Xi burst out of the kitchen.

Lao Chen stopped and looked around.

"Lao Chen," Little Xi said calmly, "let's go back to Beijing."

# PART THREE

## THREE

### EPILOGUE

*A very long night, or a warning about China's twenty-first-century age of ascendancy*

*The life of man, solitary, poor, nasty, brutish, and short.*

THOMAS HOBBES, *The Leviathan*

*Look at*
*the ants crawling round and round marshaling their troops,*
*the bees roiling in confused chaos brewing their honey,*
*and hordes of buzzing flies fighting over the blood.*

MA ZHIYUAN, "Autumn Thoughts on a Night Voyage"

*All is for the best in the best of all possible worlds.*

DR. PANGLOSS in Voltaire's *Candide*

*Idealism Chinese style*

H undreds of millions of Chinese lived through an age that witnessed a storm of idealism and were baptized in that flood of idealism. Even though later on their ideals turned to nightmares and disillusionment, and an entire generation of people lost their ideals, still they didn't abandon idealism.

Fang Caodi and Little Xi had grown up in that turbulent era. They themselves were probably not even aware of the fact that no matter how much the times and the environment had changed, they still retained the strong character of idealism they had learned in their youth.

Even though the People's Republic of China has been established for over sixty years, China remains a great nation of idealists. The population of China is so large that even though the percentage of idealists is small, if they were placed in some other country, their actual number would be overwhelming.

Just think of all those people currently languishing in prison or under government surveillance—human rights lawyers, political dissidents, promoters of a democratic constitution, leaders of nongovernmental civil organizations, promoters of independent political parties, public intellectuals, whistle-blowers, and missionaries of the underground churches—no doubt all of them are hopelessly incorrigible idealists whom the People's Republic of China version 2.0 can never cure.

No society can afford to be without idealists—especially not contemporary China.

Of course, contemporary China is fertile soil for realists, opportunists, careerists, hedonists, appeasers, nihilists, and escapists. In this age of prosperity with 90 percent freedom, they've found their golden opportunity and are living exceptionally well. In this age, if you are lucky enough to be born into a hereditary Party and government-aristocracy family and your roots are a deep crimson red, then all the heartier congratulations to you. In the future you will have a tremendous competitive advantage and many business resources will be looking to you to cooperate with them. If China has an aristocracy, you are that aristocracy. From the point of view of a Chinese Communist Party that intends to govern China forever, you are one of them and the Party trusts you.

At this point, before our plot takes a dramatic turn, and before we bid farewell to our heroes, let me first build somewhat on the story of three of our characters whose roots are as deeply red as red can be—Wei Guo, Wen Lan, and Ban Cuntou. It goes without saying that they are all riding the wave of China's age of prosperity; they are big winners under the Chinese social, political, and economic model. I'm not going to spend time relating to you how they catapulted into prominence like leaping dragons and bounding tigers. I just want to tell you I predict that these three are flourishing now and they will continue to be in the ascendant—a rich, many-splendored life awaits them. Is this, perhaps, China's destiny?

Let us return to Fang Caodi and Little Xi. That the two of them felt like old friends the minute they met and regretted they had not met earlier was wholly to be expected. They had a common language and similar life experiences. Even more importantly, for over two years the two of them had been searching for like-minded individuals, and finally they could prove that "my way is not a solitary one."

When Lao Chen introduced them, they saw at once that they were indeed like-minded. They then seriously attempted to analyze why, when everyone around them experienced an ineffable feeling of happiness and a mild form of euphoria, they always remained clearheaded and aware. Fang Caodi said the American Food and Drug Administration had issued a warning in 2009 that some common medicines given to treat asthma, such as Montelukast, Zafirlukast, and Zileuton, could cause depression, anxiety, insomnia, and even suicidal tendencies. Maybe the asthma medicines prescribed in China had the same side effects.

Little Xi, however, said that this was pretty strange, because the antidepressant medicines she took should have had the opposite effect. These medicines stimulated the brain to secrete more monoamines like serotonin and norepinephrine, which caused people to become excited. So people like her on antidepressants should not have been able so easily to notice that other people were high. She had read a report stating that mood-altering antidepressants had already surpassed blood-pressure medicines as the most commonly used prescription drugs in America. When over-the-counter drugs were also considered, antidepressants were now *the* number-one most-used drugs in America. Many Americans who were not really suffering from clinical depression, but who didn't feel good, whose spirits were low, or who were unhappy in their work, resorted to some kind of antidepressant. Little Xi wondered if perhaps many Chinese people were also taking antidepressants on their own initiative and feeling high all day.

Fang Caodi corrected her by reminding her that no matter how prevalent antidepressants were in China, there was no way that *everyone* was taking them. The phenomenon they needed to explain was why almost the entire nation was experiencing a feeling of a high, while clearheaded and sober people were so few.

During the entire trip from Henan to Beijing, the two of them exchanged stories of the things they had experienced during the past two years. Lao Chen could only listen until Fang Caodi drove his dust-covered Cherokee into the village where Zhang Dou and Miaomiao lived.

When Zhang Dou heard Little Xi's voice he thought it sounded familiar. Little Xi also felt that she had seen Zhang Dou before, but could not quite remember where.

That night, Zhang Dou and Miaomiao put up a tent in their yard and gave their bedroom to Little Xi, while Fang Caodi put up a folding cot in his room for Lao Chen to sleep on.

Little Xi had already said she wanted to be with Lao Chen, but she needed a little time to adjust, a hint that she didn't want to move in and live with him straightaway. Fang Caodi said Little Xi could stay in Miaomiao's room for the time being, and when the weather was a little cooler, he and Zhang Dou could build on another room for her.

Lao Chen speculated that if for the moment Little Xi didn't want to move in with him, that didn't mean she wanted to live for a long time in the countryside. He didn't, however, push her to decide straightaway; he thought that by staying for a while with Miaomiao and Zhang Dou and having Fang Caodi to talk to, she would avoid the prying eyes of the government, and this was not a bad idea at all.

It was very difficult for an outsider like Lao Chen to anticipate what sort of a powerful fighting spirit might be generated when people like Fang Caodi and Little Xi, who had been without a comrade to share her Chinese-style idealism for such a long time, came together. Not to mention with a strong young man like Zhang Dou as their ally.

After a detailed discussion with Fang Caodi and Zhang Dou, Little Xi gradually began to regain her memory of the first day of that lost month. It was on the eighth day of the first lunar month, after the Spring Festival holiday had ended and people started to return to work, that the television, papers, and Internet reports all carried the same news: the global economy had entered a new period of crisis.

We all suddenly felt we were facing imminent disaster, they recalled. A roller-coaster ride of varying accounts appeared on the Internet and mobile phones. In the beginning, everybody cursed America for its runaway inflation and for the overnight 30 percent drop in the value of the dollar that caused the Chinese people to lose a vast amount of their hard-earned foreign-exchange reserves. Then we heard that the southern factories had closed down, the peasant workers could not return to the cities to work, and the Chinese economy was really going to collapse this time. Next came the news that the price of gold had risen to $2,000 an ounce, that the Shanghai and Shenzhen stock markets had completely shut down to avoid further losses, and that martial law had already been declared in Xinjiang and Tibet. The atmosphere in Beijing changed instantly. Office workers headed for home, causing a huge traffic snarl-up, while gossip of all kinds continued to circulate. By the afternoon, the people's response was to start stocking up on food and everyday essentials.

Zhang Dou described how at that point he and Miaomiao had gone out immediately to buy dog and cat food, and a good thing too, because after it ran out there was none available for over a month.

In any system (especially an economic system), if everyone's activity is duplicated and multiplied so that there is only one sort of feedback without any opposing message, that system will surely collapse, they concluded. Stocking up on food and essentials worked like that. At first everyone was afraid of prices rocketing, so they bought everything, cleaned out the shelves, and stockpiled stuff at home. When everyone did the same thing, the supply was soon insufficient to meet the demand, and then genuine panic buying set in.

It was equally strange that while Beijing's official Central Television was broadcasting news reports of social chaos all around the world, no one came on to reassure the public that supplies of food and other essentials would be sufficient to meet people's needs. Fang Caodi said the government could not simply have been so slow to act. He and Little Xi at the time both believed that there was something suspicious about the situation—there had to be another reason for the government's inaction.

Little Xi remembered that she had phoned around all that afternoon to various intellectuals and media people she knew to see if they had any ideas about what to do, or if they wanted to get together to discuss the situation. Everyone was too busy stocking up on food and other supplies for their own families, and nobody had the time to talk about formulating a response. In the late afternoon, Little Xi and Big Sister Song decided to close the restaurant and go home. On the way home, they noticed how few people and cars there were on the streets, just as after June 4, 1989, and during the 2003 SARS epidemic. They were carrying food back from the restaurant when someone rode by on a bicycle and grabbed a big turnip right out of Big Sister Song's hands.

Rumors circulated on the Internet, television, and mobile networks, while police car, ambulance, and fire-truck sirens could be heard howling outside. But no night curfew was announced, so people in the courtyard organized their own mutual defense squad.

Little Xi could still not remember the events of the second day. The effort of recalling gave her a headache and made her feel sick.

She knew only that one night when she came home she had shouted, "They're going to crack down again!" She could not sleep all night and kept mumbling to herself. Early the next morning, she went out into the courtyard to curse the Communist Party, the government, and the neighbors, and shouted that the law courts were all bullshit. She fainted soon after, and when she woke up she was in a mental hospital. This was what her mother told her after she was discharged but, strangely enough, after a while even Big Sister Song could no longer remember any of it.

Fang Caodi said he was in Guangdong at the time, and the state of anarchy lasted for seven days. For the first six, everybody was already terribly frightened because they had heard there was great chaos in various other regions. Fang Caodi had been in those areas, however, and they had not really been that chaotic. But he was given the third degree because he was an outsider. On the twelfth of the month, he slipped away to the border area where Guangdong, Jiangxi, and Hunan come together and stayed in a peasant's house. Later on, he heard that the fourteenth had been the worst day because a riot, with looting and arson, had broken out. Many local residents tried to escape by going to the county seat, where they heard things were safer. Lots of people received the same message over and over again: "I have just had this news from the highest authorities—the country is in chaos, the government has lost control, take care of yourselves, everybody!"

Is China going to collapse? This was a question many had been asking for years. Will the Chinese government lose control? Fang Caodi had traveled all over the country, in the western regions, the central plains, and elsewhere, and he had always told everyone, "Relax, there's no way for the disaffected to join forces; China will always experience small disturbances, but never complete chaos; the disturbances will be local in nature and will never spread to the whole country."

During those seven days, however, the people felt like they were in purgatory; every day was too long, and by the seventh day they had put up with as much as they could stand and were about to go to pieces. As you can imagine, various criminal elements were keen to do their worst, so the population felt terrorized. There was almost mass hysteria. It looked as if total anarchy would soon break out—a fight of neighbor against neighbor to protect one's life and property. People had just one hope in their minds—that the machine of state would soon go into action.

Fang Caodi had also begun to think by then that if the situation didn't improve soon, China really would collapse into total chaos.

On the eighth day of the troubles, the fifteenth of the first lunar month, a small detachment of the People's Liberation Army entered the township where he was and received an enthusiastic welcome from the populace.

Zhang Dou said this was the way he had heard it, too. On the fifteenth day of the first lunar month, two years earlier when the People's Liberation Army entered Beijing to restore order, the people of Beijing turned out in full force on the streets to welcome them. That afternoon the Public Security Bureau, the armed police, and the People's Liberation Army issued a joint communiqué that a crackdown had begun. Zhang Dou didn't have a Beijing residence permit and didn't dare go out on the streets; instead, he hid out at home for three weeks.

Little Xi wondered whether she herself had actually gone out to welcome the People's Liberation Army troops. Then she really *must* have lost her marbles. Maybe it was because she heard a crackdown was coming that she lost control of herself and went berserk that afternoon.

Fang Caodi told Little Xi that once the crackdown started, any suspicious person would have been locked up. He himself was turned in by a peasant and taken to the local Public Security Bureau, where he was almost sentenced to death. Luckily for him, there had been a young female judge who stood her ground against her colleagues and insisted that they handle his case on the basis of the law and the constitution. She had saved his life.

Little Xi wept profusely that night as she recalled in sorrow everything she had been through. The crackdown of 1983, and the People's Liberation Army tanks rolling into Beijing in 1989 to suppress the students, had frightened her to death and left her with an immense feeling of frustration that called into question her life choices and her abilities. But now she felt she could sense her original vitality returning. From her online disputes with those middle-aged "angry youths" where she expressed her own opinions about the government, to defending peasants' land rights with the fellowship, through to listening to Fang Caodi tell his story of a young female judge who argued strongly for right and justice, Little Xi felt that she was growing stronger and stronger, that she had finally found her true self again.

Whose idealism is the most radical, Fang Caodi's or Little Xi's? The answer is Little Xi's. What do we mean by radical? The original classical meaning of radical is *root* (from the Latin *radix*), to find the essential root of something. Fang Caodi has a plain and simple sense of justice, of working on behalf of Heaven's Way; added to his naturally stubborn character, this sense of justice spurs him on to search tirelessly for that missing month. Little Xi's sense of justice is more abstract, more philosophical. The socialist and internationalist education that she received as a child engraved the bright words *equality*, *justice*, *friendship*, and *mutual aid* firmly on her heart. She really didn't understand the hypocrisy of the Chinese Communist Party. In college she studied the Roman and Napoleonic law that was taught again after the Cultural Revolution ended. During the 1980s and 1990s she was baptized in the tide of Enlightenment values such as Reason, Liberty, Democracy, Truth, and Human Rights. Both romanticism and rationalism made deep impressions on her, and she adopted the idealism of a typical contemporary Westernized Chinese intellectual. Although her idealism is not without its blind spots and intrinsic limitations, due to all of the above, we know that Little Xi is more radical, and hers is a radicalism that will remain steadfastly loyal to the end.

*Think about it. What was it that sustained Little Xi for the past few years as she underwent such great suffering and social marginalization? We have already read how she was the female host of an intellectual salon in the 1980s and 1990s. During those years, she mainly listened to the views of prominent personalities of the time, and very rarely offered her own opinions. In the last two years, though, when the intellectuals appeased the government or were "harmonized," Little Xi rose up in opposition and threw herself into solitary combat. Without a backward glance, she argued strongly for truth and justice, expressing her opinions* on the Internet. *This process forced her to clarify her own thoughts and use rational arguments to state her case in the face of her opponents, who used emotive language, rhetoric, populism, and even violence. She's become increasingly dispassionate and clearheaded. We should not, therefore, make the mistake of thinking that Little Xi is still the weak legal clerk-secretary with a sense of justice that she used to be, or a Petöfi Club salon woman, or an unemployed and helpless mother who cannot even control her own son, or a crazy woman who scurries around like a frightened animal. She is already an obscure but genuine public intellectual, though she would never consider herself as such. This is her armor, her vocation, the air she breathes to live, her loveliness and her repulsiveness. She is willing to endure the greatest suffering, hardship, and personal humiliation as long as it brings her closer to the truth.*

### To live or die together

After staying at Miaomiao's house for a couple of days, on the weekend Lao Chen went back to his Happiness Village Number Two apartment, changed into a set of clean clothes, and went to Starbucks for a latte grande. On Sunday evening, he attended another one of Jian Lin's old-movie screenings. In recent months only Jian Lin, He Dongsheng, and Lao Chen had been present at these monthly soirées. To tell the truth, these screenings had become events that Jian Lin organized just in order to accommodate his cousin, the Party and national leader He Dongsheng. Lao Chen was simply a guest necessary to keep He Dongsheng company. If Lao Chen didn't go, and there were only the two cousins there, it would be rather embarrassing and hard to continue the screenings. For friendship's sake Lao Chen felt he had a responsibility to attend. He explained patiently to Little Xi and Fang Caodi why he had to be there, and besides, he said, he had become rather addicted to hearing He Dongsheng give his long monthly lecture apropos the subject of the film.

The film they saw that night was *Setting Sun Street* from 1981, and the wine they drank was more of the 1989 Château Lafite. Jian Lin had instructed a broker to buy five cases of this at auction, so, for the next few months to come, they would probably be drinking this same vintage. Of course, Lao Chen could hardly complain about drinking 1989 Château Lafite every month.

The film had been shot in a district around the Buddhist Setting Sun Temple on Liang Guang Road on the edge of Beijing's Second Ring Road. The film depicted the lives of a number of ordinary people at the start of the Reform and Opening era, and from it you could see the new market-economy model. One of the characters depicted was a conman pretending to be from Hong Kong, who wore a showy white suit, spoke a fake Cantonese, bragged, and extorted money and sex. Young Chen Peisi played an unemployed youth, euphemistically called "a youth waiting for work," who raised pigeons and whose favorite phrase was "Byebye, all!"

When the film had finished, He Dongsheng recited a poem by the Yuan dynasty poet Ma Zhiyuan:

"Look at
the ants crawling round and round marshaling their troops,
the bees roiling in confused chaos brewing their honey,
and hordes of buzzing flies fighting over the blood."

Then he went on: "The market economy can spur on people's initiative and enthusiasm, but sometimes it looks chaotic, like it isn't working. The key thing is to have a firm grasp of its regular rhythms—the government should not manage anything, but it has

to manage everything. It taxed the mental capacity of two generations, with us going back and forth and round and round, working
ourselves to death—even now I break out in a cold sweat dreaming
about it at night."

Lao Chen almost laughed out loud. He was thinking that He
Dongsheng would not even have gone to bed at midnight and, even
if he did, he would have insomnia. How could he dream back to an
earlier time? After that brief reverie, Lao Chen pretended to listen to
He Dongsheng's long-winded lecture about the many political con-
frontations that had occurred during the thirty-plus years of Reform
and Opening. Lao Chen was really thinking about Little Xi, whom
he had not seen for a mere two days.

At the end of his speech, He Dongsheng said, "There will always
be flies, but we can't stop eating just because there are flies around."
Then he went quiet, and the three of them just drank their wine in
silence as usual until midnight.

He Dongsheng went to the toilet and then asked Lao Chen if
he wanted a lift home. Lao Chen was afraid that He Dongsheng
would want to cruise the streets again and keep him up too late, so
he politely declined.

He Dongsheng left and Lao Chen stayed behind. Jian Lin told
him he was going to London to attend a wine auction and to buy
himself a few cases of Burgundy. Lao Chen was happy to see that
Jian Lin was over Wen Lan. When he took his leave, Jian Lin said
"Byebye, all!" in the manner of the film actor Chen Peisi.

It was an early summer evening, and Lao Chen was feeling
particularly good—his feeling of happiness was back again. As he
started to walk home he thought to himself that before he went back

to Miaomiao's house, he had to remember to pack up and take along his big bag of cholesterol-lowering oatmeal. He came out of Jian Lin's apartment complex, turned a corner, and had just reached the street, when he was startled by a big black SUV pulling up next to him. He thought he recognized He Dongsheng's car, but he noticed that it was Fang Caodi driving. Little Xi and Zhang Dou were in the backseat, and the three of them were shouting at him to get in.

"Hurry!" they yelled.

"Whose car is this?" Lao Chen asked as he opened the passenger door.

"Just get in," they said.

Lao Chen hadn't fully got his mind around what was going on before he was already in the car and it was taking off down the street.

"Isn't this He Dongsheng's car?" he asked after a while. "How come . . . ?"

Lao Chen looked around at the backseat and saw that Little Xi and Zhang Dou had a man pinned down on the floor under their feet. He stared at them, speechless.

"Lao Chen, calm down," said Little Xi. "Everything's been arranged. There's nothing to worry about."

"He's fine," said Zhang Dou. "I used the best brand of chloroform; puppies and kittens get no side effects from it; the worst he might have is a headache for a couple of hours."

"He won't wake up for at least two hours," chimed in Fang Caodi as he drove along. "No matter how loudly we speak, he won't be able to hear a thing. I've tried this chloroform myself. It puts you out completely for over two hours and it's perfectly reliable."

"Have you all gone crazy?" shouted Lao Chen, glancing in terror at He Dongsheng.

"We won't hurt him," said Little Xi. "We just want to ask him some questions."

"After that, we'll set him free," said Fang Caodi.

"You really are crazy!" said Lao Chen in dismay. "We're fucked! Really fucked!"

"Shit!" said Fang Caodi suddenly. "Trouble up ahead!"

Lao Chen turned back to look through the windshield. Traffic police were conducting vehicle checks. "Now we're really fucked!" he said, paralyzed in his seat.

"Everybody sit up straight . . ." said Fang Caodi. He looked like he was going to ram the roadblock.

Just then Lao Chen saw hurrying toward them that same fat traffic cop who had stopped He Dongsheng a couple of months before. He grabbed Fang Caodi's arm and said, "Don't try anything stupid. Slow down."

As Lao Chen expected, the portly traffic cop prevented the other officers from stopping their car and just waved them through the checkpoint.

"Okay, now drive slowly," Lao Chen instructed Fang Caodi, "and gradually increase your speed."

As the SUV passed through the checkpoint, Lao Chen made eye contact with the fat cop and gave him an army salute.

He finally relaxed and the three others heaved a sigh of relief.

"That was close," said Zhang Dou.

"A miracle," said Fang Caodi.

Lao Chen signaled to Zhang Dou to move over a bit and then let his front seat recline at a 45-degree angle. He turned on his side and reached over to search in He Dongsheng's pockets for the anti-surveillance device. He took it out and pressed the button; a few seconds later the three little green lights came on. "Good," he said, "nobody is following us or listening in on us." He handed Zhang Dou the antisurveillance device and told him to put it back in the left-inside pocket of He Dongsheng's suit.

Lao Chen sat back exhausted, in a sad silence.

"Lao Chen," said Little Xi, "you mustn't blame us. Old Fang and I debated for a long time, and then decided that we had to question someone who has inside information. Otherwise, no matter how hard we try, we'll never be able to figure out the truth about that lost month. There's no way we can resign ourselves to not knowing what really happened."

"We figured," continued Fang Caodi, "that in China, where all information is controlled by the government, only a Party and national leader would have knowledge of the entire internal situation. But how could we meet a national leader? That was when we thought about this Professor He you told us about. Then we decided to find him and get him to explain things to us, but we figured he wouldn't want to talk to us, so we had to take a few risks. Anyway, we believe that our national leaders have a responsibility to tell the common people the truth. Unless we scare them a bit, they will never talk."

Lao Chen remained silent.

"Old Fang and I," said Little Xi, "were afraid that you wouldn't agree, so we didn't include you in our plans. You can honestly say that you're not a part of this grab. If you want to pull out now, we won't try to stop you. We can let you out to take a taxi back, and it will be just like all this never happened. You won't know anything about it."

Lao Chen sighed loudly.

"Of course," continued Fang Caodi, "we all hope that you'll stay with us and hear Professor He's explanations. We've already set everything up. We're going to use remote video equipment in two separate rooms to tape our questions and his answers. He will never see our faces, and our voices will be electronically modified. He'll never know who we are."

"Just now in the parking lot," explained Zhang Dou, "we all wore masks. We can be quite certain that before he was unconscious, Professor He didn't see our faces."

"How can you be so stupid?" Lao Chen finally spoke.

"You have a witness," said Fang Caodi, "that you were not in on it! When we grabbed him, you were still inside with your friend Jian Lin. We've thought of everything."

"That's not the most important point," said Lao Chen.

They didn't understand what he meant.

"The most important point," he continued, "is that very few people know about He Dongsheng coming to this monthly film screening; maybe only Jian Lin and I do, and the secretary—at most three people besides He Dongsheng know about it. I'm sure to be investigated; I can't get out of it, and I'm sure to be the prime suspect. Even if they assume I wasn't one of the actual planners, when they ask me who I've seen lately, I will naturally give them your names and you will be investigated. Now that you've let me know what you're up to, even before they torture me, I'll be so scared I'll probably squeal. This time we're totally fucked."

The three of them suddenly understood. They went quiet for a long time.

"Lao Chen." Little Xi finally broke the silence. "I'm sorry we got you into this. It was my idea to grab a national leader and ask him what has really been going on. I was so angry and now I've got everyone in trouble."

"I can't let you take the responsibility," said Fang Caodi. "This was all my rotten idea and I owe you all an apology."

"Let's find a place to stop the car," said Zhang Dou, "put Professor He in the driver's seat, get out, and go home like nothing ever happened. Professor He will wake up alone in less than two hours from now."

"Will he be able to remember what happened before he was unconscious?" asked Lao Chen.

"When I grabbed him," said Zhang Dou, "and put the chloroform rag over his mouth, he only struggled for six or seven seconds before he passed out."

"When he wakes up," Lao Chen said dejectedly, "he'll have a headache and he'll remember those six or seven seconds. Then he'll definitely phone his secretary and activate the whole security system; they'll check all the CCTV street-monitoring tapes, and probably call that fat traffic cop for corroboration. Then they'll start investigating me . . . the result being that I'll be scared shitless and give you all up. This time we're definitely fucked."

They all went quiet again; they were probably each thinking about various possible ways out of this dilemma.

"We could kill him . . ." said Fang Caodi after a while, and everybody gasped, but Fang went on. "I could never kill someone to keep him quiet. I'll do everything myself and take all the blame. You all get out of the car. I'll drive down south, contact the government, and ask for a big ransom to divert attention from all of you. You can all get out of the car here, okay? Zhang Dou, leave the chloroform with me."

"How can we do that?" asked Little Xi.

"It's just my one rotten life," said Fang Caodi, "so why not? What do you say, Lao Chen?"

"Old Fang," said Lao Chen, "this may be disappointing for you to hear, but even if you make it down south and kill yourself before they catch you, it still won't solve the problem that only a few people knew of He Dongsheng's movements this evening. They'll definitely investigate me, and I'm one hundred percent certain that I'm a coward and scared of pain. As soon as they start on me, I'll confess everything. Even if you make your sacrifice, it won't prevent this inevitable outcome. We'll still be fucked." Lao Chen turned to Zhang Dou. "What is your safest estimation of how long we have before he wakes up?"

"The earliest he could wake up would be in ninety minutes, but I could give him some more chloroform," answered Zhang Dou with a glance at his cell phone.

"Now that things have gone this far," said Lao Chen, "there's no point hurrying. We still have some time, so let me see if I can think of something."

While Lao Chen was mulling over various possible escape strategies, he remembered that in his detective novel *Thirteen Months* there was a plot twist that he called "live or die together." It got him thinking. When they reached Miaomiao's house, he sat down by himself in a corner and didn't say a word. He closed his eyes and saw his wasted life pass before him, his ruined reputation, his happiness drifting away in a mist, the impermanence of life, and himself in prison and on the execution ground. His hands were trembling and he broke out in a cold sweat, but he pulled himself back to reality and tried over and over again to calculate the possible implications of using his "live or die together" plot twist. In theory, it could just work, but in practice, he didn't have much confidence. He kept struggling back and forth in his mind until he was exhausted. He knew time was not on his side; the moment to make a final decision was upon him, and four lives hung in the balance.

Zhang Dou and Fang Caodi had already carried He Dongsheng

into the house, tied him up in a big armchair that had been bolted to the floor in one of the two rooms. A digital camera was set up so that they could watch their prisoner from the other room to check when he woke up.

Little Xi pulled a chair over in front of Lao Chen and took his hand in hers. Being close to her made him feel calm; he had been considering one particular element of the situation. His "live or die together" plot might not have any effect on an ordinary bureaucrat, but it might just have a chance with He Dongsheng. This was because He Dongsheng was no ordinary unimaginative bureaucratic official. He Dongsheng was intelligent enough and his mind was nimble enough to understand how to play this game. So Lao Chen came to his final decision to gamble everything on his idea.

"Lao Chen," said Fang Caodi, walking over with a tense expression on his face, "whatever you decide, we'll all do what you tell us. I have a premonition that we can turn this situation to our advantage."

"Is he coming around?" asked Lao Chen.

"Sure is," answered Fang.

"Is the camera connected properly to the computer, and ready to broadcast onto the Internet?" asked Lao Chen.

"A digital camera, an MP3 player, a desktop computer, and a laptop are all linked together to broadband," said Zhang Dou, settling down beside the TV monitor. "Also, three cell phones with cameras are all aimed at Professor He and are all ready to broadcast simultaneously."

"Perfect. You all have a lot of questions you want to ask him, right?"

They nodded.

"Good," said Lao Chen. "When he comes to, don't utter a

sound; listen to what I say. When I tell you to start talking, you can ask him all the questions you can think of. Okay?"

"Okay, we'll follow your lead."

"Even if I tell you to do something you don't want to do, you must still do it. Are we agreed on that?"

"Agreed."

"Now let's go in the other room and question him," said Lao Chen.

"But we can question him from this room," said Fang Caodi.

"We can't communicate properly that way," said Lao Chen. "It has to be face-to-face."

"I'll go in and question him for you," offered Fang Caodi.

"I have to do it myself," insisted Lao Chen.

"Then you better put on a mask."

"Old Fang, will it make any difference if I wear a mask or not? The moment you kidnapped He Dongsheng, I was already in on it with all of you, past the point of no return. I'm going in there now. You can all choose to remain in this room and keep well out of it, if you want."

Lao Chen took the lead and walked into the other room. Then Little Xi pulled off her mask and followed; Fang Caodi and Zhang Dou went in together behind her.

He Dongsheng was an extremely analytical person. As soon as he woke up, despite a raging headache, he seemed to be considering the possibilities behind what had happened to him. He soon came to the conclusion that either his secretary, or Jian Lin, or Lao Chen had kidnapped him. He remained calm and collected, without letting on to the kidnappers what his thoughts were. Otherwise they might kill him. So when he saw Lao Chen enter the room without a mask, his reaction was not surprise but despair. The worst thing had already happened. Lao Chen had not been afraid to reveal his identity. This could only mean that these kidnappers had already decided not to let him go alive. The question he could not understand was: why?

"Mr. He," began Lao Chen, "have some water and take a couple of aspirins." Zhang Dou brought a glass of water, but He Dongsheng didn't respond.

"Mr. He," said Lao Chen, "if we wanted to harm you, we wouldn't bother to trick you into drinking poisoned water, would we?

"Do you have any imported bottled water?" asked He Dongsheng without looking up.

Lao Chen and the others shook their heads.

"Oh . . ." He Dongsheng heaved a long sigh and then motioned to Zhang Dou to put the glass to his mouth and let him drink. He quickly gulped down the entire glass of water.

Lao Chen waited until he'd finished drinking and then said, "Mr. He, you are an intelligent man, so let's be perfectly frank with each other—let's say whatever we want to say, all right?"

"Why?" asked He Dongsheng through gritted teeth.

"You mean," said Lao Chen, "you want to know why we invited you here, or, more correctly, why we have brought you here against your will and tied you up? It's very simple. Because we have some questions we want to ask you."

He Dongsheng laughed sarcastically.

"Truly, it's that simple." Lao Chen was calm. "You can't believe what's happening. But just answer a few simple questions, and we'll let you go."

"Nonsense!" He Dongsheng was angry, but he spoke as though talking weakly to himself.

"I know what you're thinking," said Lao Chen. "You think we will not let you go because I've already let you see who I am.

Actually, even if I hadn't revealed my face, I think you would have thought of a few names, including mine. Of course, you can foresee that if something happened to you, your people would definitely investigate me, and sooner or later, in order to avoid a complete mental and physical collapse, I would confess everything. Then death would be the only option for these friends of mine."

He Dongsheng had begun to pay attention.

"We want to live, too," Lao Chen continued, "and we can only live if you live."

"So," said He Dongsheng, "if you want to live, then let me go immediately."

"Don't be so hasty," said Lao Chen. "If we just casually let you go, you wouldn't just shrug your shoulders and act as though nothing had happened; you would turn around and send somebody to arrest us. So even if we let you go this very minute, we have already committed a capital offense. It would be hard for us to escape execution; and even if you spoke up for us and we avoided the death sentence, we still wouldn't escape being punished for a major crime. No, we don't need your forgiveness now, and we're not asking you for an extrajudicial favor."

"Then what the hell *do* you want?" asked He Dongsheng.

"We just want you to understand that we are all now in a 'live together or die together' situation. Live, and we all live, or die, and we all die—and the choice is up to you. Do you want to hear my explanation?"

"Let's hear it!"

"First, let me explain the die-together part," said Lao Chen. "Consider for a moment that our camera and sound recorder are all set up and connected to the Internet and to our cell phones; all we have to do is press a button and they will all start broadcasting. If we do this, the whole world will know that you have been kidnapped.

No doubt you would soon be rescued and we would be up shit creek, but how do you think your precious Communist Party would treat you after that? How would the Party interpret this absurd situation? No matter how any of us explained it to the Party, who among them would believe our *unbelievable* reason for kidnapping you? All our interrogators would wonder about the 'genuine' reasons behind your case. Leaving aside for the moment the fact that your nocturnal car rides around Beijing would lead to some wild speculation, do you think your great Communist Party would ever trust or employ you again? Of course, before we got arrested, we would broadcast as much genuine and false written material as possible, detailing how you revealed state secrets for us to send out on the Internet. Don't you think that your official career would then bid you an abrupt adieu? You're better informed than we are on the modus operandi of your precious Party. You figure it out."

"You'll definitely die if you do that," said He Dongsheng.

"We're done for now, with one foot in the grave already. If we die, though, we'll have you buried with us; even if we don't actually kill you, we *will* ruin your official career."

"Ha!" laughed He Dongsheng. "So you call that dying together?"

"Exactly," said Lao Chen. "You could also call it mutual suicide."

"What about the live-together part?"

"First off, in a minute we'll ask you some questions, and you will answer every one of them to our satisfaction. If you do, then in the morning we'll simply let you go."

"Tomorrow morning, you'll just let me go? I don't believe you!"

"It doesn't matter whether you believe it or not," said Lao Chen. "What matters is whether or not you're willing to play this game of live or die together. If you're not, then you're choosing for us all to die together. We're going to die anyway, but first we'll kill off your official career; later on, we'll decide if we want to really kill you as well. If you're willing to play, it will be game over when the sun comes up. You can drive your Land Rover home as usual. At night when you can't sleep, you can go out and drive all around town, take a nap when you're tired, and return home when the sun comes up. You know that others also know that this Politburo member regularly stays out all night, so no one will ask any questions."

"And later on?" asked He Dongsheng.

"Later on? There isn't any later on. That is, you continue on your glorious road and we continue on our ordinary paths; we keep our lives and you keep your official position. Nobody will say a word about what took place tonight; after tonight, every one of us keeps mum, as though nothing ever happened."

"How can I believe you won't talk?"

"Obviously, you don't believe we won't talk, but if we said anything we would probably be hunted down and executed; so to save our own lives, we won't talk. On the other hand, we don't much believe that you won't try to take revenge on us. After you go home, you might still worry about us and send someone to kill us to keep us quiet. Killing someone to keep them quiet requires recruiting others to do the killing, and one of us might still escape long enough to broadcast tonight's events on the Internet for all the world to see. There are dangers either way. You can figure out the odds yourself. You can surely understand that, rationally, the best thing to protect our own interests is for *all* of us to maintain complete silence and not make any unnecessary moves, or attract any unwanted attention. In other words, both sides should abide strictly by this 'live or die together' agreement."

"Rationally? Agreement?" exclaimed He Dongsheng. "You seem to have too much faith in human nature."

"I am willing to take a gamble," said Lao Chen. "Are you?"

"You know the story of the frog who carried a scorpion across the river, don't you? The scorpion could not help himself from killing the frog, and then it drowned—that was its nature."

"True enough, true enough. Both sides are taking a risk. I have to admit that this is a dangerous gambit that we are forced to employ. If there was another way, I would not want to risk my life in such a dangerous fashion. Four lives balanced against your official position. I'd have to say that we are risking much more than you are. To tell you the truth, I suggested this plan because I couldn't think of any other strategy that would meet the demands of both sides in this situation. Brother Dongsheng, can you come up with a better win-win solution? Take your time and think it over."

He Dongsheng thought the whole situation was preposterous. But he was not in the middle of a dream. This "live or die together" idea was a mug's game, but Lao Chen and the others seemed to be quite serious about it. They are risking their lives to ask me a few questions and will then let me go. What on earth are these lunatics thinking? But it looks like all I have to do is agree to play the game and I can stay alive, at least temporarily. After I get out, I'll have the initiative and everything will be easier to handle.

"You can ask your questions," said He Dongsheng, "but I can't reveal any state secrets."

"That's not up to you," said Lao Chen. "We're not here to haggle over prices like we do on Xiushui Street. The four of us have risked everything, and we want you to answer all our questions until we are completely satisfied. We have already put aside all considerations of death, so if we are not fully satisfied with your answers, this would all become meaningless. We are all prepared to see the jade smashed to pieces and face death together. Besides, Brother Dongsheng, whether or not you give away any state secrets, if your honorable Party suspects you of doing so, then you *have* given away state secrets. If we broadcast this scene up to this point only, I think you would never get clean even if you jumped into the Yellow River. 'Live or die together' is a complete, indivisible, perfectly unbreakable circle of agreement. Both sides either abide by it completely, or the deal is off. What do you say?"

"I have to leave at daybreak," said He Dongsheng, afraid that if he stalled any longer Lao Chen might change his mind.

"It's a promise."

"Give me another glass of water."

As Zhang Dou gave He Dongsheng another glass of water, Lao Chen took the opportunity to give instructions to Little Xi and Fang Caodi. Speaking also for He Dongsheng's benefit, he said, "Whatever is asked and answered here tonight is only for the five of us to hear. None of it is ever to be leaked to the outside world, even if you think it should be. This is the key element of the 'live or die together' agreement."

No one responded.

"You all agreed already," said Lao Chen, "to follow my instructions even if I told you to do something you didn't want to do. So you'll do as I say, okay?"

They nodded.

"What are you waiting for?" asked He Dongsheng. "If you don't ask me something soon, it will be daylight. Fire away."

### The Chinese Leviathan

The interrogation: He Dongsheng began to speak, and once he started talking, he had an irrepressible charisma. His listeners occasionally interrupted him with a question.

In the last twenty years, Chinese official discourse has hardly ever mentioned the events of 1989, as though not mentioning them would make them disappear from history. In order to avoid trouble, popular discourse also avoided discussing the entire year of 1989. Even when recalling events of the 1980s, discussions always ended with the end of 1988. So everybody joked that in China 1988 was immediately followed by 1990.

One year was not to be mentioned. Had it disappeared?

For some people that year was an indelible memory. It was just like the title of a book commemorating the June 4, 1989, Tiananmen Massacre by the Hong Kong Journalists' Association: *The People Will Never Forget*.

But will the people really never forget?

For the great majority of young mainland Chinese, the events of the Tiananmen Massacre have never entered their consciousness; they have never seen the photographs and news reports about it, and even fewer have had it explained to them by their family or teachers. They have not forgotten it; they have never *known* anything about it. In theory, after a period of time has elapsed, an entire year can indeed disappear from history—because no one says anything about it.

According to He Dongsheng, 2009 was the ninetieth anniversary of the 1919 May Fourth Movement, the sixtieth anniversary of the establishment of the Chinese communist government, the fiftieth anniversary of the Dalai Lama's escape from China, the twentieth anniversary of the 1989 Tiananmen Incident, and the tenth anniversary of the suppression of the Falun Gong Movement. The so-called 90-60-50-20-10 anniversaries made everybody very nervous. So people jokingly made another suggestion: from now on, after eight we should just go straight to ten; after 2018, let's just go on to 2020.

The fourth of June 1989 had little direct connection, however, to He Dongsheng and his generation of Communist Party and national leaders. They had all risen into the government's inner circles of power after 1995, and were not tainted by the "original sin" of June 4, 1989. After the events of 2009 had passed, He Dongsheng believed that that year had been alarming but not dangerous, certainly not as fraught with danger as 2008. A couple of years later, the external situation suddenly changed again, when the world economy entered a new period of crisis that was certain to unleash long-suppressed internal contradictions. Added to that was the party-state's imminent change of leadership in 2012, and that was the period when the Communist Party's mettle was most severely tested.

From 2008 onward, a whole series of incidents took place: a riot in Wan-an in Guizhou Province of over ten thousand people accusing the police of covering up the death of a young girl; the July 2009 riot of over ten thousand Tonghua Iron and Steel workers in Jilin Province, against a takeover by a privately owned company; the June 2009 Shishou City riot in Hubei Province due to the suspicious death of Tu Yuangao, a chef at the Yonglong Hotel, and to widespread anger at alleged drug trafficking and official corruption. Government-reported "large-scale collective public security incidents" of over five hundred people had risen to over a hundred thousand a year. All these incidents made He Dongsheng realize that local governments were very weak in the face of collective protest riots. In Wan-an, the government and police simply threw down their weapons and ran away; and in Tonghua, if the central-government machine had gone into action, it would have had to suppress industrial workers. If the Communist Party suppressed industrial workers, what would become of its legitimacy?

After these incidents, He Dongsheng was assigned to a top-secret small group in the central government tasked with drawing up contingency plans for any future large-scale disturbance. They came up with a number of proposals. At the same time, Party Central held a series of joint planning meetings with the military, the Public Security police, and the special armed police, a force organized in the wake of the Tiananmen Incident. They also brought several thousand county-level Party secretaries and leading Public Security Bureau cadres to Beijing to undergo intensive training.

In 2009, He Dongsheng was already clearly aware that the world economy was going to experience another crisis even greater than the one before. If the Chinese government handled it properly, though, it might actually present just the right set of circumstances for China to find a solution to its long-unresolved internal problems, and turn a danger into an opportunity. He Dongsheng even believed that whether or not China could enter an era of ascendancy earlier than expected depended on only two things: the international situation, and the appearance of some stroke of luck in China's internal situation that would allow the government to take full advantage of the opportunity to bring order out of chaos, and complete all the unfinished business of the last thirty-plus years of "Reform and Opening." What he meant by a stroke of luck was, to put it frankly, a major crisis. Only a major crisis could induce the ordinary Chinese people to accept willingly a huge government dictatorship.

There were two major reasons that could induce the Chinese people to accept the Chinese model of one-party rule: it would promote social stability, and it would concentrate resources to accomplish "big things." That is to say, the preservation of social stability would be only a necessary condition of the party-state's legitimacy. This is because democratic systems are not necessarily unable to maintain stability themselves. Take Taiwan, for example: we ridicule them for their democratic chaos, but they carried off a peaceful transition of power and their political situation remained quite stable. Thus, just saying we can maintain social stability is not enough. We have to prove that our one-party rule can accomplish big things that democratic systems are unable to accomplish. If we cannot do this, the value of maintaining our one-party rule will be open to challenge.

He Dongsheng was just waiting for a major stroke of luck that would allow for the accomplishment of big things. Privately his plan was known as the "Action Plan for Ruling the Nation and Pacifying the World." This title followed the old neo-Confucian slogan, but no matter how many sleepless nights he spent thinking about it, with its echoes of imperial Confucianism, he just couldn't come up with a new name.

If a major crisis didn't occur in a timely fashion, the transition from the then ruling group to a new ruling group would be fraught with danger. On the one hand, the Communist Party's transfers of power have always been dangerous—full of fierce power struggles between various inner-party factions. On the other hand, there have certainly been many problems during the past few years, starting with the 2008 financial tsunami. Contradictions in Chinese society have intensified, Party officials have been shown to be at fault at every turn and have indeed grown extremely weak; they have given their enemies much food for criticism. If things continued like that right up to the next Party Congress, the ruling group would certainly have had to step down. He Dongsheng was not a member of the ruling group's inner circle; at the time, he was merely a major figure who had served consecutive Party leaderships. He had a pretty good idea, though, who was slightly less reprehensible, and who was much more unscrupulous. He rather preferred to support the empowerment of some of those technocrats who had little family background to recommend them. Be that as it may, he didn't want to be dragged into a power struggle between various factions; he didn't want to see China's political situation thrown into greater turmoil due to transfer of power within the Party.

He needed Heaven's help. If, about a year before the scheduled transfer of power, a major crisis occurred and the Politburo decided to scrupulously follow his "Action Plan for Ruling the Nation and Pacifying the World"—with that, He Dongsheng believed, China would certainly be saved. Of course, future generations would never know how much blood, sweat, and tears he, He Dongsheng, had contributed to the perfection of this strategy. They would never know that his plan was his own ingenious design to preserve Communist Party rule in China forever. All the credit would go to the existing party-state leadership.

He Dongsheng had grasped very early on the imminence of another crisis in Western capitalism. His own investment strategy was to bet *against* the U.S. dollar. He had been in Zhongnanhai for so many years, and at first, like all the other high officials, he spent as much as possible of his Chinese renminbi in purchasing dollars. About ten years earlier, he became less confident about his dollar assets. At that point, he exchanged his American currency for Canadian dollars, to pay for his only son's school fees overseas. He also purchased a mansion in an old bourgeois neighborhood called Shaughnessy in Vancouver. With the remainder of his American funds, he bought into gold, petroleum, and other mineral and energy stocks with the intention of hanging on to them long term. Even more importantly, he decided to retain a good deal of renminbi and invest them in the Chinese real estate market. He didn't play the Chinese stock market because he couldn't spare the time, didn't like the duplicity and lack of transparency of the whole game, and didn't want to appear greedy. Over these past few years, his anti-

American investment strategy had returned a hefty profit, and con-firmed him in his view of international economics.

The 2008 financial tsunami caused him to reflect deeply on his economic theory, to reconstruct his mental image of the world economy and China's road to development, and cleverly to incorporate his further ideas into his "Action Plan."

He saw that the American-led developed countries, due to their two-party or even multiparty democratic political systems, had neither the ability nor the resolve to tame the monster known as globalized finance capitalism. America's elected politicians were beholden to a plethora of interest groups: Wall Street, big business, the arms industry, local power groups, the churches, labor unions, and various public-relations lobbies; they also had to take care of popular and media opinion. So when it was necessary for them to unite to accomplish something big and important, all they could do was look around, to the left and right, and fight meaningless little battles; they didn't dare to cut to the bone and heal the body politic, and were even less likely to take bold and decisive action. American market fundamentalists and the right wing of the Republican Party constantly dragged their feet and added to the confusion; they were completely out of touch with reality and could certainly mess things up, but they could not make any positive contributions. He Dongsheng was completely discouraged by Western representative democracy; he didn't have the slightest hope for it. He was even less hopeful that those government financial decision-makers, with their multifarious connections to Wall Street, had the *cojones* to make correct decisions that would save the world economy. On the contrary, he was more and more convinced that China's vast post-totalitarian government really did have the ability to manage and direct this historical stage of globalized finance capitalism—that is, if China had the correct understanding of the globalization of capital.

He Dongsheng realized, however, that in the Chinese system, merely having a correct understanding of any situation was not enough. This was because every level of the party-state-government was under the excessive control of interest groups and corrupt officials, and they would distort or reject even the most correct policy if it didn't profit them directly. Thus, He Dongsheng thought that only a major, unprecedented crisis would permit the current ruling group to implement a genuine dictatorship, guarantee action at the bottom on every order from the top, and build a firm foundation for China's Golden Age of Ascendancy that was just waiting to blossom out of the nation's growing power.

He Dongsheng had never imagined the 2008 global crisis would happen so soon. Nor had he imagined that on the first frenetic day, the Chinese Politburo would set in motion a completely new plan for tackling the situation. The policy proposal was called the "Action Plan for Achieving Prosperity amid Crisis." This proposal, of course, represented the collective wisdom of the entire Politburo Standing Committee, but very many of its elements were in accord with He Dongsheng's own secret plan.

First, let's answer the question: What about the United States? How did they start learning from our Chinese state-run system?

The United States government printed money and sold bonds, tried to save the bankrupt car manufacturers, poured money into already defunct banks . . . spending all that money in the wrong places. The result was that credit didn't revive, the market continued to contract, house prices continued to plunge, the unemployment rate edged up as before, and the value of the U.S. dollar steadily declined. American investors didn't want dollars and international investors didn't want them either; even the central banks of Japan, Russia, and Taiwan didn't dare to hold only American currency. American bonds, both long- and short-term, were hard to sell no matter how good their interest rates were. The dollar rose for a while at the beginning of 2009, but a little later it again lost twenty-five percentage points. In the end, worldwide confidence in the dollar reached a critical low, and, in one trading day in February, panic selling began. This was followed by the collapse of the American stock market. The chairman of the Federal Reserve Board, the secretary of the Treasury, and economics Nobel laureates such as Joseph Stiglitz and Paul Krugman all agreed that the United States was in a state of high-inflation decline or "stagflation"—what the Chinese media called an economic crisis of "fire and ice."

While the world economy was floundering, what was the situation in China?

China was also in danger as exports came to a standstill, the number of unemployed suddenly rose steeply, and stock markets fell until trading was halted to forestall further losses. This time China's economic growth would probably not avoid slipping from positive to negative figures.

The economic stimulus of 2009—relying on the National Treasury to allocate funds for direct investment to stimulate the economy—helped maintain the national GDP, but didn't genuinely encourage domestic consumer demand. Much of the stimulus money was invested in dubious mega-projects and fixed-capital assets, and the chief beneficiaries were the bureaucrats, state-run enterprises, and the interest groups tied to their apron strings. In other words, the stimulus helped increase the monopoly of state-run enterprises over the market, and further decreased the scope of private businesses.

The most troublesome thing was still the huge decline in the value of the dollar. Before 2004, China's annual trade surplus had not been very large. After 2004, however, China had less and less need to import foreign manufactured goods, and its exports grew at an ever more ferocious pace. China's foreign-exchange reserves abruptly rose to over two trillion dollars. Then, all of a sudden, those dollars lost more than a third of their value.

Although China had originally made a lot of noise about the dollar, it had not actually been selling off dollars the way Japan, Russia, and Taiwan had; China held on to its dollars and kept buying American-dollar assets right up to the end. It wasn't that China didn't want progressively to distance itself from the dollar, but it lacked an alternative place to invest its money. The government was already trying to reach mutual currency-exchange arrangements with Japan, South Korea, the ASEAN, and the Shanghai Cooperation Organization nations, and was already actively urging the United States to issue some bonds payable in renminbi—what the foreign press had dubbed "Panda Bonds." So it wasn't that the government wasn't making crisis preparations, it was that time was against them; they could only pray that the dollar would not decline further—they certainly could not imagine that it would go under so quickly.

Politics is a cruel business. Just the "crime" of allowing our sovereign wealth to shrink so much was bad enough. Add to that the negative growth in the national economy that was certain to follow, and the ruling group at that time would have completely lost its prestige within the Party. The following year, that governing group would not have had the strength to resist the opposition, and would certainly have fallen from power; it would have been a time for their friends to weep and their enemies to laugh. And this is the most important reason why they resolutely decided to put the "Action Plan for Achieving Prosperity amid Crisis" into operation.

So. Since they were going to die anyway, they thought they might as well make one last stand, and take drastic measures to alter the course of the heavens, an attempt to turn a bad situation into a victory. If they won, it would be a complete victory. And if they lost . . . well . . . if they lost, the great deluge that came after them would be a problem for the next Party leadership to resolve.

The day that the dollar fell so precipitously in 2011 was the eighth day of the first lunar month. The New Year vacation period had just ended, and, except for a few factories, every place was open again for business. That morning virtually all the news media reported that the global economy had entered a period of "fire and ice" crisis.

*Where was the machine of state?*

In fact, the Public Security police, the armed police, and the army were all in a state of readiness that day. Party Central had announced to all levels of government that the entire nation was in a state of emergency, and that the "Action Plan for Achieving Prosperity amid Crisis" had gone into operation. This was a coordinated chain of actions. The entire nation had to be regarded as a single chessboard and each move had to scrupulously follow the planned schedule if complete success, total victory, was to be achieved.

In the first phase, except for establishing martial law in Xinjiang and Tibet, the machine of state was forbidden to do anything without express orders from Party Central. In other words, the party-state machine was going to wait. Why? They were waiting to see how long it would take for genuine chaos to materialize. Waiting to see how long the common people could endure a state of anarchy. When that moment arrived, the people themselves would call on the government not to abandon them; they would beg the government to save them. The machine of state was waiting for the people of the entire nation once again to voluntarily and wholeheartedly give themselves into the care of the Leviathan.

If large-scale rioting or a mass exodus of people occurred, that would be the signal for the machine of state to go into action. As things turned out, the people went through six days of being so scared they couldn't face another such day, rumors were circulating wildly, and by the seventh day, many regions reported to Party Central that a genuine upheaval had broken out in their area. Still, in this situation, only a few places experienced large-scale rioting and mass exodus. On the eighth day, the fifteenth of the first lunar month, token forces of the People's Liberation Army and the armed police entered over six hundred cities around the country, and, as expected, were welcomed with open arms by the local population. This demonstrated the fact that in a moderately well-off society, the people fear chaos more than they fear dictatorship. And besides, Chinese society was really not as disorderly as was imagined; the vast majority of the Chinese people crave stability. As long as the government was not a target of attack, everything could be easily taken care of.

That afternoon, the national security police, the armed police, and the People's Liberation Army jointly announced the beginning of a crackdown on criminal elements, and social order was restored almost immediately; even petty looting came to an abrupt halt. The government also announced that it would start distributing rice from its grain reserves. Rations would be handed out every day, completely free of charge, and no one would be refused; the people's livelihood would be guaranteed and they need have no fear of hunger. The most interesting thing, however, was that the people grumbled that the reserve rice, having been harvested over a number of years, tasted bad. They didn't want to eat it, and they certainly weren't going to line up for it. Also, due to the crackdown on criminal activity, the usual opportunists didn't dare to buy up the reserve grain to sell off to rice-wine distilleries.

"Why? Why did you have to terrorize the common people like that?" Fang Caodi indignantly interrupted He Dongsheng.

He Dongsheng answered as though he were delivering a classroom lecture: "The beginning of the crisis was the key; if handled poorly at first, it would be hard to clean up the mess later. This crisis was extraordinarily serious, serious enough to give rise to mass disturbances on a nationwide scale. It started as an economic crisis, but it was capable of causing the long-smoldering volcanic contradictions deep under the surface of society to erupt. If the government reaction was too mild and too fragmentary, the people would remain dissatisfied and their resentment would be even greater. If the government acted too harshly, dispensing strong medicine too hastily, some strata of society would not accept it and would fight back. No matter what the government did then, it would be the only target.

"The situation at the time was as follows: except for incidents involving conflict between Han and minority ethnic nationalities, in general most of the major protests involved a confrontation between the masses and the government. For years many of the common people had long made up their minds and believed that the only way to solve their problems was to create a disturbance. The smallest thing, the pettiest grievance, was enough to set off a collective protest.

"If mass protest riots broke out at the same time all over the country, and all the criticism and resentment were aimed at the government, the machine of state would have collapsed.

"On the other hand, as long as all the complaints were not aimed at the government, mass protests would be difficult to start. A few lawless elements stirring up trouble would be insufficient to start a series of mass protests."

"So what did the leadership do to prevent the popular masses from aiming all their resentment and criticism at the government?" asked Fang Caodi.

"Well, after considering the situation from every angle, the leadership decided to allow the Chinese people to frighten themselves, let them be afraid of the government abandoning them, afraid of anarchy. The condition of anarchy is what Thomas Hobbes called 'the war of all against all.' In an anarchic state of nature, to quote his book *The Leviathan*, the 'life of man' is 'solitary, poor, nasty, brutish, and short.' To have no security for their life and property is, indeed, the people's ultimate terror. And because they are afraid of anarchy and chaos, everyone is willing to bow down voluntarily before the power of a really quite unlovely Leviathan. Only this Leviathan of a government can guarantee their lives and property. That means the party-state can win only by making the people feel that our Communist Party is their only hope in a major crisis, that the party-state is the only power great enough to concentrate our resources to do big things."

"Now you're talking about having a government *or* having anarchy," Little Xi needled He Dongsheng. "Nobody said that the government has to be your Communist Party!"

"It's fruitless to argue that," said He Dongsheng. "The government and the Party are one and the same."

"After you created a state of anarchy," asked Little Xi, "and fooled everyone so that even the people of Beijing filled the streets to welcome the People's Liberation Army into the city, what did you want to do then? Why did you have to have a crackdown? Do you know how many people die every time there's a crackdown?"

"I was almost executed in that crackdown," said Fang Caodi.

"In good faith, I also hope that this was our last crackdown," said He Dongsheng. "But the government in power at the time had no other choice but to take a hard line in the face of the upcoming transfer of power.

"With the global economy in a deep freeze, China had to save itself. That required administering strong medicine to the economy, but the government might lose control of society, its orders might be distorted, and the people might protest. The government had to have complete control over society and tame the masses; everybody had to be submissive to government orders. But how does the Chinese government usually tame the masses? In 1983, when the market economy experienced turmoil, didn't Old Deng order a crackdown? And June 4, 1989, was another big crackdown. Do you see? Sacrifices are inevitable if we want to accomplish something big and important."

Little Xi and Fang Caodi felt He Dongsheng was being unreasonable and they were anxious to refute his arguments, but he motioned for them to let him finish first.

"In 1816, the year after the end of the Napoleonic Wars," He Dongsheng went on, "the effects of the war faded and Britain suffered an economic recession; its national debt was two and a half times its GDP. Most unfortunately, in 1815, the Mount Tambora volcano in Indonesia erupted, the worst eruption in history, and spread volcanic ash all around the world. The next year was called 'the year without a summer' and there was virtually no agricultural harvest in Europe. The British prime minister at the time was Lord Liverpool, and who do you think his adviser was? None other than the celebrated economist David Ricardo. In the face of an imminent economic depression potentially leading to great social unrest, they instituted a program of crisis management. And what was it? Liverpool got Parliament to agree to a suspension of habeas corpus, Britain's protection of personal freedom. The government could round up and imprison anyone who caused trouble or didn't do what they were told, without following the law or legal procedures. In modern language, the government could trample human rights at will. The result of this policy was that during the entire period of

economic decline, the usual troublemakers didn't dare start anything, and in one year the national economy recovered. Wasn't that
pretty amazing?"

Little Xi and Fang Caodi sat grimly with their arms folded.

"Of course the people were going to suffer and be hungry during this crisis, and, besides, such recessions have always been a cycli-
cal phenomenon of capitalism in the past; they would last a year or
two, and after getting through them, everything would return to
normal. But this latest crisis was like the great depression of the
1930s, and it might have lasted for a decade or more. The government couldn't just ride it out; they had to go into action. My main
point is that stability is always the number-one priority, but stability
is not the ultimate goal—we need stability in order to accomplish
great things. Therefore, in extraordinary times or emergency situ-
ations, we have to order a crackdown. We have to beat the grass to
frighten the tigers. After that, while the effects of the crackdown are
still in play, we are free to implement new policies."

### The Chinese model

According to He Dongsheng, the crackdown was the second
phase of the "Action Plan for Achieving Prosperity amid Crisis."
The third phase was to put forth a set of five new policies.

*Number One:* Twenty-five percent of all the balance of every
National Bank savings accounts was to be converted into vouchers
for use in China only. One-third of these had to be spent within
ninety days, and two-thirds within six months. Beyond that time
limit they would no longer be valid.

The Chinese people's excessive savings were one of the reasons
for insufficient domestic demand. Personal savings equaled more

than 20 percent of the nation's annual GDP, and business savings were more than 30 percent. When the foreign economic environment was bad, people with surplus cash held on to their money and spent even less. With everyone doing this, how could the economy avoid recession? Merely lowering bank interest rates and moral suasion were no longer enough to make the Chinese people spend their money. The government had to rely on coercive measures of the sort Western countries would not dare dream of.

The greatest thing about this government order was that it was so simple to enforce. All the banks are computerized, so it was easy to cut into the savings accounts. The second virtue of this policy was that it affected only people who had money. It primarily impacted the urban middle or moderately well-off classes who had "got rich quick" in the Reform era. These included civil servants, professionals, white-collar workers, staff in government enterprises, small-business entrepreneurs, and pensioners. The government could easily get away with making them spend 25 percent of their savings on themselves in order to stimulate the national economy and help China make it through the crisis. Consumers and businesses all started spending money.

The third benefit of this policy was that it did not need the National Treasury to allocate major funds or follow Keynesian "job creation" to turn the recession around. At the very least it would successfully jump-start the engine of an economic growth driven by domestic demand. This policy was estimated to have increased the GDP by at least five percentage points. The urban population with savings was busy trying to decide where to spend the vouchers and on what commodities or services.

*Number Two:* Since demand had been created, it had to be supplied. The second set of new policies was to repeal over three thousand regulations governing the manufacturing and service sectors, making it easier for private capital to invest in business, relaxing credit policies for companies catering to domestic demand, and encouraging entrepreneurship.

At the same time, the function of government was transformed in accordance with the slogan: "The officials retreat and the people move in." The government removed the restrictions on all businesses except those involving national security and government monopolies.

"Now anyone can start a publishing company," said He Dongsheng, looking straight at Lao Chen. "You can just publish your books without a government-issued book number."

"But all books still have to be sent in for approval," countered Lao Chen, "and many subjects are still forbidden."

"But at least today there are private publishers everywhere," said He Dongsheng. "There are even Chinese and foreign joint-venture publishing companies, all in complete accord with WTO requirements."

These policies were extremely effective. In a short time, it looked like everyone in China was in business. Everybody was talking business regardless of age, sex, location, or trade; everybody was trying to make money, looking for talented employees, or being sought out themselves, searching for raw materials or for people to buy or sell some resource. The Chinese people, you know—just give them a chance to do something and they can make a great success of it.

It was almost a miracle how quickly Guangdong, Jiangsu, and Zhejiang's underused industrial capacity was changed over from manufacture for export to production for the domestic market. New products and new services flooded the market in the space of a couple of months. In six months, China successfully transformed itself from an economy dependent on investment and exports to one driven by domestic demand.

How successful were these policies? asked He Dongsheng rhetorically.

Then he continued: The target for the first phase was to return to the situation of the 1980s, when domestic demand made up half of the GDP, and this goal was accomplished. The optimum target, however, was to equal the situation of the United States before the 1970s, when internal consumption was 60 percent of their GDP, ideal for a large country. After that the Americans went overboard by relying *too much* on domestic consumption. They let it go over 70 percent of the GDP, they had insufficient investments and exports, debt was excessive, and private individuals had no savings—all this leading to big trouble.

In many areas China can be self-sufficient and doesn't need to rely too much on exports to foreign countries; in other words, from now on China does not have to be overly influenced by the fluctuations of the U.S. dollar. China's domestic demand has so far been raised from 35 percent of its GDP only to close to 50 percent. Investment and foreign trade still account for more than 50 percent, and China is still investing too much in capital construction and real estate. Also, after the world economy recovers, the foreign-trade proportion of GDP will still increase slightly, but in general terms the domestic-demand proportion has been significantly readjusted upward. As people's wages are raised and with good returns on business investments, taxes will also be increased accordingly. China will have successfully eliminated the threat of a domestic economic recession that existed before these policies, and also rectified the most serious structural bias in the economy since the beginning of Reform and Openness.

And the policies killed two birds with one stone because with the rise and expansion of new businesses everywhere the unemployment problem in both urban and rural areas was solved.

*Number Three:* During this period many peasants returned to the cities and, taking advantage of the labor shortage, moved into well-paid jobs. But what did the peasants who stayed behind do? They, too, were busy taking care of their own property.

The third set of policies enhanced peasants' property rights to their farmland. This move had been discussed for years. One of the chief motives behind this policy was to divert the peasants' attention from any grievances and maintain social stability in a time of economic crisis. And, as expected, the peasants all got busy taking care of their private property.

"What about privatization?" Little Xi asked with accusation in her voice.

He Dongsheng himself was not exactly certain whether the farmland should have been privatized. The privatization experiences of other countries had not been completely positive, but he could not change anybody else's opinion on the matter. One thing was certain and it left him without an argument: the peasants fully supported the privatization policy. "After this China can never go back again," he said rather wistfully.

*Number Four:* This was a period of great enthusiasm throughout the country. It looked like it was pretty chaotic, but it was a necessary and constructive chaos.

What this chaos meant, though, was that having liberated the nation's forces of production and activated people's economic enthusiasm, the leadership's next most important task was to guard rigorously against fraud and the sabotage of government policies by corrupt officials. The "severe and rapid" crackdown of three weeks earlier had first neutralized the power of many criminal elements, including gangsters, hooligans, human traffickers, and gangs of pick-pockets and beggars. While the memory of the early crackdown was still fresh, three new targets were announced: crackdowns on graft and corruption, on manufacturing fake products, and on spreading misinformation. This announcement put the fear of death into everybody.

The Communist Party is most proficient at swatting flies. Rounding up a few usual suspects and summarily executing them does a lot to intimidate the local officials; it makes them toe the line and thus achieves the desired goal. As long as the local administrations improve somewhat, officials will not dare conspire to defraud the government. With that, the first three sets of new economic policies had comparatively better odds for success.

*Number Five:* He Dongsheng was in favor of a market economy, but he didn't believe the market was infallible, and he certainly didn't believe in laissez-faire economics. He knew that at certain points the government had to step in. The above four sets of policies created real aggregate demand and stimulated a corresponding level of production to meet it. There was a great increase in the circulation of money and in the amount of credit available in the market, and there were temporary shortfalls in some commodities and services. Even if there was no wild speculation, simply letting the market regulate itself was bound to give rise to inflation. Commodity prices would experience irregular upward swings, and if this developed into hyperinflation, it would put enormous pressure on this stage of economic reform, perhaps even bringing it to a halt. So the government had to implement price controls.

"I believe that this was the most controversial aspect of the 'Prosperity amid Crisis' plan," said He Dongsheng. It was also the policy that required the greatest amount of technical expertise to implement. Those scholars who had been brainwashed by Western economic ideas would probably have a negative conditioned reflex when they heard the dreaded words "price control." He Dongsheng was self-taught in economics, and he had originally had the same reaction to the idea of price control. It was not until recent years, after he'd immersed himself in the study of Western economic history, that he discovered that in the last century developed Western countries had on several occasions successfully implemented large-scale price-control policies; and these were all capitalist countries. His eyes were certainly opened when he read how Walther Rathenau had successfully managed the economic plan of the German Empire during the First World War period. During the Second World War, the Third Reich had also successfully combined aspects of capitalism and a planned economy.

"Most encouraging," said He Dongsheng, "were President Franklin Roosevelt's Second World War economic policies, including price controls, that not only supported an enormous military expenditure but also allowed the United States to free itself from the Great Depression that had bedeviled the nation for twelve years."

The economist John Kenneth Galbraith served at the time as deputy head of the Office of Price Administration with a staff of some sixteen thousand employees. Before becoming president of the American Economic Association in 1972, Galbraith wrote a book on price-control policies, and in the 1970s during a period of economic stagflation, he again advocated them. All Western economists are not, then, opposed to price-control policies. It is just that in the last forty years, the ideas of the Chicago School of market fundamentalists had so much influence that no one remembered that price control is a good strategy for regulating a market economy. In France right up to the 1980s, 40 percent of economic activity was still regulated by price controls.

This was the breakthrough He Dongsheng had made in his

understanding of economics. After that, he combined his new knowledge with China's actual circumstances and tried to sell his ideas to his other comrades. Fortunately, many Chinese officials had just emerged from the socialist command economy, and were willing, on the surface at least, to accept a market economy. In their heart of hearts, however, they were elated to hear about price-control policies. In a period of economic transition, price controls were actually a necessity; they would assist the market, and save this newly emerged market from self-destruction, but would not usurp the functions of a mature market economy.

None of the officials in He Dongsheng's Price Control Group were dyed-in-the-wool ideologues. The core members of the group were technocrats in their fifties who had accumulated the price-control experience of thirty years of Reform and Openness. They had recruited a large number of the best students of statistics and econometrics from China's premier universities to set up a database and develop software for a nationwide network of a kind not available in an earlier age of planned economy. This made it possible for producers and consumers throughout the world to go online and locate the most up-to-date price-control information.

Price controls make real prices transparent. They are intended to allow businesspeople to make money and encourage them to produce, but prevent them from entertaining ideas of speculation, hoarding, and profiteering.

What should be regulated, what should not be regulated, and what is the influence on supply and demand? These are the things that have to be handled just right in order to inhibit major fluctuations in prices. Even more necessary is relinquishing control at just the right time to allow the market's own regulatory mechanism to take over.

This sort of large-scale regulatory feedback system implemented in China was a startling revelation to the initially skeptical foreign media. To put it bluntly, even a more authoritarian dictatorial government would be able to implement this "command economy for a new age" by employing twenty-first-century automated information and calculation systems. Price controls provided a kind of armed escort to smooth the path of China's latest large-scale economic reform.

"In the world today," said He Dongsheng, his voice beginning to break, "China is truly the only country that could accomplish all five of these policy changes at the same time."

While the global economy was in great difficulty, and Western countries were in shambles, this was China's opportunity of the century. An originally almost moribund top leadership had in a very short time transformed the social and political crisis caused by an economic meltdown into a golden opportunity. All of which made the rest of the world accept the idea of China's ascendant prosperity. At the Party Congress the following year, the top-leadership transition proceeded smoothly. He Dongsheng admitted he didn't do as well as he had hoped. His plan to be promoted to secretary in the Central Party Secretariat came to nothing, and he was merely promoted from an alternate to a full member of the Politburo; he was now an old veteran of three leadership changes. On the first anniversary of the "Action Plan for Achieving Prosperity amid Crisis," He Dongsheng had wryly congratulated himself: "He Dongsheng, you did brilliantly."

### A century-old dream comes true

Fang Caodi and Little Xi were quite stupefied by this lecture, and they still had many questions they wanted to ask about that week of anarchy, but they were swept along by He Dongsheng's monologue. He Dongsheng went to the bathroom, came back, drank another glass of water, and carried on speaking even more bombastically.

Fang Caodi and Little Xi didn't deny that in the last two years China's economic situation had been good, but they believed that the political situation had become much worse. China was moving further and further away from constitutional democracy. They complained that everyone seemed to be satisfied with the status quo.

"Everyone seems to be perennially happy," said Little Xi.

Then Lao Chen spoke up. "I was one of those people," he said. Before meeting Little Xi again, he'd thought that China's present society was perfectly harmonious. Every day he was moved by his own sense of happiness. It was Lao Chen's turn to hold forth now.

Not long ago he thought that Taiwan and Hong Kong were leading, and that mainland China was trailing behind, but now he felt quite the opposite was the case. Everyone used to criticize the mainland for being poor and backward, but then suddenly they started loudly proclaiming that China's Golden Age of Ascendancy had arrived. For so many years intellectuals had said that the Western system was superior, and the whole world looked up to the United States, Japan, and Western Europe, but then in unison they suddenly changed their tune, and now the whole world was learning from or emulating China.

He Dongsheng interrupted and resumed his speech. He was still tied to his chair. His captors had no intention of unleashing him. "Of course there are some elements of misconception here that cannot withstand an empirical, item-by-item consideration," he said. "For example, China's per capita income is very far behind that of developed countries, environmental degradation is rampant, honest government is not to be found, human rights are not guaranteed, and freedom of speech is restricted. China has so many people, though, that its overall strength is always astonishing, and its rise is an incontestable fact. The Chinese media frequently report that in *this* area China is number one in the world, or in *that* area China is in the first rank. Not being completely clear about all that, the average Chinese person these days believes that China leads the world in everything."

In the past, foreign manufacturers had complained that China kept the value of its renminbi artificially low in order to subsidize Chinese exports, and that this created unfair competition. Western labor organizations also criticized China for exploiting its workers to maintain the preferential cost of its exports, thus lowering the living standards of workers all over the world. Now that China no longer relies on depressing export prices, the renminbi can appreciate in value, and Chinese people can buy more imported goods and go abroad as tourists, or even purchase foreign businesses. Incomes have risen across the board, companies are making good profits, and the state's tax revenue has gone up accordingly. With this extra revenue, education, health insurance, and social security can all be improved, and China can redouble its efforts to combat environmental degradation.

"If we cannot protect our workers," said He Dongsheng, "and cannot provide universal health insurance and social security, then what kind of a socialist country would we be?" For the first time, Little Xi and Fang Caodi nodded in agreement.

"Not relying excessively on exports doesn't mean not trading with other countries. China is certainly not closed to foreign contact. It is still in the process of developing its heavy industry, and so it has been necessary to buy entire production lines from developed countries such as Germany, transport them to China, and reassemble them here. Furthermore, the United States also has products that China is still unable to manufacture, like Boeing aircraft and high-tech precision instruments. China will buy as many of these as possible. At present, Europe and America still have to rely on Chinese goods, but as China exports less to these countries, it serves to reduce their trade deficit with China. In general, though, China is already able to manufacture most of the goods it needs. Whether some of these are inferior copies or not, China's domestic market is big enough and competition will produce articles of acceptable quality at appropriate prices. Then the number of industrial products that developed countries can sell to China will gradually decrease.

"China's internal market is such a juicy plum that foreign capital, big-name brands, and retail companies have willingly accepted harsh joint-venture conditions for the right to enter or remain in China. China's strict policies violate the spirit of WTO regulations, but since the protectionist and mercantilist activities of the developed nations themselves brought WTO negotiations to a standstill, the idea of global trade without barriers has turned into a pipe dream, and nobody can any longer occupy the moral high ground and lecture China.

"Our greatest needs are energy, minerals, other raw materials, and food, and most of these come from the countries of Asia, Africa, and Latin America. Now even Canada, Australia, New Zealand, and Russia are both buying Chinese goods and supplying China with these essentials. Basically, China can regard them as Third World countries. It has already reached mutually beneficial currency-exchange arrangements with the major trading nations, and the renminbi is now a globally circulating currency on a par with the dollar and the euro. China is already as important an economic entity as the United States, the European Union, and Japan. Its inflation remains at an acceptable rate of seven or eight percent, and economic growth has topped fifteen percent three years running. Such growth was seen before, during the thirty years of

Reform and Openness: from 1982 to 1984 China's GDP rose fifteen percent a year, but the total size of the GDP was small. To put it simply, China is now the only locomotive powering global economic growth. No wonder the nations of Asia, Africa, and Latin America want to be close to China, and no wonder people now say that the age of American imperialism is over, and the Chinese century has begun." He Dongsheng paused to clear his throat.

Lao Chen, Little Xi, and Fang Caodi didn't understand economics, but they were concerned about China, and knew therefore that they could not ignore the subject. They listened attentively and with narrowed eyes to He Dongsheng's explanations. What rendered them truly speechless was when He Dongsheng turned from economics to a discussion of the international political situation.

"No matter how badly off the American economy is, the United States is still, militarily, the strongest nation in the world. Only the armed forces of the United States have the power to strike anywhere in the world." He Dongsheng got back into his stride.

China cannot, therefore, follow the path taken by the Soviet Union during the Cold War: competing for world hegemony with the United States, conducting an arms race, implementing a balance-of-terror policy of mutually assured destruction. No, that is not the way to pacify the world, and not where China's permanent security interests lie. A rational person like He Dongsheng, with his deeply concealed Chinese-style idealism, knew that this road was a dead end because China's national power could not support it. To prevent the United States from starting a long-distance war, China has to employ its long-range preemptive or unilateral strike capabilities. To prevent the invasion of its territory and to safeguard its national interests, China has to become a friendly older brother to its regional neighbors and not compete with the United States for world hegemony. To use the language of international discourse, this is China's Monroe Doctrine.

"American nuclear weapons could destroy China, so it has to make the U.S. understand clearly that China will not wait for them to strike first, but will itself attack. In other words, the United States cannot viciously threaten China with its nuclear weapons because it might provoke China into using nuclear weapons first. That is the essence of China's preemptive first-strike strategy.

"China has sufficient first-strike nuclear capability to destroy only Hawaii and a few cities on the West Coast of the United States, but that is enough to inflict unacceptable levels of destruction on the Americans. Even if the U.S. counterattack could then produce a hundred times more destruction in China, the American people would still regard the damage on their own soil as too high a price to pay. China employs these two threats—preemptive first-strike and long-range unilateral attack—to frighten the Americans out of the idea of launching a nuclear war against it.

"Even the victor in a nuclear war will pay too great a price— this is also a tacit 'live and die together' agreement. China's strategy is open and made perfectly clear to the United States in order to avoid any misunderstanding on their part. At the same time, China has consistently urged the Americans not to establish an antimissile defense network in the eastern Pacific because that would give rise to a Sino-American nuclear-arms race, and force China to develop intercontinental ballistic missiles capable of breaking through the American antimissile shield, as well as build nuclear submarines and space-based weapons."

He Dongsheng didn't believe that nuclear war between the United States and China was likely, and he believed that the probability of the U.S. launching a conventional-warfare invasion of Chinese territory was virtually nil, despite the continued presence of the American military throughout East Asia.

Historically, he said, the Chinese nation's greatest fear had always been invasion by non-Chinese ethnic groups, the division of China's national territory, and rule by non-Chinese conquerors. Such fears are quite unnecessary now. China's current national-defense systems are the strongest they have ever been in the five-thousand-year history of the Chinese race.

"Who would dare invade Chinese territory today?" he asked emphatically.

Since the founding of the People's Republic, leaving aside conflicts involving Taiwan, Tibet, and Xinjiang, China has had short-term military clashes on its borders with India, the Soviet Union, the former South Vietnam, and Vietnam. The only conflict that truly threatened Chinese national security was the "Resist the United States, Assist North Korea" conflict of sixty years ago.

There are fourteen nations with which China has land borders, and six with adjacent territorial waters. Since 1949 China has already settled fourteen land-border disputes and three offshore-island disputes, but there are still some disputes that cannot be settled in the immediate future. These include India's refusal to recognize Chinese ownership of the 38,000-square-kilometer Aksai Chin region on the Tibetan plateau; China's refusal to recognize the 84,000-square-kilometer South Tibet region as part of the Arunachal Pradesh Province of northeast India bordering on Tibet and Bhutan; disputes in the South China Sea between China and each of Vietnam, Singapore, Malaysia, the Philippines, and Brunei; Sino-Japanese disputes in the East China Sea; and even with the small Himalayan nation of Bhutan.

Furthermore, Chinese plans to build large dams in Tibet and Yunnan to change the river courses there are coming under increasing criticism and have given rise to heated disputes over transnational water sources because, except for the Ganges, the headwaters of all the major rivers that flow into the countries of South and Southeast Asia are in China's Himalayan region. Still, none of these disputes or even occasional armed clashes are very likely to develop into full-scale warfare between China and some other country.

He Dongsheng knew, of course, that there were elements in the military that didn't like his views because of possible effects on their budgets. Although he didn't agree with the tireless calls by these military interest groups for the government to increase spending on the armed forces, he was not so naïve as to imagine that a large nation could rise without the support of military power. He was a realist, and he wanted only to optimize the national interest most effectively without depending on the military to achieve the victory. To do this, it was necessary to consider grand strategy.

He believed that if a country claims the moral high ground too much, it will make other countries suspicious. In the past, when China was always proclaiming that it would never seek hegemony, and talking about its peaceful rise and a harmonious world order, did other countries believe it? This is a time when other nations worry about China, and so it is a good idea for China to make its national strategic interests perfectly clear so that others will know where to draw the line. That is why China recently put forth the idea of a Chinese Monroe Doctrine.

In the 1820s, President James Monroe announced that a rising United States didn't intend to contend for hegemony with the great powers of Europe, but that they must not invade any part of the American continent. They especially must not try to colonize parts of Latin America again. The Americas were for the Americans— that was the Monroe Doctrine.

Now China has emulated the nineteenth-century United States

and announced that it has absolutely no intention of contending with other great powers for global hegemony. But East Asia is for the East Asians, and China has invited the Euro-American great powers, primarily the United States, to leave East Asia. (What China means by East Asia also includes Northeast Asia and Southeast Asia, Japan, and all the nations that were historically part of the Chinese tributary system.)

During the long period of history when a steppe civilization of northern and western Asia was continually colliding and mixing with a European civilization derived from the Mediterranean area, China was shielded behind the Gobi Desert and high mountain ranges. The self-sufficient Chinese autarchy considered itself a *Tianxia* or "All Under Heaven," a world unto itself with a high level of cultural unity. Perhaps due to geographical reasons, the ancient Chinese empire didn't have as great a penchant for foreign invasion and expansion as so many other nations over the centuries: Alexander, the Romans, Attila, the Crusaders, the Mongols, Timur, the Ottomans, Napoleon, or the European powers and Japan during the age of exploration and colonization, or the post–Cold War United States of today with its 850 military bases located all over the world.

"China," He Dongsheng said with force and getting hoarse now, "certainly does not want to take on the arduous and thankless task of policing the world, nor does it want to govern other countries. Have you ever heard of the People's Republic of China trying to occupy other people's territory?"

According to his understanding, the Chinese century is not a century to be enjoyed by China only. The Chinese century means that China has finally regained the rightful historical position that it occupied before the nineteenth century. The European powers and the United States have to understand China's intentions. It does not want to take over the world, but Europe and the United States should not imagine that they can prevent the rise and optimal development of East Asia under Chinese direction. If only the United States would leave East Asia, China, the United States, and Europe could maintain their own spheres of influence without mutual interference, and they could all prosper. Replacing a struggle for global hegemony with the regionalization of political influence would guarantee world peace during this period of the unstoppable rise of China.

In the economic realm beyond politics, the world is already divided into three main regions: the European Union, the North American free-trade countries, and the Asia Pacific region. The total internal trade and direct investment *within* each region is greater than the economic activity *between* the regions. The European nations' chief trading partners are other European Union nations, and Canada's is the United States, not Japan or China. Starting in 2007, over half of the trade of Asian countries, excluding the Middle East, but also adding in Australia and New Zealand, has been with other Asian nations. All that remains is to link politics and economics together on the same footing and you will have regionalization.

Then Europe, America, and China can do business within their own territories and spheres of influence and can both cooperate and compete on investments and development in Africa, Asia, and Latin America based always on economic criteria. For example, in Angola, China, France, and the United States can all seek offshore oil-drilling rights, and the local government will have more choices and not be easily controlled by any one country.

The second Iraq War convinced China to invest heavily in Africa. Angola is now China's largest single supplier of oil. Other African nations that supply us with fossil fuels include Sudan, the Republic of the Congo, Equatorial Guinea, Nigeria, Chad, Mauritania, Mali, Niger, Benin, and Gabon, while Algeria provides natural gas. Over

30 percent of our petroleum imports come from Africa, second only to the supply from the Middle East. Besides energy, China is also active in mining and forestry in Africa. Large areas of farmland are under contract to meet Chinese demands. China has also built roads, hospitals, harbors, airports, and communication networks. China has always advocated trade, friendship, and non-interference in other nations' internal politics, and African leaders welcome this attitude. It is not surprising that our power and influence in Africa will soon surpass that of America, France, and Great Britain to become Africa's number-one trading partner.

In South Asia and the Middle East, China has friendly relations with Iran and has expended a great deal of thought and money on its longtime friend Pakistan. This is an important strategic national-security consideration: to contain America's ally India, our so-called "cold to India, warm to Islam" policy, and to protect our oil-supply lines—the shortest route for the shipment of African and Middle Eastern oil is by sea or overland to the port of Gwadar in southwest Pakistan, and then north along the Chinese-built Gwadar–Dalbandin railway to meet up with the Karakoram highway in China's Xinjiang Province. This avoids a long sea journey from Africa or the Middle East, and bypasses the Indian Ocean and South China Sea shipping lanes—especially the narrow and busy Strait of Malacca, where the navies of India, the United States, Singapore, Thailand, Indonesia, the Philippines, Australia, and Japan frequently conduct joint naval exercises.

China has also not failed to grab any energy resources that have slipped out of the grasp of other great powers. In 2008, when the price of oil fell from $147 to $33 a barrel, China greatly increased its oil imports from Venezuela and Iran. In 2009, when Russia reneged on its contract and stopped importing natural gas from Turkmenistan, China reached out its helping hand and signed a thirty-year contract with Turkmenistan that included building a gas pipeline across Turkmenistan, Uzbekistan, Kyrgyzstan, and Kazakhstan all the way to China. The same goes for oil from Kazakhstan. China not only participated in its extraction, but built three thousand kilometers of oil pipelines. With the exception of Russia and Iran, the nations in the region are all landlocked, and their energy exports have to be shipped through other countries. Therefore they all support China's ultimate strategic goal in Central Asia—that is, the construction of a "Pan Eurasian Energy Bridge," an oil pipeline from the Middle East, through Iran, Russia, Azerbaijan, and Kazakhstan to Xinjiang.

Today, in its own national interest, China wants to promote regional stability in Africa, the Middle East, Central Asia, Iran, and Pakistan. It wants to prevent any manipulation by other great powers and to block the influence of religious extremists, separatists, and terrorists who want to undermine or overthrow the governments in those regions. In order to isolate the Xinjiang independence forces, China has offered special friendship to the six "Stans" of Central Asia, and to Turkey. Turkey has long been denied entry into the European Union, but China has offered it observer status in the Shanghai Cooperation Organization, and has given Iran official membership. Most unexpectedly, even Israel has to be friendly toward China; because Israel is afraid that China will export high-tech weaponry, including nuclear weapons, to Islamic countries, it is selling sophisticated technology to China.

China also did not oppose Russian efforts to counteract American influence in the continental-heartland regions of Central Asia, the Caucasus, and the Ukraine. These multiethnic nations didn't, however, want to throw themselves back into the Russian embrace. Kazakhstan, for example, has not forgotten the great suffering it endured as a result of Stalin's forced-removal policies and on the

Soviet collective farms. Uzbekistan was even casting amorous glances toward the United States and NATO. All the Central Asian nations agreed that China had no political ambitions in the region, and so they felt more confident in doing business with China. On the contrary, it was China that didn't want Russia to get the idea that they were trying to muscle in on Russia's sphere of influence. The new foreign-policy term for the Chinese and Russian governments was "coordinated diplomacy," and that explains why the Chinese provided a huge loan to the small nation of Moldova, to the west of the Black Sea, with which China had never had any affiliation. It was to collaborate with the Russians in their effort to prevent Western power from moving East.

China has for a long time endured much humiliation to accomplish the task of making Russia a friendly ally. Through more than a century, Russia has occupied over 1.5 million square kilometers of Chinese territory, an area three times the size of France. Many years ago China gave up any claim on these lands and the two nations jointly declared the Sino–Russian borders fixed. As long as China doesn't bring this matter up again, there is no further reason why China and Russia should have any major conflicts. Russia is very large, its population is in decline, and it is under threat militarily from the power of NATO on its western front. It is expending all its strength on managing the instability of its income from energy resources, controlling its non-Russian ethnic-minority populations, and reasserting the power and influence of the former Soviet Union.

Russia is overdependent on energy exports, and so this latest round of global economic decline hit it very hard. Fortunately, when Europe reduced its imports of natural gas from Russia, China immediately increased its purchases of Russian energy. From then on, Russian oil and natural gas and other staple exports, such as heavy weaponry and Siberian timber, were guaranteed a Chinese market. In 2010, Russian oil was already flowing through the Siberian Pacific pipeline from Skovorodina to Daqing in Heilongjiang Province, and now natural gas also comes into China from Yakutia through the 6,700-kilometer Yakutia–Khabarovsk–Vladivostok gas pipeline. All this reduces Russia's dependence on the European market, as well as diversifying China's supplies of fossil-fuel resources. Due to their lack of capital and their close ties to the government, several Russian oligarchic enterprises competed to accept China's friendly state-enterprise investments in joint monopolies of Russian titanium, gold, and other precious metals. We can thus say that in economic terms China and Russia are mutually supportive.

Having noticed this fact, recently many Russian regions bordering on China have altered their attitudes and tacitly allowed or even openly welcomed Chinese capital, businesses, and workers to come in and cooperate in their development. For the sake of our two nations' core interests and in consideration of our grand strategies, as long as China doesn't bring up the question of its lost territory, China and Russia are perfectly able to live in peaceful coexistence.

He Dongsheng said that this great recent shift in the global center of gravity presented China with the opportunity of a century. In the past few years, China had been developing quite smoothly, but in order to have long-term security and to "rule the nation and pacify the world" (as the traditional phrase goes), He Dongsheng believed there was still one key move remaining: an alliance with Japan, "to make 'East Asia for the East Asians' a reality," he said.

Only when Japan changed its attitude, shook off the United States, and entered Asia could American imperialism be removed from East Asia, and the Cold War arrangements finally collapse. Once the two Asian superpowers, China and Japan, joined hands, a new world order appeared, and a new post-Western, post-white era was ineluctably created. There was nothing Europe and America could do but accept it. This prospect was what had motivated Sun Yat-sen in 1924, when he went to Japan to promote Asianism and urged the Japanese not to emulate Western imperialism, but instead to join hands with China and make the traditional Chinese "Kingly Way" a reality. Sun Yat-sen was a nationalist.

"Do you think he didn't see Japan's ambitions?" He Dongsheng asked his audience.

He did, but he understood that neither China nor Japan alone had the might to force the Western powers out of Asia, but if they worked together, nothing could stop the rejuvenation of Asia. Sadly, though, Japan didn't heed Sun Yat-sen's good advice, and went on to invade China and the rest of East Asia, ruining themselves and many others, and causing both countries to suffer tremendous losses.

Now the opportunity had come again. The leaders of China and Japan risked overwhelming internal opposition to conclude an alliance, signing the most comprehensive security treaty in the history of their two nations, and an extremely close bilateral economic-cooperation agreement.

"You probably don't know," said He Dongsheng, "that Japanese military might is second only to that of the United States and China." He went on to relate that, in theory, Japan's defense spending is only 1 percent of its GDP, but the Japanese economy is very large, and, just as in China, much of its military spending is hidden in other budget items. These include naval forces, its space program, and its weapons research and development, none of which show up in the national defense budget. Although Japan's official military spending is slightly less than China's, Japan leads in advanced technology, and many of Japan's civilian industries can be easily converted to military use.

With Japan having a conventional military might equal to that of China and being so geographically close, it made China extremely nervous when it was not viewed as a friendly state—not to mention the continued presence of American troops in Japan, the island of Okinawa, and South Korea.

By the same token, Japan had a similar feeling of unease as it witnessed China's rapid rise, which might have led it to abolish its "peace constitution," become a normal country, start an arms race with China, accept the continuing presence of the United States in East Asia, and even unilaterally develop nuclear weapons.

What sort of stability would there have been in East Asia if that happened? Both countries might have once more suffered equal and terrible losses. To disarm this time bomb, create a win-win situation for China and Japan, and force the United States to withdraw from East Asia required great wisdom or a once-in-a-century stroke of luck. That stroke of luck was the global economic stagflation.

One can say that Japan's economic depression had already lasted more than twenty years, and every time their situation seemed to improve, they would fall back again. They were growing weaker, and the latest global economic decline made recovery look too far away to imagine. Japanese industrial production, which had once looked down its nose at the rest of the world, seemed to have no hope of recovering any time soon.

Chinese leaders saw this period of Japan's greatest weakness as an opportunity too good to pass up. They demanded that the isolationist and protectionist Japanese market immediately be opened up to China, especially to allow China to purchase Japanese companies. If Japan refused, China would take retaliatory measures to restrict the access of Japanese goods and businesses to the Chinese market. These demands were the straw that broke the Japanese camel's back. Now China is Japan's number-one trading partner, and the Japanese economy recovered somewhat between 2002 and 2008, largely due to its trade with China.

In the end, and in the name of free trade, with great pomp and circumstance the two nations concluded a most-favored-nation agreement. Both countries can now go in and out of each other's markets, without restriction, just as in China's close bilateral economic-cooperation agreement with its Hong Kong special economic zone. This was the first time in history that Japan had freely opened its doors to another country. As these two markets rapidly became integrated, they were soon able to challenge the American and European economies.

When China and Japan joined hands, South Korea and other Asian countries all expressed a desire to collaborate with them to establish an East Asian common market. Even Australia, New Zealand, Canada's two western provinces, and the Latin American members of APEC all wanted to organize a Pacific and East Asian community.

Besides expanding their free-trade area, China and Japan also signed an unprecedented agreement to allow the free movement between the two countries of workers with special expertise or capital investors. To assist Japan with its problem of an aging population, Chinese immigrants to Japan have to be under forty-five, while no such limit was placed on Japanese immigrants to China. On the basis of this agreement, an estimated fifty thousand or more Chinese will emigrate to Japan every year, about the same number that were going to Canada.

These Chinese have various reasons for emigrating: to find employment, because travel is easier with a Japanese passport, because of the quality of the Japanese lifestyle, or because they don't want their children to endure the fierce competition for advancement in the Chinese education system. Most of the Japanese immigrants to China are senior citizens who can get much better value for money out of their pensions there, giving them both a higher standard of care and more enjoyment. China is helping Japan replenish its declining population with people of excellent quality. This policy also has great symbolic meaning, since it implies that China and Japan have forgotten their former enmity, and now happily receive each other into their respective countries. The process is similar to how the traditional enemies Germany and France began to live in peaceful coexistence after the Second World War and also established a new order in Europe.

Of equal importance, China and Japan signed a mutual non-aggression and national security treaty stipulating that if one of them was attacked, the other would come to its aid. It has the same structure as the United States–Japan Mutual Defense Treaty, the NATO alliance, or similar pacts between nineteenth-century European powers. A brilliant Chinese aspect of this treaty was to allay Japanese anxiety by not demanding that Japan abrogate its mutual defense treaty with the United States. Japan is now protected by both China and the United States; it has bought two insurance policies.

The Sino-Japanese security treaty also put a restraint on North Korea. On the one hand, it meant that North Korea could no longer practice nuclear blackmail against Japan, because if Japan was attacked China would come to its aid. On the other hand, Japan could no longer use the threat from North Korea to justify military expansion. After the stubborn South Korean regime began to feel isolated, they too considered signing a similar security treaty with China to further curb the power of North Korean militarism.

"That's China for you," said He Dongsheng with a smile. "All you have to do is recognize China as your friendly older brother, and everything can be easily accomplished, even if China has to give up some of its advantages."

In the last century, Japan invaded China and the Chinese people hate the Japanese to this day, but today's Japanese certainly do not hate the Chinese. They used to look down on us or even despise us, but now they fear us. In the past they were the invaders, but surprisingly they have no hate-China complex. This is easily understood if we think about it: if you inflicted terrible harm on us in the past, naturally you do not hate us now. The Japanese believe they were defeated by the Americans. Japanese territory had never before been occupied by a foreign power until the American postwar occupation, and there are still fifty thousand U.S. troops stationed on Japanese territory. Therefore, to this very day, the Japanese harbor a wish to see the Americans suffer a setback. This is part of the subtle but deep psychology between powerful and weak peoples, the invaders and the invaded, the victorious and the defeated in war—another war is not necessarily the only way to take revenge and wipe away the shame. A reversal in the status of the high and the low, or at least a new equality in status, might suffice.

This is why the East Asian Monroe Doctrine and the Sino-Japanese mutual security treaty actually had so many supporters in Japan—because they were a slap in the face to the Americans. The subtext of the extremely close Sino-Japanese bilateral economic-cooperation agreement was that Japan needs China's assistance, and that also gave many Chinese a strong feeling of self-respect.

If Sun Yat-sen were alive today he would surely congratulate China on the realization of its century-old dream. "Well done! Well done!" was He Dongsheng's proud conclusion.

### The best option in the real world

"Ha! The realization of his century-old dream?" protested Little Xi. "If Sun Yat-sen were alive today, he'd die of anger. Sun's Three People's Principles were nationality, rights, and livelihood.

Where are the people's rights now? In the last hundred years, their rights have been trampled all over by your Communist Party. Every time we turn around, you're cracking down, snatching people, and throwing them in prison." She stamped her foot for emphasis.

"Right," said Fang Caodi. "You say social order is in danger, there are great contradictions, and evildoers are running amok, but who's really responsible for stirring up all this social unrest? Isn't it all due to the corruption and incompetence of your Communist Party? It's been over sixty years since the founding of the People's Republic! Is the Nationalist KMT Party in power now?"

"According to you," said Little Xi, "China has already entered an age of ascendancy and prosperity. If that's so, why are you still unable to govern the country by the rule of law? Do you believe that China should never have the rule of law? After over sixty years in power, you're still unable to practice good government! The problem is that your Communist Party is fundamentally opposed to real political reform. Every new policy is designed to be a cash cow for your corrupt cadres and officials, on every level. Can one-party dictatorship solve the problem of your Party's own corruption? Just look at your 'second generation rich,' all those children of entrepreneurs, and 'second generation officials,' all those children of the Party elite. They're disgusting. They're all fat cats of crony capitalism!" She folded her arms in rebuke.

"The Chinese Communist Party is completely hypocritical," said Fang Caodi. "They're always lying, hiding the truth, distorting history—you cheat me and I cheat you. It starts with the top leadership and the lower echelons emulate them; even the younger generation has been corrupted. When a nation that used to pride itself on its honesty has become so morally degenerate, how can you talk about prosperity and ascendancy?"

"You've just been talking back and forth about the old ideal of 'enriching the state and strengthening the military,'" Lao Chen chimed in now, "about how to grab resources, how to stimulate economic growth, overtake Japan, and catch up with the United States, but the costs of your economic development have been tremendous. You've ruined the environment and exhausted all the resources of even your grandchildren's generation. Following the Western industrial nations' model of development, sooner or later you'll come to a dead end and be stopped in your tracks."

Fang Caodi had done business in Africa and had seen a very different scene from the one He Dongsheng described. When Chinese enterprises worked on major infrastructure projects, they hired only Chinese workers; they didn't employ local workers and didn't help reduce the high levels of local unemployment. Cheap Chinese products flooded the African market and ruined those few manufacturing industries still in existence there. The Chinese were no different from the former European colonialists. They colluded with corrupt local ruling elites to exploit Africa's natural resources, and they didn't help the African people with any long-lasting economic development that could be of genuine assistance.

"Why is such a powerful nation so weak that it can't accept even the smallest amount of criticism?" asked Little Xi. "Why do you stifle freedom of speech? Look how frightened you are of the Internet—not at all like a great nation."

After Fang Caodi had returned to China, he had traveled all over the minority peoples' regions; because he was particularly looking for traces of his father and the former Xinjiang warlord Sheng Shicai, he went everywhere in North and South Xinjiang. His overall assessment was that the Communist Party's nationalities policy was a total failure. The Han Chinese complained about the injustice of positive discrimination, while the Uighurs and Tibetans felt humiliated and oppressed. The local communist cadres in Xinjiang and Tibet were corrupt to the core and grew rich on the ethnic conflicts. With old hatreds and new complaints, Xinjiang and Tibet would never be at peace. "If China doesn't institute a federal system, there will be dire consequences!" shouted Fang Caodi.

"He Dongsheng," added Lao Chen more calmly, "you're a typical old-style Chinese scholar. You have a head full of ideas about 'ruling the nation and pacifying the world' and you're dying to become an official and a state tutor. When you're close to power, you get all excited, and as soon as you enter the inner circle of power, you immediately support authoritarian dictatorship. You pretty it up with fancy words about needing absolute power to accomplish big things, but in fact you are consumed by a burning personal ambition. Doing something big doesn't necessarily mean doing something good. You can also do something very bad that will have terrible and incalculable consequences for years to come. In the last several decades, there has been no lack of such examples, right?"

He Dongsheng listened with a smile, as if he was lapping up their criticism. "Everything you've said is true," he said, "but all the information you normally have can't possibly compare with the information *I* have access to; the two are completely out of balance. I can tell you several things that are even more terrible and absurd than those things you already know about. A couple of days ago, we had a meeting to discuss what kind of a major catastrophe would arise given the hypothesis that so much mud has eroded off the hillsides along the Three Gorges Dam that it blocks the Yangtze River. Everybody knows that this is going to happen sooner or later—we just don't know which leadership group is going to be so unlucky as to have to clean up the fucking mess. But I'll tell you something for sure: you can't just watch other people do all the heavy lifting while you just reap the benefits. You always have to give up something. Some lousy and irresponsible work will always be done here and there in a big country, but that's the only way it can function. I can tell you another thing straight from the heart: there is no possible way for China to be any better than it is today."

"What do you mean there's no way China could be any better than it is today?" asked Little Xi indignantly. She threw up her hands.

"Doesn't the West believe in God?" asked He Dongsheng, ignoring her. "God created the world and God is completely good. So God could not have deliberately created a bad world, right? But there are many things in the world that are not totally good. Many have struggled with this—the German philosopher Leibniz's theodicy set out to defend God on this score. He proposed that, although the world is indeed not perfect, a better world is an impossibility because God had created the best possible world he could. If God can't even do it, how can China? China's current situation is as good as it can be under the existing circumstances, and it's a practical impossibility to make it better. You cannot just assume that China has Britain's parliamentary tradition, or northern Europe's social democracy, or America's vast land resources . . . China is just China, and history is not a blank page that you can fill in any way you want to; you can't turn back the clock either; you can only start from the present situation. I firmly believe that today's China has already chosen the best option in the real world."

"Voltaire long ago ridiculed Leibniz's philosophy that the world could not improve," said Lao Chen, "in the words of Dr. Pangloss: 'All is for the best in the best of all possible worlds.'"

Fang Caodi wrinkled his brow in confusion.

"Whatever you say," said Little Xi, "you're just defending your one-party dictatorship."

"Well, can you propose a better, more complete, and more feasible option?" asked He Dongsheng.

"Just because I can't do it," answered Little Xi, "doesn't mean that I want to accept your option."

He Dongsheng understood very well all the arguments and charges made by his captors. He knew that everything was due to the double-edged sword that was the Communist Party. Maybe the blame belonged to Lenin and Trotsky for first devising a one-party dictatorship.

"But can the dictatorship's 'Chinese capitalism with socialist characteristics' be replaced by any other system? Or is it already the best option in the world as it really exists?

"One-party dictatorship is indeed incapable of eliminating its own corruption, and one-party dictatorship has to stifle freedom of speech and suppress any and all dissidents. But can China be controlled without a one-party dictatorship? Can any other system feed and clothe one billion, three hundred and fifty million people? Or successfully administer an 'Action Plan for Achieving Prosperity amid Crisis'? Could China rise so fast without the leadership of a one-party dictatorship?" He Dongsheng allowed his words to settle in his captors' ears before continuing.

Some people might think that now that China has risen and its age of prosperity has begun, China can end its one-party dictatorship! The He Dongsheng of twenty years ago might even have thought that. He might have joined the democratic-reform faction within the Party and even supported a Chinese Gorbachev. But now He Dongsheng has absolutely no faith in the Western democratic system. Even more importantly, he knows that since June 1989, the Chinese Communist Party no longer has any ideals. As a party-state regime with a total monopoly of power in China, the Communist Party rules only to preserve its own power. Today He Dongsheng not only has no passion for political reform, but he even cynically believes there should be no such thing, there *must not be* any such reform, because any reform would lead to chaos.

"Just let China maintain the status quo," he said, "and continue to develop smoothly for twenty more years, then we can see about reform. At the most we can institute a few small reforms and gradually move toward good government."

"What would a post–Communist Party democratic China be like?" asked Little Xi.

He Dongsheng had no idea.

"Political reform?" he said with a sneer. "Is it that easy? The result of political reform will not be the federalism that you want, or European-style social democracy, or American-style freedom and constitutional democracy. The result of such a political transition will be a Chinese-style fascist dictatorship made up of a combination of collective nationalism, populism, statism, and Chinese traditionalism."

"Your communist party-state is already fascism," responded Little Xi, raising her voice. "You don't need any transition!"

"Even if we are fascist," He Dongsheng replied calmly, "we are only in the early stages of fascism now. You still haven't tasted the full flavor of violent fascist despotism. From the way you talk, I can see that you lack the imagination to comprehend genuine evil."

At that, the faces of a few Communist Party leaders he knew who harbored true fascist ambitions rose before his mind's eye, and he thought that if any of these men came to power, not only China but the whole world would be in for terrible trouble. He even had a certain sense of mission, a feeling that he must stop such people from coming to power.

He Dongsheng knew for certain that the opponents of the

present leadership group came from both the left and the right, but
the most dangerous threat was from the ultraright. The "Action
Plan for Achieving Prosperity amid Crisis" was a continuation of
the market-economy policies of Reform and Openness, and it had
offended many powerful people and created many enemies. The Old
Left and the New Left both opposed the privatization of agricultural
land; many large state-operated enterprises were unhappy with the
challenge posed by private businesses, where they had long enjoyed
a monopoly; and, finally, abolishing official control and encouraging
competition had decreased the scope for collusion between bureaucrats and businesspeople, as well as the officials' opportunities for
graft. For a Party in which deeply rooted corruption was endemic,
the current leadership's attempt to put into effect a "sunshine
law"—mandating that officials reveal their overall financial worth
in order to uncover the discrepancies between their legal incomes
and their actual wealth—so angered many corrupt officials that
they resolved to work together to overthrow the current party-state
leadership.

Ambitious factions within the Party always looked for the current leadership's weak spots. The two weak spots of this current one
were none other than their alliance with Japan, and their postpone-
ment of border disputes. Anti-Japanese sentiment had widespread
popular appeal that united several generations. Suddenly signing
an oath of brotherhood with the Japanese was quite unacceptable
to many, even though it was in accord with China's core national
interests. It was also easy for joint development of border areas to be
interpreted as a humiliating forfeiture of Chinese sovereignty. The
ambitious faction within the Party knew that all they had to do was
fan the flames of nationalist sentiment and accuse the leadership
of pandering to the foreigners, hinting at surrender, or even trea-

son, and the present leadership group might not be able to hold up. At the very least their reputation with the people would collapse, and when the rest of the world saw the ensuing violent upsurge of Chinese nationalist sentiment, they would also come to believe that China was an expansionist and aggressive new empire. They would be convinced that the "China menace theory" was correct, and they would prepare for mutual hostilities and cease to trust the Chinese government. To see the present leadership group damned from inside and outside the country would be just exactly what that faction had in mind. He Dongsheng feared that if this went on for very long, Chinese popular opinion would be hijacked by the ambitious fascist faction.

He even began to reflect fondly on the now-defunct liberal faction of intellectuals. Without them as a target, all the antiliberal forces—the Old Left and the New Left, the nationalists, populists, traditionalists, and ultraright—directly concentrated all their attacks on the present leadership group. Unfortunately, when the global economy went into decline and China's Age of Prosperity officially began, the liberal faction, accused of being pro-Western, sharply declined, and the market for their ideas dried up. After a period of reflection, most of the members of the liberal faction came to support the present pragmatic authoritarian leadership. They now believed that China could not follow the path of the Western nations, and that the present Chinese model was the best option in the world as it really exists. Those few well-known liberals who stubbornly refused to change their minds were effectively forbidden to voice their opinions—they could not appear in the media, publish, lecture, or teach. There was now only the occasional small fry, like Little Xi—his eyes met hers—who went on the net and carried on a very weak guerrilla resistance.

### Heaven save the Communist Party

This was certainly a long, slow night. As Lao Chen, Little Xi, and Fang Caodi listened to He Dongsheng bombard them with information, their emotions went on a roller-coaster ride; they were totally exhausted, and yawning continuously. Zhang Dou had already dozed off several times, the tiny camera dandling on his knee.

By contrast, the more He Dongsheng talked, the more energized he became. It was as though he had been hosting a one-man marathon talk show, and he didn't have to hold anything back, he could say whatever he wanted. It's great, he thought, to be able to say whatever I want; I haven't felt so happy in a long time. He also realized that he was saying things that he normally could not say, but if he didn't say them today, he would probably be measured for his coffin before he'd ever have another chance to talk like this. He was also fully aware that he had never before drunk Beijing tap water, but today he had downed several glasses and he was bound to have an unusual reaction to it.

He Dongsheng thought of a strange thing that had recently transpired and he just had to talk about it, would not feel right if he didn't.

"I'm going to tell you," he said to his captors, "a state secret. Last month a terrorist organization infiltrated a top-secret state-run chemical plant and tried to blow it up. Luckily our security forces were tipped off in advance and killed them all on the spot. The astonishing thing was that those six terrorists were all members of a fascist cell centered on Beijing—they were all students from the elite Peking and Qinghua universities. After we learned their identities, we kept it a secret and reported that they had died in an automobile accident, but not being given access to their bodies, for a while their parents raised a fuss. I'm telling you all this so you will understand that real fascism already has a firm foothold in China. For these university students to know about this secret chemical factory, they would have to have accomplices in the Party, the government, and the army. And these people have their own agenda; they have not been true Communist Party members or socialists for some time, and only 'fascist' can describe them."

"Was one of the dead students named Wei?" asked Little Xi slowly.

"Wei? No," answered He Dongsheng.

"Are you absolutely certain?" she pressed him.

"You don't need to doubt my memory," said He Dongsheng, "and besides Wei is not a common surname. If there was a Wei, I would definitely remember."

Seeing that Little Xi looked relieved, Lao Chen knew she was thinking of her son, Wei Guo. His heart went out to her.

"How did you come to have advance warning?" Lao Chen asked randomly to change the subject.

"Lao Chen, you shouldn't underestimate our security apparatus," said He Dongsheng. "We have eyes and ears everywhere. In general, wherever people gather, we have informants . . . but then, how the fuck did we miss you three?"

"Why did they want to blow up that chemical factory?" Fang Caodi suddenly asked in all seriousness.

Since he had already told them about the "Prosperity amid Crisis" and the "Ruling the Nation and Pacifying The World" plans, and the nation's grand international strategy, what else was there that He Dongsheng could not talk about?

"Let me put it this way," He Dongsheng said. "At China's present stage of development, the difference between our government and those fascist elements is that we want the people to have a loving and compassionate nature, not a martial spirit. But the fascists want to promote a martial or combative spirit. The chemical manufactured in that factory makes the Chinese people happy and full of love and compassion, and for that reason the fascist elements wanted to destroy it. Do you understand what I'm saying?" He looked directly into Fang Caodi's eyes.

"Is it the chemical factory near Happy Village in the Mount Taihang region of Hebei?" Fang Caodi asked, following a sudden intuition. "The one that has its own airport?"

"You seem very well informed," He Dongsheng said, his eyebrows raised. "It seems that there's been a leak in our security system."

"What does that chemical factory make that causes the people to feel happy?" asked Fang Caodi, pressing his line of inquiry. "Professor He, you agreed that you would answer whatever question we asked."

"There's no harm in telling you," said He Dongsheng, "and anyway, I don't think it's a bad thing. If you have never heard of MDMA, surely you have heard of Ecstasy. We manufacture 'generation N' of MDMA. It's mild, nonaddictive, and has no bad side effects. After you take it, you feel really great, you feel like the world is full of love, you want to hug other people and tell them everything, but you're clearheaded and don't have any hallucinations, just like I am now."

"What do you want such a big factory to make Ecstasy tablets for?" asked Fang Caodi, looking puzzled.

"It's not making tablets," explained He Dongsheng as though Fang Caodi should know, "there aren't any tablets at all, and it's not to sell Ecstasy to other countries. China is a big country, we're not North Korea, so don't get the wrong idea. We're merely producing this chemical for our own use."

"Just as in Aldous Huxley's novel *Brave New World?*" interjected Lao Chen, happy to contribute a literary reference.

"I know what you're trying to say," said He Dongsheng a little defensively, "but we were not at all influenced by him. We have an Office of Stability Maintenance staffed by specialist scholars who conduct research on ancient and modern techniques for maintaining stability both inside and outside China. One of the scholars was working on British materials. You know that young people in Western countries like to drink and party wildly on New Year's Eve, and when they get drunk they often cause trouble. Just look at their soccer games—the British fans are very unruly. For the last few years of the twentieth century, though, when Ecstasy became popular, New Year's Eve violence suddenly decreased. It turned out that after those British youths took Ecstasy, they just wanted to dance around bobbing their heads, to listen to music, embrace each other, love everybody, and pour out their hearts to everybody around them. This is the effect MDMA or Ecstasy has on people, and it's very different from the effects of alcohol or other hallucinatory drugs. Alcohol messes up people's minds, and releases their animal instincts. Psychedelic drugs cause hallucinations and interfere with normal social communication. Our Office of Stability Maintenance had the Harbin Institute of Technology make up some pure samples of MDMA. At first they didn't know what it would be good for; they just wanted to experiment.

"Then, when the Politburo was studying the 'Action Plan for Achieving Prosperity amid Crisis,' one of the standing members was worried that the crackdown was going to make the people depressed and passive. That would have a negative impact on the people's enthusiasm just when we were trying to implement the second set of our new economic-reform policies. He wondered if there wasn't some substance that would make people feel good and positive, but without any violent tendencies that would disrupt our harmonious society. There was a spokesman from the Ministry of Public Security at the meeting who had trained at Harvard's Kennedy School of Government. He had been studying the American drug problem, and he jokingly said that we could have that sort of effect on society only if everyone in China took methylene-dioxy-methamphetamine, or MDMA—Ecstasy.

"That's how it started and the more we discussed it, the more we thought it might just work. One standing member said he'd never imagined there was anything like it in the world. The chief ingredient for the manufacture of MDMA Ecstasy is sassafras oil, or safrole. You know what country produces the most safrole in the world? China. What a perfect coincidence." He Dongsheng would have slapped his thighs, but his hands were still tied up. "Both Western and Chinese researchers have found that ingesting a small amount of MDMA is not harmful to human health, and they have not discovered any dangerous long-term side effects either. Since we could use it to make everyone in the country happy and thus improve our national stability, why shouldn't we do it?

"Didn't I say ours is a government that can accomplish big things? Once we said we'd do it, we did it. We built a well-managed high-spec factory in Hebei to turn out a product of scientifically guaranteed quality. Then we added MDMA to all our drinking-water reservoirs and to cow's milk, soya milk, fizzy drinks, fruit juice, bottled water, beer, and rice wine. Except for some very isolated areas, we covered over ninety-nine percent of the urban population, and over seventy percent of the rural population. Everyone drank such a small amount that it was totally undetectable in a standard urine test. People would never know they drank it, and it would only make them experience a mild euphoria. This was only a small supplementary program in support of our economic-reform project. The real success of our 'Action Plan for Achieving Prosperity amid Crisis' was due to the correctness of our overall grand strategy."

As the others listened to He Dongsheng, they broke out in a cold sweat.

"No wonder we've all been feeling a small-small high!" exclaimed Lao Chen in a burst of relieved enlightenment.

"Exactly," said Fang Caodi, "over ninety-nine percent of people in the cities are high all day, every day!"

"How could you do this to the people without letting them know?" asked Little Xi a little disingenuously.

"Almost everything the Communist Party does, it does without informing the people," replied He Dongsheng. "It's always been that way. Many other countries put chemicals in their drinking water. In Hong Kong they put fluoride in the water to prevent tooth decay. It's all for the people's own good."

"Your policy," said Little Xi, "is designed only to keep the people ignorant so they won't complain and just let you get away with everything."

"That was precisely our goal."

"Once you'd achieved your goal," asked Lao Chen, "why didn't you stop?"

"With things going so well, why would we stop? What's wrong with having the whole population happy and maintaining a harmonious society? China today has the highest happiness index in the world. Religious believers are rapidly increasing while domestic violence and the suicide rate for rural women are noticeably declining . . . What's wrong with all that? And besides, we really don't dare to stop now. If we do, the people might grow unhappy. Some foreigners who've lived in China for a long time begin to feel very strange when they go home. They don't feel as happy as they did in China, and they always want to come back. We have a great many international friends like them! When other foreigners criticize China, they stand up and defend us, telling their compatriots that if they went to live in China for a while, they'd see that the Chinese people are the happiest in the world."

"Not everyone has the same reaction," said Fang Caodi. "There are four of us here who have never been controlled by your drugged water."

"I'm telling you," said He Dongsheng, "this is a good drug, but it's only a minor drug. There's no way it can control people. It just changes their feelings a bit. Whatever the people have to do, they can still do it. Our follow-up studies indicate that over ninety-nine percent of people have the same positive reaction, but perhaps there is an extremely small number of people who for some reason or another don't have any reaction. It's good enough that the great majority feel happy, because any minority will have their emotions influenced by the majority. Of course, there are some exceptions among the exceptions. I can see that you all belong to the extremely small minority made up of an extremely small number of people who remain unhappy. Just like me! I deliberately don't drink our Chinese water or other beverages, just to experience what it feels like to see everybody else high when I'm sober. But today I 'fell off the wagon,' as the Americans say. The effect is best the first time. Just look how much I talked after I drank a couple of glasses of your tap water. I've talked so much . . . including telling you all sorts of things I never should have."

"When did you start putting Ecstasy in the water?" the hitherto silent Zhang Dou suddenly asked. "Exactly what day was it?"

"The exact day is very clear," answered He Dongsheng, beginning to cough. "It was the last day of the three-week crackdown. On that day, the water works of all first-, second-, and third-level cities and all provincial cities put it in the drinking water at the same time. That was because we were going to officially announce the start of China's Age of Ascendancy the next day and we had to properly calibrate the people's emotions."

"I'll kill you, you bastard!" shouted Zhang Dou. He sprang onto He Dongsheng and pressed He's feeble body down into the chair with the full weight of his hulking frame. "I'll kill you, you bastard!"

The others frantically tried to pull him off, but Zhang Dou was too strong and they couldn't restrain him.

"Zhang Dou, let him go! Are you mad?" the three of them shouted.

He Dongsheng was making choking noises. His face had gone a deep red.

"He hurt Miaomiao! He's the bastard who poisoned Miaomiao!" shouted Zhang Dou with his hands closing around He Dongsheng's throat. It looked like he was going to choke He Dongsheng to death right there in front of them.

Suddenly Miaomiao gave a big scream. Zhang Dou loosened his grip on He Dongsheng and turned to look at her. Miaomiao was standing in the doorway with a plate of cookies in her hand; she was glaring at Zhang Dou. Zhang Dou climbed off gingerly.

He had almost murdered their hostage, and the other three were very shaken. He Dongsheng, rescued from the grip of death, still had not caught his breath and was struggling to speak.

"He's the one who poisoned Miaomiao," repeated Zhang Dou. "Miaomiao started to act strange, like she was sick, the day the crackdown ended, and it was all because they put that shit in the water."

"You're mad! You're all stark raving mad! You . . ." gasped He Dongsheng hoarsely. For a moment he thought he'd just dare them to kill him and get it over with, but his logic took hold and he decided that daring these kidnappers to do such a thing might not be in his best interests.

Lao Chen was still the most cool-headed. He approached He Dongsheng with a glass of water, but He Dongsheng looked away. "I'll untie you so you can drink some water, okay?" Lao Chen said gently.

He Dongsheng was somewhat moved. Lao Chen loosened the rope. "What just happened was unplanned," he said, "whether you believe it or not. The roosters are just about to crow and then it'll be light. Your long dark night is about over. Just be patient a little while longer, all right? Do you have any more questions to ask?" Lao Chen addressed the other three while he helped pour water into He Dongsheng's dry throat.

"Yes. I almost forgot," said Fang Caodi. "That lost month. Or, strictly speaking, that lost twenty-eight days. Professor He, the one week of anarchy and the three-week crackdown that you just told us about—except for the three of us and you, everyone I've asked about it doesn't remember that time. Lao Chen, you don't remember either, do you?"

"I really don't have any memory at all," answered Lao Chen.

He Dongsheng started to laugh—a sort of gurgling from his throat—it was still hard for him to talk. "I'd like another glass of water," he said as he swallowed to clear his throat.

"Professor He," pressed Fang Caodi, "can you explain it to us? That year when everyone was given a bird flu vaccination. It was really a drug created by the Office of Stability Maintenance to make us all forget, right?"

"No, it wasn't," corrected He Dongsheng. "The bird flu vaccination was to prevent bird flu, and only ten or twenty million people were actually vaccinated. Where would the Office of Stability Maintenance find such an amazing amnesiac drug? It would be wonderful if we did have one. Then our Communist Party could rewrite its history any way it wanted to."

"Then what was the real reason why everyone forgot?" asked Fang Caodi.

"Was it the Ecstasy in the water?" asked Little Xi.

"How should I know?" He Dongsheng began to laugh again, a genuine, mirthful laugh. "If you ask me for the real reason, I can only tell you that I haven't a clue! Don't think we can control everything. Many things happen that are beyond our expectations. We never dreamed that the month you're talking about would just disappear from people's memories."

"If you don't know, then who does?" asked Fang Caodi. "Don't try to keep anything from us . . ."

"I'm not trying to hide anything. Let me tell you everything I know. After the 'Action Plan for Achieving Prosperity amid Crisis' began to meet with some success, the first sentence in a *People's Daily* editorial was 'Since the global economy has entered a period of crisis, China's Golden Age of Ascendancy has officially begun . . .' It was only editorial rhetoric to put these two events together in the same sentence. After that, the sentence was picked up. It ricocheted across the media until everybody could recite it by heart.

"At that time, the Central Propaganda Bureau issued another report that mention of the intervening twenty-eight days was dwindling, even on the Internet. We thought people couldn't stand to remember those hard times, and everyone was too busy making and spending money.

"This was very good for the Party. Anarchy and suppression are not exactly splendid states—they're bloody affairs, even sinful, if you're a religious person. So the Propaganda Bureau took advantage of the situation and forbade all news media, including the Internet, from discussing those twenty-eight days. You know China's Internet-control techniques are the best in the world, and of course the traditional media wouldn't dare disobey our orders. Besides that, after China's prosperity and ascendancy began, everybody lost interest in the West. Now the Chinese people prefer to watch our own colorful media, and only a tiny minority still watch non-Chinese media sources. In this way those already rarely discussed twenty-eight days completely disappeared from our public discourse.

"And then something unimaginable happened that to this day I still cannot fathom: more and more people genuinely forgot those twenty-eight days, and it was not just temporary memory loss, but they absolutely could not remember that time, just as though the whole country had unconsciously erased some painful childhood trauma.

"People in middle age and above had not really forgotten the earlier Cultural Revolution and June 4, 1989. It was just that during these two years of China's ascendancy, everybody was living very well and very few people had any interest in recalling the Cultural Revolution and June 1989, so those memories just naturally faded away.

"But people were *really* unable to remember those twenty-eight days. Whether this was related to the water or not, I can't say for sure. The leaders living in Zhongnanhai have their own drinking water. We don't drink what the rest of the people drink, although there might have been a few of us without sufficient self-discipline who went around drinking ordinary water, I can't say for certain. What I can tell you is that most of the leaders in Zhongnanhai can definitely recall those twenty-eight days, and they are also fully aware that the whole nation is suffering from a form of both collective and selective amnesia.

"When I first realized what was happening, I went around sounding out various groups, including mid- and low-level cadres and specialist scholars. Just as I expected, they really had no recollection of that time; it was like they had brainwashed themselves. It was all so strange, but it was definitely true.

"It was for the best that they didn't remember. The previous leadership group, having the blood of those twenty-eight days on their hands, was very eager for everyone to forget the events of that month. So they started to revise any materials that reported on that time. For example, they ordered that all newspapers in all public libraries should be in digital form only. We totally rewrote the history of those twenty-eight days. Most importantly, we brought the date that China's ascendancy officially began forward to match the date that the global economy entered the period of crisis and stagflation, thus erasing the historical existence of that week of anarchy and those three weeks of harsh crackdown. No one objected to this distortion of reality, and practically no one even noticed it. Once in a while, when someone in or outside the country mentioned those events, we simply filtered them out. Very soon the new version of things became the only available version. To tell you the truth, even I was pretty surprised: how could the Chinese people so easily forget such events?

"What I want to tell you is that, definitely, the Central Propaganda organs did do their work, but they were only pushing along a boat that was already on the move. If the Chinese people themselves

had not already wanted to forget, we could not have forced them to
do so. The Chinese people voluntarily gave themselves a large dose
of amnesia medicine."

"Why?" asked Little Xi and Fang Caodi together. "Why did the
Chinese people do it? How could they? There must be some explanation."

"Didn't I tell you already," insisted He Dongsheng. "I don't
know!"

Little Xi and Fang Caodi were dumbfounded.

"I'm quite puzzled, too," added He Dongsheng, seeing that they
were all speechless. "Real life isn't like a detective novel, and everything doesn't have a perfect explanation. I have to admit this is one
big riddle that I can't solve. It could be that human beings are simply forgetful animals and they long to forget some aspects of their
history. It could be that the Chinese Communist Party is just plain
lucky. It could be that the Chinese people deserve to be governed
by the Communist Party, and sixty-plus years is still not enough.
It could be a miracle, or the Chinese people's common karma. Too
bad I'm a materialist, otherwise I would certainly say that it was the
Will of Heaven, that Heaven wants the Chinese Communist Party
to go on governing. Heaven saved my Party!" He gave another deep
laugh.

Little Xi and Fang Caodi sat there expressionless and depressed.
He Dongsheng looked victorious. Lao Chen sat there staring blankly
at nothing. After a long while he regained his composure and saw
that it was already growing light outside.

"Brother Dongsheng, let me remind you again that we have all
made a 'live or die together' pact. No one is going to reveal anything
that was said here last night. That way we can continue living our
ordinary lives and you can continue living your official-promotion-

and-money-spinning life. You think it over carefully. People, if there's nothing else, I'll let Mr. He go home."

The others remained silent, so Lao Chen gently addressed their captive. "You can go now."

He Dongsheng hesitated for a moment, rose, felt his arms up and down, and walked slowly to the door. Then he turned around and said by way of justification, "You think I care about official promotion and making money? I do what I do for the sake of the nation and the people."

They all looked at him expressionlessly.

"Believe it or not, as you wish," added He Dongsheng serenely, and then he walked out the door. A few moments later, they heard his SUV drive away.

Lao Chen, Little Xi, and Fang Caodi sat there in silence.

They walked slowly outside into the dawn light.

"I'd better go," said Fang Caodi.

"Fine," said Lao Chen.

"Can I give you a lift into town?" asked Fang Caodi.

"No, thanks," said Lao Chen. "It's light now. Little Xi and I will go and catch a bus. You'd better get going."

Fang Caodi gave each one of them a hug, said his good-byes, climbed into his Jeep Cherokee, and drove off.

"Master Chen," asked Zhang Dou, "are we going to be in any trouble?"

"I guess it's a fifty-fifty chance," said Lao Chen.

Zhang Dou nodded.

"Take good care of Miaomiao," said Little Xi.

The three of them hugged for a long time and said good-bye.

"I have some friends on the Yunnan border," Lao Chen said to Little Xi, "who have never had that small-small high feeling. Shall we go and visit them?"

"If it's no trouble," Little Xi answered after a moment's thought, "I'd like to bring my mother, too."

"No trouble at all," said Lao Chen with a smile.

The eastern sky was bright, and the two of them shaded their eyes as they walked arm in arm into the harsh light of day.

*The Fat Years* is a unique combination of a mystery novel with a realistic exposé of the political, economic, and social system of China as it is today, and will be for the foreseeable future.

The novel posits a mystery while at the same time offering a social and political critique of the nation in which the mystery takes place. We don't learn how the mystery came about or why until very near the end. In the meantime, there are several related questions: what happened during a spell of exactly twenty-eight days in the spring of 2011 when the government carried out one of the Chinese Communist Party's periodic violent crackdowns? Why are most Chinese people unable to remember the violence and the economic panic of this crackdown? Or, in fact, any of the other even more violent episodes in the sixty-plus-year history of Chinese Communist Party rule?

Some of the story may initially seem to follow a familiar theme: two people suddenly meet again, some twenty years after a period when they were spending a great deal of time together, which for them was in the liberal days of the mid- to late 1980s. At that time the male protagonist, Lao Chen, had been attracted to Little Xi, but nothing ever really happened between them. When he meets her again, he is once more intrigued by her, but she doesn't trust anyone who trusts the party-state regime. Chen's pursuit of Little Xi leads us through both the very significant underground Christian movement and a land-rights protection campaign that demonstrates the flexibility of local Party officials.

The realistic exposé, with only one or two exaggerations, reveals the Chinese Communist party-state control system, and the Chinese Communist Party's plans to replace the United States as the most dominant superpower in the world.

The original title of the book could be literally translated as "China in the Ascendant," and the novel is indeed primarily concerned with that subject. The main theme is that China is yet another "rough beast, its hour come round at last," and what that may mean for the world and the Chinese people. This theme is in basic agreement with recent works of nonfiction, and also dovetails with many proposals by young ultranationalist Chinese and high officers in the Chinese armed forces who champion what can only be labeled as fascist ideas. It also reflects several recent warnings by old retired Party leaders who fear these ultranationalists and how they want China to develop.

Unlike a work of nonfiction, however edifying, *The Fat Years* gives you a full taste of what it feels like to be one of the characters living in the "counterfeit paradise" that is China today. In its original form it was circulated throughout China among concerned Chinese intellectuals, students, and so on, jumping the Great Firewall of censorship. Probably many high-ranking Chinese Communist Party officials have read it. The Chinese scholars who sent the novel to my wife, and many other Chinese intellectuals we've talked to, have all said that this book is "the best description of the way they live today." I believe it is destined to become a classic in China in the *Brave New World* rather than the *1984* tradition. Less futuristic than *Brave New World,* the book is still prophetic and will long be relevant to our understanding of a modern dictatorship of the kind that exists in China today.

In the realism of the novel's character depictions, we meet a very wide spectrum of almost all the elements of China's three hundred to four hundred million urban population. They include ultranationalist wannabe fascist students, professors, and Party officials (Wei Guo, Professors X, Y, & Z); "ordinary" professors, members of the Chinese Academy of Social Sciences (CASS), who conduct "ordinary" research (Hu Yan); well-heeled real estate moguls (Jian Lin) and high-ranking officials in the party-state apparatus to whom they are firmly tied by interest and blood relationships (He Dongsheng); editors, writers, and media types (Zhuang Zizhong and unnamed *Reading Journal* contributors); sons and daughters of "Red Aristocrats"—longtime loyal Party families—who serve the party-state's interests at home and around the world (Ban Cuntou, Wen Lan); young people of the lumpen proletariat, some of them escapees from slave-labor camps (Zhang Dou); other young professionals who have dropped out of the state-controlled media (Miaomiao); leaders and their followers in the rapidly growing underground Christian movement (Gao Shengchan and Li Tiejun); young and old netizens who argue for and against ultranationalism and government policies; foreigners who like Lao Chen have opted to live the good life in a communist dictatorship because it is a good life for them and it does not frighten them; high-priced female escorts and drug addicts who work in places with names like the Paradise Club, catering to the newly rich, the Party powerful, and foreigners (Dong Niang and her boyfriend); youthful dissidents who protested and then escaped abroad or went silent after the Tiananmen Massacre (Shi Ping); and, finally, professional dissidents like Little Xi who refuse to accept the party-state's version of past, present,

and future reality; she is joined by the older, more experienced peri-
patetic cook and small-time entrepreneur Fang Caodi, and Zhang
Dou, the young escapee from slave labor.

A number of groups are, however, missing from *The Fat Years*.
From the urban population, these are the many professors, lawyers,
and other professionals who are actively working to change the dictatorship. Also missing are the urban working class and peasant
workers (migrant laborers) who toil in the harsh working conditions
of mostly foreign-owned factories (owned by American, Taiwanese,
Japanese, and Hong Kong consortia), and who by 2010 acquired the
unfortunate habit of committing suicide as a way out of their misery.
Missing also are the other eight hundred to nine hundred million
Chinese who live in rural China. Although, as the fictional CASS
scholar Hu Yan says, their aggregate income has indeed increased
in the last thirty-two years, they are certainly not enjoying the "fat
years" that some, but not all, Chinese urbanites enjoy. Missing,
too, except for Wei Guo's ineffectual fascist cell, are any detailed
descriptions of the special People's Armed Police, the military,
and the thugs who maintain the party-state's stability by routinely
harassing anyone who balks at having his or her house demolished,
or farmland stolen as part of party-state real estate deals, or who
calls for any sort of liberal democratic reforms, including genuine
implementation of the existing constitution of the People's Republic
of China.

Many people interpret the China of this novel as a dystopia, but
I do not believe it presents China as a dystopia. Dystopia is thought
of as "an imagined place or state in which everything is unpleasant
or bad, typically a totalitarian or environmentally degraded one, the
opposite of utopia." That is an accurate description of the state presented in Orwell's classic dystopian novel *1984* that was modeled on

Stalinist Russia. It would also describe China under Mao Zedong, especially from the Great Leap Forward to the Cultural Revolution, 1956 to 1976. The former occasioned the greatest man-made famine ever in world history in which some forty-five million people perished, and totally destroyed almost every aspect of China's social, cultural, economic, and environmental infrastructure; the latter did more or less the same, except for the famine; fatalities in the Cultural Revolution were usually the result of intellectuals and teachers being beaten to death by young Red Guards, suicide, murder, or civil warfare.

China today and for the foreseeable future is not a dystopia, nor is it a utopia; it's not even trying to be a utopia. It is a Leviathan-like Leninist party-state that is, by the Chinese Communist Party's standards, a great success, a putatively "harmonious society" that aims to give everyone a "moderately decent standard of living." Some people call it a fascist state, but if it is, it is a truly successful fascist state. A fascist state, however, has to have an ardent ideology and a Great Leader, but China today has neither. The semifascist ultranationalists, like Wei Guo in the novel, are a minority, and their passion does not extend to the nine men of the Politburo Standing Committee who actually govern China—Party Central, represented in the novel by one of its secretaries, He Dongsheng.

China is a party-state in which the Communist Party is both the state and the government and controls every institution in the society. Since 1979, the Chinese Communist Party has achieved tremendous economic successes by abandoning any residual socialist or communist ideals, and by becoming the director of a capitalist economy without the rule of law, a capitalist society claiming to be a dictatorship of the proletariat that rules for the people and in their interests. With the Communist Party at the center of everything, this modern Leviathan works by attracting direct foreign investment, selling to foreign consumers, and buying off most of the professional urban class, and many of the peasants, while brutally suppressing any dissent and treating the entire population as a "reserve army" that labors for the benefit of the Communist Party and its party-state apparatus.

The Party leaders have no dream of utopia, only a dream of amassing more wealth and power for themselves and their dependents while suppressing all malcontents in the name of national stability. In this, they still resemble O'Brien's Party mentioned in Professor Lovell's Preface. In a recent interview, CASS professor Yu Jianrong, an outspoken advocate of individual rights, makes an interesting comparison between the "stability" of Taiwan and that of China. His comments on the two different kinds of "stability" are that, in his view, "when judging stability in Taiwan the criterion" is "whether or not the situation will influence the stability of the law," while the standard for judging stability on the mainland is mainly "whether or not the situation will influence the stability of the Chinese Communist Party regime . . . In order to consolidate its regime, the Chinese Communist Party views every action that might remove their pressure on the people to be a destabilizing element . . . In order to eliminate all the destabilizing elements, the Chinese Communist Party then continuously practices suppression, i.e., takes suppression for stability . . . I believe that the core belief of the Chinese Communist Party is not economic development. There is only one goal of everything it does: the exclusiveness of its political power. Without realizing this, one cannot really understand the Chinese Communist Party . . . It has long since become a party without belief, a party of pragmatism. The only thing that will influence it is the pressure of reality."

The only vision the Chinese Communist Party has is the overall vision of coming world hegemony, related in *The Fat Years* through He Dongsheng's lengthy monologue. Some readers may regard this as a tedious "soap box monologue" lacking in drama, but they would be mistaken. Most liberal ethnic-Chinese scholars living in China and abroad regard the last section of the work as very dramatic and the most important part of the book. Important both in He Dongsheng's manner of delivery, and in the content of his monologue.

The way He Dongsheng talks to, or rather lectures at, his kidnappers is exactly the way the Party leadership talks to the 1.3 billion Chinese. It is how "President" Hu Jintao addresses the ordinary people, while Premier Wen Jiabao seems to have tried to imitate the so-called populism of Mao's behind-the-scenes hatchet man Zhou Enlai (a performance that has been criticized by the dissident Yu Jie, in a book published this year in Hong Kong). Several Chinese intellectuals and reporters from the popular liberal paper *Southern Weekly* (itself mentioned in the novel) who visited Taiwan in November 2010 witnessed the way President Ma Ying-jeou interacted with the ordinary people and with other officials. Then they publicly lamented the fact that no dialogue of that sort could possibly take place in the People's Republic.

Reality has already caught up with He Dongsheng's monologue, and many of the plans he describes have already been fulfilled, especially China's buying up of much of the world's natural resources to fuel its economic behemoth. Everything else, except for the genuine fantasy of an alliance with Japan, is in preparation or in progress. All these plans are intended to fulfill the goals of a China that its leaders and many of its people believe is in ascendance and destined to become the main power in the world.

This idea that the U.S.-led West is suffering an unstoppable decline while China is enjoying an unstoppable rise is why in 2010 Chinese foreign policy became exceedingly aggressive and, as a

result, China antagonized much of the world and drove all its neighbors either to increase their defense budgets or seek a rapprochement
with the United States for protection. As political commentator Ste-
phen Hill points out, "Beyond economic and ecological indicators,
the hallmark of a great power is when other nations want to emulate
you . . . But no one is banging down doors to get into China, and only
the poorest countries aim to be like the People's Republic." Some
nonpolitical Chinese scholars do return to China to work, even after
obtaining their getaway pass in the form of permanent residency or
citizenship in the United States or some other democratic country;
while most of the poor nations that want to follow the Beijing model
of development are ruled by unscrupulous dictators out for the main
chance.

Further evidence of the realism and relevance of this novel has
just appeared. As I write these pages, two autocratic regimes have
fallen in the Middle East due to popular protests, and some others
are in danger of falling. The reaction of the Chinese Communist
party-state was to mandate a ban on independent media reports
on the Middle East and on any local disturbances; the government
called for increased control of the Internet, cell phone messages,
Twitter, and microblogs, and made preparations for a complete
Internet shutdown; it also stepped up police detention and harass-
ment of all known democracy advocates. This is all of a piece with
their treatment of Nobel Peace Prize winner Liu Xiaobo, whose
wife is presently under house arrest.

In *The Fat Years*, even those chic intellectuals like Lao Chen
may become uneasy about China's potential to become frightening
in the future; all they can do about their unease, however, is what
the 2000 Nobel Prize–winning novelist Gao Xingjian advised—
escape. The reality of geopolitics demonstrates that it will probably
be a long time before He Dongsheng and the Chinese Communist

Party's dream of Chinese world hegemony is fulfilled, if ever. But the question remains: would this hegemony be the free, just, and civilized power that so many of its concerned citizens hope for? In the meantime, *The Fat Years* provides the most interesting and enlightening way for us to understand both the possible future of China and what it is like for many urban Chinese to live in the belly of the Chinese Leviathan.

I would like to thank Josephine Chiu-Duke for her thoughtful suggestions concerning the interpretation of this novel and for considerable help with the translation.

MICHAEL DUKE, FEBRUARY 2011

8    *Master Chen:* The literal translation would be "Teacher Chen," but this is not a recognized form of address in English.

10    *The sweet smell of books in a literary society:* A common Chinese saying, as in "a whiff of refinement."

20    *Deng Xiaoping's 1992 southern tour:* After Deng Xiaoping formally retired, he still remained in power. His "reform" policies were threatened after the 1989 Tiananmen Massacre, so in 1992 Deng took a long tour through southern China and made several speeches announcing his continued support for economic reforms. At this time he may or may not have said "to get rich is glorious." Deng's reforms continued under the new leader, Jiang Zemin.

23    *Ji Xianlin said the twenty-first century is the Chinese century:* Ji Xianlin (1911–2009) was a celebrated Chinese linguist and Indologist.

26    *This year is the year of my zodiac sign, and a lot of strange things are bound to happen:* The Chinese believe that the year of a person's zodiac sign, coming once every twelve years, is unlucky, and so one has to be very careful throughout that year.

27    *They treat the Taiwanese like their little brothers:* China's party-state government has long regarded Taiwan as a renegade province, and the 85 percent of Taiwanese on the island (as opposed to 15 percent of mainlanders) are considered of lower status than mainlanders.

27    *The Tiu Keng Leng refugee camp:* Also known as Rennie's Mill, this was a special settlement created by the Hong Kong government for Nationalist (Kuomintang) soldiers and supporters after they lost the Chinese civil war in 1949.

28    *Chen Yingzhen:* A Taiwanese leftist writer and political activist (b. 1936) who spent several years in prison in the late 1960s and early 1970s.

30    *ethnic conflict was growing increasingly acrimonious:* This is a reference to the feuds between the Taiwanese and the mainlanders. Chen Shuibian, president of Taiwan from 2000 to 2008, pressed for independence for the island, causing fears that the Chinese would invade.

34    *I loved to watch those post-1949 Chinese films:* All the films from 1949 to the 1980s were Communist propaganda for any campaign that was running at the time. They are now known as part of China's "Red Legacy."

35    *The Three Years Natural Disaster:* A Chinese Communist euphemism for the greatest famine in world history, which resulted from Mao Zedong's Great Leap Forward policies and led to the death of some 45 million Chinese.

40    *Politburo:* The Chinese Communist Party is organized on the Leninist model created in the old Soviet Union. The twenty-five-member Politburo, short for Political Bureau, is its second-highest organization. Only the nine members of the Politburo Standing Committee have more power. Both groups are announced at Party congresses held at least every five years (cf. *three Party Congresses,* following note). For details, see Richard McGregor, *The Party: The Secret World of China's Communist Rulers,* Harper, 2010.

40    *three Party Congresses:* A Communist Party congress is held every five years. The next congress is due in 2012. At these congresses, the new top level of leadership (the Politburo, Politburo Standing Committee [nine members who are the heart of Chinese rule], president and premier) is presented to the nation, having been chosen in secret by the outgoing leadership in fierce factional infighting.

40    *Party Secretariat:* The Secretariat of the Communist Party of China Central Committee is the CCP's permanent bureaucracy. There are

several secretaries and they manage the work of the Politburo and its Standing Committee.

42 *feichengwuraook:* A genuine URL, but actually a phishing site designed to harm your computer.

44 *monsters and demons:* A phrase made popular by Mao Zedong to attack specialists, scholars, and other so-called class enemies during the Cultural Revolution. On June 1, 1966, the *People's Daily* published an editorial entitled "Sweep Away All Monsters and Demons." Soon after, the Red Guards went on the rampage for victims.

44 *1983 crackdown:* During the Anti-Spiritual Pollution Campaign in late 1983 to early 1984, some factions of the Chinese Communist Party tried to stamp out the influence of Western liberal ideas and cultural practices coming into China due to the "Reforms and Openness" policies that began in 1979. It was a short-lived and largely ineffective campaign, but it did involve many public executions, often of young people, in Shanghai and other cities.

45 *the trial of the Gang of Four:* The name given to a powerful radical leftist faction of the Chinese Communist Party during the Cultural Revolution. They included Jiang Qing, Mao Zedong's wife, and Zhang Chunqiao, Yao Wenyuan, and Wang Hongwen. They were imprisoned shortly after Mao's death in 1976 and given a show trial in 1981 that resulted in prison sentences ranging from twenty years to life, and a death sentence for Jiang Qing that was commuted to life. Jiang Qing was famously defiant at the trial, claiming with considerable correctness that she was only carrying out Chairman Mao's orders. She committed suicide in 1991. For details, see Roderick MacFarquhar and Michael Schoenhals, *Mao's Last Revolution*, Harvard Belknap Press, 2006.

45 *Rightist status:* Under Mao Zedong's rule in China, Communist Party members who disagreed with Mao's policies were frequently branded as Rightists. Some seven hundred thousand or more people were so labeled during the Anti-Rightist Campaign in the late 1950s because they disagreed with the collectivization movement later known as the Great Leap Forward that led to Mao's great famine. Deng Xiaoping played a prominent role in carrying out this persecution. In the 1980s, these people began to be rehabilitated, many of them posthumously.

46    *Public Security Bureau:* The PSB is the main arm of the Chinese police; they operate under the Ministry of Public Security. China also has a very powerful People's Armed Police Force, a uniformed paramilitary group that is in charge of internal security, crowd control, crackdowns, etc. Many ad hoc groups of mercenaries, sometimes referred to as thugs, also perform similar duties in local areas.

52    *Reforms and Openness:* The current reform era in China began in 1979 under the leadership of Deng Xiaoping. Known in China as "Reforms and Openness," it refers to the policy of reforming China's economy into a putatively market economy, so-called "market socialism" or "capitalism with Chinese characteristics," and opening up to the world to allow an influx of foreign investment and cultural influences.

54    *I present the strict facts and employ reasoned arguments, and I argue exclusively from the point of view of the Constitution of the People's Republic of China. This infuriates them, and they all attack me:* This summarizes the activities, and their consequences for him, of the 2010 Nobel Peace Prize recipient Liu Xiaobo, who was sentenced to thirteen years in prison for more or less the same things Little Xi does in this novel, only in concert with others and at a more intellectual level.

56    *It was then that I was abducted at the railway station and taken to do slave labor in an illegal brick kiln in Shanxi Province:* This part of Zhang Dou's story is based on the 2007 Chinese slave-labor scandal, also known as the Shanxi Black Brick Kiln Incident, in which it was revealed that thousands of Chinese, children included, had been forced to work in illegal brick kilns, where they were tortured. Local Party officials were complicit in this activity.

57    *"harmonized" off the net by the Web police:* A reference to Hu Jintao's idea that China is a "harmonious society." It has become a verb with a satirical meaning—as here, to suppress—on the Internet.

64    *the SS Study Group:* "SS" has obvious Nazi overtones for English readers, and Wei Guo's group certainly has fascist tendencies of the kind many older Chinese establishment intellectuals warned against in 2010. "SS" probably stands for Carl Schmitt and Leo Strauss, two Western thinkers from whom youthful ultranationalists derive antiliberal and statist ideas.

65    *state tutors:* An archaic term from the days of imperial rule, referring to the emperor's tutors. Here it is used ironically to indicate the similarities between Chinese Communist Party rule and imperial rule.

67    *the New Whampoa Academy:* Whampoa, or Huangpu, is a district in Guangzhou where the Nationalist Party (KMT/Kuomintang) and Chinese Communist Party (CCP) military officers were trained from June 1924 to 1928, before the academy was shifted to Nanjing.

68    *politics is the art of distinguishing between the enemy and ourselves:* In Mao Zedong's 1957 speech "On the Correct Handling of Contradictions Among the People," Mao distinguished between two social contradictions: "between the enemy and us" and "among the people." This kind of Maoist thought is still part of the Chinese Communist Party's thought and practice.

68    *the politics of the ancient Confucian Gongyang School:* The *Gongyang Zhuan* places particular emphasis on the thinking of respected rulers of the period, promoting the "One Great Unity" and "Bringing Order out of Chaos" points of view. To criticize this school of ancient thought could be seen as criticizing the Communist Party dictatorship.

69    *appreciated by the government:* in Chinese, *guojia* means either "the nation," "the state," or "the government." China is a Communist Party state in which the Communist Party is both the government and the state.

71    *we must identify our enemies and let our hatred rise against them:* This way of thinking fits in with China's increasingly aggressive posture, for example, in claiming the South China Sea as their "core interest" and initiating conflict with Japan (September 2010) over the Senkaku islands. This mind-set resembles that of Hitler's Germany from 1933 to 1945—with Hitler's goon squads and stormtroopers—and Japan's ultranationalist *bushido* spirit from the 1930s to 1945.

73    *PS: The "SS" in the SS Study Group refers to two Germans:* Leo Strauss and Carl Schmitt, as mentioned in the note to p. 64. Strauss was Jewish and Schmitt was anti-Semitic and antiliberal.

82    *White areas:* As opposed to Communist Red areas, these were under the Nationalist (Kuomintang) government at the time.

90     *wanted to write only about new people and new things:* "new people and new things" is a Cultural Revolution phrase referring to the Maoist Communist utopian idea of remolding human nature to produce a new type of human being.

99     *the complete works of Jin Yong, Zhang Ailing, and Lu Xun:* Jin Yong is the pen name of Louis Cha (b. 1924), GBM, OBE, the most famous writer of martial arts fiction, many of whose works are available in English translation. He was a cofounder of the Hong Kong daily *Mingbao.*

99     *Zhang Ailing:* Eileen Chang (1920–1995) was a Chinese modernist writer and is regarded by many to be China's finest writer of the twentieth century. Her short stories are most highly prized, but her novels have also attracted critical acclaim, many being made into feature films. Zhang's *Lust, Caution* was translated by Julia Lovell in 2007 and made into a popular film by the Taiwanese director Lee Ang in the same year. Her writing is characterized by its domestic detail and nicknamed "boudoir realism."

99     *Lu Xun:* The pen name of Zhou Shuren (1881–1936), a celebrated Chinese writer. His twenty-six short stories have been repeatedly translated, most recently as *The Real Story of Ah-Q, and Other Tales of China* by Julia Lovell (Penguin, 2009). He is considered to be the founder of modern Chinese literature and was also lionized by Mao Zedong as a great "revolutionary."

104     *Maotai:* A powerful liquor produced in Maotai in southwestern China. It is distilled from fermented sorghum.

104     *You can drink it without any worries:* A reference to the many bogus products in China, including liquor and wine, such as that discovered in a major wine scandal in December 2010.

105     *He was seeking an absolute self-reliance:* This is Chinese Communist Party propaganda and not exactly what Mao did. While rejecting the West, China relied heavily on Stalin and the Soviet Union, until Khrushchev's Twentieth Congress speech against Stalin made Mao worry that he might also be criticized in a similar way. After that, Mao tried to dominate the world communist movement, declared that nuclear war would be an acceptable option if only half the Chinese people were

killed, and so on. His actions led to a Sino-Soviet break when Khrushchev ordered all Russian technicians out of China.

119    *Qiong Yao, Yan Qin, Cen Kailun, Yi Shu, and Zhang Xiaoxian:* Qiong Yao (Ch'iung Yao, b. 1938) was the most popular and prolific romance-novel writer in Taiwan for over thirty years, from 1963 into the 1990s. Many of her works have been made into feature-length films and television series. In the 1990s, her work began to be read on the mainland and she became one of the bestselling writers in China. Yan Qin, Cen Kailun, Yi Shu, and Zhang Xiaoxian are all popular Hong Kong Chinese writers of romance fiction who are very popular on the mainland.

134    *The Bible says that when the world is full of masters, then the end of our days is in sight:* Matthew 24:14, "And this gospel of the kingdom shall be preached in the whole world for a witness to all the nations, and then the end shall come."

138    *Yang Jiang:* The wife (b. 1911) of the celebrated scholar Qian Zhongshu, and a major writer in her own right. Her *Six Chapters from My Life "Downunder"* is a classic memoir of their difficult life on a farm during the Cultural Revolution, including an account of their son's suicide.

161    *we Chinese are not happy:* A satirical allusion to the popular 2009 book *China Is Not Happy* (or *Unhappy China*) by Song Xiaojun and others that encourages China to seek world hegemony.

162    *inedia:* The ability to live without food, i.e., to fast. Fang Caodi is referring to Buddhist fasting traditions.

167    *Pangu:* There are several myths about Pangu. In the prevailing one, Pangu (usually depicted as a primitive hairy giant with horns) emerged from a cosmic egg that had coalesced from the formless chaos of the universe. He set about creating the world, and separating Yin (the earth) from Yang (the sky).

168    *Yandi:* Another name for Shennong, the Divine Farmer, who was one of the mythological bearers of culture at the beginning of civilization. His main achievement, according to Han historians, was to have led humanity out of a state of hunting and savagery, toward agrarian utopia.

169    *home church:* China's Christian population has swelled to around fifty million since the government began loosening controls on the

practice of religion in the 1970s. Private gatherings have proliferated, and as the government requires Christians to meet only in officially registered places of worship, these are often cracked down upon by officials. The home was the original setting for the early church.

177    *Mencius:* Mengzi (Master Meng) is the Saint Paul of China. He upheld and greatly elaborated the philosophy of Confucius, as Paul did the religion of Jesus, and, in a sense, was the real inventor of Confucianism. He is most famous for the idea that man's original nature is good, but it has to be taught to remain good.

178    *the people's Central Discipline Committee:* The Chinese Communist Party's internal policing organization, put in place because only the Communist Party investigates wrongdoing in the Communist Party.

179    *old Laozi:* Master Lao (the Old One) is the reputed founder of Daoism, an ancient Chinese tradition of philosophy and religious belief.

192    *auntie and uncle:* These words appear in Japanese in the original (*obasan* and *ojisan*) and are meant as terms of affection.

209    *a Petöfi Club salon woman:* Sándor Petöfi (1823–1849) was a Hungarian poet and leader of the Hungarian Revolution of 1848. Petöfi circles or clubs were popular among intellectuals before the Hungarian Revolt of 1956. At various times in China, government or leftist leaders have denounced so-called Rightist groups as Chinese Petöfi Clubs.

224    *We are all prepared to see the jade smashed to pieces:* This means being prepared to die heroically rather than live in shame. It is a saying that dates from the seventh century: "A true man would rather be a shattered jade than a perfect pottery tile."

237    *Han:* The name given to the vast majority (over 90 percent) of Chinese today. It is an ethnic term for a constructed "race" that is essentially, like the Europeans, made up of many "races." The name comes from the Han Dynasty (206 BCE–220 CE), the name of which came from the Han River.

239    *a suspension of habeas corpus:* The emergency situation described here has been the permanent situation under Chinese Communist Party rule ever since 1949, and still is. The British Parliament restored habeas corpus in March 1818. China has no habeas corpus law.

253    *China's Monroe Doctrine:* The Chinese do not use the term "Chinese Monroe doctrine" (its application is the author's), but it seems the Chinese party-state's long-term plan is to surpass and replace the United States and European powers everywhere in the world. They would like to start by ejecting the Americans from East Asia, where they believe they should be the most important power, as they were in the imperial glory days. However, other nations in the area are keen to keep American military might in the area to defend them. The idea that the Chinese would make an alliance with Japan is pure fantasy—it would be a powerful blow against the United States.

Almost all of the economic planning described in He Dongsheng's speech is accomplished or in the planning. China's greatest successes have thus far occurred in Central Asia. They are also making headway in Africa and Latin America. Recently, the Chinese have begun to face the sort of anti-imperial, anticolonial resistance that Britain and France faced when they were imperial powers. He Dongsheng's statements about making the RMB (renminbi) an international currency are, it seems, unlikely to happen.

292    *basic agreement with recent works of nonfiction:* See Mark Leonard's *What Does China Think?* (2008), Richard McGregor's *The Party: The Secret World of China's Communist Rulers* (2010), and Mark Lilla's "Reading Strauss in Beijing: China's Strange Taste in Western Philosophers" (*The New Republic*, December 8, 2010).

294    *"an imagined place or state in which everything is unpleasant or bad, typically a totalitarian or environmentally degraded one, the opposite of utopia":* Mac Dictionary definition of "dystopia."

296    *In a recent interview:* Published in the Taiwan academic journal *Sixiang* (*Reflexion*, No. 17, January 2011). Translated by Josephine Chiu-Duke, from pp. 114 and 115.

298    *China antagonized much of the world:* See Minxin Pei, "2010 Was the Worst Year for Chinese Diplomacy Since 1989," Carnegie Endowment for International Peace pdf.

298    *"Beyond economic and ecological indicators":* "The China Superpower Hoax," *Huffington Post*, February 10, 2011.

298    *reaction of the Chinese Communist Party state:* Perry Link, "The Secret Politburo Meeting Behind China's New Democracy Crackdown," *New York Review of Books* blog, February 20, 2011.

Chan Koonchung was born in Shanghai and raised in Hong Kong. He has previously written several works of nonfiction, a novel, and short stories. This is his first novel to be translated into English. In 1976 Chan founded the influential *City* magazine in Hong Kong, where he was editor in chief and then publisher for twenty-three years. He lives in Beijing.

Michael S. Duke received his doctorate in Chinese from the University of California, Berkeley, in 1975. After thirty years of teaching, he is Professor Emeritus of Chinese and Comparative Literature from the University of British Columbia.

Julia Lovell teaches modern Chinese history and literature at Birkbeck College, University of London. She is the author of *The Great Wall: China Against the World* and *The Opium War: Drugs, Dreams and the Making of China* and writes on China for the *Guardian*, the *Independent* and the *Times Literary Supplement*. Her many translations of modern Chinese fiction include, most recently, Lu Xun's *The Real Story of Ah-Q* and *Other Tales of China*.

A NOTE
ABOUT THE TYPE

The text of this book is set in Epic Thin, one of six
weights in a contemporary and versatile font family,
with many subtleties in its construction. Epic is a true
workhorse and is effective both as a readable text face
and one that is visually interesting when used in display.